Never Back Down

a novel

by Ernest Hebert

David R. Godine, Publisher
Boston

First published in 2012 by
DAVID R. GODINE · *Publisher*
Post Office Box 450
Jaffrey, New Hampshire 03452
www.godine.com

Copyright © 2012 by Ernest Hebert

All rights reserved. No part of this book may be used or reproduced
in any manner whatsoever without written permission from the
publisher, except in the case of brief excerpts embodied in critical
articles and reviews. For information contact Permissions,
David R. Godine, Publisher, Fifteen Court Square,
Suite 320, Boston, Massachusetts 02108.

Author photograph by Medora Hebert

LIBRARY OF CONGRESS
CATALOGING-IN-PUBLICATION DATA

Hebert, Ernest.
Never back down / by Ernest Hebert.
    p. cm.
ISBN-13: 978-1-56792-432-9
ISBN-10: 1-56792-432-8
I. Title.
PS3558.E277N48 2012
813´.54—dc22
2010049796

FIRST EDITION
Printed in the United States

Recently I read a piece in a quality magazine about an artist who was quoted describing one of his portraiture characters as "a kind of lowlife, the one who parks your car." Such casual slander against working people is so common it's hardly noticed. I've heard people who would never use sexist or racist language refer to people who work at McDonald's as "losers" and working people as "trailer trash," "white trash," and worse.

You who park the cars, cook and serve the burgers, mop the floors, pick up the trash, plow the roads, stock the shelves, make change at the check-out counter, drive trucks, log the pine, catch the cod, pound the nails and pour the concrete, walk high steel, wipe the asses and empty the bedpans – people like my father, Elphege Hebert, who worked without complaint for more than four decades, fifty-five hours a week in a textile mill; people like Harold Archer, a telephone man who inspired me with his work ethic and skill wiring Number 5 Crossbar bays; people like Alphonse Pierre who worked by day teaching schoolchildren and by night as an attendant at DePaul Hospital in New Orleans to provide for his family; people (nearly all of them women) like the ones who labored in nursing homes to care for my parents in their last years – you, the lowlifes, the losers, the trailer trash, my book is dedicated to you, the unsung heroes of America.

Contents

Part One
Love and Loss

We were American as tarte aux pommes.
                                                        – Memere

You rarely get what you want and when you do,
there's always a sorrow.   *– Memere*

Lark, lovely Lark
Lark, I am going to pluck you
I am going to pluck your head.   *– Memere*

That Word

Never Back Down, Never Instigate
July 1953

I slipped my baseball glove through the right handlebar of my black, balloon-tire Schwinn bicycle and pedaled from my house on 19 Oak Street up to the top of Roxbury Street hill. I rested for a few seconds, hopped on, and started downhill, pedaling hard until the houses on each side blurred. I removed my feet from the pedals and put them against the inside of the handlebars and coasted, steering with my thin-soled sneakers. I did not worry about crashing; I did not worry about cars nor pedestrians. I worried about dogs chasing me down and biting me; I worried about the hell the nuns told me about; I worried about humiliation when you say the wrong thing or somebody mocks you in the presence of others, who laugh the way they did when I was in kindergarten struggling to speak English.

The sensation of speed and air blowing against my face brought to mind Superman and Rocket Man serials at the Scenic Theater on Saturday afternoons. I never believed I could fly like Superman, but Rocket Man was within the realm of possibility, because he was an ordinary man with a rocket unit strapped to his back. I would have traded my bike, but not my baseball glove, for a rocket unit.

The grade of the hill eased, and I coasted to a stop. Then I turned the Schwinn around and pedaled to Mrs. Doan's Corner Store at Beaver and Lincoln, really just a distressed wood-framed house, in which the living room had been remodeled into a mini-grocery. I grabbed my baseball glove and went inside. I might leave my bike unattended for a minute or so, risking its loss to Billy Winters and his gang of bicycle thieves in the North End, but I carried my baseball glove everywhere and was willing to fight to the death to keep it in my possession.

Mrs. Doan sold bread and canned goods, no refrigerated items. My interest was in the display case of candy: bubble gum, Tootsie Rolls, Cracker Jack, Turkish taffy, and Hershey bars. I had tried them all, but M&M's was my candy of choice.

The bell overhead tinkled musically as I entered. Mrs. Doan stood behind her counter, dignified and still as a figure in a wax museum, while I stared with wonder at the candy behind the glass displays. I was impressed by Mrs. Doan's white hair, which she kept in a bun and which was always in place.

I pointed to one of the display cases.

Mrs. Doan reached in for M&M's and put the pack on the counter. Her hand had big blue and red knuckles, bony fingers, bulging veins, thin loose skin. It was like a crude imitation of a hand you'd make with Tinker Toys wrapped with crepe paper.

I grabbed the M&M's, pulled a quarter from my pocket, and put it in the center of the creased W in Mrs. Doan's palm. I watched while the hand moved to the register. The other hand pulled a crank, and the register opened, making a musical note that I always took pleasure in. Mrs. Doan gave me two dimes in change. Not a word passed between the ghostly widow and the virgin boy.

I pedaled hard down Beaver Street. For a minute I was so happy and lost in the joy of speed that I failed to realize that I had drifted into the left lane. When I saw a car coming toward me, I veered into my own lane, then off the road onto the sidewalk, where I nearly hit a woman carrying a shopping bag. Then, for no better reason than the fun of it, I cut sharply into the entry of Green Lawn Cemetery. The moment the front tires hit the dirt road, the bike went out from under me. For a split second I was flying like Rocket Man. If only I could keep going, swoop up into the sky, and land in a time long ago where I would belong. And then I was rolling on the gravel.

I was up on my feet almost instantly. I went over to the Schwinn to make sure it was all right before I inspected myself for wounds. Blood on both elbows. Scrapes with dirt in them. I was trying to figure out how to lick my elbow when I saw a boy about my own age. He was short but ruggedly built, dark like me, and I knew without thinking about it that his people had come down from French Canada. He was carrying a catcher's mitt with a scuffed baseball in the pocket.

He came over and looked at my bruises, and said, "I like it when they get infected and ooze pus."

"The yellow," I said.

"I can pus green," he said.

"You never pussed green," I said, challenging his veracity.

"Fuck I haven't."

It was the first time I'd heard a boy my age say *fuck* with author- ity, and the sound coming from his lips, so natural and expressive, sent a thrill through me. I decided right then and there that if I was going to improve myself I would have to learn to speak the word *fuck* with the gusto of my new friend. I framed a response in my mind, complete with exclamation point. *Well, fuck!* But I couldn't get the phrase out. *Never use that word*, Memere said. I had only a vague idea what the word meant. My father never spoke of sex in my presence; my mother explained the facts of life to me in her nurse language and added that it was a beautiful experience designed to make babies. My mother never used the word *fuck*, and though I came to understand that *fuck* represented this "beautiful experience," there actually was nothing beautiful about the word. It seemed to express something different from making babies: excitement, danger, but also disgust and rage, and something else that was as mysterious and scary. But what? I did not know, and because I did not know, I could not utter the word. It stalled somewhere between my brain and my vocal cords in its journey to my groin.

Finally, I said, "I like to pick off the scab and chew it after it dries out."

"Oh, yeah, that's the best. Do you like the crunch or the taste?"

"I like the taste but I don't swallow."

"Me neither, because it feels so good to spit it out." The boy made a spitting sound.

We looked at each other and as if on cue we started to *howdy-har-har* like hyenas at a lion wake. In our sardonic laughter, I knew I'd found a friend for life.

"I'm Jack Landry," I said.

"Me, I'm Elphege Beaupre."

Without him having to tell me, I knew to call him Beaupre, not Elphege. He'd just moved into town with his mother and her latest boyfriend. I offered him my pack of M&M's, and he accepted a modest number.

Beaupre hopped on the crossbar of my bike and we rode among the gravestones and pine trees downgrade to Beaver Brook. We got off the bike and listened to the water flow over rocks.

"Someday I'm going to live beside a brook like this," I whispered. I was thinking of my favorite piece of literature, the magazine called *Fur, Fish, and Game*.

Beaupre nodded.

Even at the beginning of our friendship Beaupre knew when to kid me and when to respect my moody moments.

"Let's play catch," I said and pulled my glove from the handlebar.

Beaupre tossed me the ball, walked to a flat spot among the gravestones, and squatted like a catcher behind the plate. "Chuck it," he said.

I wound up and threw my best fastball.

"Ball one!" Beaupre shouted, stood, and turned to the imaginary umpire and said, "Ball one, my ass. That was a fucking strike!"

I pitched an imaginary shut-out inning, issuing one walk, striking out two. Pop fly in foul territory. Beaupre flipped up an imaginary mask, ran around a couple of gravestones, and made a diving catch for out number three.

We pedaled to the western edge of the cemetery where there was a big oak tree that included a rope swing and a tree house built by Billy Winters and his gang. A crude ladder of short boards had been nailed into the tree to reach the tree house, which rested in a crotch of the oak. I leaned my bike against a gravestone, walked over to the tree, and swung on the rope a couple times. Then I watched Beaupre do the same thing.

Something hit me on the head. Another. Acorns. "Hey, there's somebody up there," I said.

Beaupre hollered at the tree house, "What's the matter, you chicken?" He made a *puck-puck* sound.

Two boys stepped out of the tree house and started pelting us with acorns. We picked up acorns and returned fire. The boys were a year younger than we, so we didn't feel threatened. It was just fun having an acorn fight.

"You're dead," repeated the skinny boy over and over again, making gunfire noises. The skinnier boy never said a word.

"Okay, we're dead – let's move on," I said. "See you later, Chalky," I yelled up to the tree house.

"Don't tell my mother we went to the cemetery," Chalky yelled down.

"I never squealed on you and I never will," I said.

Beaupre and I took off on the bike.

"Who are those guys?" Beaupre asked.

"The mouthy one is Chalky Landry, my cousin, and his buddy Spud Polix."

"Brave little bastards, aren't they?"

"Chalky and Spud are actually both chicken, but they get brave when they're together."

"Do they have a fucking motto?"

"No, they're too stupid," I said, but I was thinking that I must be stupid, too, since I didn't have a motto either.

The dirt lane of the cemetery gave way to street pavement and a lazy residential neighborhood. On the sidewalk, we saw a half a dozen boys coming out of the Franklin School playground. In my household, public schools were called "Protestant schools." Anyone who was not a Catholic was referred to as a Protestant. Never mind that Keene included Baptists, Lutherans, Methodists, Presbyterians, Unitarians, Jews, nonbelievers, and half-believers. As far as my family was concerned they were all Protestants. I recognized Billy Winters, leader of the North End gang of Protestant boys.

Outnumbered six to two, we stood a good chance of getting beaten up.

"We could pedal by them," I said.

"They'll think we're chicken – never back down," Beaupre said.

"And never instigate," I said. I stopped the bike, Beaupre hopped off, and I walked the bike toward the boys.

"Hi, Billy," I said.

"Nice bike," Billy said. It was rumored that you could buy a bike cheap from Billy and that Billy was very good at fixing bikes.

"Nice rope swing." Beaupre pointed in the direction of the cemetery. I hopped on the Schwinn, Beaupre hopped on the cross-bar, and I slowly pedaled off. When the gang was out of sight, we both started laughing.

"Never back down, never instigate," Beaupre said.

"That will be our motto," I said.

"Our fucking code of honor," Beaupre said.

The Nail

When we arrived at the Hephaestus Dynamite building, we dismounted from my bike and we walked it slowly along the sidewalk, in awe of the place. The abandoned single-story factory was near the old armory in the North End. The sidewalk concrete was so distressed I found it impossible to obey my rule never to walk on the cracks.

Hephaestus Dynamite had long ago closed, but rumors persisted that stashes of explosives lingered in the abandoned factory. I could hear the building calling out to me. *Enter my domain*, it said, *and you will find a stick of dynamite. Pick it up, stroke it, light the fuse, admire it, hurl it. Enjoy it going boom. Dale Evans will admire you.*

"I bet there's a dynamite stick in there," I said.

"Let's check it out," Beaupre said.

Because the building was uninhabited, with broken windows and wild nature growing all over it, pilfering its contents did not register with me as stealing. I would never steal. I was a good boy, or so I had been told. Goodness was an awful burden to carry, with responsibilities such as serving as a good example for my sisters, Gemma and Denise, by frequent washing of hands, brushing of teeth, combing of hair, refraining from nose-picking, farting, burping, and leaning my bottom on the pew bench during kneeling times at mass.

Beaupre and I went around to the front of the building, me walking my bicycle, Beaupre lagging a step or two. Beaupre found a place behind some *pricka* bushes where a dog had dug a hole under the wall, allowing us to wiggle through to the other side. Never mind that we could easily have scaled the wall by climbing the vines or even scrambling over the fence that blocked what had been the driveway; it was more fun to crawl under the wall. I used my baseball glove as a shovel. The dirt caked in the blood of my scraped elbows.

What had been lawn and a gravel parking lot was now a jungle of briars, bushes, tall grasses, and wildflowers. We found a door to the building that was slightly ajar but stuck.

"If we had a crowbar, we could jimmy this door," I said and voiced an explosion sound.

"We'll go to my house and get a fucking hammer. That'll do it," Beaupre said.

Beaupre hopped on the crossbar of my Schwinn, and we rode somewhat precariously half a mile or so to his house, in the floodplain of Beaver Brook, below the street.

The yard was a fascinating new world, littered with junk cars and various discarded appliances, including a white enameled gas range upon which Beaupre, as I later learned, had painted "fuck" in red. The written word so excited me that I wanted to do a somersault. So I did. Once again I tried to voice the word, but a choir of nuns, priests, parents, and a clan dating back three centuries in Catholic Canada, all of them led by Memere, began to sing "Ave Maria" in my head, and I could not bring myself to break the harmony by saying "fuck" aloud.

"Fuck," grunted Beaupre. Oh, how I admired him.

We went into the house, entering from a back porch into the kitchen; there was no grown-up to greet us. It was difficult for me to process the sights. My mother and father conspired to do dishes immediately after every meal. Floors were regularly swept and mopped. Dust mites could not make a living in the Landry house. This place was deep in the clutter of dirty dishes, crushed empty beer cans, food left out too long, newspapers and magazines strewn on the floor.

Beaupre read the expression on my face. "It's a shit hole, but I don't give a fuck," he said, though something in his voice told me he did give a fuck.

"Where's your mom?" I said.

"Who knows?"

"Where's your dad?"

"Dead, I hope." Beaupre spat on the floor.

We found a hammer down cellar. I hefted it, enjoying its weight in my pitching hand.

"Let's get the fuck out of here," Beaupre said.

And we did.

Back at the Hephaestus building, I wedged the claw of the hammer between jamb and door, and pulled. The door groaned and opened an inch. We put our shoulders to the door and shoved. The door gave way just enough to allow us to squeeze through. We clutched our baseball gloves like amulets.

I vividly remember spiderwebs illuminated by sunlight through broken glass. Against the walls were torn-open wooden crates piled high to the ceilings. The pitted concrete floor was littered with boards and nails. I brushed against a crate, and a metal pipe from above fell at my feet. The echoing pipe rolling on the concrete floor jarred Memere from her cloud in heaven. *Sing*, she shouted to the French-Canadian choir, and they sang, *You're going to hell, Jack; you're going to rot in the everlasting fires of hell.*

"I don't like it here anymore," I said.

"Okay, let's get out of here and play catch," Beaupre said.

We were almost at the door when I stepped on a rusted twenty-penny nail. It drove easily through the thin rubber sole of the sneaker, hit bone, slid around and upward through flesh, poked through a lace hole, and stopped. For a second it was a minor annoyance. With the next step, the pain hit me so hard it knocked me down. I lay writhing on the concrete like a worm on a fishhook.

Beaupre knelt beside me and lifted my foot. "Fuck, it went right through."

I lay on my side, listening to my quick breaths. Trickles of blood oozed through the lace hole of the sneaker. My parents would have to buy a new pair. Maybe I could salvage the laces. I unlaced the sneaker and put the lace in my pocket.

Even if you are rescued, you will be brought to court for burglary, said Memere. *You will be shamed, sent to reform school, our family disgraced. It would be better for you just to die here. Maybe the neighborhood dogs will eat your face, so that when your remains are discovered you cannot be identified.*

"I'll go for help," Beaupre said.

"No, they'll put us in jail," I said.

"So fucking what?"

"I can't shame my family, Beaupre," I said.

"Okay, I'll get that fucking nail out." He grabbed my baseball glove and shoved it in my mouth. "Bite it," he said.

I'd seen enough movies to understand the routine. I bit.

He picked up the hammer from the floor, hooked the claw around the nail head, and pulled. I saw bright colors and slashes of light through my closed eyelids. The colors dimmed, the light mellowed, the world turned rosy. I opened my eyes. The nail slid out, slick and wet with blood. My drool had soaked into the tooth marks on my baseball glove. The nail in the claw of the hammer was as slimy as a leech from Robinhood Park Pond.

Beaupre wrapped my T-shirt around my injured foot and tied it with the bloody sneaker lace. I reached in my pocket and counted nine M&M's. No breaks in the sugar crust – good. I put five M&M's one at a time on the tray of my tongue. They would give me energy and will. I kept the others in reserve – in case of emergency.

I stood and put my arm around Beaupre's shoulder, and he helped me out the door.

I started that word with breath over curled lower lip, whispering the *k* sound against the roof of my mouth. I whispered it again to give me courage to voice it, until I shouted the word so loud that it came back in echo, blowing in my face like spit into a wind, "Fuck. Fuck. Fuck!"

Beaupre's Bat

Coach
February 1956

Like the late uncle he was named after, a beloved pastor of St. Bernard's Church, Cormac "Skitzy" MacDonald bore a resemblance to actor James Cagney, both in his appearance and in his feisty attitude and demeanor. As a youth, he taught himself to speak in an Irish brogue, and he stuck with that way of talking all his life. MacDonald was quite the man about town – Keene City Councilor, president of the Granite Lake Property Owners Association, proprietor of Liberty Taxi, collector of sports memorabilia, and coach of Post 7 American Legion baseball team, which represented Cheshire County.

Every Sunday in the winter after ten o'clock high mass at St. Bernard's Church, MacDonald left his wife and three daughters and drove the ten miles from his home in Keene to the family's three-room camp on Granite Lake. It was understood by Mrs. MacDonald, after much persuasion, that her husband needed this time for masculine company. Skitzy MacDonald loved to entertain his political buddies, local sports enthusiasts, and neighbors on the lake. There was always a blaze of birch and maple logs going in the fireplace and plenty of beer and potato chips. Men sat around, gabbed, told jokes, and played dominoes until sunset, when Skitzy announced that it was time to clear out.

On this particular Sunday in February, MacDonald brought

two fourteen-year-old boys with him to the camp, myself and Elphege Beaupre. We knew why he'd invited us, and so did his pals at the lake. We were prospects for his Post 7 baseball team in the coming summer. Beaupre and I believed we were hot stuff. We could play for John Watterson and Post 4 or Cormac MacDonald and Post 7. We were leaning toward Watterson. Everybody knew he was the better coach who produced better teams. But Coach MacDonald had informed me that he had an in with the Boston Red Sox organization. "Jack, you're a prospect," he said.

So here we were, in the back seat of Coach MacDonald's Oldsmobile. I was thinking about my own personal and dark history at Granite Lake. On the twenty-minute drive from Keene, Coach talked to us and talked to us and talked to us.

"Boys, I have set goals in my life," he said. "I want to raise my daughters right, I want to be mayor of Keene, I want to make enough money to buy a Chris-Craft and a Cadillac, and I want to prepare a local ballplayer for the big leagues. I know a lot about you fellas. You're wondering, *like what, for instance*. Like nobody calls Elphege Beaupre by his first name. You're *Boh-pray*. I know that you're half French and half Heinz 57 variety, that your natural father went back to Canada and left his American family behind. I'm sorry, Beaupre. That's the way the ball bounces. Jack, I know that you had problems in kindergarten, that you couldn't speak English. You *parlez-vous* today?"

"No."

"You banished that language – good boy," MacDonald said. "You're catching on to what America is all about. I've been following your careers since Jack threw that no-hitter in Little League. Beaupre, you're going to be a quality catcher for my team in a couple years. You only have an average arm and under average foot speed, even for a catcher. You have power at the plate, but no eye for the strike zone, and you often swing at bad pitches. We'll work on that. You're going to be a feared hitter. You'll grow thick in the chest with piston-like legs. I bet you wind up a pulling guard on the football team."

"Geez," mumbled Beaupre.

"You have two strengths I have noted," MacDonald said. "Anybody ever push you around?"

"You mean besides my old man, no," Beaupre said. "I never had a fight in my life."

"You're the kind of kid a bully is afraid to pick on. Isn't that right?"

"If you say so, Coach," Beaupre said, and I wondered whether Coach MacDonald heard the sarcasm in Beaupre's tone.

"You want to know your second strength?" MacDonald asked.

"Sure, why not?" Beaupre said.

"Your second strength is that you're Jack Landry's best friend and his catcher."

"Jesus Christ," Beaupre said.

"Never use the Lord's name in vain in my presence, understand?"

Beaupre didn't answer, but Coach MacDonald said, "That's better," as if Beaupre had apologized. "You're rangy, Jack. You'll top six feet. We'll have to cut back that wild black hair, keep it out of your eyes. You have a serious, sometimes unnerving demeanor, and you don't even know it. You got lips like a girl, curious eyes, a stubborn streak, typical Frenchman – right?" I was about to answer in defense of my people, but Coach MacDonald kept right on talking over his question. "And you have the strongest throwing arm that I have ever seen in a boy your age, plus you can put the ball over the plate. I like your ability to concentrate. I like that you're a passable student in school, that you study hitters. A good pitcher has to have a brain."

He tapped his temple and talked on as if we were already his players. He cared about me; he admired my talent. I wanted to play for him.

"Jack, you're more intense and nervy than Beaupre, which means you have moments when you let your emotions take hold of you. Isn't that right?" he said.

"Yes, that's right," I said, hoping I'd given him the correct answer.

"I will teach you to use your emotions constructively, such as learning how to stare down hitters and how to intimidate them by pitching inside," he said. "Tell me how badly you want to win."

I didn't know what to say. Part of me did not care about winning and losing. Another part of me realized that winning baseball games for Post 7 would bring me that much closer to the major leagues. I struggled to explain myself in a way that would be honest but still please this man, but I couldn't find a word.

"Well?" said Coach.

"We just want to play," Beaupre said.

"That's it," I said.

Coach MacDonald shook his head in disgust. "Without the exhilaration of winning and the despair of defeat, the game is trivial," he said. "Without the struggle to love and honor, to value victory and lament defeat, a man's life is reduced to making a buck, raising kids, assuaging women, and burying the old folks."

I was deeply moved by the speech. Not Beaupre. He whispered in my ear, "What a fucking windbag."

The Camp

We arrived at the camp, entering through the back foyer into the tiny kitchen; the door was unlocked and the place was warm. Coach had left a key with one of the ice fishermen, who had started a fire. Half a dozen men sat around two card tables shoved together in front of the fireplace. They were drinking, snacking, and playing dominoes.

We stopped at the refrigerator door to stare at a snapshot of a very pretty blond-haired girl in a yellow bathing suit.

"Eye that picture with respect; that's my daughter Katie," Coach MacDonald said.

"Gee," I said, and turned my head away.

"Gee," Beaupre said, but he didn't stop looking.

I tried to feel comfortable, but all I could do was stand stock-still, hands awkwardly at my side. Off the mound, I didn't know how to posture.

The kitchen exhibited a woman's touch – walls painted a cheerful yellow, a welcome mat to wipe your feet, and embroidered napkin holders – but the main room was very masculine, with fir-paneled walls, a stone fireplace, the head of a ten-point buck mounted over it, lots of windows that looked out on a porch that ran the length of the camp and faced the ice down slope about fifty feet away, a map of the mile-long lake that showed its depths, and framed glossies of baseball teams that Coach MacDonald had either played on or coached.

"Someday you'll be on that wall," Coach said.

"Yeah, me and Beaupre," I said, but I was looking at the deer head. Somebody had put a cigar stub in its mouth. I took offense. It was as if these men were mocking the spirit of the deer.

"The place is full of jokers," Coach said. "Do you smoke?"

"No, I heard it cuts your wind," I said.

"Good boy. Beaupre, do you smoke?"

"No."

"Yes, you do, I could smell it on you in the car," Coach said.

"I've been smoking Camels since I was eleven," Beaupre said.

"More doctors smoke Camels than any other cigarette," Coach said.

"I'd walk a mile for a Camel," Beaupre said.

"If you play for me, you do your smoking out of my sight and away from the ballfield, okay?"

"Okay, coach," Beaupre said, a smirk on his face.

I didn't know it at the time, but Coach MacDonald was not at all upset by Beaupre's insolence. He liked his players to be cocky, a little mean.

The men smoked, drank beer, and snacked on Wise potato chips and sardines from the can as they played dominos. I liked the clucking sound as the pieces smacked the table, but I didn't like the men, who seemed coarse by comparison to my mild-mannered father.

Coach introduced us as ballplayers. I looked around the room, sizing it up. Beaupre helped himself to potato chips, and hung around with the men. He had no fear. Coach's eyes followed me as I gravitated toward the fire and stared at dancing figures in the flames. I wished everybody in the room would leave so I could concentrate on listening to the music of the ages in the burning logs.

Suddenly, Memere took hold of me, and I grabbed a chair, stood on it, pulled the cigar stub out of the buck's mouth, and flung it in the fireplace.

For a split second the men were caught up by the effrontery of my action, then one of them laughed and then they all laughed, and then the laughter died suddenly, leaving a embarrassed silence.

To break the awkward moment, one of the ice fishermen said, "Hey, Skitzy, tell these ballplayers how to vote, will yah?" The men's laughter revived for a beat, then degraded into shit-eating grins.

"Okay, boys, listen up," Coach said. "This is a lesson in civics. First, you vote for all the French names."

"Hey, the last time you told this one it was the Irish names," said one of the domino players.

"These are the sons of French Canada. I'm advising them to stick with their own."

"I threw my mother down the stairs a kiss," said one of the men, voicing a local joke deriding the diction of French-Canadian Americans. The men at the card table may have noted my shamed, embarrassed smile, but only Beaupre read the anger beneath the veneer of the smile.

I turned my eyes toward the windows, and I could tell by Coach MacDonald's face that he was a little peeved that I was not paying attention to his performance.

"After you check off the French names," he went on, "vote for known Catholics." He paused. "Then anybody who lives near you, then anybody you've met, especially if they shook your hand." Another pause.

One of the men, a political ally in local government, gave Coach the setup line. "When all else fails?"

"When all else fails – ." Coach paused again, this time with an expression of feigned forgetfulness on his face. Then he brightened and prompted the men at the card table with a gesture of his hands.

They chimed in, "Vote for the candidate with the best head of hair."

The men guffawed, Skitzy MacDonald guffawing loudest, but Beaupre and I did not guffaw. We believed we were being made fun of. Coach tried to smooth it over: "Don't listen to these old farts, they're living in the past."

Beaupre went back into the kitchen to stare at the picture of Katie MacDonald in a bathing suit.

I left the fire and walked over to the windows. The view included a dozen or so bob houses, the tiny figures of men checking their tip-ups, and swirls of snow lifted by the wind. The beauty gave me that old ache to live a different life, in a different time. Coach joined me at the window.

"You never seen a bob house before?" he said.

"Oh, yeah. I've been on Granite Lake before, and I wondered, does it have a name?" I asked.

"Does what have a name?"

"The island." I pointed. It was about half a mile away, maybe a couple acres in size, and completely forested over with white pines and a few hardwoods. The shore was rocky and on one side of the island was a ledge, perhaps ten feet up from the water.

"Oh, that. That's Mystery Island. It's owned by the Granite Lake Property Owners Association."

"Why is it called Mystery Island?"

"Oh, I don't know. Indian reasoning? You're just brimming with curiosity, aren't you?"

I answered with a bare nod. I was thinking about the first time I'd seen the island, that fateful moment on the ice when I was five years old.

"The story goes that in bygone days an old Indian brave and his granddaughter lived on the island," Coach MacDonald said. "She farmed corn, pumpkins, and blueberries, and the old buck fished. One day they were visited by a handsome voyageur from Quebec.

He had a broken leg or some damn thing and the Indian maiden nursed him back to health and fell in love with him. But he had a wife up there on the St. Lawrence River. When he spurned the Indian maiden, she was so distraught, she jumped off the ledge and drowned herself. What do you think of that?"

"How did he get to the island if had a broken leg?"

"For all I know he took a Liberty Taxi from Keene – it's just a story, Jack."

"Probably he had a birchbark canoe," I said. I was thinking about my magazine, *Fur, Fish, and Game.*

Coach gave me an *oh, brother* look, picked up a brochure from a shelf, and said, "Get a load of this." I liked the way he spoke, as if taking me into his confidence; I could tell he liked me even if he didn't respect my question.

He showed me a picture of a speedboat with a brown wooden hull, a steering wheel, and a windshield. Suddenly, I was thinking of a movie that had scared me, *The Creature from the Black Lagoon*.

"This is my dream boat, a Chris-Craft," Coach said.

"It looks like a car."

"Exactly, a car that says 'successful man behind the wheel.' Nobody in Europe could have made this boat. This boat is as American as apple pie. If Liberty Taxi ever gets to Venice we'll sink the gondolas and bring in the Chris-Crafts." Coach laughed as if he'd made a joke and I laughed, too, but I didn't understand the humor. I hoped Coach MacDonald didn't realize how stupid I was.

I went over to the map. Granite Lake was a little more than a mile long, half a mile wide, 111 feet deep in the middle. I turned back to Coach and said, "Is the lake water clear?"

"Very clear, except in the spring and fall when the bottom turns over, and then it's murky."

"Can we go out to the island?"

"My camp not good enough for you?" Coach watched me while I tried to make sense of his question, and when I couldn't seem to answer, he said, "I was just kidding, go ahead."

"Hey, Beaupre," I hollered, "Let's walk out to the island."

While Beaupre and I put on our coats and boots, the men talked about us as if we were not in the room.

"That kid, the tall one – Jack Landry – he's going to pitch in the big leagues, mark my words," Coach MacDonald said. He meant for me to hear him.

Suddenly, the men were all yammering at once, and I could not tell who was speaking.

"Frenchmen choke, he'll never make the bigs."

"Hey, watch it, I'm French."

"The Beaupre kid didn't act French."

"His mother's Irish and who knows what else," said Coach Mac-Donald.

"That explains it."

"This is all horseshit. These kids are going to act the way they are and never mind their blood."

"No. Blood counts. I'd trust an Irishman over a Frenchman with two out in the ninth, if you can keep him sober."

"It's not the French blood, it's the fact that most of these Frogs got Indian blood mixed in, and who knows what the effect is."

"Well, I'm part Indian, and that part of me takes part offense."

"Well, fuck you, Tonto."

Guffaws all the way around.

"The sperm count in this state is watered down. All the ballsy ones went West after the Civil War, leaving behind the timid and the weak-minded, like us yokels sitting here when we could be home putting it to the old lady."

"Same thing happened in Canada, except the reverse. The ballsy ones toughed it out at home, and we ended up with the bottom of the barrel."

"Skitzy, suppose you had five guys in the dugout to pinch-hit in a testicular situation. They're all batting .275. A Frog, a Harp, a Pollack, a Wop, and a Yankee, which one do you pick?"

"That's for me to know and you to find out."

"Hey, are there any Americans here?"

Mystery Island

Without having to discuss the matter, Beaupre and I were happy to rid ourselves of the men, graceless, ugly, smelly, and full of stupid jokes and slanted attacks on youth. I pulled my father's wool navy watchman's hat over my ears. Old Man Winter might be harsh, but he was not critical, nor full of mockery.

We stopped at a tree in the yard in front of the camp. On a branch hung a thermometer that said 22 degrees, balmy for this time of year. I tapped the bulb of the thermometer. It dropped to 18. Beaupre took baseball-type practice swings with the ax he'd grabbed from the woodpile on the way out.

"Guess what kind of tree this is?" I said, because I wanted to show off my knowledge.

"Gotta be a fucking pine tree," Beaupre said.

"No, it's an Eastern hemlock. See, reddish bark, tiny soft needles."

"How do you fucking know that?"

"From my magazines. My memere told me that in the old life I was a *coureur du bois.*"

Beaupre gave the tree a hug and pretended to hump it. "Sorry, old girl," he said.

We walked down to the shore, me with my pitching hand in the pocket of my coat to keep it warm, Beaupre with the ax on his shoulder, both hands gripping the handle as if he were on deck with a baseball bat. We could hear the American flag flapping majestically from the top of a homemade pole made of metal water pipes. We walked out onto the frozen, snow-covered lake.

The air on the lake hurt because it blew from the northwest in our faces. I pulled the watchman's hat over my ears. Wind drifted snow into crested waves here, whisked the blue-gray ice clean there.

We halted, thrilled by a deep rumbling noise under our feet that went on for half a minute.

"The lake is making ice," I said. The beauty and immensity of it gave me a terrible longing for that lost home in a previous lifetime. "This is about the spot where my memere fell."

"She cracked her head, right?" Beaupre said.

"Yeah, it was after a rain and the lake had frozen over, and my Dad took us out to go skating. Memere was supposed to be waiting in the car, but she came out onto the ice. She called me over and I skated to her. 'I have something to tell you,' she said in French. I think I bumped her. Maybe on purpose even. I don't know, I just don't know. She fell, Beaupre – she fell."

"You killed her, Jack. You're a fucking granny mugger."

Even Beaupre's bluntness couldn't bring me out of my wistful mood. "She's still alive somewhere inside of me, Beaupre – I know it." I tapped my head. "Out here I'm thinking that there really is a God."

"I hope not," Beaupre said in that droll voice that announced his cynicism regarding human goodness and a benevolent despot of the universe.

"Because he's reading our thoughts about Coach's daughter," I said.

"Hey, never mind *our* thoughts – she's mine, take note, friend."

We laughed, but we both knew that I would step aside in the quest to meet the prettiest girl in Keene.

I stared out at the island and thought about the old Indian and his daughter, the huge pumpkins in her garden. "I wonder," I said, and repeated, "I wonder," because, really, there was nothing but wonder inside of me.

Beaupre grabbed a Camel out of the pack with his teeth and lit it with his Zippo lighter. I liked the branch-break noise of the lighter when he flicked it.

We trudged on. Beaupre had yet to perfect his John Wayne walk, but carrying the ax helped. I had just finished telling Beaupre the sad tale of the Indian maiden when we arrived at the island, shaped like a hand cupped to throw a curveball, with a rocky point where the thumb would be and a shallow cove between imaginary thumb and curled index finger. Tall pines came right to the rocky shoreline. The only inviting harbor for a small boat or someone on foot on the ice was the cove, which ended at some rocks and a path. I scrambled up the rocks to a ledge that overlooked the cove some ten feet below.

From this prospect, I could just make out the MacDonald camp, cloistered behind the hemlock tree where Beaupre and I had discovered the thermometer. Camps and a few year-round houses dotted the rocky shoreline of the lake. One place stood out. Local people called it Shinbone Shack, though it was not a shack at all, but a stone and shingled mansion of a type of "cottage" architecture that reached its grandeur in Newport, Rhode Island, in the early years of the twentieth century.

"This has got to be the spot where she jumped," I said.

"Who?"

"The Indian maiden."

"She lived on an island, you figure she'd know how to swim."

"Maybe she tied a rock around herself," I said.

Beaupre laughed. "It never happened, Jack. It's just a damn story."

"No, it happened."

"How would you know?"

"Because I remember it."

"Your memere tells you things in dreams in French, and you don't understand French, but when you wake up they come to you in English."

"That's right." I smiled.

"You know why I hang around with you?" Beaupre asked.

"Because I take pity on you."

"No, because next to you, I appear to be fucking sane."

"Not to me you don't."

We both laughed.

We explored the paths on the island. Beaupre scouted around for a tree to chop down. I searched for the Indian maiden's garden, but after three hundred years I could find no trace. The only clearings on the island were the tops of ledges. Everything else was over-grown with forest or *puckah* brush.

I was looking up admiring a couple of crows in a white pine tree when I heard Beaupre hollering, his voice full of the excitement of discovery. "Hey, get a load of this!"

Beaupre stood at the base of the most magnificent tree on the island, a sugar maple of great age. The tree's gray bark was streaked with orange, green, and black mold. Burls protruded from the trunk. I liked to think that the old Indian brave and his grand-daughter tapped the then young tree for maple sap. Perhaps the Indian maiden and her voyageur lover sat under the tree in the summer and talked about their hopes and dreams, not knowing the tragedy that lay ahead. I put myself under the tree with the Indian maiden, who wore a headband around her dark, braided hair.

"I should have married her," I said.

"What?"

"Never mind."

Beaupre pointed up at the tree. "Do you see what I see?"

It took a minute, but I saw what Beaupre was pointing at. One of the malformed branches of the old maple tree was shaped like a baseball bat.

"It's not hickory, but sugar maple is just as hard. It should make a good bat," I said.

"I knew it, I knew it in my fucking gut," Beaupre said.

We spent the next couple hours tearing up the landscape to reach the bat. We took turns swinging the ax to chop down some small trees to lean against His Lordship the Maple. We scrambled up this crude ladder until we reached the first great crotch of His Lordship. I gave Beaupre a boost to the next branch. Beaupre strad-dled it, and I handed him the ax.

Beaupre chopped at the smaller branch below until it parted from the tree and dropped into the crusty snow.

We were about to leave when I noted our confused footprints in the snow, the raw wounds of the stumps, the slash we created with our wild use of the ax. I stood in horror at the mess. Everything was well ordered and pleasing except where Beaupre and I had done our business.

That Saturday I confessed my sin against the island to the priest who gave me absolution without comment and a penance of three Hail Marys and two Our Fathers. I never did figure out why confessors preferred Hail Marys over Our Fathers for penances. I did not believe myself absolved. My shame was not for my sin alone. It was for the sin of humankind, the mess we make. I wanted to ask the priest: What does God think of us? If there was one. I had doubts. You couldn't say such things to a priest. He would be too shocked. Beaupre's right, I thought, I am crazier than he is. Memere's voice echoed in my head: *Find a priest to talk to – every Catholic needs a confessor*.

Beaupre spent the next couple weeks whittling the branch with a hunting knife. He scraped the bark off, refined the shape of the barrel of the bat, and carved a knob at the bottom. He smoothed the bat with a piece of glass, and finally he sanded it with three different grits. With a nail that we heated at a campfire at Sunset Rock on Beech Hill in Keene, Beaupre burned a label into the wood: Beaupre's Bat.

The bat was almost white with faint traces of pink and little auburn-colored lines peculiar to the maple tree family. The bat was too heavy to get around on a fastball, but once the cells dried out it would be just right. My uncle, William "Three-Fingered Willie" Landry, Chalky's dad, who worked at the Furniture Factory, advised Beaupre to let the bat season a year before using it to hit a baseball. The drying process should be retarded by keeping the bat moist; otherwise the wood might split.

In the daytime, Beaupre kept the bat under his mattress with his dirty books. At night, after everyone had used the bathroom, Beaupre put the bat in the bathtub wrapped in wet towels.

In the summer of 1956, our first year playing American Legion baseball for Post 7, Elphege Beaupre was the second-string catcher.

He hit .255. The following year, after he put on twenty pounds and started using the bat that he'd chopped out from His Lordship, he led the team in home runs and doubles, and hit .366.

We had picked Skitzy MacDonald over John Watterson for our own private reasons. Beaupre hoped to see more of Katie Mac-Donald. I was counting on Coach's "in" with the Red Sox. I knew I was being selfish. I knew that my sin of pride eventually would lead to some kind of chaos; sin always does.

The Web Boy

The Landrys
June 1957

In the Landry household, the midday meal was called *dinnah* and the evening meal *suppah*, the words spoken in my parents' peculiar accent, half French Canada, half up-country New England Yankee. *Lunch* was something you took to work in a brown paper bag or lunch pail. Sunday dinnah was always an event in the house, because it followed directly after 10 A.M. high mass. This particular Sunday, my mother served one of my favorites, tourtiere (pork pie from an old Quebec recipe), mashed potatoes with gravy, canned peas, and dinner rolls. The disappointing part of the meal was the dessert, tapioca pudding. I would have preferred apple pie with vanilla ice cream from the Sealtest people.

After the meal I went into the living room to wait for Beaupre to show up in his '49 Ford so we could go to American Legion baseball practice at two. I sat cross-legged on the rug reading the funny papers of the *Boston Daily Record*, a Sunday afternoon ritual. The *Keene Sentinel* did not come out on Sundays, so my father bought the *Record*. I read only the sports page and the funnies, but even so, I believed myself better informed and maybe a little smarter for holding a big-city newspaper in my big hands.

I had turned sixteen the previous month. At six feet I was now taller than my father by five inches. I had long arms, a lean raw-boned body that had yet to fill out, and black hair so thick I struggled to pull a comb through it, but the whiskers on my dimpled chinny-chin-chin were skimpy and did not require the daily shaves that I administered. My skin was clear, cheekbones prominent, but the brown eyes were too small, appearing suspicious when they were merely fuddledbeebed by the sights they perceived.

I was reading Prince Valiant in the comics. The Prince had long hair with trimmed bangs and he wore a tunic that could have been mistaken for a skirt. It occurred to me that Prince Valiant was a fairy. I planned to discuss this matter with Beaupre. After baseball practice, Beaupre and I would drive around in the Ford in search of girls. If we had some luck, which was not very often, we would take the girls to the dead end of the road at Otter Brook dam and neck in the car.

My sisters cleared out directly after the meal. The Landry household was not a welcoming one for youth. It was too clean and picked up, and the shrine to St. Anthony and holy pictures on the walls disconcerted the Protestant friends of Gemma and Denise, my sisters. My mother did not believe in in-between meals, so she banned snacking, except when she made doughnuts, in which case the aroma attracted dogs and children alike. When my father was working nights, and therefore sleeping days, she suppressed loud talk and laughter from us children.

For the moment I was alone with my parents. My mother sat at her new electric sewing machine, which saddened me. I missed listening to the foot-operated Singer with its gentle *clickity-clack*. Above the sewing machine was a gutted cuckoo clock. Inside the empty clock frame was a foot-tall plaster statue of St. Anthony, patron saint of lost things and missing persons, my mother's favorite saint. On an oak dresser were framed pictures of family:

Father clowning on his Indian motorcycle while Memere frowned in the sidecar as she held the infant me in her arms, my mother in shadow on the sidewalk, holding the camera.

Me after my no-hitter in Little League with my best friend and catcher, Elphege Beaupre.

Gemma and Denise at the Cheshire Fair petting a horse. Gemma, like me and my mother, was very dark by the standards of Keene. She was a goodie-goodie girl. Denise was pretty, with my father's fair skin and blue eyes. My childhood memories are of Denise getting scolded by my mother for dirtying her dresses by playing in puddles and Gemma standing by, appearing above it all. One of my regrets in life is that I was never close to my sisters. These were the days when boys and girls were kept apart, even in school.

A formal portrait of Memere glaring critically at the camera, the picture taken a week before her death falling on the ice at Granite Lake, that terrible year of kindergarten. She was dark with a glum face, and she wore thick glasses. I never remembered her smiling. She'd worked in a shoe shop to raise her children after Pepere had a stroke that paralyzed him. Thanks to Memere, I was at the center of the most vivid and often-told family story. I had been born sickly with jaundice and it was thought I might not survive. The priest was called, but Memere beat him to it by baptizing me. Later, she insisted that I was the reincarnation of her only son, who had died mysteriously as an infant.

My father sat in his easy chair by the window rubbing my mother's lotion on his hands to make them soft. For a few seconds, I flashed back to a time when I was four years old, sitting on the floor playing with a toy pistol.

It's morning. My father comes downstairs as he has for the last four months, in his sailor suit, peacoat, and watchman's hat, walking right past me as if I am invisible.

I aim my toy six-shooter at him. "Bang! Bang! You're dead."

He doesn't respond. He sits in the big easy chair, removes his watchman's hat, and rests it on his lap.

My father stares out the window all day, rising only to eat, to go to the bathroom, and to go to bed, when my mother leads him by the hand.

Upon his return from World War II, my father had lingered in this distraught state of mind for six months. When he resumed his life, he was a different person, no longer the wild young man who raced his motorcycle.

St. Anthony, Memere, what happened to my father during the war to make him lose himself?

I watched my father rub my mother's lotion into his hands. He took great care of those hands and grew the fingernails very long with filed edges so they were never rough, because he needed his hands to be clean and soft for his work as a weaver at Narrow Textiles, Inc. Just what that work was I did not know, because my father was not a talker and because I had never stepped foot in the factory building that everyone I knew called "the shop." When I was younger and deserved a spanking, my mother did the deed, because my father did not want to risk damage to his hands – or maybe that was not the real reason. Maybe Alcide Landry shied from violence of any kind. Who could say? Not Alcide. The main power he wielded in his family was inferentially through his work ethic and inscrutability.

I thought about my own hands, the left the glove hand, the right the throwing hand. The legs, hips, right shoulder, arm, elbow, and wrist supplied the power and snap; but it was the fingertips, their sensitivity to the seams of the ball as it left the hand, that made the difference between a well-placed pitch and a perfectly placed pitch.

My mother worked as a practical nurse at Elliot Community Hospital on weekdays and tended to her house on weekends. When she washed floors, she got down on her hands and knees with a bucket of water and brush, so she had need for hand lotion but she had stopped using it. She reasoned that Jesus was a carpenter; surely, the Son of God and Man loved calloused hands.

She finished her work on the sewing machine and called out to her husband: "Al, I think now is the time to talk to Jack."

"Good idea," Alcide said.

I didn't like the tone in their voices. My parents never argued in front of their children. For all I knew they never argued at all. When they had something to say to me or one of my sisters, they presented a united front so that the child was outnumbered. It didn't seem fair to me. I pretended to be engrossed in the newspaper.

"I do not like it when you slouch; it is not good for your posture to sit on the floor like that," my mother said.

I looked up as if I had not heard. "What?" I said.

"We have something to tell you," my mother said. She looked at my father. He looked back at her as if to say, *you do the talking*.

My mother always spoke slowly and deliberately, and she never apostrophized her verbs. She was not a cuddler mom. She was all business, but a very good business. She cultivated mysteries. She prayed constantly to St. Anthony, the patron saint of lost objects, but she wouldn't say what she had lost. As a kid I had it in my mind that there was something about myself that I didn't know, and that my mother held the key to that knowledge. There were times when I wanted to shout: *What is it, tell me?* I held my tongue; we were not the kind of family that spilled our guts to one another.

"You are sixteen years old," she said, as she stood over me and looked down. "You have a license to drive the car. You are eligible for the workforce. Have you been thinking about getting a job for the summer?"

"Yes," I said with a flash of guilt, because I was speaking a half-truth. How could I tell my parents that I already had a "job" – baseball pitcher? How could I voice my grandiose dreams of playing in the big leagues to these good people whose main values were humility and self-abnegation? Why couldn't my parents be like Beaupre's mother and latest husband, unpredictable and selfish?

"Have you opened the paper to the want ads?" my mother interrogated.

I glowered down at the newspaper, and spoke as if to the paper. "It's the *Record*. Why would I look for want ads in a Boston paper?"

"Get your nose out of that paper and look up at me," my mother said, triggering my anger now. I tossed the paper away and stood, towering over my tiny mother, so she had to bend her neck to see my face.

"That is better," she said, which further annoyed me, because she didn't seem to notice that I was looking down and not up at her.

My father stared out the window and continued working the lotion through his hands as my mother and I debated my deportment. I knew he would not enter the argument unless he thought I was winning. Which of course I was not. I didn't surrender with an apology, but with a tone in my voice, "Okay, Mummuh."

Satisfied with her victory, my mother turned to my father and said, "Alcide, tell him."

My father was relaxed now. He could see that there was not going to be a blow-up. He removed his handkerchief, wiped his hands dry, stood, and walked over to me, stopping three feet away, just out of touching range.

"They need a web boy at the shop," he said. "I can get you in."

I didn't respond, but it didn't matter. I knew that my parents had made up their minds and that I would be a web boy for Narrow Textiles, Inc.

"Do not forget to tell him to stay away from that bad priest," my mother said.

"He's not bad, Jeanne – he's just Commie," my father said.

I must have appeared puzzled, because my mother turned to me to explain, "There is a priest working at the shop, a trouble-making Jesuit with modern ideas."

"Father Gonzaga is an instigator and a union man," my father said in a matter-of-fact, nonaccusatory tone.

The notion that a priest would involve himself in secular activities was so alien to me that my parents' information hardly sunk in. All I knew was that I was going to hold down two jobs during the summer – baseball pitcher by night and web boy by day. Perhaps I would discover what my father did for work to require him to keep his fingernails long, his hands soft and clean.

The Shop

The shop was a low, mean red-brick building with a flat roof and a faded sign that said NARROW TEXTILES, INC. That first day, all the windows in the factory were open, because even though it was early morning the temperature was already warm. In the parking lot a hundred yards away, the din drummed in my ears.

My father left me in the reception room of the office, a smaller brick building across a narrow green from the shop. I watched my father through the window, walking slightly bowlegged and with just a hint of a limp, the result of a motorcycle accident from that ancient time before the war when he was known as a hellraiser, before he met Jeanne St. Vincent de Paul and fell in love, before the war trauma that had changed his personality from rambunctious to restrained. He carried his dented, fifteen-year-old, dull-black lunch pail in his left hand. Like one of my idols, Mel Parnell, Alcide Landry was a southpaw. Just as he was about to enter the shop, he stopped and turned in my direction. It was obvious he had some concern for me. Suddenly, it was as if I was ten years old again, weak and in need of a father's protection. I turned away from the window and found myself looking at a pinched-faced middle-aged woman holding papers in her hand.

"Can you write okay?" the clerk said.

"Uh-huh." I gave her a bare nod. I was still thinking about my father, and I was trying not to look as if I was about to cry.

"Well, then, you won't need my help, will you?" the clerk said. My Nathan Detroit behavior suggested to her I was a wise guy. At the moment I wished I was a wise guy. Wise guys didn't trepidate.

She shoved the papers into my hand, left the room, and shut the door. I sat down beside my brown-bag lunch.

It was hard for me to concentrate because of the noise from the shop coming in through the open window, a heavy complex Spike Jones number that included rattles, clicks, roars, whirs, and what seemed to my ear the muffled wails of innocents being tortured.

After I filled out the papers, it passed through my mind that I should return them to the clerk, but the closed door glued me to the chair. I sat up straight, hands on my knees, trying to appear stalwart for the eyes of the powers that be that I imagined were observing me through a secret peephole.

Ten minutes later, "stalwart" had lost its appeal, and I slouched and reached into my pocket for a handful of M&M's and their sweet solace. Just then, the door from the outside opened.

A rotund man in a suit and tie appeared, followed by a woman and a girl. The man had ruddy skin and freckles. His curly reddish blond hair was balding at the crown. His eyes were blue and vibrant, but he unsettled me with a faint, mysterious, thin-lipped smile of condescension. I wanted to grab him by the throat and say, *watch me pitch*. In high-heeled shoes, the woman was as tall as the man, about five-foot-seven, very blond and very pregnant. She appeared much younger than the man.

The girl was a couple inches shorter, wearing a white tennis skirt, white tennis shoes with pink laces, and white bobby socks. The sight of her bare tanned legs made me gulp for oxygen. She had long dark hair, an Annette Funicello face and complexion, a nose with a slight Roman spread, and inquisitive almond eyes that studied me. I imagined her as some kind of girl-scientist with an obsession to measure everything in her line of sight. The girl's eyes traveled from my face to my pitching hand; when she saw the M&M's, the eyes lit up with such brightness that the room went suddenly starburst white, as if I'd died and heaven lay behind the gate.

I extended my hand. The girl took one of the M&M's. The brush of her fingertips against my palm sent a snake exploring my lower spinal column.

"M&M's," I said.

"Mother Marys," the girl whispered so low that only I could hear her, and she popped the Mother Mary in her mouth and crunched it, her eyes still on me. She wanted me as a witness. She took another.

"Come on, Alouette," said the man, soft-spoken but impatient. He swiveled his head in my direction and gave me that insincere smile.

I averted my eyes. I wasn't used to making eye contact with strangers. A second later, the encounter was over. The three of them went through the office door and closed it behind them. I shut my eyes and imagined myself with Alouette. She holds a tennis racket. I pitch a tennis ball to her. She swings the racket, and her skirt flies up to reveal more of those beautiful tanned legs. I was jarred back into the material world by the sound of the outside door opening.

A man in his forties wearing a blue work shirt and matching trousers entered. At his hip hung a leather holster carrying a pair of long scissors. Still partially in my delirium, I thought: *It's J. Edgar Hoover, I'm under arrest for thinking about that girl.* Actually, the man was taller than the FBI director, but he had the same type of smooshed face. The man walked past me without a glance, went into the office, came out a couple minutes later holding a punch card.

"Jack Landry?" he said, hovering over me.

I couldn't seem to speak, but I had enough sense to stand up and nod.

"This is your time card." The man handed it to me. "I am your overseer. You're going to be my web boy. I'm going to break you in. Let's go. Don't forget your brown bag."

My overseer walked me across the skimpy green to the shop. As we approached, the noise grew louder. We went in. Directly in front of us was a punch card machine.

"Slide it in," the overseer said. "You got enough behind you to get it in, haven't you?"

Was he making a dirty joke? Was I supposed to smirk in appreciation? I didn't know the proper etiquette for behaving in front of an overseer. In the end, I followed the procedure for meeting a stranger. Avoid his eyes, say nothing, speak only in response to a question.

I slid in the card, and the machine made a sound like the jaws of a snapping turtle as it stamped the card with the time and date.

The overseer showed me a slot in which to store the card. Other slots had names in capital letters under them – OLYMPIA TROY, SEBASTIAN GONZAGA, ALCIDE LANDRY, and so forth. Mine would be added later. I liked the idea of my name in type-script, on a card, in a particular place, in capital letters. It gave me some status I didn't have before.

Hey, Memere, hey, Coach, see? My name. I'm somebody. I'm some-body! I'm Special, capital S!

We walked through the canteen, which included a bulletin board, bins to store thermos bottles and lunches. Management provided hard benches but neither chairs nor tables. Management didn't want the workers' refuge to be too comfortable, lest the workers spend too much time away from the looms. My overseer pointed. I put my lunch in a bin.

My overseer opened the double doors to the great hall and the power looms. The heat and noise slammed me in the solar plexus and stopped my breath. I'd fallen into the maw of a lion in the mid-dle of its roar. The noise rippled the concrete floor under the soles of my feet, pain shooting up through the scar where I'd put the nail in my foot five years ago. Daylight streamed through the windows like the fires of my boyhood nightmares. *How do you like that, Old Soul?* I had entered the hell that Memere had harangued about but that, until now, I had doubted.

The overseer pushed a funny-looking wheeled machine to the rear of a power loom. His cigarette breath tickled my ear, and he shouted over the din, "This is your web horse, web boy." The web horse included a crank and a reel.

He bent down behind the power loom, where fabric had wound automatically on a roll, and said, "This is web." I could just barely hear.

He pulled the long scissors from his holster, snapped them open and shut, and cut the web. He holstered the scissors, stood, unhitched the rig from his hip and handed it to me.

I tied the rig around my waist. Suddenly I was full of the con-fidence and false modesty of a gunslinger.

I watched my overseer work the edge of the cut web onto a notch on the reel and crank web off the loom. After a couple of winds, he pointed to the web horse.

I cranked. Sweat flowed down my forehead and itched my nose, but with the overseer looking over my shoulder I didn't dare scratch. When I finished, I had a roll of web a foot in diameter and three inches wide. The overseer pulled the roll off the reel and put it in a cart. He started walking away, and it took me a second or two to realize he wanted me to push the cart and follow him. I left the web horse and pushed the cart.

We went through the canteen to storage bins lining a long hallway. It was quieter here, and the overseer did not have to shout to be heard.

"You put the rolls in the bins – they're all marked, see?" He pointed and explained the coded numbers.

I bobbed my head.

"That's it, that's the job," he said. "Just keep up with the web. If a roll winds over and touches the floor and gets dirty, your ass is grass and I'm a lawnmower." The overseer took my hands in his and clamped them. "The enemy of web is dirt. Keep your hands clean." Then the overseer released my hands and said a few words to me in mock French.

I blinked at him.

"You don't *parlez-vous*?" the overseer said.

"Only when I dream."

"A Frog that don't *parlez-vous* except in his dreams, what's the world coming to?" The overseer shook his head, his mouth twisting into the mockery of a smile. Big joke. My pulse jumped and I clenched my fists.

The morning dragged on. The work was not hard, but it was tedious, the environment hot, ugly, and dangerous. Exposed whirring belts and metal gears the size of bicycle wheels could chew off a finger or even an arm. There was no ear protection from the din.

Cotton lint floating in the air burrowed through my sweat and made me itch, flew into my eyes, ears, up my nose and down my throat, collected in white puffs that dove and sailed on currents of heated air like dandelion parachutes until they finally fell to the floor, gathered, and rolled down the aisles like tumbleweeds on the streets of an Old West town.

I was grateful for the half an hour off for lunch. My mother had packed a meat loaf sandwich, celery stalks, a couple of raw peeled carrots, and a piece of her magnificent chocolate cake wrapped in wax paper. Milk in the thermos was almost cold. Some of the men sat around on wooden benches and played pitch on a big wooden box. Others chatted. Among them my father.

Alcide Landry was not an educated man, but he always tried to make good use of his time. At the moment, he was conversing with Jon Tamulus, who had taught my father to count to ten in Lithuanian. My father was reciprocating by teaching Jon to count to ten in French. My father counted in his patois, and Jon repeated as best as he could, Lithuanian-American patois superimposed onto French-Canadian New England American patois to create words for a new language: *err, derr, tworr, cart, sank, cease, set, wheat, neff, dzeez.*

I was just finishing my lunch when one of the woman weavers brushed by me on the way to the ladies' room. Busty, full-figured women ruled movies and magazine covers: Marilyn Monroe, Anita Ekberg, Elizabeth Taylor, Sophia Loren, and my favorite, Gina Lollobrigida. The woman weaver at Narrow Fabrics, Inc., held her own with the glamour queens. She wore a white blouse open a couple of buttons so that her cleavage was exposed. She kept her coal-black hair in a Grace Metalious ponytail with a red ribbon around it. As she walked by me, I caught a whiff of her scent, sweat and perfume. It was a faint aroma but it went from my nostrils right to my groin.

A moment later I sensed another presence. I turned to see the overseer standing over me. He had a grin on his J. Edgar Hoover face that told me he'd caught me gaping at the woman with the big bazooms, curvaceous ass, and Lollobrigida lips.

"You like that?" the overseer asked.

I was still excited, my shyness suppressed. "What's not to like?"
I said.

"How about a dose of the clap? That's Olympia Troy."

"That's Olympia Troy?" I had heard the name bandied about
in high school, a loose woman originally from White River Junction, Vermont, sixty-something miles away.

I blushed.

The overseer laughed.

Dye Man

Late in the afternoon, the overseer ordered me to wheel a load of
web to the finishing room. I pushed the cart through the double
doors, into the canteen, and down a long concrete runway. Bins
of web, rising above me on both sides, made good sound insula-
tion, so the noise of the power looms receded. By the time I
reached the finishing room, it was relatively quiet, the lion's roar
replaced by soothing clicks, hums, and sad romantic sighs that
reminded me of Christmas wind-up toys.

It was even hotter in the finishing room than in the shop, the
air moist and thick, the heat and humidity inoculating me with a
mild potion of equal parts drowsiness, dizziness, and forgetfulness.
The floor did not shake, and my pores opened and flushed lint
worms from my skin.

Streams of white web snaked through rollers all the way to the
high ceiling and back down again, into dye vats that resembled
witches' cauldrons in children's books. The web emerged red or
violet or yellow or orange or blue onto drying racks. Colored vapor
rose off the vats. I felt like a man walking barefoot into the heart of
a dying sunset.

A staircase corkscrewed to a platform, where on a throne-like
chair sat the finishing room's sole attendant, a fat man about age
thirty with hair the noncolor of dust, two-day stubble of beard,

dressed in black trousers held up by black suspenders, wearing black spit-shined shoes, bare-chested with volumes of dark curly hair that roused my envy, a priest's Roman collar around his throat. He wiped fog from black, thick-rimmed glasses, and his lips twitched as if about to pose a profound question.

"No doubt you are the new web *bonhomme*, and I am Sebastian Gonzaga," he said, sounding like a French-Canadian hockey announcer, which made me think of Habitant pea soup, which, unlike Campbell's, came uncondensed in big cans.

I remembered now seeing the name Sebastian Gonzaga on a punch card. This man must be the seditious priest my mother had warned me against. Because she wanted me to keep my distance from the man, I wanted to get to know him better. I had it in the back of my mind that true knowledge of the world had eluded my parents, so I had to look elsewhere for guides.

"I'm the new web boy – Jack Landry."

"Joseph Jacques St. Vincent de Paul Landry."

"Gee, you know my name, all of it," I said.

"I have my sources. I'm your priest for life, *bonhomme*. Like your memere I recognized you right away as an old soul. What are your aspirations?" He talked to me as if we were family, as if he'd been with me all along. My guardian angel? Beaupre and I had had many arguments about the existence of celestial beings. He was a non-believer. I was a maybe believer.

In an effort to impress Father Gonzaga, I told him of my ambitions to pitch in the major leagues and my accomplishments so far.

"Yes, you have become a regular in the *Keene Sentinel*. Sports is another ploy the oppressors use to distract the masses from their true concerns, but I won't hold you personally responsible. You're just a dupe." He broke off his rant, stood up from his chair, did a fair imitation of a Sammy Davis Jr. tap dance.

I gazed up at the platform in delight and awe. I felt as if I had been transported into a Bing Crosby/Bob Hope road movie in which the finishing room was the exotic set and the man on the platform played the role of Pooh-Bah.

"Are you really a priest?" I asked.

"Is Pope Pius XII preparing himself for beatification? I was ordained as Father Sebastian Gonzaga, but my formal title at Narrow Textiles is Dye Man." He started to sing, "Come dye with me, come dye with me, on my way to the stars." He grinned at heaven and sat down on his royal throne.

"I never met a priest like you before."

"It's both the triumph and the failing of the Church that she embraces all kinds, even an Experimentalist such as myself."

"A what?"

"Experimentalism, *bonhomme*, is an *-ism* I've invented to describe a restless, relentless spirit dissatisfied with *-isms* of every stripe, inspired in part by my mentors, Doctor Norman Vincent Peale, Bishop Fulton J. Sheen, and Leon Trotsky. Think of the failures: Fascism, Communism, Capitalism, Socialism, Protestantism, Judaism, the list is unending; even our beloved Catholicism requires acts of faith, without which it would make no sense. The motto of Experimentalism is: Try, try, try again. The Experimentalist seeks the *-ism* that God wants us to adopt, and when that day comes Experimentalism will no longer be necessary."

"What's a priest doing working in the finishing room of a textile mill?"

"I would have preferred to be with the weavers, but management has isolated me. The finishing room is my mission, you are among my flock, and never mind that I am officially on disciplinary leave from my reactionary and militant order." Father Gonzaga spoke these words as if telling a big joke, but then his voice turned serious. "How much are they paying you?"

"Ninety cents an hour."

"Minimum wage." Father Gonzaga wiped his glasses again. "Have you heard the phrase 'workers' paradise?' No, of course not. Do you like Ike?"

I gave the priest/Pooh-Bah/Dye Man one of my signature teenage shrugs that said: *trick question, leave me alone*.

"I don't like Ike," Father Gonzaga said. "He works for them, not for you and me. Them – you know who I'm talking about? You understand me?"

I shook my head.

"That's okay, nobody else does either. Even I don't understand me. I exist in a state of constant stimulation, because I never know what God wants me to say and do next. He speaks through me in fits and starts, mainly fits. My words are His words. You like the shop?"

Another trick question. "It's all right," I mumbled.

"That was not an honest answer. You are never entirely honest, are you, Jack? This is what the oppressors do: They punish honesty, decency, kindness, so that one loses touch with TRUTH. After that it's easy to fall prey to the big lie, war hysteria, prejudice, self-loathing, and false gods. Do you believe in God?"

The biggest trick question of all. "Sometimes," I said.

"Your faith, it weighs on you, doesn't it?"

"I worry about hurting my mother if I left the Church," I said, speaking honestly now, and startling myself with self-discovery. I had not known what lay behind the dam of confusion and doubt until the words spilled out: the presumed feelings of my mother.

"That's better," Father Gonzaga said. "Jack, what is the single most pressing question that has consumed your mind today? Ask and I shall help you find an answer."

I looked at him slack-jawed and uncomprehending.

"You are the new web boy – your first real job. What you think today, what you feel today, will linger on for years to guide or torment you. Now think, what is on your mind? Tell me and I will give you my blessing." Father Gonzaga wiped his glasses.

I looked away from Father Gonzaga and took in the wonders of the finishing room: the serpentine web in long strips of white going through the dye vats, coming out in colors, the moist cleansing heat, the torrent of Father Gonzaga's oratory flowing out from the platform, his voice piercing and haunting as a train whistle waking you at 2:00 A.M. – all of it so exalted and strange to this teenage boy. In the beauty of the moment, I found what I wanted to say.

"When I was in the reception room this morning filling out forms, a big shot came in with a good-looking pregnant wife and a better-looking daughter. I heard the man call the girl Alouette. I gave her a couple of my M&M's, and she called them Mother Marys. My question is: Who is she?"

"Did the man have an impressive vestibule?" Father Gonzaga patted his tummy. "And did he lance you with his smile?"

"That's the guy."

"The man is Hiram Williams, the scion of an old Bean Town family with a Southern branch, post-Civil War carpetbaggers with connections to the government. The females would be the current wife and the daughter from a previous marriage. Narrow Textiles used to be locally owned, by a Swede who sold out to the Williamses' company down South. The Williams family has a manse on Granite Lake."

"Hiram Williams is an overseer?"

"He oversees the overseers; he's the general manager. He sticks around two or three years, and then . . ." Father Gonzaga made a cut sign across his throat. "Big layoff. Then he's on to the next trouble spot. That's why I'm here: to warn the workers, to organize them, to prepare them. Narrow Textiles is not a workers' paradise." Father Gonzaga read my impatience and paused for a long moment to wipe his glasses yet again.

"But you don't care," he said. "You're too young to appreciate the struggle. It's the Williams daughter that's on your mind, or perhaps I should say on your private parts. She's thirteen or fourteen, a student at a boarding school in New Orleans. That girl is a trap for a youth like you. Stay with your own kind, *bonhomme*, lest you please the Devil."

What to think about this man, this priest, this angel, whatever he was? What to think about Alouette Williams? Olympia Troy? The overseer? My parents? Memere? My sisters? My baseball coach? My best friend and Katie MacDonald, the prettiest girl in Keene? The people of planet Earth and my relationship to them?

"What's on your mind now, Jack?" Father Gonzaga asked. "You

look like one of those souls more frightened by the confessional than by the Judgment."

"I want to learn how to figure out people like the overseer."

"Listen to me, Jack. You already know how to deal with the world, you just don't know how you know. That knowledge was passed down to you by the Holy Ghost when you were baptized. It is now emerging from its chrysalis. Come up here." Father Gonzaga summoned me with a twitch of his index finger.

His glasses were steamed again and I could not see his eyes. Hypnotized, I climbed the winding staircase to the platform. Father Gonzaga held his hand over my head and without even touching me guided me to my knees. I folded my hands in prayer, and bowed. When I looked up, Father Gonzaga was wearing a confessor's stole around his shoulders.

"Bless me, Father, for I have sinned," I said, making the sign of the cross.

"Begin with an old sin," he said in a soft voice.

"When I was eleven years old another boy and I broke into an abandoned building," I said.

"Do you have a particular, recurring impure thought?"

"I imagine myself a major league pitcher, and the city of Keene names a street after me."

"That's a good one," Father Gonzaga said.

After that I'm not sure exactly what happened, because there's a hole in my memory. The next thing I remember is a vivid mental image of Father Gonzaga and his hairy chest, and he's giving me absolution and mumbling something in Latin that I do not understand.

"What did you say?" I asked.

"I prayed to the Holy Ghost to infuse you with grace. Now unload your cart and go; the Dye Man has work to do."

On my way back to the shop, I met my overseer striding toward me in the hallway.

"You dawdled in the finishing room, didn't you?" the overseer said.

"I'm sorry," I said. "I got to talking with the dye man."

"Let me tell you something about the dye man," the overseer said. "The dye man knows his dyes, he does his job, I'll give him that. But he's a troublemaker, a union guy, a nonconformist, and probably a Communist, who's damn lucky he hasn't been bounced. Don't let him bamboozle you with his talk."

"Is he really a priest?"

"Am I really General Patton?"

How to pitch to the overseer? He could hit the long ball. He was patient at the plate. He could not be intimidated by brushing him back with an inside pitch. He would be waiting on the fastball. A mistake hitter. But he had other things on his mind, so you could sneak a pitch by him. Throw him off-speed stuff on the corners. Catch him looking or swinging ahead of the pitch. If he doesn't go for the slow curve or the straight change-up and you find yourself down two and oh, or three and oh, don't give him anything to hit. Better to walk him and take your chances with the next hitter. After all, he can't run, so there's virtually no chance he'll steal a base on you.

Once I had determined how I would pitch to the overseer, my anger and anxiety lifted. I would get through this purgatorial summer, thanks to Father Gonzaga, who had forgiven me my sins and taught me how to use the knowledge I already possessed and infused me with the spirit of the Holy Ghost.

Broken Thread

All the rest of the afternoon I rode the web horse, wound web, and stacked it in bins. A few minutes before the five o'clock whistle, I happened to be watching my father at his looms. A thread broke. Alcide immediately shut down the power. With quick, deft movements he found the two ends of the broken thread, and faster than you could sing "Bony Moronie Peggy Sue" he made the repair. I suddenly understood why my father's fingernails were so long. He needed them to tie knots to join broken threads. I looked at my own hands; the hand-quickness that I was so proud of – my meager athletic talent – had been inherited from my father. I wanted to tell him at this moment of realization that I loved him, but such expressions were not part of my upbringing, nor my own developing idea of manhood, so I kept my feelings to myself.

The next day I was eager to talk to Father Gonzaga, but my overseer assigned somebody else the task of delivering web to the finishing room. I looked for Father Gonzaga in the canteen, but he never showed. Finally, on the fifth day, Friday, my overseer sent me to the finishing room. A new dye man was on duty. He informed me that Father Gonzaga had been fired by Mr. Hiram Williams himself.

Olympia

I didn't know myself very well during my teen years, but deep down I knew I wasn't the wandering type. I wanted to settle down with one girl. As a star athlete at Keene High School, I certainly had opportunities to meet pretty and interesting girls, but the fact was that I couldn't go very far with a girl. It was a strange feeling. If I found myself liking a girl too much I began to feel unfaithful. My thoughts always went back to the Indian maiden on Mystery Island and to Alouette Williams, the brush of her fingertips as she took my M&M's. In my twisted imagination, the Indian maiden and Alouette were the same person. In my mind it was not as if I were creating a mental script; it was as if the idea that I was in love with a girl from a past life had been inside all along, and I was just discovering it. We would not be happy until we were reunited. To be so entranced by a girl I'd seen only once no doubt was a sin. Happiness itself was sin. I wanted so much to confess to Father Gonzaga and seek his advice, but he had left the area, his whereabouts unknown.

That's the frame of mind I was in one night after an American Legion ball game at Alumni Field. I had pitched very well. In fact, I had a perfect game going into the last inning. No one had ever pitched a perfect game for Post 7. With two outs and only one batter to go, my right fielder and cousin, Chalky Landry, misjudged a high fly ball that fell for a questionable double. That put a man on second base, who scored when Chalky dropped yet another fly ball for an obvious error. We lost 1–0 to John Watterson's Post 4. Coach MacDonald had drummed it into our heads that we should feel bad after a loss, especially one to our local rival, but the truth was I was always interested primarily in my own performance. If I pitched well, I'd be satisfied; if I pitched poorly, I'd be depressed. I wanted to make history with a perfect game more than I wanted to win for my team. Selfishness was one of my many sins.

"I bet you think I dropped it on purpose," Chalky said after the game.

"What, me worry?" I said, and I pulled my ears to remind Chalky of his big ears.

I should have felt bad for Chalky. His father, my Uncle Three Fingers, was a drinker who whapped his loved ones when he was on the bottle. My mother told me that since I was a year older than Chalky and a star on the baseball team I should serve as a good example. But the truth was, I didn't much like Chalky. He annoyed me and I went out of my way not to go out of my way for my only male cousin.

Chalky took off with Spud Polix in a beat-up Chevy. It was Spud's car, but he and Chalky took turns driving it. Beaupre dropped me off in downtown Keene so he could go parking with Katie MacDonald in his '49 Ford. Lucky guy! He wouldn't admit that they were going all the way, but in recent days I'd noticed that his John Wayne walk appeared more assured. I was thinking that I was making a sacrifice and perhaps that would mediate against my sin of selfishness. Before walking the mile home, I stopped at the Crystal Restaurant for a bite to eat.

I never got through the vestibule. I was halted at the door by the sight of a beautiful woman. She wore her dark hair in a flow like Jane Russell that fell over bare shoulders and a slinky black dress that displayed her *wow!* cleavage. Her smell of sweat, perfume, and booze made my penis jump inside my pants.

"Hey, you're Al Landry's kid, right? You worked at the shop last summer." Usually adults talked to me as if I were a kid, which made me dislike them as a group, but this woman's voice was matter of fact, as if we were peers.

"Yeah, I'm Jack Landry. You're Olympia Troy, right? A weaver like my father?"

"So I am. Going in for some chow?"

"Yeah, we had a game and I'm always hungry afterwards. I was going to get a Western." I spoke very carefully, the way I'd been taught to speak to grown-ups.

Olympia gave me a look that no other girl or woman ever had. I didn't know what it meant, but I was interested.

"I got some leftover ham," she said. "I'll make you the best Western this side of El Paso."

I don't know what I said. Next thing I remember we were walking, heading for her place on 152 Church Street near the Eagle Club. I winced as we crossed the Beaver Brook bridge, where years earlier I'd stuck my tongue on the iron rail one winter day. The geography might have been familiar, but the territory was unknown, and I had no idea how to behave, so I told her all about the game. I almost never talked much, but nervousness made my mouth go into overdrive. Finally, Olympia interrupted me somewhere in the fifth inning.

"So how come it's ten o'clock at night and you're eating alone?" she asked.

I didn't know what to tell her. I didn't want to squeal on Beaupre and Katie, but I didn't want to lie either. I didn't say anything.

"Go ahead, I don't spill no secrets," Olympia said.

"My friend Beaupre has got this girl that he's been saving himself for."

"She must be special."

"Prettiest girl in Keene, Katie MacDonald."

"That's Skitzy's daughter. I know Skitzy."

I got the impression from her tone of voice and faint Cheshire (County) cat smile that she knew Coach MacDonald all too well.

"Coach doesn't want any of us ballplayers going out with his daughters," I said.

"So your pal and Katie slunk off wanting to be alone to go parking and you got left out."

"Not completely. Beaupre promised to let me use his car if I get a girl I'm serious about."

"You don't work at the shop no more?" Olympia said.

"My uncle Three-Fingered Willie got me a summer job at the Furniture Factory."

"You like that work better?"

"I do. I like working with wood." Without even thinking about it, I held out my hands like a offering. Olympia reached over from the sidewalk edge and took my left hand in her right hand and squeezed gently. We were holding hands. For a moment, I felt ten feet tall. Here I was, a youth of seventeen, with an older woman. I was excited and terrified thinking about what was going to happen next.

Olympia's apartment was plain, but very neat. While she puttered in the kitchen, I watched her tropical fish. Four tanks took up a lot of space and made the tiny living room feel cramped. Now it seemed to be her turn to be nervous, because she started to chatter away.

"That one's a twenty-gallon tank. Couple of plecos and a redtail shark. Three angelfish, some neon danios, dwarf gouramis. You're looking right now at a blue gourami. Good starter fish if you're interested."

She babbled on about the fish, but I stopped listening until I heard the magic words. "How do you like your Western? Heavy or light on the onions?"

I kept staring at the fish. I didn't dare look at her. Memere babbled something in French that I roughly translated as, *Tsee-yuh, what are you doing here?* I raised my voice ever so slightly, and said, "No onions."

"Jack, a Western omelet without no onions is called an Eastern."

Suddenly, I wasn't shy anymore. Watching the fish had allowed me to calm my mind, think through this alien situation. I turned away from the aquarium, and looked directly at Olympia Troy, and I said, "No wonder waitresses always look at me cuckoo when I ask for a Western with no onions."

That comment made her laugh. "Have a seat, cowpoke, and keep me company." She nodded at the kitchen table. I was pleased with myself and sat down. I felt as if I was in a movie watching me watching her.

She broke three eggs in a breakfast bowl, scrambled them in a little milk with a fork, added diced ham, sprinkled in salt and pepper, and poured the mix into a hot fry pan greased with half a wallop of Crisco and half of butter. When the eggs were cooked through on the bottom she folded up the sides with a spatula and flipped the pile over. I thought: Holy smoke, so that's how you make an omelet. She put two slices of bread in the toaster. When the toast popped, the omelet was ready. I was impressed by the timing.

I was hungry and ate two of those Western Easterns or Eastern Westerns with half a bottle of ketchup and drank a tall glass of milk. Olympia cleaned the table and did dishes while I ate.

"Finished?" Olympia said with a sly smile.

"Yep," I said, after I downed the last of the milk.

"You gotta a white mustache," Olympia said. She came over, bent, licked it clean. That got my attention.

We made out on the couch with our clothes on for a while, doing the kind of blue-ball stuff I was used to. I didn't have that feeling that I was cheating on the girl in my past life. What was happening was different. It wasn't love. It was a form of masturbation. A sin, but not a serious sin. And not a betrayal of my dream girl.

Olympia Troy was experienced, and I had no experience, so I decided to let her set the agenda. She was like a coach, and I was a rookie. It was heavenly touching her here and there.

"I like breasts," I said.

"I like hands, so we're even." She pulled away from me and lit a cigarette.

"The Old Golds keep me steady," she said, as she drew the smoke into her lungs.

"Not a cough in a carton." I repeated the company's advertising slogan.

"Jack, when did you first have the feeling for a woman?"

The question brought back my shyness for a moment, but then I started to talk and it felt good to say things I would never say to a friend or even a priest.

"I was, I don't know, maybe eleven or twelve. It was a Saturday afternoon Roy Rogers movie at the Scenic Theater. I suddenly started noticing Dale Evans instead of Gabby Hayes, the fringe on her buckskin blouse hanging there sticking out. All during that movie I watched the fringe jump around."

Olympia laughed. I could tell I was charming her, and I loved the feeling. She butted her cigarette in an ashtray. "Don't go away," she said, ducked into the bedroom and closed the door. She came out in a Western woman's outfit, like Dale Evans.

"This is what I wear at contra dances," she said, and went back in the bedroom, leaving the door open this time. I followed. She flopped on the bed, lying on her back. "Rope me," she said.

As far as I was concerned, she was Dale Evans. Olympia hiked up her skirt. No underpants. I lost myself in paradise. I could hear Dale Evans chanting Olympia's words, "Rope me, rope me." Olympia unzipped my fly. I lasted inside of her all of ten seconds, though they were the best ten seconds of my life thus far.

Half an hour, an Old Gold, and some conversation later, Olympia said, "Here, let me," as if she were reading my mind. She pulled my T-shirt up over my head. I shut my eyes while she undressed me. Then I watched while she stood by the bed and took her own clothes off in a businesslike way, as I imagined Dale undressed for Roy Rogers. I was ready again and lasted longer.

We lay in bed, content. "When you were looking at my fish wondering what the hell to do with an older woman you suddenly found some confidence," Olympia said. "What happened to set your mind?"

"When I meet somebody new I always figure out how I would pitch to them if we were playing baseball."

"Pitching a baseball is that involved?"

"It is for me. Watching the fish helped me concentrate on you. I thought experience at the plate. Weakness, maybe a little over the hill, needing to compensate for a bat that's not so quick anymore. She's going to wait on my curve because she knows she can get the bat around on that pitch. So I'm just going to throw her heat. Fastballs in different locations because she's going to be guessing on the location as well. Odds are in my favor I'll get her out."

Olympia laughed as if I were Red Skelton. "I don't have no idea what you are talking about, which I suppose is the great gulch between man and woman or maybe teenager and grown-up or maybe just me and everybody else. In my wanderings, I've cradled a robber and now I've robbed the cradle." And she laughed.

Olympia and I made a deal. We would see each other from time to time. "Now that you've had me, you're not going to be satisfied by no high school girl," Olympia said.

Olympia was right. After that episode I lost interest in high school girls as lovers. In one respect, I had the perfect deal for a young man. A sexy older woman who made no demands on him. But the relationship brought me some anguish, too. It upset me that I was only one of Olympia's boyfriends. I never fantasized about Olympia. She was all too real. My imaginary lover was a combination of the Indian maiden and Alouette Williams, who wore a yellow bathing suit like Katie MacDonald's. She was quite vivid in my imagination, this girl, but I was not. I could not imagine myself. Something about me was missing. In those moments when my faith was relatively strong I prayed to St. Anthony to help me find whatever it was that I had lost. *He who schemes for his own happiness hurts his loved ones*, Memere said.

Alouette

Bonus Baby?
July 1959

It was a beautiful July day for the annual Granite Lake Property Owners Association clambake in the field behind the beach. Earlier in the week, the Red Sox organization had been in touch with me through Coach MacDonald. The Red Sox did not offer me a contract, but they did invite me to attend a rookie camp in the Gulf Coast League in February.

My grades in high school were okay if not great, and I thought about going to a college that had a good baseball team, but my mother was terrified of the idea. "You'll lose your faith," she said. My father suggested that there was plenty of work in Keene these days, so why would I want to go to college or run off to play baseball – what kind of job was baseball? I went to Coach MacDonald and told him about my confusion. He asked me if I considered myself a snob. I said no. He told me that a person could go to college anytime, but a chance to play in the big leagues was a once in a lifetime opportunity. "Make your mother happy, make your town proud," he said. So I ruled out college.

Coach MacDonald had assured me that the Red Sox would offer me a bonus and that Beaupre would also be signed. Coach was wrong on both counts. The Red Sox showed no interest in Beaupre; a scout gave me a bare-bones offer: expenses and a modest allowance during rookie camp. I could have made more money working at the Furniture Factory. Coach assured me that if I did well, the Red Sox would assign me to one of their farm clubs. I'd be in the big leagues before I was old enough to buy beer.

Meanwhile, in his role as president of the Granite Lake Property Owners Association, Coach had hired me as Mystery Island caretaker for the summer, employment that Uncle Three-Fingers referred to as a "tit job." I would be required to sleep every night on the island as a guard to frustrate revelers and vandals. Ever since someone had chopped down trees on the island some years back, Coach was determined to protect the association's property. Naturally, I didn't tell Coach that it was Beaupre and I that cut down those trees, and with Coach's ax. "It will be a good job for you, Jack," Coach said. "It will keep you out of trouble. I want you ready for rookie camp, no distractions."

My chores included picking up litter: Dixie cups, Coke bottles, beer cans and beer bottles, paper in various guises, and cigarette butts. Whatever I couldn't burn in a fire pit, I ferried to shore in whichever boat Coach wanted to lend me that day: the Old Town canoe, the leaky wooden rowboat with the five-horsepower Johnson, and once in a great great while his new Chris-Craft, the only inboard runabout on the small lake.

Coach had invited my parents to the clambake as his guests. More than a hundred people sat around picnic tables and consumed boiled lobsters, steamed clams, clam chowder, corn on the cob, potato salad, dinner rolls, and strawberry shortcake. Just before the dessert line formed, Coach made a speech, a man obviously born to the megaphone he held in his hands. He cracked a few jokes about Ike's golf game; predicted the presidential candidates for the coming election, Democratic Senator Estes Kefauver and Republican Senator Robert Taft ("Remember where you heard it first"); thanked association members for their support; and introduced me as Mystery Island's caretaker for the summer; but he didn't stop there.

"Our Jack is a bonus baby," he announced. "He has signed a contract with our beloved Bosox, and has been ordered to rookie school in the Gulf Coast League, isn't that so, Jack?"

He made a motion for me to stand, and I stood, and the gathered gave me a warm round of applause. I smiled with forced bashfulness, but I felt like a phony. Bonus baby? Bonus babies were given big money to sign contracts. I tried to orient myself. Was I a bonus baby?

Coach was so persuasive that my mother whispered into my ear, "Is he right, Tsee-Guh? Are we rich?"

"No, Mummuh, there's no money involved."

"Good, I worry a little less," she said.

"Worry about what?"

"Worry that riches and glory will go to your head. Remember the teachings of the sisters. It is the meek who inherit the earth and the poor who gain the keys to the gates of heaven."

"The poor part is coming easy; it's the meek part I'm having problems with," I said.

"Don't be no Ernie Kovacs," my father said. "Listen to your mother."

"Sorry, Pop, I was just kidding."

My mother turned to my father and said to him, as if I were not there, "You think Skitzy MacDonald is a good man who does bad things or a bad man who does good things?"

"He's a politician, so it's hard to tell," my father said.

My parents rose to fetch their strawberry shortcake, and I left the picnic table with them, but I wanted to be alone and I didn't go to the food line. I walked through a few scrub gray birches and young white pines to the beach.

The Girl in the Dream

I sat in the wet sand at the lake's edge, and I didn't care that the water soaked through my dungarees. I had an idea to swim out to the island where, miraculously, I would find the Indian maiden who had been scorned by the voyageur three hundred or so years ago. I would not scorn her. I would hold her hand . . . and . . . and what? I was thinking about Olympia Troy now. Desire for the Indian maiden wasn't the same thing as desire for Olympia. So what was it, what did I want, what did I need? Tell me, St. Anthony what I have lost.

I kicked off my sneakers and threw them over my shoulder. "Hey, watch it!"

I turned, almost expecting the Indian girl to be there, and in the next instant I knew . . . somewhere deep inside I knew, I knew that my life was framed before me in the image of the girl standing in the sand in a Brigitte Bardot red and yellow bikini bathing suit, dark hair thrown back, mischievous eyes and mouth. I knew everything about her that had happened and the tragedy yet to come. It was Alouette Williams. I knew that I would love her until the end of our days. I knew that our epoch had begun long before either of us had been born. I knew that she knew that underneath my surface I bubbled molten lava millions of years old. She knew because she too resided in those depths, flowing and seeking to unite. That was how the moment hit me.

"You followed me out here, and I know why," I said, my voice casual and under control, because I knew we were sharing the same thoughts and feelings.

"I saw a bulge in your front pocket – let me have a nibble," Alouette said, taking a seat beside me in the sand.

I reached into the right thigh pocket of my dungarees, whipped out my pack of M&M's, poured a half dozen into Alouette's hand. She tipped her head back, dropped one in, crunched it, took another. Crunch. Another. Crunch. Until all six had been crunched. I watched with the awe of a child witnessing his first sword-swallow at the carnival.

I dumped four M&M's in my hand and nested them on my tongue, which I pressed against the roof of my mouth so I could feel the sugar slowly break down, then I shut my eyes. Hundreds of years of bliss went by. When I opened my eyes, the chocolate had been released and Alouette was looking me over.

"Can I see?" she said in a reverent whisper.

I opened my mouth, and she peered inside.

"That's how you eat Mother Marys?" she whispered. "Melt the sugar, then just let the chocolate sit there and seep down?"

"It's the only way for me," I whispered.

"I smash them between my teeth. I like the graininess. When you had your eyes closed, you went back in time, didn't you?"

"Yes, I was looking for you," I said, and it was not an idle comment. It came from that volcanic chamber deep inside myself.

"You're an old soul," she said.

"That's what my memere used to say."

"I'm an old soul, too, and I love my Mother Marys."

I gave her some more M&M's, and the two of us, each in our own way, ate the rest in silent pleasure. I was so at ease I didn't even leave backups for an emergency. The awesome responsibility I felt for succeeding as a baseball player, not for myself but for my coach and my town and for the idea that talent must not be wasted; my sadness that my best friend would not be joining me at Red Sox rookie camp; my secret glee that I alone had been chosen; my guilt that I was betraying my parents and my French-Canadian American heritage by seeking success; my vanity that I could strike out the world; my guilt for carrying on an affair with an older woman and without the element of love; my suspicion that I was as much fraud as Frog: these conflicts, roiling inside of me, fell away. All that mattered was this moment with this girl.

When we were finished with the M&M's, we continued our whispered conversation. In our minds we had been transported to that place in time past where only we lived and where only soft speech was permissible.

"I've been thinking about you ever since I first saw you two summers ago at Narrow Textiles," I said.

"I knew that when I followed you out here from the clambake."

"Your name is Alouette, and you're Mr. Williams's daughter."

"Yes, my father and his wife and baby are staying at my father's family summer house on the lake."

"Shinbone Shack?"

Alouette laughed. "Don't call it that when Daddy's around. Your father works for my father at the plant."

"The plant? We call it the shop. That's where I first saw you."

"I remember. I had just got off the plane for a visit with Daddy, and I was disoriented, which is why I needed the Mother Marys you gave me."

"Do you remember the noises in the shop, the din from the machine room?"

"No. My father doesn't allow me in. He says it's too disagreeable."

"I never saw you again until now. You don't go to Keene High."

"I'm only around for the summer. I live with my mother and her new husband on the Gulf Coast, and I go to a Catholic boarding school in New Orleans."

"You're a Catholic?"

"Oh, yes." Alouette thumped her chest with her right fist. "Sometimes I think Jesus is my only friend. My mother sends me to a Catholic school, but my parents are not believers." She paused, and something in her eyes – an anguish – touched my heart. "My family is scattered, my friends are scattered, my beliefs are scattered, my entire being is scattered. I'm not a whole person, I'm just blowing in the wind." Though her words were despairing, her tone was rich with hope, hurt, rage, and a kind of excitement, as if she had just discovered some great truth exploring a Roman catacomb. Her breath punched through my eardrum, slipped around the side of my neck and down my spinal column.

"I heard Mr. MacDonald call you Jack," Alouette said.

"That's me, Jack Landry, full name Joseph Jacques St. Vincent de Paul Landry," I whispered. "My memere named me after the son she lost in childbirth. When she was old and her mind was addled she used to think I was the son she never had."

"They don't call you Joe?"

"The French-Canadian farmers along the St. Lawrence River named all their boys Joseph and all their girls Marie – get it?"

"Yeah, too many Joes, so they gave you another name to go by. How did you become a Jack?"

"When I was a little kid I was Jacques. By the time I reached kindergarten I spoke only a few words in English. They laughed at me. I came home from school and told my parents I was never going to speak that awful French language again. They held a family meeting and, over the objections of Memere, they stopped talking French in the house and started calling me Jack. Memere countered by falling on the ice right here on Granite Lake and cracking her head open. I saw her die, I saw her eyes searching for heaven. She's been haunting me ever since, because I don't *parlez-vous.*"

"You're like me, Jacques, trapped in time. I could never love a boy named Jack, but Jacques, oh, Jacques, that's a name I can taste."

A moment later a wave broke across our feet, and suddenly the spiritual feeling that had come over us vanished, and we were back in the material world. We stared at each other, embarrassed as Adam and Eve upon their discovery of television. Finally, I took Alouette's hand and we walked along the beach, a very short beach, only a hundred feet or so long, when it gave way to narrow camp lots, each with a small boat dock, homemade barbecue pits of cinder blocks, scraggly lawns under hemlocks, red spruces, white pines, and birches, wood-frame cabins that we called camps. We trespassed through yards until we reached the MacDonald place. No one home; all the MacDonalds were at the clambake.

We walked out to the end of the T of the dock and sat in fold-up wooden lounge chairs, at our feet a set of water skis and a snorkel. Faintly smelling of dead perch, the rowboat with the five-horsepower Johnson was tied to one side of the dock, the Chris-Craft to the other. The Old Town canoe was pulled up on the grass beside the dock.

"You like the lake?" I asked.

"I like the lake house; my grandfather was rich and he built it for my grandmother, Mirriam, but she committed suicide anyway. I like my father, I like Moses our poodle, I don't like his wife . . ."

I interrupted, "The poodle has a wife?"

"That's correct," Alouette said with a straight face. "I'm jealous of the poodle's wife, the bitch. You ought to see her, sticks her face in the plate to eat, goes to the toilet on the front steps, refuses to wear a sanitary napkin when she's having her period, bites for no reason at all. Just had a litter of puppies, ate all but one who I'm supposed to think of as my brother. Do you think the poodle husband will be upset if I put the bitch in a sack and drown her in the lake?"

"The bitch might resurface when the lake turns over."

"Lake turns over – what does that mean?"

"Every spring and fall, the bottom of the lake roils up. The waters become muddy and dirty, and strange things float to the top."

Alouette clicked her tongue. "You're a ballplayer and bonus baby, that sounds exciting."

I knew I should be honest with Alouette, but I wanted to impress her so I was only half honest.

"I am a ballplayer, a pitcher," I said, and I told her about my desire for a baseball career and my job as caretaker of Mystery Island. I omitted telling her I was not a bonus baby. "Coach has been good to me, but I feel like his prisoner, and he's got a warped mind. The only time I can relax is when I'm on the island – it's intense."

"Is that because Boy Scouts and Girl Scouts live on the island?"

"What?" I asked.

"Who else lives in tents? What do you call a girl with snarly hair?" Alouette asked.

"I don't know – what do you call a girl with snarly hair?"

"Heather."

I was beginning to understand; I thought for a minute and said, "What do you call a guy who has been run over by a steam roller?"

"I don't know."

"Mat."

"What do you call a girl with a taste for martinis?" Alouette asked.

"I don't know."

"Ginny?"

We both laughed.

I told Alouette the tragic tale of the Indian maiden of Mystery Island, how peaceful it was in my tent at night with the sounds of water kissing rocks on the shore, birds in the trees, crickets, and the wails of Indian ghosts lamenting the passing of their way of life.

Alouette pointed to the Chris-Craft with its windshield and steering wheel, and said, "It looks like my grandfather Preston's Lincoln."

"It starts and steers like a car, too. You just turn the key, put it in gear, and off it goes."

"Drive me out to the island." Alouette spoke in a tone that told me she was not begging nor asking nor demanding. She was voicing our mutual desire.

I sometimes operated the Chris-Craft when the MacDonald girls and their friends wanted to go water-skiing, but it had never occurred to me until now to take the boat for my own uses and without permission.

Joy Riders

I released the lines that held the Chris-Craft against old tires serving as bumpers on the dock. I turned the key, and the Chris-Craft started with a sound like a dragon clearing his throat and farting at the same time. I eased the throttle until I knew I was in deep enough water to gun it. "Hang on," I said, and I pushed the throttle forward as far as it would go.

The engine heaved, foam bubbled from the stern, the bow arced toward the planet Venus, and the boat shot forward. Alouette wasn't expecting the sudden G-forces and she fell backward onto the deck.

"Are you all right?" I shouted above the roar.

"I'm happy, I'm happy," she said with hysterical glee. She sucked on her arm, and I could see blood on her lips.

"It's just a scratch," she said, responding to the alarm on my face.

"Coach says you can't turn this boat over no matter how hard you try – well, I'm going to try," I shouted. "Hang on."

I cut the wheel so that the hull was almost sideways to the lake, and the propeller came out of the water with a falsetto whine. I turned into the wake to make the hull bounce. No matter what I did, the Chris-Craft remained stable. Alouette sat in the back, where spray stung her skin and made her laugh/cry. I hadn't felt so free since I was a kid riding my bicycle down Roxbury Street, feet on the handlebars.

I slowed the boat as we entered the tiny cove on the eastern shore of the island. I dropped the anchor, and with the bow line in my hand, leaped out onto a rock where I fell and, like Alouette before me, scraped my arm enough to make it bleed.

"I love blood," Alouette yelled.

She stood up on the stern cowling, held her nose between thumb and forefinger, and jumped into the lake. I walked up the narrow path to the ledge, where I sat and watched Alouette dog-paddle around the boat. I smelled sun on the pine trees. I was content just to be.

Alouette came out of the water with a question. "What do you get when a masochistic girl marries a president?"

"I don't know."

"Maim me Eisenhower."

"I can't beat that," I said, laughing. "I'll get you a towel." I headed for the tent, which included a cot, my stuff in a rucksack, a rake, a long-handle shovel, a bow saw, an ax, and a porta potty, all lined up neatly on one side of the tent.

Alouette was at the tent flap by the time I found a towel. I handed it to her. She put the towel around her arm where the blood had started to clot.

"I bet you never get depressed out there," she said.

"Never – never. Depression is just a state of mind," I said.

Alouette lipped but did not voice my words: *Depression is just a state of mime.*

We went over to the ledge and sat looking out at the lake, watching water skiers, occasional fishermen trolling Dare Devil lures, and people in power boats just going up down the lake for the sheer, or maybe the pretend, fun of boating.

"You want to be a baseball player like Mickey Mantle," Alouette said.

"No, like Smoky Joe Wood. He was an old-time fireballer for the Red Sox, and there's a street named after him in Keene, down by the river. I used to imagine that they named a street after me for my exploits on the mound until I realized it was a sin."

"So you don't imagine it anymore?"

"I do – I can't seem to stop sinning."

"If you died young and tragically, they might name a street after you whether you were good at baseball or not."

"I don't think I want to die young."

"Are you afraid of death?"

"No. I'm afraid of my dreams. I see fires from the distant past. I wake with a feeling that home is far away in a different time period. What are you afraid of?"

"That I won't fulfill myself?"

"Like what?"

"Like go to a good college where I can snag a husband, preferably a doctor," Alouette said, with a big fake sigh.

"What do you really want, Alouette?"

"I want to right all the wrongs in the world and save humanity, Jacques."

I might have been tempted to joke, but there was something in Alouette's voice – a fierceness, a determination, a sincerity – that I admired too much to make fun of.

I put my arm around her shoulder. She turned toward me and shut her eyes. I kissed her, a respectful no tongue first-time kiss. Then I pulled back and held her hand in both of my own, and I took her in with my eyes: her bare tanned skin, the bloody towel, her red-painted toes, her beautiful face, a face I could believe in.

"Just looking at you makes me happy," I said.

"Show me your bloody arm."

I held up my arm. The blood had coagulated, leaving a soft, ugly sponge of red. Alouette held her own bloody arm against my bloody arm.

"There – we can do it. My blood, your blood – we can make the world all over again," she said, in a way that told me she had thought about the idea for a long time.

I could feel the stickiness of her blood.

"I like you, Alouette. From the first moment I saw you back at Narrow Textiles two years ago, I wanted you to be my girl. I tried to forget you, but I couldn't. Even Memere loved you. She talked about you in my dreams. She said we were old lovers from bad days gone by. I've been searching for you through lifetimes."

"Jacques – Jacques," she said, licking her lips with my name. "Kiss me again, kiss me and make me faint."

I kissed her. And I kissed her again. And then she kissed me. And kissed me again. In a crazy kind of way that made me a little more than kin to myself, I felt pure and holy.

I lay supine on the ledge, the pitted granite biting into my back. Alouette knelt over me exploring like a medical student. When she reached the scar on the sole of my right foot, she said, "What's this?"

"It's where I lost my virginity, sort of," I said, and I told her the strange story of how I learned say that word.

"Mary Magdalene washed Jesus's feet with her hair," Alouette said, and she kissed the scar on the bottom of my foot. "I lost my virginity playing tennis. I cried for three days."

"I'm sorry," I said.

"It wasn't the physical loss that bothered me. It was that it was so mundane, so stupid, so unromantic. I want beautiful things to happen to me. I want to be part of something extraordinary that celebrates my womanhood."

At that moment, I heard the peculiar ping of Coach MacDonald's five-horsepower Johnson. From the ledge, I watched the leaky rowboat chugging toward us. Coach sat at the stern, the steering handle of the outboard in his hand. In the middle seat, hands on his knees, staring straight ahead, was Hiram Williams.

"Oh-oh." I removed my arm from Alouette's shoulder.

We walked down to the cove. Coach brought the rowboat alongside the Chris-Craft and killed the engine. He pulled an oar out of the oarlock and extended it toward me. I grabbed the end of the oar and pulled the rowboat to the rocky shore. Coach drew the oar in and returned it to the oarlock. Then he reached down and tossed my sneakers at me, first the right, then the left. I felt good catching them. It was like snagging fungoes.

Coach stepped out of the boat onto the shore, then offered a hand to Hiram Williams. It seemed to me that Hiram Williams, who two years ago was pudgy, was now certifiably fat.

"Here's the deal," Coach said, giving me his Jimmy Cagney *you-dirty-rat* look. "I'm taking Mr. Williams and his daughter back to their place in the Chris-Craft. I'll leave the Johnson with you. I'll tell your parents you're on duty at the island, okay?"

"Okay, Coach." I sat down and put my sneakers on. I didn't worry that the socks were missing.

Hiram Williams looked at his daughter. "What happened to your arm?"

"I scratched it when I fell in the boat."

"Yeah, we saw you hot-dogging out there." Coach addressed me.

Hiram Williams pointed to the Chris-Craft, and Alouette stepped on board. Then Mr. Williams turned to me and smiled at me, that nasty malicious smile.

"Young man," Mr. Williams said, "you, I am told, are eighteen years old. Is that correct?"

"Yes, sir."

"My daughter is only fifteen, not of age. She is a minor under my care, you understand?"

"Yes, sir."

"If I learn that you have been keeping company with my daughter again, I will contact the authorities. Is that clear?"

"Yes, sir."

"Alouette, you brought reading matter from Mississippi with you, did you not?"

"Yes, Daddy."

"Well, you will have time to catch up on that reading, because you will not be leaving the lake house for two weeks."

"Okay, Daddy. Goodbye, Jacques," Alouette said, her voice thin and far away, belonging, it seemed, to a different person than the one I had just kissed.

An idea firmed in my mind: Alouette was the reincarnation of the Indian maiden of Mystery Island. I cupped my hands and hollered through the hole, "What do you call a girl home run hitter?"

"Ruth," Alouette said. "Ruth."

The Chris-Craft suddenly roared as if protesting the word play, or perhaps any play at all, and lurched forward. I watched Alouette grow obscure in the spray and the bend of lake light as the boat sped off. "Ruth! Ruth!" I shouted to no one.

A Warning

After dark, I heard the farting/belching/snorting of the Chris-Craft as it started up half a mile away. That's what it was like at the island: Depending on the wind, you might be entirely insulated from noises on the lake shore; at other times, you could hear conversations, music, cars, laughter, and boat engines, but the sounds never seemed real. It was as if I were eavesdropping on events that were occurring outside my own epoch.

From the ledge, I watched the running lights of the Chris-Craft as it approached the island. Coach was coming out to see me, no doubt to deliver one of his signature lectures.

What could he do to me? Fire me? Tell me to stop chasing girls? No doubt he was going to chew me out because I took his Chris-Craft. He had cause to be angry.

I went down with a flashlight to the cove to meet Coach. His Lordship, the maple tree of Beaupre's bat, loomed over us like a chortling judge laughing at the fools that come before his bench. Coach grabbed my flashlight, led the way, as we walked the hundred or so feet to my tent.

I had a campfire going, and Coach and I sat on the log to watch the flames. Coach gave me the flashlight, grabbed a stick, and poked at the flames.

"You know what your problem is, Jack?" Coach posed a question, but I knew I was not expected to answer. "Your problem is you're French."

I was outraged on behalf of my family as well as myself. "I have never been to France, my parents have never been to France, so how can we be French?"

"France is in your bloodstream like bacteria. It's not your fault. See, Jack, unlike you, I have been to France, I liberated France. *Libertay, fraternitay*, and whatever else. I've seen the French. They are a sneaky people. Appear to be submissive and law-abiding, but when you turn your back they'll joyride your Chris-Craft with the teak decking and mahogany hull that you paid an arm and a leg for, so you could give your daughters the best water-ski boat on Granite Lake, and you give this French kid a dream job – caretaker of Mystery Island. If you're going to make it in the bigs, not just for yourself, you ungrateful piss-aunt but for the greater glory of Post 7 American Legion baseball, then you must stop thinking with your pecker."

Men on first and third, one out. Sacrifice fly will bring in a run. Coach will wait for a pitch he can lift. I better keep the ball down. Low curve on the outside corner – call strike one. He steps closer to the plate. Fastball on the fists. Ball one. Fastball on the fists. Ball two. Fastball on the fists. Foul ball. Two and two. Fastball down the middle, but low and off speed. Grounder to short. Double play.

"Stop mumbling and listen to me," Coach said. "There's certain things you have to understand. The age of consent is sixteen. That girl is fifteen. Normally, you could get away with it because you're a young fellow yourself, but this girl's father is a big shot and he doesn't like you, especially when he saw the blood on her arm and on your arm. What the hell did you do to her? Don't answer the question. I don't want to know anything in case this winds up in a court of law. Let's just say you made a rookie mistake. It's not only you that's at risk, it's our team getting beat yet again by John Watterson's boys, but more important to you, it's Alcide."

I was suddenly paying attention. "My father, what does he have to do with this?"

Coach poked viciously at the fire, raising sparks, scattering embers. He turned to me and said in a soft voice, "What do you think of me?"

"You're the best baseball coach in American Legion ball," I said, hating myself.

"And you're the best young arm in northern New England," Coach said. "Now, Jack, you know you screwed up today."

"Coach, I know I shouldn't have taken the Chris-Craft – I went a little crazy. But I never touched that girl except in a tender way."

"I'll forget the boat, you forget the girl. By the way, you couldn't tip it over, could you?" Coach gave me a little triumphant laugh. Then he added, poking in my direction with the fiery stick, "Just remember: You owe me. You . . . owe me."

"What did you mean about my father?"

"If Hiram Williams gets wind that you're seeing his daughter again, I guarantee he will take retaliatory action not just against you but against Al and me. I need Williams's support on the council. Your father needs his job to support his family."

"You think he'd fire my father?"

"I wouldn't put it past him."

"I never thought of that, I never thought . . ."

"That's right – you never thought. Jack, I told Williams you were a prospect for the big leagues, I told him, but all he knows is you're the son of an ignorant Frog who works for him. He doesn't want his daughter cavorting with a factory worker's son. That's all you need to know. Stay away, okay? Stay away. Make the big leagues and then maybe, just maybe, you'll have a chance for a girl like that."

Slippery Water

Heartsick

The day after Coach MacDonald warned me about the dangers of seeing Alouette Williams, I had the worst outing of my career pitching for Post 7. I couldn't find home plate, I hit a batter, and Coach pulled me out of the game in the second inning after I'd allowed five earned runs. Coach asked me if I was all right and I said I couldn't concentrate.

"You look a little off balance, like you have an inner ear problem," Coach said. "I'll give you some aspirin – you'll be hunky dory."

The next day I had another visitor at Mystery Island. I could see him a long ways off paddling toward me in the MacDonalds' Old Town canoe. It wasn't until he was in the cove that I recognized the true identity of the paddler.

"Father Gonzaga!" I shouted.

"Have you been to confession?" He pointed with the paddle and almost tipped the canoe.

"Not for a while, Father." I crossed myself, and grabbed his hand as he hopped awkwardly from the canoe to the rocky shore.

We sat on a fallen log under His Lordship the maple tree. Father Gonzaga wore a red-and-black checkered woodsman's shirt, heavy work pants, and a floppy green hat at a rakish angle. He spoke with a strong Quebecois accent. It took a minute or so for me to figure out who he reminded me of, myself in some previous epoch.

"You look like a voyageur of old," I said.

"Of course," Father Gonzaga said. "This is a transitional period. During such times one adopts an historical garb. Only temporary."

He explained that he had come out of a monastery in French Canada where he had gone for a retreat.

"Kneel." Father Gonzaga pointed to the ground.

I knelt in the forest duff while Father Gonzaga remained on a fallen log, the stole around his neck. I confessed the old sins of breaking into the abandoned building, of cutting Beaupre's bat out of the tree under whose shade we now resided. I confessed taunting my cousin Chalky after he ruined my perfect game.

"Taunting him – how so?" Father Gonzaga asked.

"Well, he looks like Alfred E. Neuman, and he's sensitive about it," I said.

"You rubbed it in."

"Yes, I rubbed it in."

I confessed mocking my sisters and their chatty friends. I confessed my affair with Olympia Troy. (I tried to sneak it in by burying it among lesser sins.) I confessed borrowing Coach MacDonald's Chris-Craft without permission and operating it recklessly.

For sure, I thought, he's going to ask for details about my shenanigans with Olympia, but he only shrugged, and said, "There's something else, isn't there?"

"No," I said.

"What about the girl?" His lips twisted with accusation, and his breath quickened.

"How do you know about her?"

"I keep tabs on my flock."

"All I did was kiss her. That's not a sin."

"No impure thoughts?"

"No, Father. My thoughts about Alouette were and are mysterious, beautiful, historical, and very, very pure." I took a deep breath. Father Gonzaga's question had brought out my best thought in my best language. He appeared disappointed.

"It's not normal," he said. "It could be the work of the Devil. You have to confess the details of your machinations with this girl or I can't give you absolution."

I stood from my kneeling position. His words turned me against him, turned me against God. "I don't want absolution. I don't believe anymore," I said.

As usual, Father Gonzaga surprised me. Instead of acting disappointed by my behavior he returned a sly smile of amusement.

"It's all right, Jack. You're just heartsick. It's a common ailment among young persons, though usually at an earlier age. The fact that it's hitting you at eighteen means you have a more severe case. You'll get over it. But let me add one cautionary element. The fact that you won't confess . . ." He paused, then continued. "Let us say it does not bode well. I will pray for you."

He stood, pulled the stole off his neck, folded it, and put it in his pocket. I resisted an urge to step on his new work boots to scuff them. I watched him walk to the canoe, the stole popping out of the pocket and dangling from his pants, an unnecessary appendage.

Textures of a Baseball

Four days later, I was on the mound again. I pitched like a robot, and through eight innings I had a no-hitter going. In the ninth inning, it was as if I suddenly woke up out of a dream. I deliberately threw a fastball down the middle of the plate to the number-three hitter in the lineup. The batter swung and missed. I threw another lazier fastball, and the batter fouled that one off.

I yelled at the batter, "You want me to put it on a tee for you?"

Beaupre turned to the umpire, called time, stood, raised his catcher's mask onto his head, like a knight raising his visor, and walked slowly to the mound, left hand in his mitt, right hand holding the ball. Beaupre was not tall, but he was built solid as an old apple tree. As a boy, Beaupre had copied John Wayne's wiggle-walk to give himself confidence. In those days the walk appeared a little ridiculous on one so young. Over the next few years, he made the walk his own; the walk said *I can get it up any time I want.*

"Your fucking arm getting tired? You're missing the corners, Jack, and the fastball is not jumping," Beaupre said.

"I'm not tired," I said.

"What's the fucking matter, Jack?"

"Shut up, and give me the ball."

Beaupre laughed a little, gave me the ball, lowered his mask, and returned to his position behind the plate.

I knew I was acting crazy, but I didn't feel crazy. I felt as if I was close to being the man I wanted to be, a person who made his own decisions according to his own desires, and did not need a God, a coach, nor even a friend.

I held my right hand behind my back, turning the ball, feeling the seams on my fingertips. I bent and peered at Beaupre's mitt. I hardly noticed the batter. Beaupre held up two fingers – curveball, outside corner. I threw another fastball down the middle, and the batter finally caught up with it and pasted it hard down the line for a stand-up double.

I didn't care that the no-hitter had gone by the boards. I was secretly gleeful.

The next batter hit the first pitch over the second baseman's head for a single and scored the man on second.

Coach MacDonald rose from the bench seat in the dugout and stood, one foot on the top step, the other foot below. He couldn't have been too worried. He had a big lead and there was one out in the last inning, but he didn't like the way his pitcher was throwing.

The next batter hit a long fly ball that was caught by Chalky in front of the fence.

Beaupre again came out to the mound.

"Jack, why are you throwing fucking fastballs down the middle of the plate when I'm calling for fucking curves on the corners?"

"Fuck you."

Beaupre turned his head toward the dugout, and Coach Mac-Donald jogged to the mound. "What the hell is going on?" he asked.

Beaupre looked at me and said, "Jack?"

I stared off in the direction of Alpha Centauri. "I'll nail this last guy, no problem," I said.

Coach took the ball out of Beaupre's hand and put it in mine.

I struck out the last batter on three pitches, all fastballs.

In victory I was thinking about the ball in my hand behind my back as I prepared to pitch: the white cowhide, the red seams, sewn like the way my mother sewed, like the way my father wove, the feel of the colors on the tips of my fingers, the texture of color, the texture of a curveball, the texture of a fastball, the texture of a sinker, the texture of a screwball, the texture of a change-up. *That's what it's about, I thought.* It's about ignoring the tricks of sight to apprehend color and texture, because the hands are more sensitive and knowledgeable than the eyes or brain. Was I a ballplayer? I didn't know anymore.

On the Ledge

I did not celebrate that night with Beaupre and the other players. I returned to the lake with Coach in his new Cadillac; he yakked on about his plans to run for mayor. Perhaps he talked with an Irish brogue to get votes. His last words were, "Good game. I like the way you snapped out of it. Too bad about the no-hitter."

"Thanks, Coach," I said, but even in that simple response I knew I was lying, and I despised myself for not standing up to Skitzy MacDonald and his twists on truth, and I hated my team and the very idea of baseball, my long dedication to that sport an anguish, for it seemed to me that I had missed out on matters that were so much more important and meaningful. *What matters, Jack? What are you talking about?* The questions were in English, but the voice in my head belonged to Memere.

Later that night, on Mystery Island, unable to sleep, I stripped naked and went outside for the late-night mosquito wave and stood under the moon and let the little crucifiers have at me until I couldn't take it anymore and I screamed, my echo frightening me for the desperation I heard in the voice of that stranger I was trying so hard to acquaint myself with.

Back in the cabin on the cot, I writhed in discomfort the remainder of the night. Finally, at dawn I fell asleep, and Memere appeared, babbling to me in her New England French-Canada patois.

"Memere," I said, "*Je ne peux plus comprendre français dans mes rêves.*"

Memere stopped talking and pointed to the ledge at the island, which in the dream was much higher up from the water than the mere ten-foot height of the ledge of waking reality.

On the ledge stood the Indian maiden of Mystery Island, looking at me with pleading eyes. "Marry me to unite our warring peoples," she said in perfect mid-twentieth-century New England English.

I wanted to say, "Yes, yes, I will," but the words that came out of my mouth were in corrupted French, and the Indian maiden did not understand and leaped off the ledge and disappeared into the depths. I was left alone and bereft.

I slept all day. When I woke, mosquito bites stippled my body, but the itching had gone away and I knew the welts would recede by evening.

That night, I stood on the ledge and made a resolution. Not my coach, not my parents, not my half-assed loyalty to Olympia Troy, not my best friend Elphege Beaupre, not Hiram Williams, not Father Gonzaga, not the Catholic God, nor the ghost of Memere was going to keep me from Alouette Williams. Only a word from her would drive me away. I almost hoped she would refuse me so I could return to my comfortable life of Olympia Troy, baseball, baseball, and baseball.

Love

A little after 1 A.M., I slipped into the canoe and paddled to Shin-bone Shack. It was a sultry summer night, the lake almost perfectly flat, moon glow leaving hieroglyphics of light on the lake's surface. I left the canoe half in the water, half on the narrow beach beside the dock.

A dog barked, no doubt Moses, the poodle that Alouette had referred to in her tirade against her stepmother. I waited a few minutes, and the barking stopped.

I guessed that Alouette's bedroom was on the second floor, the one with the window open at the end of the house. It did not occur to me that I might be approaching the bedroom of Mr. and Mrs. Williams, or perhaps the bedroom of the couple's baby, or merely one of the many other rooms in the Williams mansion.

I moved out of the shadow of the trees into the moonlight and tossed a stone. It hit the screen. Tossed another. Another. Each one hit the screen dead center. I picked up a bigger rock and aimed my fourth toss at the wall above the window. I heard it thunk.

"Ball one," I spoke aloud.

Seconds later the screen went up, and Alouette poked her head out, and said just as perfectly natural as if we were in the middle of a conversation, "What do you call a girl with a wooden leg?"

"Peg," I said. "I've got Coach's canoe. What do you call a girl named after the Confederate army without its greatest general?"

"Less Lee – Leslie. I'll get dressed and meet you at the back door. I knew you'd come."

Minutes later, I put my arms around Alouette's waist and kissed her. She wore yellow shorts and she carried a canvas bag. I smelled her scent, some kind of magic substance for which I had no name nor experience with but that I knew would guide our actions.

We walked holding hands to the beach. The silhouette of the island stood out in front of the distant hills. I imagined myself in outer space gripping the craters of the moon, winding up, pitching it over a corner of the island. Strike one.

We kicked off our shoes and dropped them into the canoe.

"Hop in," I said.

Alouette eased into the front rawhide weave seat and faced the stern so she could see me. I slid the canoe over the sand into the water, warm and tactile as touch on my bare feet. I stepped into the canoe, knelt, pushed off with the paddle. A scraping sound, then quiet as water caressed the hull.

"We've left that sad world behind," Alouette said, her soft southland voice in union with this sultry night.

I J-stroked to keep the bow toward the island. "I wonder if the ghosts of grandpa Indian and his heartsick granddaughter are haunting tonight," I said.

"I hope so," Alouette said.

I told her about the games I'd pitched, how unimportant they seemed since I'd met her. Alouette talked about her "incarceration" in Shinbone Shack.

"I read *Evangeline* over and over again," Alouette said. "I didn't mind being alone with just books for company. What bothered me was not being allowed to leave. I want to be free, Jacques, I want to be free."

After minute or so, when the only sound was the paddle parting the waters, I asked, "Alouette, what does your father do?"

"He's the general manager of Narrow Textiles – you know that."

"But what does he do? I mean, I know what my father does. I've seen him work on the looms. I've seen him twist the threads with his long fingernails to make knots. What does a general manager do? What does Hiram Williams do for his company?"

"He doesn't make knots. I don't really know what he does. Lots of meetings. Traveling. I've lived with him in five different towns in four different states with two different wives and a girlfriend, and that doesn't include my mother's house in Bay St. Louis. He goes to work at nine o'clock in the morning, and sometimes he's not back until midnight. Lately he's been calling himself Paladin, have gun will travel." Her voice fell, because as she spoke the words, it must have suddenly occurred to her what her father had meant by referring to himself as Paladin.

I remembered what Father Gonzaga had told me about Hiram Williams. He's a fast gun. Sticks around two or three years, then a big layoff.

"I don't understand," I said.

"Me either," Alouette said.

There was a quiet moment. We both knew we were lying; we were both ashamed.

"I know this much: His work keeps him up at night," Alouette said.

"Well, not tonight it didn't, lucky for us."

Alouette laughed, I laughed, and suddenly we were quiet again, because the sound of our laughter, not the laughter of mirth but the laughter of scorn and deceit, seemed a violation of the night.

When we reached the island, I pulled the canoe up on a rock and the present moment was so shockingly alive with the sounds of the island that as we stepped out of the canoe we found ourselves temporarily welded to the rock. I heard the Indian grandfather whisper in my ear, *Listen.* We listened to peepers and frogs and insects and strange sounds emanating from who knows where and that we could not identify.

"What's that noise?" Alouette asked.

"I don't know."

"I think it's the voyageur in his canoe singing to the rhythm of his paddling," Alouette said. "Let's go swimming."

"Did you bring a suit?" I asked.

"No, but I brought a blanket and a towel." She spoke in a very serious tone.

I helped Alouette lay the blanket out smooth on pine needles. I did not watch Alouette undress under moonlight. I did not believe I deserved that privilege. My impulse was to run into the water and make a big splash like a kid, but Alouette took my hand

and led me in slowly. It was the right way to enter, silently like a pair of snakes.

We broke the flat surface into ripples that bent the reflected moon glow into boomerangs of light, water warm and slippery against our skin. We swam with only our heads above water to make as little noise as possible. We swam and embraced and did not speak. It was as if we were in a great cathedral and it would be disrespectful to raise our voices. We swam and kissed and swam some more and kissed again. Without discussion or even gesture, we both knew what would happen next.

We came out of the water holding hands and lay down on the blanket on the pine needles.

"We're purified now," Alouette said. "We can't fool each other here. We can't lie."

"It's the island, it doesn't allow lies," I said.

"I've been waiting for this moment for hundreds of years," she said.

Everything about Alouette – hands, mouth, breasts, curves of her hips – was smaller than Olympia Troy. Olympia could be whatever she wanted to be with a man. Alouette could only be herself. Making love to her, I felt as if I were performing a rite in a sacred ceremony. We remained on the blanket for a long time in each other's arms weeping softly, crazy with love and sorrow.

Let's Play Chicken

Mad, Mad Youth
Early August 1959

Alouette and I had gone to the Ice Creamery in Beaupre's '49 Ford, while Beaupre and Katie MacDonald went to see *The Horse Soldiers*. I ate a hot fudge sundae with M&M's and Alouette a banana split with M&M's. We drove around town in that pleasant euphoric state produced by ice cream and chocolate.

"Do you think everybody will go to hell after the atomic war, or just the bad people?" Alouette asked.

"You mean God will punish us all? It doesn't seem fair."

"That's what scares me most. That God is not fair."

"Beaupre and Katie don't believe in God. Me, I don't know what to believe. One day I'm a Catholic, next day a pagan. What do you believe, Alouette?"

"I believe in you and me and past lives, Jacques. I'm Evangeline and you're Gabriel, and we were separated on our wedding day. We've been chasing each other through history."

"You're being metaphorical, right?"

"No, I'm speaking the truth of profound reality."

Alouette's talk might have been crazy, but the way she spoke her words, with deep conviction and a faraway look in her eyes, made me love her all the more, even if I didn't understand her.

I slowed to a stop at the Main Street lights. Ahead was Central Square with its Civil War soldier in bronze, the park benches where

vagrants had passed the time since the 1700s, a bubbler that produced only a trickle of tin-tasting water. Overlooking all was the
Protestant God in the belfry of the whitewashed First Congregational Church. First Congo, we teenagers called it. Beaupre had
installed a glass-pack muffler in the Ford, and the vehicle backed
off impressively while I casually revved the engine as we waited for
the light to turn green.

On one side of us was Wes Leb on a Harley motorcycle. He wore
a leather jacket, black engineer boots, and dark sunglasses. He
was a couple years older than I, an Elvis look-alike who got all
the girls.

Chalky and Spud in the newly pin-striped Chevy pulled up on
the other side of the Ford. Chalky was driving.

"Hey, Jack, want to play chicken?" asked Chalky.

"Not with you, Chalky."

"Because you're chicken."

"What, me worry?" I shouted loud enough so that Wes Leb
would hear, a move that I knew would tick Chalky off.

Chalky peeled out with tires squealing as the light turned green,
but the Chevy still lagged behind Wes Leb and his Harley.

I drove slowly away from the light.

"Who are they?" Alouette asked.

"My goofy cousin, Chalky Landry, and his pal, Spud Polix."

"Chalky looks like Alfred E. Neuman."

"Yeah, he hates it when I say 'What, me worry?' It always shuts
him up."

"What's chicken?" Alouette asked.

"Two cars drive down the middle of the road from opposite
directions. First guy turns into his lane is chicken."

"Can girls play?"

"Why would you want to? It's stupid."

"The thrill. I want to play chicken," Alouette said.

"We need two cars. Anyway I wouldn't play with Chalky. He's
on my team, right-fielder. He's crazy and Spud eggs him on and I
don't think he'd turn. I'd be the one chicken or we'd crash."

"I thought your code of honor was 'never back down.'"

"You forgot the 'never instigate' part – I am not chicken," I said in an emphatic tone.

"*Puck puck, puck puck, puck puck puck-puckkkkkk!*" Alouette was enjoying herself teasing me.

What I wanted to say to Alouette was *stop behaving like my sisters, it gives me the creeps*. Instead, I sulked and schemed, and drove another mile out of town to the flats. Garish sunset over tree-covered hills. Fields tall with corn. While his wife shops for cold cuts, farmer in a deli contemplates the sale of his land to a developer.

"Let's play one-car chicken," I said in a calm, even voice. "I'm going to floor it. If I take my foot off the gas, I'm chicken. If you tell me to slow down, you're chicken."

"Great idea!" Alouette said in a whisper full of wonder.

I glanced at the speedometer – forty-eight. I gradually depressed the accelerator until my foot felt the floorboard.

The moment was grave. I was no longer petulant. It was as if I had stepped through a gate and the gate had slammed shut behind me. Now I must go on into unknown territory.

"Jacques, are you afraid to die?" said Alouette, her voice thin and uncertain now.

"I don't know – I never faced death."

"Do you want to?" Alouette said.

"No."

"I do, I want the experience. I want to know what it feels like to be dizzy with terror." Her voice, low and passionate, frightened me.

Fifty-five.

"That doesn't mean you want to die," I said. "You want the experience of death without actually dying."

"I want to know what happens after death. I want to know whether my faith is real. Jacques, do you believe what the sisters teach us? Do you believe we're going to purgatory or hell or, with a good Act of Contrition, heaven?"

Sixty.

"I don't know," I said. "Religion, God – it's all over my head. I try not to think about it."

"I think about it all the time. I have these strange imaginings."

"Like what?"

"Like the sisters say you should love Jesus, but it's different for me. See, I'm *in* love with Jesus. I want to marry him, I want to bear his children."

I felt a stab of jealousy. "What bothers me is that heaven doesn't seem very exciting," I said. "You just sit around in adoration. I want to be able to play ball, at least pee-gee ball."

Seventy.

"I want to live in the desert with Jesus and walk on burning sands," Alouette said. "I want to die with him on the cross." She spread her arms and dropped her head.

"I don't want to die until I find out why I'm here in the first place," I said. And then I thought about something more than myself. "And I don't want you to die."

"You could take your foot off the accelerator," Alouette said, her voice halfway between sincere and sardonic.

"Does that mean you're chickening out?"

"No, I am not chickening out. I want you to chicken out."

"I will not chicken out," I said.

"Do it because you love me."

"Now you're trying to trick me."

"That's true. I apologize. But I will not chicken out," Alouette said.

"Me, neither."

"You don't like the idea of a girl being braver than a boy."

"That's right," I said.

Eighty.

"What difference does it make?" Alouette said.

"If girls are braver, the world as we know it falls apart," I said. Where had I heard that? Father Gonzaga?

"Maybe it should. Maybe the reason for our love is to take it apart. Maybe the Holy Ghost wants it that way. That's why He brought us together. Jacques, you're going eighty-five."

"No, I'm going eighty-eight. Tell me to slow down, Alouette. Tell me before we die."

Alouette started to speak, but stopped when the Ford began to shake. Her eyes grew wide as if she were seeing something terrible through the windshield. At that moment, I went to a place in my mind that I had never visited before in waking reality. I was still driving Beaupre's Ford, but I was no longer in Keene, New Hampshire. Up ahead I could see houses burning, barns burning, soldiers herding people onto sailing ships.

Ninety-five.

It was time to end this silly game of chicken, and I tried to lift my foot from the accelerator, but I could not command my body to act. Alouette had transported me to that other place, that other time, and my powers in the present moment no longer existed. Up ahead, through the windshield I saw flames. Soon we would reach the end of the flats and begin a series of tight curves. We would go off the road and we would hit a tree, or the car would roll over and over and over, and the flames would engulf us.

One hundred.

The violent shaking of the car, reminding me of another noise, jerked me back to time present.

"Alouette, this is what it's like in your father's shop, the vibrations, the chaos, the screams of a hundred power looms."

Alouette had not returned from that far place. She was not listening to me; she was listening to the din. We prepared to die.

At one hundred and five miles an hour, Alouette suddenly must have understood everything, because she yelled out, "Jacques! Jacques!" Her voice released the force that held my foot to the accelerator.

I pumped the brakes, pumped the brakes, pumped the brakes – we entered the first curve. The car went up onto two wheels, balanced like a cart in a carnival ride, then after what seemed like minutes, but was only a few seconds, settled down on four wheels, and we knew we would be all right. I pulled off the road in front of a sandbank.

Alouette reached for me, and we embraced and laughed, shaking and shimmying, as if to imitate the vibrating Ford at high speed. Outside, the sun dropped over the horizon, leaving lurid colors in the clouds.

Alouette Williams and I tore off each other's clothes and made love in the Ford with the passion of desperadoes.

By the time we started back for town it was dark and we were late for our rendezvous with Beaupre and Katie at Lindy's Diner.

"Jacques, you never would have driven like that with anybody else, would you?"

"No, I guess not."

"What do you think it was that made us do it?" she asked.

"I don't know," I said.

"I think it was telepathy."

"Telepathy? Are you kidding?"

"I'm not kidding. Something happened to us."

I stopped and thought for a moment. "I had this vision. It was like a memory. I could see a village of houses with thatched roofs burning."

"I've seen those fires since I was a little girl. Jacques, we went back to the old doom of Le Grand Derangement."

For a moment I didn't know what she was talking about. "Wait a minute, that's *Evangeline*, right? You weren't kidding when you said you were Evangeline."

"Le Grand Derangement when our people, the Belliveaus and the Landrys, the Acadians were deported from their homelands." She spoke in that wild but confident voice.

"We read it in seventh grade at St. Joes's," I said. "I guess I wasn't paying attention."

"Evangeline and Gabriel are teenage lovers. They get separated by soldiers on their wedding day. They spend a lifetime looking for each other:

"'Wives were torn from their husbands, and mothers, too late, saw their children

"'Left on the land, extending their arms, with wildest entreaties. "'So unto separate ships were Basil and Gabriel carried. . .'"

"Who's Basil?" I asked.

"Gabriel's father, the village blacksmith."

"It's just a made-up poem, not real people," I said.

"It's based on hundreds of real stories. Twenty thousand people were deported from their homes. It's our story, Jacques. When you saw the fires, where were you?"

"I was in the woods. I ran away. I felt like a coward for not coming out and fighting. But I didn't have a gun."

"I saw the same scenes you did, but I was on a ship. We were separated, Jacques. Now we're together after two hundred years. We can save the world, Jacques. Our love can do it."

I looked into her beautiful mad eyes. No doubt she was crazy, no doubt I was crazy. It didn't matter. She made me feel magnificent and fated. I had never been closer to myself or to another person and certainly not to that God I could not quite conjure than when I was with Alouette Williams.

We found Beaupre and Katie at a booth at Lindy's Diner. They were playing the jukebox. Elvis was singing, "A Fool Such as I." We sat down and ordered coffees.

"Don't tell anybody," Beaupre said, "but I'm joining the Army in December, and me and Katie are going to elope."

Shinbone Shack

Dagwood Sandwich

A few days later, around 6:00 P.M., I sat on a branch in a pine tree watching Shinbone Shack and waiting for Mr. and Mrs. Williams to leave. I was thinking of the game I'd pitched and won, listening to my teammates and their girlfriends carrying on.

"You coming with us to the Ice Creamery?"

"No, I'm going back to the lake with Coach."

"Sneaking off with his Southern belle again."

"Come on, that's a secret."

"Everybody knows, even Coach."

"I never told him, and he didn't say anything to me."

"That's because you're special, the bonus baby."

"That bonus has given you a swell head."

"Who said I got any bonus money?"

"Coach. You never denied it."

"Coach said your girlfriend is Ted Williams's love child?"

"Coach never said that."

"Cross my heart hope to die he did, didn't he, Beaupre?"

"You know Coach," Beaupre had said and laughed. He enjoyed watching me squirm, because he was the only one who knew the truth. In fact, I had moments when I wasn't sure of the truth myself. Was spreading the rumor that I was a bonus baby Coach MacDonald's subtle way of giving me confidence? Did Coach know something I didn't know? Were the Red Sox actually going to give me some money? Was it possible that Alouette was Ted

Williams's secret daughter? Why would Coach say such a crazy thing? Maybe Alouette and I could start new someplace else, maybe the Mississippi Gulf Coast where her mother lived. Start a life based on honesty.

So went my *House of Wax* thoughts as I sat in that tree. I peeked through the greenery as the Williamses' Lincoln left the long driveway of the estate, pulled onto the lake road, and vanished into the embrace of the forest canopy.

I scampered down the tree, catching pine pitch on my hands. The second I was on the move, my discouraging thoughts vanished, and I was full of excitement with the prospect of being with the girl I loved. I walked swiftly among the pines and over granite outcroppings with their multicolored lichen maps of the confusing, heartbreaking, ineffable cosmos onto the lawn and around the back. I could have entered through the front door, but I liked sneaking around. It brought out the boy in me.

I walked past the remnants of what once had been Mirriam Williams's perennial garden. The current Mrs. Williams had made a few feeble attempts to bring back the garden, but unlike Mirriam, she had no servant help, and the area was full of bugs, and she was pregnant, and really she was happier on the dock, catching some sun from the prospect of a padded Adirondack chair as she read the *New Yorker* or the books everybody was talking about, such as the one by that dope fiend, William Burgles, or Borrows, or whatever his name was.

A few flowers fought their way through tall unmowed field grass. The garden was quite beautiful in its distressed state. Or was it? Is beauty *only* in the eye of the beholder? I shook the question out of my head. One of Memere's favorite sayings: *The philosopher is always glum, which is why we have the Church to do our thinking*.

Alouette and Moses the poodle met me at the door. I did not kiss Alouette; I dropped to bended knee and kissed Moses. I loved the dog's nappy coat and the feel of his musculature and I knew from experience that if I did not kiss him he would follow me around the house morose and resentful.

"What do you call a town in Alabama named for an elephant with a dental problem?" Alouette asked.

"I don't know." I stood.

"Tusk-ah-loosa."

"What do you call a town in Alabama named for an elephant with a sinus condition?" I asked.

"I don't know."

"Tusk-ah-gig-gee."

"Gig-gee, what's a gig-gee?" Alouette asked.

"Snot."

"Gig-gee s'not in my lexicon. What do you call a girl with threads hanging from her skirt?"

"I don't know," I said.

"Unseamly," Alouette said, and she reached to kiss me, and she kissed me, and I kissed her back, and we kissed together while Moses whined and lay his jaw on the floor and put his paws over his head as if trying not to listen to Bill Haley and the Comets singing *one o'clock, two o'clock, three o'clock rock.*

"Jealous boy," Alouette said and broke the embrace.

The dog bounded up on his feet, wagged his tail in relief, and interposed himself between Alouette and me.

"Moses," I addressed the dog, "what do you call the hide of a tree?" I flicked his nose.

"Bark," said Moses.

"See, a talking dog," I said.

For that one moment the richness of Alouette's laugh made me the happiest human being that ever walked the face of the earth.

Girl, boy, and dog entered Shinbone Shack.

Henry Mancini's rendition of the theme for the Peter Gunn television show played on the hi-fi. Alouette changed the record, and Elvis sang, "You ain't nothing but a hound dog," a tune appreciated by Alouette and me but perhaps bitterly resented by the poodle for its casual slander of the canine species.

I raided the refrigerator and started building myself a Dagwood sandwich of leftover roast pork, pickles, lettuce, stinky cheese,

Sunbeam white bread with French's mustard, Hellmann's Real Mayonnaise, and a remaining slather of leftover pâté. The food in Shinbone Shack was so much more interesting than the food in my parents' house or Coach MacDonald's.

"They must think you eat a lot," I said as I constructed my sandwich.

"I don't know what they think."

"Your stepmother doesn't question you?"

"She's not my stepmother. She's Moses's bitch. My father married her out of pity. We don't say much to each other, and my father, well, it's guesswork trying to figure him." Alouette suddenly stopped, realizing perhaps that she was being petty. She changed the subject.

"Listen," she said. "I've been memorizing *Evangeline*."

"'Soon she extinguished her lamp, for the mellow and radiant moonlight/Streamed through the windows, and lighted the room, till the heart of the maiden' – That's me. – 'Swelled and obeyed its power, like the tremulous tides of the ocean./Ah! she was fair, exceeding fair to behold, as she stood with/Naked snow-white feet on the gleaming floor of her chamber!/Little she dreamed that below, among the trees of the orchard,/Waited her lover' – That's you. – 'and watched for the gleam of her lamp and her shadow./Yet were her thoughts of him, and at times a feeling of sadness/Passed o'er her soul, as the sailing shade of clouds in the moonlight/Flitted across the floor and darkened the room for a moment.'"

As she recited the poem, all of Alouette's smart-aleckiness vanished. I understood just how vulnerable she was.

"That's beautiful," I said. "I like the 'naked snow-white feet on the gleaming floor.'"

I took a giant bite out of my Dagwood sandwich. Moses whined, and I tossed him a piece of pork. He chased it down.

"What room are we going to explore today?" I asked.

"I'm thinking about it," Alouette said. "Maybe the Secret Room."

Just for the adventure of it, Alouette and I made love in a different room every chance we got in Shinbone Shack, but one room in the house was locked, the window shutters nailed down so you couldn't see inside. Alouette called it the Secret Room.

"This is a great sandwich," I said, "if I do say so myself, a real treat, especially the pâté. You'll never see that stuff in my parents' house. Can I have some milk?"

"I like it when you talk with your mouth full," Alouette said. "It's like listening to a gorilla eat a banana underwater."

Alouette brought me a tall glass and a bottle of unpasteurized milk. I shook the bottle to mix the cream and milk, and poured the glass full.

"Do you know any more lines from the poem?" I asked.

Alouette clasped her hands together, and looked out at an imaginary audience. "'Tears then filled her eyes, and, eagerly running to meet him,/Clasped she his hands, and laid her head on his shoulder and whispered – ?'" Alouette lay her head on my shoulder, then continued her recitation. "'Gabriel! be of good cheer! for if we love one another,/Nothing, in truth, can harm us.'"

"'Nothing, in truth, can harm us.'" I repeated the line, trying to believe it.

Alouette and I kissed, then I finished my sandwich and drank my milk while we talked.

"A couple days ago," Alouette said, "three men showed up, talked to my father, and went into the Secret Room. I asked him what they were doing. 'Cleaning up and checking for vermin,' he said. I asked him to let me in, but he wouldn't. 'There are things in there that can hurt you,' he said, and for a second he broke down. It's the first time I've ever seen my father not in control."

"That would be a better treat than even pâté."

"That's a mean thing to say, Jacques."

"I'm sorry, Alouette. You bring out the liverwurst in me."

"What do you call a witty, wandering girl?" Alouette asked.

"Sally. What do you call a wise-ass, lecherous guy?"

"Sully. What do you call chaos among Chinese bears?"

"Pandemonium," I said, and I reached into my pocket and gave Alouette some M&M's.

"Thanks. Jacques, whatever happens between us, every time I crunch a Mother Mary I'll think of you. Wait here. I have to check on the baby." Alouette left the room and Moses followed.

I did not wait in the kitchen, as Alouette requested, but went into the living room and changed the record to Gregorian chants sung by Benedictine nuns. The music would help me concentrate and last longer at lovemaking. "Where have you been all my life, music?" I said to nobody, and lay down on the carpeted floor to contemplate my happiness.

When Alouette returned, she hopped on my pelvis, her legs straddling me. I opened my eyes. Alouette was holding a key between the thumb and index finger of her right hand.

"Let's go to the Secret Room," she said. "There's something special I want to tell you."

The Secret Room

We walked through the formal dining room, the foyer, the library, and a short hall, and stopped at a heavy oak door that led to the Secret Room.

Alouette fumbled with the key until it eventually turned, but the door stuck and I had to give it a shove with my shoulder to persuade it to open. The scar on the instep of my foot tingled. For a second, I flashed back to the day Beaupre and I broke into the Hephaestus building. Inside, the place had smelled musty, and something else – raw and close to the bone of human fears and desires. The same smell hit me in the Secret Room.

Alouette flipped a switch and the room filled with light.

On one wall were mounted the heads of African buffalo, American bison, a gazelle, and other ruminants. On another wall were big cats – a tiger, a lion, a leopard, a black panther, a lynx, and a cougar. On the third wall were weapons used down through the

ages to kill animals – big game guns, spears, bows and arrows, har-
poons, clubs, even a slingshot. On the fourth wall was a rhino horn,
elephant tusks, walrus tusks, whales' teeth, and photographs of big
game safaris, along with framed letters, hunting licenses, and pass-
ports. Preston Williams had gone to a great deal of trouble to doc-
ument his hunts.

In front of the huge stone fireplace was a polar bear rug, the head
uplifted, jaws open. In the hearth, artfully cemented in between
stones on each side of the fireplace, were human shin bones with
a plaque that said, IN MEMORY OF EDVARD EUCHARISTE,
BELOVED GUIDE, KILLED BY A HIPPO.

For a couple minutes, Alouette and I went our separate ways.
I was fascinated by the animal heads, teeth, hides, glass eyes, claws
and paws, horns sticking out of heads. How to pitch to a lion: He's
nothing more than a big cat and therefore likely to go after bad
pitches, so tease him with slow curveballs outside the strike zone.

The weapons and stuffed animals held no allure for Alouette;
she went right for the photographs on the wall and searched each
one carefully.

"Look at this, Jacques," she called, and I came over. Alouette
pointed to an eight-by-ten glossy of a blond woman and a man
who looked like William Howard Taft, America's heaviest president. Between them hung the body of a dead leopard strung from
the limb of a gnarled tree.

"She's beautiful," I said.

"My grandmother Mirriam," Alouette said. "I knew she'd killed
herself in the trophy room, but I thought it was in the Atlanta mansion they sold. Now I know she died in this room and the real reason why my father didn't want me here. It wasn't because he
thought it would upset me. It was because it upset him. That's why
this room has been closed all these years. I always thought he was
so strong, even insensitive, but he's not. He's as frail as the rest of us."

"The fat guy, that's your grandfather?"

"Yes, Preston Williams."

"Was he, maybe, related to Ted Williams?"

"Who's Ted Williams?"

"He's a baseball player, started as a pitcher, became the greatest hitter who ever lived. Was there a Preston Junior?"

"There was a Preston the Second, but he was killed in World War Two. My father says he was the favorite in the family. You must be the favorite in your family, Jacques. You're the oldest, you're the only boy, and you're a bonus baby."

"I don't know, I never thought about it," I said, but I had thought about it. I was expected to carry on the family tradition of the Landrys and the St. Vincent de Pauls, where the man subjugates himself to job, family, and Church. Memere was deeply suspect of riches, honors, and status. She believed, as did all my people, that worldly success beyond the necessities came at the expense of other people, especially one's own loved ones.

Alouette turned her eyes away from the photos and looked at me. "Jacques, do you love me?"

"I can't imagine ever loving anyone else." I reached for her, but she pulled away. The mad and beautiful Evangeline in Alouette seemed to disappear from her spirit. In that moment, Alouette was only a fifteen-year-old girl trying to understand her life.

"Jacques, I went to confession. I want to love you, Jacques. It's all I really want, but I can't do it like this anymore, going from room to room, like we're trying to prove something. I asked the priest if he'd marry us."

"Who was the priest?"

"I don't know. He was a visiting Jesuit."

"That sounds like Father Gonzaga. What did he say?"

"He said a French-Canadian American man must have the means to provide for his loved ones, like Joseph in the holy family. Jacques, my grandfather lost his fortune, well, most of it. My father had to claw his way up. Even now, we can barely afford to maintain this place. I can't let Daddy down by marrying a factory worker's son without money or prospects. If only you were going to college."

"I can't marry you now, you're not of age, and I can't provide for you, but in a few years. . ." I didn't know what to say next. Alouette looked at me, hope in her eyes.

I believed that if I didn't say the right thing, I would lose her.

"Alouette, you've heard the rumor that I'm a Red Sox bonus baby, right?" I said.

"Yes, I wondered. I didn't believe it was true, because you never said anything about it."

"Suppose it is true. I could provide for you right now. I'm going to play for the Boston Red Sox, Alouette. I'll have money, fame. Everybody in America will know who Jack Landry is."

The spirit was back in Alouette's eyes. "Oh, Jacques – Jacques – we'll get married, just like Evangeline and Gabriel, and we'll have beautiful tragic lives, but only after the children are grown and graduated from college and have given us twenty grandchildren."

We lay on the polar bear rug side by side, looking into each other's eyes.

"What do you call a girl chasing a butterfly?" Alouette said.

"Annette. What do you get when you cross a cop and a vacuum cleaner?"

"J. Edgar Hoover."

The sound of our laughter, loud and uproarious and personal, rang through Shinbone Shack like an air raid warning horn.

"Kiss me, Jacques, kiss me and make me faint."

We were in the middle of the kiss when Hiram Williams entered the Secret Room.

"Alouette," he said in a Boris Karloff voice.

She jerked to her feet as if pulled by a bad-tempered puppeteer, and blushed. I rose to my knees on the rug, lost my inertia, and remained in the penitent's position.

"Alouette," Hiram repeated. "Your stepmother is pregnant again. That's why we came back. She had a food craving. At this very moment she is crying in frustration in the kitchen, because somebody ate her pâté. Who ate the pâté?" Hiram swiveled his hips toward me, his belly lagging a moment, and grinned. "You, you ate the pâté."

"Yes, I ate the pâté in my Dagwood sandwich," I said, half-defiant now.

"Stand up like a man."

I stood. "Alouette and I are in love, we're going to be married," I said, not succeeding in trying to sound firm.

"She's not of age, young man, and even if she were, how would you support her?"

"He's a bonus baby," Alouette said. "The Boston Red Sox will support us. Jack is going to pitch for them. We will live well."

"No," Hiram said. "Ball teams never conceal their bonuses to young players. It's in their interests to reveal the numbers to attract more athletes into their sport, to keep the name of their team in the newspapers, to stimulate their fans. This boy's talent is marginal. At best he'll be assigned to a minor league team and play for peanuts."

"Is that true, Jacques? Did you lie to me?"

I wanted to tell her how much I loved her and how full of shame I felt now, but I could not. I stood silent and humiliated.

"You did lie to me," Alouette said. She looked around at the jaws of the beasts in the Secret Room, the claws, the horns, the photographs of her grandmother who had committed suicide. Alouette turned away from me and ran into her father's arms.

Aftermath

The next day my father was laid off from his job at Narrow Textiles, Inc. Alcide Landry was always stoic and quiet, his face expressionless, so I could never read him to know how he felt about me, himself, our world. I learned to read my father by reading my mother. When my father was upset, my mother would talk more than usual, snap at us kids, and pray more. After my father lost his job, my mother insisted that our family say a rosary every night and afterwards say a few extra prayers to St. Anthony.

I wondered if St. Anthony blamed me for the loss of my father's job. I wanted to ask Father Gonzaga in the confessional, but he had done one of his disappearing acts. Nobody in the family raised the subject of my complicity in the firing of my father, though my sisters often burst into tears at the sight of me. Coach MacDonald never said a word, but instead gave me his famous *you asshole* look. I behaved as I thought my family and coach wished me to, with modesty and sympathy toward others. I worked very hard at being a good boy. Inside, though, I was bubbling with rage. I wished to be accused so I could defend myself. I wanted to hurt something or somebody.

I had my opportunity a week before Christmas. Beaupre and Katie MacDonald had eloped, getting married outside the Catholic Church by a justice of the peace. Beaupre had enlisted in the Army, and Katie planned to join him after basic training. The newlyweds had yet to inform their families, and they knew it would be hell to pay once they did, so they decided to have a party for their friends before they told the old folks.

The party was held at the MacDonald camp on Granite Lake. Chalky and Spud brought beer and hard stuff, which I think was probably provided by Uncle Three Fingers. I'd had very little experience with alcohol, so when I got drunk I wasn't exactly sure what was going on inside of myself. The party was winding down around 11 P.M. when the phone rang.

"Oh-oh," said Beaupre. "I bet it's Skitzy. Somehow he got the word. Let it ring."

"No, I can't do that," Katie said, and she lifted the receiver.

"Jack, it's for you," she said, and handed me the phone. I knew from the look on her face who was on the other line.

"Hello, it's me." I recognized Alouette's voice, her soft Southern accent with just a touch of Cajun French in it, and I tried to be calm and collected while the lava pushed out from my entrails.

"How did you know I'd be here?" I snapped out my words.

"It was a guess. No, it was more than a guess. It was a message from our past lives."

"You still on that kick?" Who was this girl who got my father fired from his job and now tells me she can read not only my mind but the minds of our past lives?

"It's not a kick, it's the truth."

I tried to hold back the lava. "Are you at your boarding school in New Orleans? How's the weather down there? It's colder than a witch's tit here." I sounded strange to myself. I never used ugly language like *tit* in front of her when we were going out. *She's too good for that*, Memere said.

"What? I didn't get what you said," Alouette said.

"I said how's the weather."

"It's nice and cool here, but it's not going to be a white Christmas. It's never a white Christmas on the Gulf Coast."

I started singing "I'm Dreaming of a White Christmas" in my not-Bing Crosby voice.

"Jacques, what's the matter with you?"

When she called me by my French name I couldn't stand it any more. She just ripped my soul. The lava spewed out.

"What do you want from me, what the fuck do you want, you broke up with me? You called me a liar. And a phony. Maybe, I was. Maybe I am," I babbled on.

"I have to see you, Jacques."

"You got money, hop a plane," I shouted, then repeated. "You got money, I don't, because I'm not a bonus baby, as your father pointed out, rubbing my face in the snow, and you don't love me and I don't love you and why the flaming fuck are we talking?"

At that point she started to cry, but at the time I thought she was laughing at me. I was going to hang up on her, but the line went dead.

I told myself she was mocking me. Because I was drunk and because the next day, when I woke up hung over, the incident seemed unreal to me, I dropped it into the deep recesses of memory.

Months later, Narrow Textiles in Keene was shut down, but by then my father had another job, working with Uncle Three Fingers in the furniture factory. My overseer at Narrow Textiles stayed with the company and took a position at a textile mill in North Carolina. Olympia Troy went to work for her cousin, who owned the WRJ Diner in White River Junction, Vermont. Jon Tamulus started a landscaping business that went on to great success locally. I headed south for spring training with the Red Sox rookie school.

Three Strikes

In the News
Early March 1960

I liked the long bus ride from the rookie camp in north Florida to Red Sox spring training camp in Scottsdale, Arizona. I liked the Western scenery – it opened a person up – even while it made me more keenly aware of my homesickness, not for people so much as for lichen on granite boulders, the smell of white pines at Sunset Rock in Robinhood Park, the movie reel in my mind of curly black smoke of birchbark starting a campfire on Mystery Island, the music of lake water kissing the shore as you drifted off to sleep, the drum roll of the lake making ice in the hard cold of a winter day, dreams of love with the Indian maiden in a time long ago.

In a month I'd learned more about pitching than in the previous six years. After sizing myself up against other young right-handers, I'd concluded that I was somewhere between can't-miss and no-chance. Hiram Williams had been right about me. My talent for the big time was marginal. I might make it to the major leagues, if my arm stayed healthy, if I worked hard, if I was patient, if I got a break or two along the way. I'd been told I would spend the next four to six years as an underpaid minor league baseball player learning my trade, but I was happy to be in the position I was in. The life of a professional baseball player seemed more than I deserved. And never mind the vast emptiness between the Western mountain peaks and the stars above, never mind my yearning for home, and never mind that other thing, the permanent ache of a lost love.

We Red Sox rookies were scheduled to play a game against the Yankee rookies as the first part of a double-header in Scottsdale Stadium. The main attraction would be the second game, the real Yankees versus the real Red Sox. It was only spring training, but we rookies were all excited to play on the same bill as the big leaguers.

It ended up being a middling day. My team lost a close but well-played game, though I did not pitch, but the real Red Sox beat the real Yankees. It was only spring training, so no one took the games seriously except for us rookies and some of the older players on the big league clubs who were fighting for jobs. I failed to glimpse Ted Williams of the Red Sox, because he did not play. Williams was not even with the club that day. I was about to board the team bus headed for the hotel room when I heard someone yell, "Hey, bonus baby!"

Two genuine bonus babies and I swiveled our heads and saw a middle-aged man who resembled James Cagney grinning at us. The wry smile belonged to Cormac "Skitzy" MacDonald. Coach was vacationing with his wife and daughters, except for Katie. The women had gone shopping, while Coach took in the ball game. I could smell that he had been drinking.

"Let's get a bite to eat," he said. "I've got a rental. I'll drive you to your hotel," Coach said, and I nodded obediently, the way I always did when he spoke.

Coach insisted we eat at a Mexican restaurant. "You'll like the adobe architecture, the funny smells," he said.

He was right. I liked the contrast between the tan (fake) adobe walls and (fake) weathered beams. I liked the aroma of spices and refried beans.

Coach ordered a margarita and I ordered one, too. I showed the waiter my fake ID that said I was twenty-one, though I was only eighteen. In those days it was easy to change the age on your driver's license. You just erased the typescript and typed in a new number. There was no plastic covering the information. All of us ballplayers had fake IDs.

Coach smiled at me. He was impressed by my savoir faire, though actually I had no idea what a margarita consisted of.

I asked Coach how things were going, and I started to speak, but it was clear that, as always, Coach was more interested in talking than in listening. I paused for a moment, knowing that Coach would use the opening to take over the conversation.

"You and Beaupre were like sons to me, and what does he do but runs off with my daughter behind my back. She has to work as a barmaid for them to stay even. You know what an Army recruit makes? I haven't been so pee-ohed since you took that brunette for a ride in my Chris-Craft. I forgave you, Jack, but Beaupre is on my permanent shit list for stealing my pride and joy. You're all I got left, you're special, you're going to put Keene on the map."

The food arrived.

It was my first try with Mexican fare and I was puzzled by it. I didn't recognize the ingredients, which were all mooshed up so it resembled sink strudel.

"How do you like it?" Coach said with a here's-laughing-at-you grin.

"Essence of blowtorch," I said.

Coach laughed, and I got this warm feeling because I had entertained him with my little joke.

I wanted to ask Coach why he'd referred to me as a bonus baby when I was not, but I couldn't bring myself to do it. Everybody I knew, from Memere to the nuns to my parents, had taught me not to question authority, and Coach MacDonald was more than an authority, he was like a second father, giving me the guidance of a man of the world, a role Alcide Landry could not provide. Suddenly, I missed the only person who had ever really showed any interest in me. Father Gonzaga, the wandering experimentalist Jesuit, would help me organize my confused thoughts and feelings. I regretted refusing to accept his absolution. He'd told me to mark his words. *Father Gonzaga was right*, Memere said.

"Jack – Jack, you paying attention to me?"

"Sure, Coach, sure."

"You talk to yourself, you know that, Jack?"

"Yeah, I know."

"Listen, the thing that bothers me about Katie and Beaupre is not that they married – she wasn't even knocked up – no, it's not that, it's that they sneaked off and eloped. You don't know how hurt Katie's mother was. Me, well, I handled it. I said to myself, 'Self, just think of the money you saved on the wedding.' A lot of girls, they want more than nuptials, they want a banquet, which breaks the old man's pocketbook . . ." On and on Coach MacDonald talked. I interrupted when the waitress brought his second margarita.

Coach ordered another margarita for me. I timed it so I'd finish the drink when I finished the meal. Coach was talking so much he didn't eat. Finally, he stabbed his enchilada with his fork, and said, "Jack, of all the big leaguers, who would you like to pitch to and how would you do it?"

"That's easy," I said, animated now. "Ted Williams." I had the crazy idea now that Coach MacDonald was going to tell me that Alouette Williams was Ted Williams's daughter.

Instead, he said, "The greatest hitter in the history of the game."

"The greatest hitter in the history of the game," I repeated, just to taste the words.

"So, how would you pitch to him?"

Coach MacDonald went at his enchilada like a starved wolf, so I was finally able to get in some words edgewise.

"When Ted sees a new pitcher, he takes the first pitch to get a feel of what he's up against, so I would chance it and throw him a four-finger fastball right down the middle of the plate," I said. "Call strike one. And he hasn't learned anything real about me. Second pitch, I'm going to throw him another fastball, low on the outside corner. Since he's only seen me once and since this is my best pitch, he'll probably take that one, too. Umpire pumps his fist – stee-rike! Ted has two strikes and he hasn't swung the bat. He's seen me twice, he's thinking he's ready for that fastball, and he's probably heard that my curve is not prime, so he's not worrying about the curve. Normally with two strikes, I'd waste a pitch, but Ted never swings at anything outside the strike zone and I don't want him to see too much of my motion. I've learned in rookie camp that I don't yet have a major league curveball, I don't even have a double A curveball, so I'm not going to waste a curve off the plate; I'm going to throw him a strike. It's going to look just like a fastball, and he'll be sitting on the fastball, but it's not going to be a fastball; it's going to be a change-up, inside corner, high, but in the zone – just barely. With that big wide swing, it'll tie him up. Strike three, swinging. It's all about the motion. If I can fool him with my motion, he'll be too far ahead of the pitch to do anything with it."

"Jack, that's wonderful," Coach said with a mouthful. "I could see it develop in my mind when you were talking, the great Ted Williams down on strikes. It wants to happen, Jack, it will happen, it's almost as if it has happened. I can make it happen better than you, and I have a dead arm."

"What do you mean, Coach?" I asked.

"Just watch my smoke, my boy. Watch my smoke."

I didn't know what Coach meant until a week later, when I was back in rookie camp. I had gone to my room, which I shared with a Puerto Rican second baseman who was only a year older than I but married with two kids, who was even more homesick than I was, and who got drunk every night. I snapped the light on. My roommate slept like the dead. I noticed the mail on my dresser, a letter from Cormac MacDonald on Liberty Taxi stationery. I opened it, no writing, just a clipping from the *Keene Sentinel* with a year-old picture of me in my American Legion baseball uniform posing with Coach MacDonald, who had his arm around my shoulder. Coach was wearing a Liberty Taxi baseball cap.

The headline read: BONUS BABY JACK LANDRY STRIKES OUT SPLENDID SPLINTER.

The news story consisted of an interview with Cormac Mac-Donald, coach of the Post 7 American Legion baseball team. MacDonald told the *Sentinel* that he'd attended a spring training game at Scottsdale Stadium in Arizona between the Red Sox and the Yankees. Keene "phenom" Jack Landry came in on relief in the ninth inning to face Ted Williams with the bases loaded and two outs.

"Jack struck out Williams on three pitches, three fastballs, just overpowered him," MacDonald said. "It's only spring training, but it goes to show just how much potential Jack has. He could pitch in the major leagues now if they'd let him. His stuff is that good."

The reporter pressed for the sum of Jack Landry's bonus.

"Remember, Jack is not twenty-one," MacDonald said. "I don't think it's ethical to reveal whether Jack did or did not receive a bonus from the Red Sox and certainly not dollar figures when a minor is involved."

The *Sentinel* contacted Jack Landry's parents, who refused to speak to the reporter.

A Red Sox spokesman would neither confirm nor deny that Jack Landry had received a bonus, but did confirm that Jack had been invited to rookie camp and would be assigned to a Red Sox farm team if he did well.

After brooding for a while, I concluded that Coach sending me his interview with the newspaper was his way of telling me that the people back home in Cheshire County depended on me to do great things.

What's My Sin?

A Test of Character

One week later, I was back in Florida in the clubhouse with my team, scheduled to pitch the following day, and I was nervous but full of anticipation, a mood that told me I would pitch well. My manager came over, and said, "There's a phone call for you. It's your mother." Suddenly, my breath caught inside of my chest. My mother would never call me unless she had news, bad news. By now my father was well established in his job at the Furniture Factory, working with his booze brother, Three-Fingered Willie. I imagined my father, like Uncle Three Fingers years ago, had lost an appendage to one of the power tools. Worse, I was afraid that something terrible had happened to one of my sisters.

"Is everything all right with the family?" I said to the phone.

"Everything is all right with the family," my mother said in her flat, infuriatingly even-tempered voice. It was part of her mystery that the more grave the event the more calm she remained.

I was relieved. I could breathe. "What is it, then?"

"It is your cousin Charles and his friend, Steven," my mother said. It took some prodding to get a more or less complete story out of her. Chalky had crashed the Chevy into a tree and Spud had been killed. Chalky was in the hospital unconscious and in critical condition.

I took the next bus out and arrived in Keene in time for the funeral. Katie was there, but Beaupre hadn't been allowed a furlough because Spud wasn't family. After the funeral there was a gathering at Spud's parents' house. They were Polish Catholics, and they clung to the parish priest. In those days there was no kindly vernacular language to describe the relationship between Chalky and Spud. We didn't talk about it.

I visited with my parents and sisters until they went to bed, then I left the house and walked from 19 Oak Street to 152 Church Street. Olympia had seen me from the window of her upstairs apartment and she met me at the door. She was wearing a robe, her long black hair wet. I glanced down at her feet, toes painted bright red. I couldn't stop looking at those toes, and I was ashamed. The more shame I felt, the greater my desire.

"It's been a long time, Jack; I missed you," she said, and then the expression on her face changed. She could see that I was upset.

"Can you give me a glass of milk?" I asked.

I sat at the kitchen table and Olympia went to the fridge and poured me a glass of milk. I drank the milk in one long gulp.

"You hear what happened?" I said.

"Yeah, it was in the paper. I'm sorry, Jack."

"I went to see Chalky in the hospital, but he was still out. He was all broken up. I got this idea it was my fault."

"How could you be responsible?" She remained standing while I remained seated.

I don't know, Olympia. It's not a thought or an idea; it's a feeling that I have committed a grave sin. What's my sin, Olympia?"

"I can't imagine, but I think I know part of your problem." Olympia pulled the sash of the robe and it opened. I fell on my knees and kissed her red toes. I was crazed with passion. I'd been celibate ever since Alouette and hadn't known how full of need I was.

After the second time, I dressed and Olympia put her robe back on and we sat at the kitchen table. Olympia drank a glass of (in her words) ziggyfield wine and smoked an Old Gold.

"I've got to talk, Olympia," I said.

"Shoot. I have heard so many stupid stories from men that one more ain't going to bother."

"Can I have a glass of wine?"

"Sorry, no liquor until you're legal." She smiled. "Look, I know there's more to it than Chalky and Spud. What is it, Jack?"

I looked at her slack-jawed. Didn't know what to say or even what to feel.

"Tell me about the girl," Olympia said, and her insight lit me up.

"How do you know about her? Did you talk to Father Gonzaga?" I asked.

"No way am I going to take up with any damn priest. It was guesswork. Works all the time for me."

I told her most of the story about my affair with Alouette Williams, leaving out the Acadian past lives part, because, well, I'm not sure why. Maybe I didn't think Olympia would understand, or more likely I didn't understand myself.

"I hate her – she got you and Dad fired," I said. "No, I don't hate her. I hate myself for getting involved with her. The M&M's. The special jokes we had."

"What special jokes?"

"I don't want to talk about it. It's too personal."

"How old is she?"

"Fifteen."

"Jailbait," Olympia cracked a smile. "You could be in trouble. Me, I like trouble. It keeps me interested. But you, Jack, you're not the daring type. That girl ruined you for girls your own age, or was that me?"

"Is that it? Is that why I'm so screwed up in the head? I'm ruined for a steady girl my own age?"

"No, you're screwed up in the head because you still love Alouette Williams. What else is bothering you, Jack? There is something else eating at you. You tell me."

"Okay," I said. I hadn't known until Olympia confronted me just what was on my mind. "Back in December, just before Christmas, me and a few friends had a party at the MacDonald camp. There was a phone call. It was from Alouette."

I spilled out the story to Olympia.

"Anyway, the line went dead," I concluded. "She beat me to the hang up. That's the end of that, I tried to tell myself, but I had this incredible sad feeling like I'd run over my sister with a Mack truck. I've been down in the dumps ever since, even in baseball rookie school. Then when Chalky and Spud hit that tree I thought I did it, I killed Spud and maimed Chalky. I knew they were crazy when they drove and I should have had a talk with them, but me and Beaupre and the rest of the guys, we just egged them on."

"That's not your sin, Jack. That's just bullshit thinking to avoid the real thing."

"What is the real thing, Olympia? What's my sin?"

"It's not nothing you did to make Chalky crash his car that was your sin. Your sin was getting so drunk so you couldn't think straight when that girl called you." She suddenly stopped talking. It was the first time I'd seen Olympia not completely in charge. She was holding something back.

"What is it?" I said. "What's my sin, Olympia?"

"Listen, I know what it's like being pregnant at fifteen, and you can't get the father's attention. The difference is the man. I wasn't even sure who it was, but I knew this much: He didn't care about me, and I had to deal with the problem myself, which I did. You, you still love that girl, don't you?"

I buried my face in my hands. "Oh, my God, she was trying to tell me she was pregnant!" Even as I spoke I wondered whether I was actually calling upon the deity or just mouthing a familiar saying.

"This is an important moment in your life, Jack. This is the moment you have your character tested."

I was guilty of selfishness, stupidity, and youth – mainly youth – and I should have sought wise counsel, from my parents, from Coach MacDonald, from the parish priest, from Father Gonzaga, if only I could locate him. If only. If only I had been thinking straight I would have telephoned my manager of the rookie club. But my only clear thought was to reach Alouette. Olympia had made me realize that I loved Alouette Belliveau Williams, had always loved her, and always would. I had to go to her. I had to save her if I wished to save myself. If she was pregnant I had to give the child a father. I had no phone number, but she'd told me about the Belliveau house that had been in her mother's family in Bay St. Louis, Mississippi. I went to the bank, closed my account, put my life savings in my hip pocket, and took the next bus south.

On the Trail

Crazy Girl?

The house in Bay St. Louis, Mississippi, on the Gulf Coast, was shotgun-style, with a front porch held up by fake Greek pillars in a comfortable but not fancy neighborhood. The waxy leaves of azalea bushes shone in the sunlight. The back yard butted up against a cemetery. Street traffic was slow and occasional. It was a neighborhood made for lying in a hammock. A perfect place to raise a child, retire, or just live in harmony with live oak trees, flower beds, trimmed lawns, and the Gulf of Mexico only a few blocks away. When I knocked, I made myself believe Alouette herself would answer.

A heavy black woman in her forties opened the door.

"I'm looking for Alouette Williams," I said.

"Who?"

"Alouette, the daughter of Mrs. Belliveau."

"You mean Mrs. Dampier. She doesn't live here anymore."

"This your house?"

"No, we're renting."

I was trying to see into the house, but there was a lot of woman in front of me and she blocked my view. "Do you know Alouette?" I said.

"The crazy girl?" She pointed to her head and made circles with her forefinger.

I had to take a breath to speak the word yes. Then I asked, "Where can I find her?"

She didn't look at me when she said, "Who knows?"

"What about your landlady, Mrs. Dampier?" I asked.

"I pay the bank. They transfer the money. I don't have an address." She averted her eyes while she told me the lie, and then she looked at me, like, *when are you leaving, buster?*

I stood unmoving. I was going to make her slam the door in my face or talk to me.

The woman hesitated before she spoke, softer this time, tired out maybe. "They had her committed."

I blinked real fast and I could feel my jaw go slack. "A breakdown brought on because she was in a family way – is that right?"

The woman gave me a how-should-I-know shrug. "Try DePaul," the woman said. "DePaul Hospital in New Orleans." I stepped back, and she slammed the door.

New Orleans

New Orleans felt like . . . I was going to say "like home," but that wasn't it. It was as if something in my skull recognized New Orleans as congenial to Landry sensibility.

I took the St. Charles Avenue streetcar that traveled on the grassed median strip in the middle of the avenue. Most of the passengers were black women, all of whom, I guessed from their clothes and deportment, were either going to or coming back from work, their faces masks hiding their true selves. It was a warm sunny day, and the windows in the streetcar were open. Aromas, presumably from flower gardens behind high walls, intoxicated me. I glimpsed mansions in the shade of giant live oak trees, yards fecund with greenery and blossoms. I pictured myself and Alouette sitting on a bench in one of those gardens by a tiny pond. Our daughter holds a frog in the palm of her hand. Delicate flower petals rain on Alouette's bare feet. A red bird sings in Peggy Lee's voice, "Fever, fever, you give me fever."

DePaul Hospital was an imposing red brick building with a high wall around it in a residential neighborhood that bordered a city park. I learned that Alouette was a patient but that she was in a locked ward and was allowed only family for visitors.

With my knapsack flung over my shoulders, I walked to Audubon Park and the city zoo very near the hospital. I wandered around eating shell peanuts and drinking colas and taking in the sights like any tourist. I was especially fascinated by a manmade mound of earth that included trees and brush, home for the zoo's primates and known affectionately by local people as Monkey Hill, the highest point in New Orleans, or so the story went.

That night I set up my pup tent in some bushes, which ran between the back side of the zoo and the edge of the Mississippi River. I lay on my sleeping bag, but I hardly slept. All night long I listened to the monkeys carrying on. They were quite sedate during the day, but at night they fought and fucked, like the masses of us common folk the world over. I finally fell exhausted into a dead sleep and was awakened the next morning by a police officer. He didn't give me a ticket, but he did warn me not to camp behind the zoo anymore.

I got the break I needed reading the want ads in the *Times-Picayune*. "ATTENDANT: DePaul Hospital, Seton Unit, Night Shift. Must be mentally and physically fit. Head Nurse Glenda Bethanny." I thought, well, I'm half qualified.

Shock Therapy

DePaul Hospital

Nurse Bethanny was wearing street clothes, and I thought it strange she was not in nurse whites. She was about sixty, dark brown skin, a flat nose, textured lips that turned pink on the inside curve when she spoke. Her hair was shiny and black and straight with Gisele MacKenzie bangs across her forehead. Her eyes kept scanning me. Her voice was piercing and probing but without malice, her accent more New York sounding than Southern, a Ninth Ward accent as I later found out. She conducted the interview in a hallway standing up. She was carrying a clipboard.

"May I see some identification?" she said.

I showed her my draft card and driver's license, phonied up to make me twenty-one.

"You got a Cajun name but you're from the North? What brings you to New Orleans?" she asked, strip-searching my facial expressions with her eyes.

Her words hit me in the gut. While I might have a Cajun name, I was no Cajun in my behavior, habits, and life history. I was almost nineteen years old and still didn't know who I was nor what world I belonged to. I'd rehearsed a long but plausible story, but I couldn't bring myself to tell it, so I gave Nurse Bethanny a *Reader's Digest* version of my truth. "I'm looking for a girl."

"What do you want from this girl? Romance? Marriage? Maybe she owes you money?"

The questions caught me off guard. For a long moment, I didn't know what to say. What did I want?

Nurse Bethanny is potentially a friend, so treat this encounter like batting practice. Throw her that medium flat fastball down the middle and let her hit it.

"I want to save her," I said, and I looked Nurse Bethanny right in the eye.

"Save her from what, a bad man?"

"I don't know, I just don't know." I could feel my eyes tearing up as I searched for a word. "I believe . . . it's possible . . . from the information I have that she may be in a family way."

Nurse Bethanny furrowed her brow. I could see now that her hair was on a little cockeyed. A wig. There was a long uncomfortable silence. People came and went. The place looked like a hospital, but no one wore uniforms, so you couldn't tell the patients from the doctors and the nurses. It didn't smell like a hospital. It smelled like a school. I didn't see any gurneys or people on crutches or in wheelchairs.

"What's Seton Unit?" I asked.

"Seton Unit treats mainly schizophrenics. We're an experiment. We don't use drugs. We don't dress in uniform."

I blinked fast, which of recent seemed to be my most effective means of communication.

"You got muscles, but you're not a great big man," Nurse Bethanny said. "I don't want great big attendants on my unit. They scare the patients."

"I'm big enough," I said.

"You're just the right size, my boy, and you're sensitive. I'm going to go against my better judgment and hire you. When can you start?"

My work at DePaul Hospital was simply to be in attendance from 11:00 P.M. to 7 A.M., which is why my job title was Attendant. I was the only white attendant. We had no black patients. If black people came down with schizophrenia, they did not find their way to Seton Unit. I worked with a female attendant on the same floor, usually Charlet Gibson. By day she took care of her three pre-school children. Her husband, a taxidermist, worked days in a shop downtown and she worked nights at DePaul.

I made one male friend, Alphonse Pierre, another black person and a teacher in an elementary school who needed the extra pay to support his family. He'd work his eleven to seven attendant shift and then go off and teach. I covered his floor and my floor to allow him a few precious hours of shut-eye.

Occasionally, someone would, in the parlance of Seton Unit, "act out," and you would tie him or her down to a bed with leather straps. This was not the attendant's decision to make but the nurse on duty after consulting with the doctor via telephone.

Some nights I had long talks with Alphonse Pierre or the female attendant on duty, especially Charlet Gibson. She was like a big sister to me. She taught me all about her world. "In Norl'ns, it's seg-regate in the daytime and integrate at night," she'd say with a rich, throaty laugh.

She taught me the phrase "good hair," hair that was not kinky. Like Nurse Bethanny, Charlet wore a wig of "good hair." I told her that in my hometown race was in the deep recesses of people's mind and did not come up in conversation very often, but skin color was right out front. People with lighter skin had an edge over people with darker skin, but, for reasons I could never figure, tan-ning exempted you.

During this time I was making inquiries of the staff people to learn about Alouette and her condition. Olympia had been right. Alouette was pregnant. I had moments when I wanted to flee. I was not ready for fatherhood. But, in my secret heart, I believed I was not ready for the rigors of being a professional athlete either. Maybe my love for Alouette was just a smoke screen to cover my fear of competing as a professional baseball player. My confusion paralyzed me. I continued working but did nothing to make con-tact with Alouette.

Brain Scramble

One morning at seven o'clock, just as I was about go off duty, a nurse from another unit showed up on our floor, a big black woman who spoke with a Caribbean accent.

"I need an attendant for a few minutes to assist in electroshock treatment," she said. "Alphonse Pierre said you'd be available. It won't take long."

I followed her as we walked down three flights of stairs to the basement.

This part of the hospital was grim, neglected. I didn't see another person. The only sound I heard was our steps on the concrete floor and muffled whirring machine noises.

The nurse took me to a small room that smelled vaguely of medicine. There were a few shelves, an operating table, and a panel with dials and knobs. The room looked like a set for a Frankenstein movie.

The nurse left me alone for a minute, then a tall black guy in hospital orderly whites showed up.

A minute later, the doctor arrived with the black nurse who had fetched me and a white nurse almost as big as the black nurse. The doctor had a slight hunch in his back, pale skin, a bald head with veins popping out all over his skull, dried spittle in the corners of his mouth, and small, drab cockroach eyes devoid of curiosity. Like the other doctors I'd met at DePaul, he didn't bother to introduce himself nor even to acknowledge my existence with a glance. But what really sticks out in my mind was that he had only one arm. The empty sleeve was neatly pinned at the shoulder.

"When the patient arrives, you will each take an arm and hold it down," he said. "They can exert a surprising amount of force when the seizure grips them."

The doctor started to turn dials and pull knobs on the panel, his good hand working expertly and swiftly.

The nurses left for a minute and came back with the patient on a gurney. It was Alouette. Her eyes were wide with terror. She was too frightened even to speak. Her mind had moved to another realm. So had mine. You could have slapped my face and I would not have felt the sting.

The doctor said, "Let's get this show on the road."

The orderly and I lifted Alouette off the gurney and onto the operating table. The white nurse, instructed by the doctor, put jelly and electrodes on Alouette's head, while the black nurse tied her feet down with leather straps. The orderly and I each grabbed an arm and held it to the table.

I think our touch reached Alouette in some deep way, because she came out of her terror trance and locked me to her with her eyes. I bent down very close to her lips.

"Jacques, I remember our word game." I barely heard her.

I whispered, "What do you call an average working guy?"

"Norm," she whispered so only I could hear. "Take us to Acadia. Only the baby can save us." She began to cry in a desperate but dignified way so that I could tell she was weeping only by the heave of her chest.

"Don't talk to the patient," the white nurse said to me.

I turned to the doctor, and I said, "She's going to be all right without this treatment. Let me have some time with her."

"Jesus Christ," said the doctor. A wave of revulsion went through me. I thought it sacrilegious that a medical doctor would use the Lord's name in vain in a Catholic hospital. He pulled a switch.

Electricity went into Alouette's head. The muscles in her body twitched and constricted and pulled all crazy at the same time. The orderly and I had to put a good part of our strength into holding Alouette down. Foam bubbled out of her mouth. Seconds later, it was over. Alouette lay unconscious, eyes open but unseeing.

The black nurse put her index fingers on Alouette's eyelids and pulled them down.

The doctor signaled the white nurse with a glance, and she

looked at me and said, "You better go now. The doctor is not happy with you."

I pointed to Alouette. "What about her?"

The white nurse looked at the doctor but he made no response, so she turned her gaze to the black nurse, who said, "When she comes around there's a maybe that she won't feel so black and blue."

The black nurse left the room.

I tried to make eye contact with the doctor. I wanted to see what he felt, what he was really like inside, but he turned his head away from me. I wanted to voice my outrage. At what? Just what was I angry about? I could not say.

The manager comes out of the dugout. Takes the ball out of my hand, crooks his finger in the direction of the bullpen. I'm out of there.

Escape

Freedom

By this time I'd learned a few things about the main wing. For example, where the head nurse hung her keys. The night after Alouette received shock treatment I left my station on Seton Unit around 3:30 A.M. and made my way to Alouette's room. Most nights it's quiet in a mental hospital from 3 to 5 A.M. Even crazy people need their rest.

I snapped on her light and she popped awake, smiled when she looked at me.

"Geez, you look cheerful," I said.

"Well, I guess I am. Did I have a treatment?"

"Yeah, shock therapy." I remembered that patients often have temporary memory loss after shocks. "Do you know me?"

"Yes, you're Gabriel."

"And who are you?" I asked.

"Evangeline, of course."

"Close enough," I said, feeling pleasantly unreal, because Alouette's surprisingly giddy mood rubbed off on me. "Get your stuff and let's beat it. We only have a few minutes before the nurse discovers her keys are gone."

Alouette did not rush. She acted if she were on a great adventure. She packed a toiletry kit, a few clothes, too many pairs of shoes, and her paperback dictionary. It was April in New Orleans, even warmer than usual for this time of year, like a sultry July night in New Hampshire. We had some luck, leaving the hospital without seeing a soul.

"I want to walk on the levee," Alouette said.

"Great idea," I said.

The levee was a long grassed mound between the city and the channel of the Mississippi River. Along the top was a wide path. You could see the crescent of the Crescent City on one side, the great river on the other. Wisps of fog. Tugs pushing and pulling long barges up and down the river. Lights blinked from cargo ships and from houses on the other side of the river. You could see that the confined river wanted out, wanted to spread over the city in a great, murderous embrace.

Dawn began to break.

"Are you all right, is the baby all right?" I asked.

"We're fine. It's so good to be free."

We took the streetcar to the bus station.

On the Bus

We slept on the bus headed for Memphis. It wasn't until we woke, ate breakfast between bus transfers, and were on the way again for points north and east that I began to understand that the shock treatment, while alleviating the symptoms of Alouette's depression, had also taken something away from her: memory and something else, too, a perception of what most of us might consider day-to-day reality. *Tsee-guh, she was like that to begin with*, Memere said.

We sat side by side on the bus. Alouette's proximity, with her belly full with our child, was enough to make me dreamy with contentment. Even then I sensed something of the tragedy to come, just as I sensed the tragedy of our past lives, but I didn't care. Those moments of happiness being with the girl I loved were worth the purgatorial times of the past and future.

I patted my hip pocket, where I kept my life savings. I was wondering whether my money would be worth more in Canada. I calculated that I had enough to last us a month, if we were frugal. *Maybe you should write a book, The Frugal Frog*, Memere said.

"What?" said Alouette.

"Nothing, just talking to myself," I said. "What are we going to do when we get to Acadia?"

"We are going to cross," Alouette said in a whisper.

I didn't understand, but I didn't question her. I figured she'd make herself clear later on.

"Do you think they can hear us?" she said.

"Who?"

"Them."

I looked around.

"Can you see them?" she said.

"No," I said, but I could feel the malicious forces of society and history eavesdropping on our mad conversation, judging us, scorning us.

"I don't know about this, Alouette."

"Our baby is going to be our bridge over the river Kwai," she said, referring to a war movie a few years earlier.

"What do you mean?" I asked.

"Jacques. If only we pray, if only we have faith, and love. Yes, and love. Kiss me, Gabriel. Kiss me and bring me back to the world." I kissed her, and Alouette – or Evangeline, who knows – talked on and I began to believe.

For me the verb "cross" was a way of trying to understand ourselves better; Alouette meant the word literally. She believed she was a girl named Evangeline whose lover had been taken from her on her wedding day in 1755 and that the birth of our daughter would allow us to return to that awful time and somehow make it right. Alouette was either a visionary or a schizophrenic. Perhaps both. And yet the possibility that Alouette was seriously mentally ill did not bother me; what did bother me were the little things. Alouette remembered me sometimes as Jacques, sometimes as Gabriel; she'd forgotten our little personal riffs – our mutual love of M&M's, the Mother Marys, our wild and silly wordplays. She remembered our game of chicken, but not our moments of lovemaking on Mystery Island on Granite Lake. She remembered her grandmother Mirriam, but not the half brother that she babysat for, nor Moses, the family's French poodle. She remembered her mother's recipe for gumbo, but not her mother's new married name. Indeed, often she talked about her parents as if they were still together. She believed that the birth of our daughter would heal the wounds her parents inflicted upon one another. Like all good Catholics, she believed in the redemptive quality of suffering and the nobility of sorrow.

As for me, my grasp on the idea of belief itself was slip-sliding. I never had a strong faith, which meant my chances of being saved were slim. I believed in hard work, but I couldn't believe I had the talent and character to be a major league baseball pitcher. I couldn't believe in my parents and their backward ways. I couldn't believe in myself, because I had no self. I believed in my love of Alouette Belliveau Williams, but the girl was crazy so I couldn't believe in her. In the end, all I could be sure of was that though my love was real enough, it was a mistake. Love itself was error, a joke to amuse a bored God. But love was all I had. And despite my fears and misgivings and confusion, I was happy on that long bus ride.

"Where will we live in Acadia?" I asked.

"In a little farmhouse with a thatched roof," Alouette said.

I attempted to conjure a notion of renting a place in Grand Pre. *You know nothing about farming*, Memere said. My lips moved involuntarily.

"Isn't that sweet, you were talking to yourself again," Alouette said.

"Did you understand what I said?"

"No, it was some kind of garbled French."

"Sometimes, I think my mind is infiltrated by an alien, because I don't know where my thoughts come from."

"It's not just your mind, it's all minds," Alouette said. "It's the Devil. He penetrates all of us."

"I don't believe in the Devil," I said.

"If you believe in God, you have to believe in the Devil, because if you didn't then God would be responsible for the evil in the world."

"Maybe that's the way it is. Maybe God and the Devil are just two manifestations of the same force. Or farce. Whatever it is."

"Like Jesus and Judas."

"Yes. Maybe. I don't know."

"I guess that covers everything," Alouette said without any hint of irony.

Our discussions continued inconclusively. Eventually, we turned to personal matters.

"My mother grew up poor in Port Fourchon, on the prairie of the delta," Alouette said. "I remember shrimp boats coming up the bayou so that it looked like the boats floated on grass. It was beautiful and strange, and I loved it. My grandfather Belliveau was a shrimp fisherman and pretty well off by the standards of the day. He had his own boat; I mean he and the bank owned the boat. One September morning, he went out into the Gulf and never came back. Boat, crew, catch – lost to the sea. No insurance. After that my mother lived in poverty."

"Did you learn about Acadia from your Cajun relatives?"

"No, I knew about Acadia from birth. Actually, before. My memories go back hundreds of years, Jacques. I knew I was Evangeline before I read the poem in Catholic school." Alouette paused.

"Even before Evangeline, you were on Mystery Island, weren't you?" I said as one in a trance.

"Yes, yes, yes. We go back, way back, back before there was a USA and a Canada, back to the beginning of time."

Those words snapped me back into the world of the bus, the world of time, the world of logic. I tried to break the mood and bring Alouette into my realm of the present moment.

"Do you want a Mother Mary?" I asked.

"A what?"

A shudder ran through me. Alouette had forgotten her phrase for M&M's. I took some out and offered them.

"No, thank you. My mother vowed she would never be poor again. She rejected her Cajun roots and left the bayou for New Orleans. That's where she met my father. Daddy was an oil man in those days, but his investments didn't pan out, so he had to go to work in the family business. He didn't like textiles. He didn't like his job. He called himself Paladin, but he was being sarcastic. He didn't want to close the plant in Keene. I'm sorry it happened, Jacques."

"I'm sorry I blamed you, Alouette."

"You may have been right to blame me. Sometimes I actually feel better about life, about everything, when I can admit everything is my fault."

"What's your fault? You're not even sixteen yet."

"I'll be sixteen when our baby is born. Did your parents talk about old Canada?"

"Not much, but my memere did. She wanted to go back. She wanted to die in Nicolet where her infant son was buried. She used to get me mixed up with him. In fact, she baptized me. She didn't trust that the priest would get it right."

"That's pretty funny," Alouette said with a mischievous grin, and for a moment I thought: This is the girl I fell in love with; she will follow up with one of her wordplays. But her expression dimmed. It was as if her old soul woke for a moment, then went back under the covers. "What about your grandfather?" she asked.

"My Pepere. I never knew him, and my mother refused to talk about him. She said he was a bounder. There's some kind of shame attached to him, but nobody in the family will talk about it. You sure you don't want an M&M?"

"No, thank you. And your father's side, the Landrys?"

"They split off: one group ended in South Louisiana, my father's branch made their way to Quebec. My father never had any curiosity about the old days, and he wasn't a talker, so I don't know much."

That was how our journey went. Pleasant in an unreal kind of way. It was like watching the ocean horizon while you were walking the plank. For two days our life was simple: views from the tinted bus window, conversation, snacks, sleep. I had the odd, not entirely unpleasant sensation that I had died and that I was in transit to the next life. As it turned out, my mood was quite an accurate representation of what actually was taking place.

Many hours later, at night, the bus stopped in Mexico, Maine, across the river from Rumford. Mexico was like a rundown neighborhood of a big city, but there was no city. There was the wilderness and the stink of the paper mill across the river. The night was warm and humid, very unusual for this time of year in New England. It seemed like the whole town was out on the street and in a giddy mood. That's what it's like during the first warm spell after the long winter in the North Country. I was waking out of a troubled sleep. My mouth tasted like congealed lint puffs from the Narrow Textiles factory. A low yellow fog slithered through the glow of the street lights. Despite the obvious poverty, the lack of civil attention to the aesthetics of architecture, the place had vitality, the people boisterous and sardonic. The center of humanity appeared to be a bar/restaurant called the Chicken Coop.

Alouette went out to get us food. I remained on the bus, dozing. When she came back with fried chicken in a basket, something was different about her, but I wasn't paying attention. I was hungry, and I was thinking about the food. The bus pulled out and headed north. Finally, after my belly was full, I could think.

"Alouette, what's wrong?" I said.

"Jacques, I called home."

"That's okay. What did they say?"

"Jacques." She spoke my name as if I were not sitting beside her on a bus headed for Canada, but somewhere else. She was talking to a me from another lifetime.

"What is it, Alouette? Tell me."

Now she was back in the moment, and she began to cry. "Jacques, my daddy had a heart attack. We have to go back."

A Cold Rain

I convinced the bus driver to let us out on the highway. In those
days it was no big deal to hitchhike, and anyway, even if we didn't
get a ride, we could easily walk back to Rumford. I carried our stuff
tossed over my shoulder in my father's old sea bag from his World
War II Navy days. What I didn't count on was a sudden change in
the weather.

We walked about ten minutes, passed by only a single car. I talked
to Alouette. She responded, but I couldn't figure where she was in
her head. All I knew was I had taken her away from the profession-
als who could help her. Now I had to get her back to her family.

We walked maybe another mile. Two cars passed us. Alouette
began to slow, and then she doubled over and groaned.

"What's the matter?" I said.

"It's Jesus reminding me that I've betrayed him." She raised her
head up as if in prayer to heaven.

The air cooled. The sky turned black, no moon, no stars. The
only light was the faint glow of Rumford a few miles away, reflected
off in the clouds. The air grew thick and still. We trudged along.
I was so inexperienced with the ways of childbirth that I didn't
guess what was happening. Neither my parents nor the school system had educated me in this very important realm. The wind hit
first, a slam, then the rain came very quickly, a cold, slanting imper-
sonal downpour. Within seconds we were soaked to the skin.

An hour later I was standing in the middle of the road flagging
down a pickup truck. By then it was too late. I was hypothermic,
Alouette was hypothermic, and the baby was dead. Had it not been
night, had it not been raining, had I some training in childbirth,
I would have understood that I had to clear the airway. The baby
had choked on her own meconium. I was responsible for the death
of our child.

The next few months went by in a blur. Alouette was returned to DePaul Hospital. Hiram Williams recovered from his heart attack, only to be fatally struck down a couple months later. These facts and events registered with me, but I was detached from them. My soul had been wrenched from my body and it lingered outside its host, a forlorn wraith.

I was brought before a court of law and charged with kidnapping. Under Louisiana and federal statutes Alouette and I were both juveniles. Turned out that Hiram Williams's threat against me was empty. These were the days when you weren't legally an adult until you turned twenty-one. The judge rejected the prosecution's argument that I should be tried as an adult. I had no prior record; Coach MacDonald came down from New Hampshire to testify on my behalf, that I was a promising ballplayer, that I had never been in trouble, that I was just a kid who had made a mistake. Because technically I was still a juvenile my name was not made public, and my court appearance did not appear in New Hampshire papers.

In the end I was put on probation and ordered by the court to refrain from contacting Alouette Belliveau Williams. The judge agreed not to send me to reform school provided I joined the Army for a three-year hitch, a common arrangement in those days when the courts were more easygoing, especially with youthful lawbreakers of the white race. I disappeared from the roster of Red Sox rookie school. My career as a professional baseball player was on hold for three years.

Part Two
Work

Decisive moments come upon a person unawares and then vanish before they are understood or appreciated.   *– Memere*

Our people may not be as smart as the Irish or the Italians or the Yankees and certainly not the Jews, but we can outwork them all.   *– Memere*

Atomic Round

The Deal

I returned to my parents' house briefly before I entered the Army. Second day home I headed for 152 Church Street, only to discover that Olympia had moved. I sought out Father Gonzaga, but no one in our parish knew his whereabouts. Coach MacDonald treated my "kidnapping" of Alouette as a youthful adventure. He spread the word to my friends and acquaintances that I was quite the ladies' man, even if I did show bad judgment in going out with a crazy rich girl, which was how he characterized Alouette. My parents never mentioned her. A great forgetfulness seemed to come over them. Their way of dealing with the shame of my behavior was to pretend the episode that brought on the shame had never happened.

By now Alcide had become skilled in his new job at the Furniture Factory. He worked on table saws. My mother worried that he would wind up with missing digits like Uncle Three Fingers. These were the days before OSHA – open saws, no guards. Life was more or less back to normal in the Landry household.

A few days before I left for the Army, Coach MacDonald called me for a meeting at the camp. I borrowed my dad's car and drove out to Granite Lake. Though it was late April and most of the snow was gone from the countryside, the lake was still covered with ice, but the bob houses had been pulled off and the ice was rotten and corrupt, unpleasant to look at. The thermometer on the hemlock tree said forty-two degrees. Coach was alone in the camp when I walked in, sitting at the card table reading the paper. Birch logs crackled in the fireplace. Somebody had stuck a cigar in the mouth of the deer head. As I had done a number of times, I grabbed the cigar and threw it in the fire.

Coach laughed. "Your problem, Jack, is you're assertive about the wrong things."

I tried to act as if everything was normal, but I found myself blurting out a question that had been on my mind.

"You didn't happen to see Olympia Troy around town, did you?" I said.

"Olympia Troy – Jesus Christ! I should have known you were unstable when you joyrided my Chris-Craft," he said in his phony Irish brogue. "You can never know people for real, remember that and you won't be blindsided by life. Are you listening to me?"

"Yeah, Coach, sure," I said, but I was thinking that I hated hearing Coach using the Lord's name in vain, even if I doubted that such a Lord had ever existed. That's how my mind worked in those days, a traffic snarl of thoughts, beliefs, directives, feelings, prayers, and cries in the wilderness. I stared at the fire for comfort.

"You have a way of not paying attention when you want to be stubborn – typical Frenchman," Coach said. "An Irishman would take me on. That's more gutsy. You're a dreamer, Jack, and deep down you're chicken. That's your problem."

I wanted to say, *no, that's two of my problems*, but I didn't have the courage to speak up. I just hung my head.

"Sit down." Coach pointed at the chair on the other side of the table.

I sat.

"Geez, Jack, why can't you go out with normal girls your own age?"

"I don't know, Coach."

"For your information, Olympia has moved in with Pete Dubie."

"Who's he?"

"Old fart. I think probably Olympia will usher him into the next life in a happy kind of way."

"What's in it for her?" I was jealous.

"Pete's got a pretty nice trailer and a big chunk of land, and never mind that half of it is swamp. Olympia could always find a way, if you know what I mean."

I was thinking that the two women who ever meant anything to me were now unattainable.

"You understand that you let me down," Coach said. "You let down your team, you let down the Red Sox, you let down the city of Keene, and brought shame to your parents."

Head still bowed, I returned a bare nod. I was struggling not to cry.

"Have you been to confession?" Coach asked, in a raspy whisper now.

I was happy for the question, because it took me out of my passive mood. "No," I said. "I don't believe in Jesus anymore." I was thinking about Alouette losing our baby in a cold rain. *You cannot afford to disbelieve in God*, Memere said.

"Stop mumbling and look at me," Coach said. "You don't have to believe – you just have to go to confession. Jesus Christ!"

His swearing made me feel as if I wanted to puke.

"Okay, forget about the religious shit for now, but I predict you'll come crawling back to the Church eventually – they all do. Here's what I want you to think about. You owe the city of Keene, you owe your parents, and you owe me. As far as Keene is concerned, Jack Landry had to leave the Red Sox organization because he came down with a sore arm. He joined the Army to defend his country against the Reds."

"The Cincinnati Reds?"

Coach MacDonald slapped my face. It stung and I reeled back, but actually the pain and shock made me feel a little better, a little less passive. "Don't fuck with me," Coach said. "You know what I'm talking about. Do you want to disgrace your parents? They're good people."

I thought how my parents would feel if the truth came out in the *Keene Sentinel*. "Okay, Coach, I'm sorry I was a wiseass," I said, though I wasn't sorry. I was proud that I'd been able to say something that made Coach lose his temper.

"All right," he said. "I forgive you. Here's the deal. You struck out Ted Williams, and the next day you felt something in your elbow. The doctor said your arm needs rest, more than a year. So you signed on with Uncle Sam. We won't mention the business about the girl and the *Loozeeanna* court. Okay?"

"Okay, Coach," I said.

"Next year when I run for mayor you'll make a couple of appearances with me – in your Army uniform."

"Right, Coach," I said in a voice that surprised me with its cheerfulness.

"Good boy," Coach said, and I couldn't help feeling better.

I was beginning to understand that the adult world was a series of contracts and obligations between individuals and institutions in which the cunning always came out ahead. Dreams, memories, and love were obstacles to survival and needed to be suppressed, altered, or even smashed. You couldn't pitch to the world. They'd hit everything you threw.

The Shroud

I hoped that after basic training I would be sent to Germany so I could visit Beaupre and Katie, but Uncle Sam kept me stateside.

Meanwhile, my family was changing. My sister Gemma shocked my parents by marrying a Protestant. She stayed in the Catholic church, so my parents were able to adjust, that is, as much as they were capable of adjusting. Gemma and her husband, Kyle, moved to the Seattle area to be near his work with the Boeing company. During my last year in the Army, my sister Denise was a senior in high school and she was making noises about going to college. My parents were still suspicious that she would lose her faith, but even so, they were encouraging her to apply. A Catholic had been elected president, which gave my parents confidence, even if he was, to quote my mother, "a lace-curtain Irishman and just barely Catholic." Changes were in the air, though I have to say I was not consciously aware of them at the time. It's always been that way with me. The world goes this-away and that-away and I always seem to be the last one to notice. For better or for worse, I've always ridden the horses on my own merry-go-round.

I didn't really recover from the trauma of losing Alouette and our baby. My mind was blunted, my range of emotions reduced to those required of the soldier. Beaupre was a good soldier, squared away and gung-ho; I was an adequate soldier. I did what I was told, but only the minimum. I behaved myself, but I never aspired to leadership. Given my record thus far, I could not believe I was capable of good judgment, so I refrained from judgment. I did not fear going into battle; I feared that I would make some terrible mistake that would get my buddies killed. By the time I got out, three years after signing up, I'd been promoted from private to private first class, one stripe. During more or less the same time period, Beaupre went airborne and made buck sergeant, three stripes.

I did take pride in my ability to work, like my father, long hours without complaint. I volunteered for KP, extra guard duty, and details, such as picking up trash and cigarette butts (called "policing" the area). Work helped damp the guilt and self-loathing I felt for my behavior with Alouette Williams and for my culpability in the death of our baby. Even as I admitted to myself how wrong I was, I couldn't help but fall into reverie about the girl herself. She was the Indian maiden, the sweetheart of Shinbone Shack, a farm girl in old Acadia ripped from her lover by war and politics; she was the Cajun girl; she was the daughter of the Eastern establishment. My passion flowed through the ages. I could never see her again in this lifetime, but I could never stop loving her either. My memories of her were the only resource I could depend on to give me peace and a modicum of strength. I imagined that we would meet again in another realm.

For my first year as Uncle Sam's "paid killer," I was a supply clerk at Fort Dix, New Jersey, a tedious but not demanding job. During the second year I was transferred to a National Guard artillery battery stationed at Fort Bragg, North Carolina. In 1961, President Kennedy mobilized the country for the Berlin crisis. Some National Guard units were called up from the states, but they were almost all under strength, so some of us regular Army guys were transferred to fill in. I was assigned to a battery of eight-inch howitzers. Firing and caring for these big guns out in the field was a lot more fun than working in a supply room.

Did I call them guns? My battery commander will not be happy with me if he reads these words. It was drummed into us that a *gun* has a smooth bore. A *howitzer* has spiraled groves in the bore-rifling. A howitzer is not a gun, but a great big rifle. Our weapons fired 220-pound projectiles loaded with explosives. To load the round, the muzzle of the howitzer was lowered. Four men carrying the projectile on a "loading tray" would hoist the projectile into the bore. Then six to eight men carrying a long staff would "ram it home," through the bore into the breech.

I was the number-two man. It was my job to pull the lanyard on a command from the gunnery sergeant, which would fire the weapon. The entire rear of the howitzer would whoosh past me. If I didn't take care to position myself outside of the recoil I could be crunched. At night you could see flames ten feet long spit out from the end of the bore, and there would be a tremendous noise. Maybe a minute later the round would land in the impact area, two to ten miles away. You could hear the muffled *wump*. Firing the gun – er, *howitzer* – always sent a little thrill through me. Training in the field at Fort Bragg had all the excitement of warfare without the danger.

In the few times that Beaupre and I got together, usually with family and friends during holidays when we couldn't really cut loose, we agreed that the Army of our time was "piss poor." The main problem with the Army, according to Beaupre, was guys like me – draftees and men who had joined up under some kind of personal duress. "You don't really want to be a soldier, Jack. Not that I blame you. Well, actually I do blame you, so fuck you." As usual, Beaupre was right.

One incident will give the reader an idea of what the Army was like in my day. My battery got word that we had been chosen to fire a simulated atomic round from our howitzer. The round weighed . . . well, I won't say what it weighed, since that information surely is still classified. I can say it was heavier than a conventional round. It was housed in the back of a deuce-and-a-half truck in a motor pool, kept from sight by an olive-drab awning. In order to see the round, you had to have a security clearance, but if you had a security clearance, you pulled extra duty to guard the round. Part of the rigmarole for obtaining a security clearance was to pass a test. I can't remember the questions, but they were easy. I didn't have a perfect score, but close. Yet half the guys in my battery, some of them college men, deliberately flunked the test so they could avoid guard duty.

When it came time to fire the simulated atomic round in demonstration before a couple of generals and a congressman, only a few of us had clearances. Regulations said men without clearances could not view the round. One of the officers came up with a solution. We who had clearances covered the round with a black shroud and lifted it onto the loading tray. The round was brought to the muzzle like a corpse on a bier. I was one of the pallbearers. We lifted the round to the end of the bore. The men on the long staff brought it up to the rear of the round. Men without clearances were ordered to look the other way while the shroud was removed and the round was rammed home.

That was the kind of army that served this poor country on the eve of the Vietnam War.

Chris-Craft Crisis

Home Again
Summer 1963

A few months prior to my discharge from the Army, I had another meeting with Coach MacDonald. He had been working to get me back into Red Sox rookie school. With his encouragement I spent my last few months in the Army getting my arm in shape.

I was always frugal – or as Beaupre put it, cheap – so when I got out of the Army, I had enough money saved to buy myself a used pickup truck, which I outfitted with a plywood camper body, based on the one John Steinbeck drove in *Travels with Charley*. Steinbeck hit the road with a poodle named Charley, which gave me the idea to name my new pickup truck Moses, after Alouette's dog. In the few months before rookie school, my parents would expect me to get a job and earn some money, settle down with a local girl, get married in the Church, and raise a family. But my plan was to park my camper in the woods and live like a modern-day *coureur du bois*. I would hike, fish, hunt, and maybe lay a trap line.

My parents and I might consider ourselves French-Canadians living on the wrong side of the border, but we were also New Englanders and products of the mid-twentieth century, which meant that normally we embraced only under great duress, but for some reason, that day I came home from the Army in September 1963 we found ourselves hugging and kissing spontaneously until, just as suddenly, the three of us at the exact same moment became self-conscious and backed away from one another.

My parents had aged, or perhaps I was just noticing that they were no longer youthful middle-aged people, but just plain middle-aged. My father worked on at the Furniture Factory, though his hours had been cut back. I found myself checking that he still had all his fingers.

My mother mentioned that "the Commie priest" was back in town, stirring up trouble talking about ecumenism. He had this mad idea, my mother said, to replace the Latin mass with English. I hadn't been to mass in more than a year, and the prospect of bumping into Father Gonzaga filled me with dread. I wasn't entirely a nonbeliever like Beaupre. I was a maybe-there's-something-to-it-but-probably-not believer. I figured if there was divine justice, I could not be saved because of my sin against Alouette Williams and our baby. If there was no justice and no God, there was no meaning. Either way I was doomed: That was my state of mind.

After a *dinnah* of meat loaf, string beans, boiled potatoes flavored with pads of margarine, and a dessert of angel food cake, my father helped my mother clear the table and then he laid out the Sunday edition of the *Manchester Union Leader* on the table and looked at it as if it were his will. My mother sat beside my father and looked at me across the table.

"What is it?" I said.

My mother glanced over at my father. "He wants to know," she said.

"You better tell him," my father said; he kept his eyes on the newspaper.

My parents' habit of talking about me as if I were not in the room did not infuriate me less now that I was no longer a teenager. My urge was to glance at my watch and leave on some pretense, but I decided to stick it out.

"You're worried about me going to rookie school," I said.

"Yes, you will lose your faith."

I didn't have the guts to tell her that my faith was already seri-ously compromised, so I tried to change the subject. "You don't worry about Denise?"

"It is different with Denise."

I waited for her to explain, but she was silent.

"What do you mean?" I said.

"It is too early to say which way she will go, so I will not expec-torate," she said.

"You mean *speculate*," I said.

"Yes, that is what I said."

"Mummuh, I don't know what you're talking about."

"It is because you are still too young." She spoke the words to my father. His eyes remained on the newspaper.

I was now at the height of exasperation. All my life my mother had been a mystery, and now she seemed further than ever from me. I was no longer a teenager, I was a man. I had to confront her.

"Mummuh, for five years you were unaccounted for. Where were you, what happened when you were my age?"

"Now is not the time to talk about it, but one day I will. I will tell you everything and you will be astounded. You will tell your sisters. They will be astounded." Now she was talking as if my father was not at the table. I waited for him to question her, but he acted as if he had not heard.

"Dad doesn't know? You never confided in him?" I glanced at my father, who had a faraway look in his eyes. I wanted to grab him and shake him, just to make him react.

"I did not want him to know, and he did not, as you do now, push me to explain," my mother said. "He could love me without my history. It is the reason I married him. He knows that, right, Alcide?"

My father returned a bare nod.

In the Depths

Later that day, I took off in my Moses camper to visit Coach Mac-
Donald. The last time I'd seen him was when he was running for
mayor and I had appeared in my dress greens Army uniform with
him at a Rotary Club meeting as the Red Sox bonus baby. Apparently my presence didn't do much. Coach was defeated in the election. He vowed to be back on the ballot. They told me at the office
of Liberty Taxi that the MacDonalds were at the camp entertaining
some "big shots." I decided to drop in on them. After all, I was a
local big shot myself. I was the teenage phenom who had struck
out Ted Williams.

It was unusually warm for September, though most of the
camps had been closed down for the season, which traditionally
ended after Labor Day, when the kids went back to school. It was
late in the afternoon when I arrived at Granite Lake and I impul-
sively veered into the driveway of Shinbone Shack. At the end
stood the mansion, abandoned and forlorn, the grounds over-
grown with tall grass, wildflowers, and weeds. All my old feelings
for Alouette Williams came flooding back.

I got out of my truck and looked through the windows. The
furnishings had been removed. The shutters to the windows of the
Secret Room were open, and I could see inside. The mounted animal heads and everything else – gone. I felt like a character in a
ghost story arriving too late for his plot. I didn't want to see Coach
MacDonald now. I didn't want to see anybody. In my camper I
hauled out a bottle of Four Roses, poured myself a stiff shot, and
chased it down with a beer. I lay inert on my camper bed for half
an hour, thinking of Alouette and our grand summer. I tried to
keep my mind on the good moments.

I fell asleep, and when I woke in a sweat, well after dark, I was
shouting, "Speak English, goddamnit, speak English!"

In the echo of the forgotten dream I heard Memere babbling in

French. What was Memere trying to tell me? I went out into the night, warm and sultry, like the one when I'd roused Alouette out of bed and we'd made love for the first time.

At the water's edge, I shouted, "What do you call a man falling into a sausage machine?"

Alouette was not there to answer. I hollered at the sliver of moon over the island: "Frank!" A terrible loneliness came over me. I remembered that Father Gonzaga had told me that the worst pain of hell was the absence of God. I had an inkling now of the nature of that absence.

I walked over ledges and under pines, hemlocks, and birch trees, through lawns distressed by acidic pine needles, until I reached the MacDonald place. The lights were on inside. Through the window I could see Coach in Bermuda shorts and a Hawaiian shirt and Mrs. MacDonald in pedal pushers. She was serving drinks to the Keene city manager, his wife, and a couple other people I didn't recognize. Coach MacDonald was pacing back and forth, talking a mile a minute. They all gave the appearance of enjoying themselves, as drunk people will.

Everything I'd learned as a ballplayer and soldier, a meager confidence, vanished. In my head, Memere led the choirs singing "Ave Maria." Down by the dock I listened to the lake slap against pilings. The skinny moon and starlight created a black shadow of the behemoth Chris-Craft on the water. *Do something, even if it's wrong*, Memere said. I started thinking about Mystery Island. Maybe there was a clue there.

I stripped off my clothes, hung them on a tree branch, and slipped into the water. I was neither a schooled nor a strong swimmer, but I swam relaxed and I would have no trouble side-stroking to the island half a mile away. After a few minutes, the breeze died down and soon the lake was calm. I stopped to tread water so I could listen to the quiet. Then I floated on my back and stared up at the stars.

I was hardly winded when I reached Mystery Island.

Walking on rocks and sticks hurt my feet. I waited for that clue
to the mystery of life; I waited for a vision of the Indian maiden
herself. Nothing came to mind except a return of the feeling of the
absence of God I'd experienced on the lake shore.

What secrets did you expect to find here, Jack? It wasn't Memere's
voice, it was the voice of His Lordship, the maple tree from which
Beaupre and I had chopped out his baseball bat.

I jogged out to the ledge and dove into the water, making an
awful racket as I started back for the mainland. Minutes later,
clouds obscured the starlight, and serpents of fog slithered along
the surface of the lake. I swam hard in the fog, and swam some
more, and swam until I should have bumped into land. Then I saw
it, only a hundred feet away – the island. I'd gotten turned around
and had been swimming in the wrong direction. I treaded water to
calm myself and locate the lights from the MacDonald place and
started swimming again.

At about the halfway point between the island and the shore,
the fog returned, obscuring my view. At the same time I heard a
roar. For a split second, I thought a lion had escaped from Benson's
Wild Animal Farm and found its way to the lake. My next thought
was accurate: Coach MacDonald's Chris-Craft had come to life.

No doubt Coach MacDonald was taking his drunk friends for
a ride. The boat charged up and down the lake, its lights by turns
visible and invisible in the shifting fog, the roar unrelenting like
some terrible beast slouching toward Bethlehem, New Hampshire.

The roar changed pitch as the boat turned sharply and, from the
sound, bore down on me.

The boat passed me not twenty feet away, its roar fading, the
sound rather pleasant, if mournful, the lamentation of the Doppler
effect.

I rode the big, confused wake left by the boat. The soprano
notes of the propeller coming out of the water told me that Coach
had made another sharp turn and was coming toward me again.

Dive, Jack, dive, head for the bottom of the lake, where you will find

Truth, Memere said. The boat passed over me, its turbulence spinning me around. For a few seconds I was weightless with no idea which way was up.

I rose with the air bubbles churned up by the propeller, and surfaced seconds later. Miracles followed. The Chris-Craft veered away and did not come close to me again. The fog lifted, the clouds dissipated, and I had no trouble finding my way to shore. I arrived only moments ahead of the Chris-Craft. I stood naked by the hemlock tree as Coach MacDonald and his guests walked past me. I knew what I had to do now. I had to confess my terrible sin.

The Penance

Confession

Two A.M. Moses was the only moving vehicle as I drove slowly down Main Street in my hometown. When I came to the Eagle Hotel, I stopped in the middle of the road and looked up. "You'll know the room he's in," my mother had said, "because the light is on twenty-four hours a day and nobody else is on that floor." She was right. One light shone from a window on the third floor. I thought I saw the vague shape of a figure.

I parked Moses behind the building, no longer a hotel but a rooming house. The hallway was dimly lit, with no sign of life. The staircase was renovated with new carpeting and refinished wooden banisters; newly installed lights illuminated paintings of the St. Lawrence Valley in French Canada and peasant scenes in old France. A drawing in charcoal stopped my breath for a moment. A girl, bearing a remarkable resemblance to Alouette, held a water bucket. Below her was a young man who looked like me, pulling a rope attached to the bucket, his fingers curled as if to throw a curveball. Under the painting a plaque said, AT THE WELL, AUGUSTE-ANTOINE-ERNEST HEBERT 1817–1908.

At the top of the stairs was a sign over a door that said, ECUMENICAL CHAPEL. A faint whiff of incense tickled my nostrils and threw me back in time. I'm in church and the priest in his colorful vestments swings a smoking metal pot. My father kneels beside me, the war trauma on his face. Memere grips my hand. "You were born to be a *coureur du bois*," she whispers.

Down the hall was Father Gonzaga's room, 314. I didn't have to knock. The priest opened the door when I was still ten feet from reaching it. "Jack, come in," Father Gonzaga said, with a faint smile and familiarity, as if he'd expected me.

Father Gonzaga was wearing a black Jesuit robe from another century. He was barefoot with long toenails, and he wore his hair perfectly combed, Peter Gunn style. He wore thick horn-rimmed glasses. He'd lost quite a bit of weight.

The room had high ceilings with two huge windows that afforded a view of Main Street. There was no bed. He slept in a big leather chair, if he slept at all. Furnishings included an electric hot plate, a liquor cabinet, bookshelves, a kneeler of shellacked oak, a Leica M4 camera on a tripod by the window. On the creamy walls above the dark wainscoting were prints of Pope Pius XII, Pope John XXIII, St. Ignatius of Loyola, and on posterboard, black and white photographs of Keene street scenes – the Star Cafe, Miller Brothers Newton, Newberry's, and the lobby at the Latchis Theater, where the manager, Keene's only black man, George Miller, took tickets. Beside the window and chair was a coffee table with an ashtray overflowing with crushed Gauloises cigarettes and a clothespin.

I stared at the clothespin, its presence seeming so incongruous.

"If I should have a seizure, clamp it over my tongue so I don't bite it off," Father Gonzaga said.

"You won't be able to speak."

"Yes, the fit is God's way of shutting me up and inspiring me all at the same time."

"The stairwell with the paintings and the chapel – " I struggled to find a verb, but failed, and I let my sentence hang unfinished.

"I prefer austere surroundings for my private quarters, but I've made improvements to the Eagle Hotel for my mission to spread the word of ecumenism." He pronounced the name of the place the French way, Hotel l'Aigle.

"You? You made improvements?" I said, puzzled.

"My mission bought the building, Jack," Father Gonzaga said. "Sit down."

I sat in a wooden chair and Father Gonzaga in the big plush chair beside the window.

"I didn't know Jesuits had that kind of money," I said.

"Well, most don't, but I am a man of some means these days. I went to Rome to participate in the Second Vatican Council and made the rounds of the cardinals. Cardinal Spellman told me how he acquired his fortune. Like myself he was an amateur photographer. He attended seminary in Rome where he visited the homes of rich American Catholics, introduced himself as a young seminarian, and offered to photograph the children of these wealthy families. Photography was his entry into their lives. Soon they were lending him money and giving him inside tips on the stock and bond markets. By the time he was ordained, he was financially secure. I did the same thing with the help of my Leica and mentor, Henri Cartier-Bresson, who has some connections on the Continent. My mission now has fair financial underpinnings. Ignore my enemies who will tell you that my riches come from a recent inheritance. We are in the Age of Ecumenism, Jack. You, me, all of us, even the Church must adapt."

"The union organizer priest, the buttoned-down conformist priest, now this?"

"The Experimentalist philosophy is a restless one," Father Gonzaga said. "We are forever searching for the way to heaven. The day of the so-called working class, its protective unions, its confrontational identity, its sense of solidarity, its left lean is in eclipse. As for the conformists, they will always be with us, but they no longer have power to control the tick-tock of this country." He smiled at me in pity. "I'm sorry to upset you, Jack. The Experimentalist is unrelenting in his quest for God and Truth and harsh in his critique of the world of men. I know you've come here out of desperation, and I do not mean to take advantage of you when you are vulnerable."

"How could you know I was desperate?" I said, amazed.

"No one would visit me at this hour unless he had a reason charged with need and emotion."

I put my elbows on my knees and dropped my head into my hands. "I don't know who I am, Father, or what I should do with my life," I said. "I'm supposed to return to baseball rookie school, but I'm full of doubt and despair."

"You wish to confess your sins in hopes of absolution." He was breathing hard. I was hardly breathing.

"Yes, I have sinned."

Father Gonzaga pointed to the kneeler.

I rose from the chair, brought the kneeler to the table, and knelt. "Bless me, Father, for I have sinned." I made the sign of the cross. "My faith has lapsed. I have doubts, Father."

"That's all right," Father Gonzaga said, his tone full of resonance and echoes in the catacombs of my mind. "Doubt is good. Cynics, Skeptics, Epicureans give our faith something to push against. Tell me everything, and together we will discover the sin and how to purge it."

Father Gonzaga bent his head and rested his chin in the crook between thumb and index finger. On my knees, I bowed my head and talked into my folded hands.

When I'd finished my story, Father Gonzaga asked, "Why this girl?"

"It's hard to explain. We were lovers long ago. We were fated. It's like looking for her is what my life has always been about."

A crooked smile of irony crossed Father Gonzaga's face for just a moment and cut me. "Before you locate her, whether in time or in space, you must locate yourself. Your sin was in getting drunk and rejecting her when she needed you most. All that followed, Hiram's untimely heart attack, her mental breakdown, and, of course, let us not forget the loss of your child, resulted from the first sin. Do you accept the responsibility?"

"Yes, Father."

Father Gonzaga looked up, and I raised my head to see him.

"You're obviously contrite, Jack. What do you think led to your sin?"

"I don't know, Father."

"Yes, you do. Examine your conscience. In youth what obsessed you, alienated you from yourself, but mainly made you insensitive to the needs of your cousin Chalky?"

"You know about Chalky?"

"Of course. I know that he recovered more or less from his injuries and left home with a bad attitude and a copy of Jack Kerouac's book, *On the Road*. Give me your answer – what desensitized you?"

"Baseball. It was all I thought about from the time I was eleven."

"That's the symptom. Go a little deeper."

"Pitching?"

"You think pitchers sin more than catchers and basemen? I don't think so. Go deeper."

"When Coach MacDonald started the rumor that I was a bonus baby, I pretended to be upset, but I was secretly gleeful, and when he said I struck out Ted Williams and came down with a sore arm, I began to believe it myself."

"You're getting warm."

I thought for what seemed like a long time, but it was probably only a minute or two.

"It was my ambition," I said.

"Good. Now push further into your soul."

"My pride?"

"Yes, it was your pride," Father Gonzaga said. "Sin always comes down to pride. Now elaborate on your insight."

"I made my desire to pitch in the big leagues me – nothing existed but that desire. When Alouette came into my life, I took what I could from her but without giving anything in return. She was only fifteen. I loved her, I can truly say that."

"Perhaps, but in the end you loved your ambition to be a big leaguer more."

"Yes, Father."

"You let your ambition – your pride – blind you and get in the way not only of your love for Alouette Williams but in the way of your love for your family and friends, and even for yourself, which by extension estranged you from our Lord Jesus Christ. Is it any wonder you doubt your faith, since you doubt yourself? You can't pitch to the Devil and get him out, Jack. You must hand the ball to God."

I waited for his blessing, absolution, and penance, the usual say-some-Hail-Marys and offer-up-your-communion, but Father Gonzaga had another idea.

"Since I've attended the Vatican Two council and joined the ecumenical movement, I've come to believe that the individual must devise his own penance, with the confessor's approval, of course. Since your sin was grievous, the penance must be severe."

"I don't know what would be the right thing."

"Yes, you do."

For a long moment, my mind was blank, and then I could see a road ahead of me and it was not a yellow brick highway. I thought about my father, my mother, Uncle Three Fingers, my cousin Chalky, and I thought about our French-Canadian American heritage of work and more work and never complaining. "I will not go to rookie school. I will serve others by my work."

"Yes, a common laborer. Burn that phrase into your brain. You will live by the sweat of your brow and by the calluses on your hands. You will labor in the fields, in the forests, in the factories, and in the ditches to enable others to prosper, advance, and relax."

"Yes, Father, that is what I will do. That is my penance. I will offer my labor to my country."

"Say a good act of contrition."

I bowed my head and prayed: "O my God, I am heartily sorry for having offended Thee, and I detest all my sins because I dread the loss of Heaven and the pains of Hell; but most of all because they offend Thee, my God, Who art all-good and deserving of all my love. I firmly resolve, with the help of Thy grace, to confess my sins, to do penance, and to amend my life. Amen."

Father Gonzaga raised his hand and gave me absolution. "I forgive thee in the name of the Father, the Son, and the Holy Ghost. Now go forth and live as a common laborer, unnoticed and uncelebrated by the great masses. Your life lies before you. You have my love and the love of our Creator. How I envy you."

"Envy? Me?"

"Yes, your life is set, mine is at sea." He pulled off his stole, stood and hung the stole on a nail, walked over to the window, and stared down at the empty street.

I remained kneeling with head bowed. *Your life is destined to be like your father's, and like his father before him, and like the earthly father of Jesus,* Memere said. *You are the St. Josephs of the world. Without you there is no Jesus, no pyramids, no long wall in China, no grand presentments.*

"Yes," I whispered so low that Father Gonzaga would not hear. And of course there would be no Alouette Belliveau Williams. She deserved more than the likes of me. My life as a prospect for the big leagues – any big league – was over. For the first time since I turned eleven and devoted myself to becoming the best pitcher I could, I experienced the peace of humility.

Jobs

Under the Chute

My mother helped get me a job in the laundry room of Elliot Community Hospital. My parents were relieved that I was not going to rookie school. For them there was no such thing as menial labor. After you reached the age of sixteen you sought out a job, and as long as you arrived at work on time, did what you were told, did not complain, and did not tell the boss to go fuck himself, you were considered an honorable person.

Laundry room employees at Elliot Community Hospital were encouraged to enter through a back door on the loading dock, but I came in through the front entry so I could look at the murals on the walls depicting old Keene: the Congregational Church at the head of Central Square, cows grazing on the green, a horse pulling a plow beside a passenger train, a meetinghouse with people milling about on the steps, a maple tree holding a sap bucket. I longed to go back to a time more suited to my temperament and needs than the one I was living in.

The laundry room was in the basement of a brick building, the basement walls consisting of huge mortared stones, the floor concrete. Overhead there was no ceiling; visible were joists of the floor above and tangles of wires and asbestos-insulated hot-water pipes that hissed and groaned and shuddered in torment. The room was dominated by half a dozen washing machines and dryers the size of VW Bugs.

I devised a couple rules to live by in the laundry room. One: Never stand under the chute. Forty pounds of dirty laundry tightly bundled in a sheet with the corners knotted could build up quite a bit of attitude in its plunge three stories down to the basement. Two: Always look before you reach, because you never know what you will touch. Working with dirty clothes in a hospital gave me an appreciation of the complexity and variety of the corporeal experience, especially the concept of gooey.

Under the chute was a mountain of dirty laundry left by the night nurses. The challenge was to keep up with the flow, whittle the pile down to zero by 5 P.M., and start again the next day.

I wheeled a cart from Mount Laundry (no doubt Alouette would have referred to it as Mount Landry) to a washer, shoved in the dirty clothes and bedding, added soap, and started the machine. After the first load was done, I pulled out the damp, heavy fabrics, put them in a cart, and wheeled them to a dryer. Around 8 A.M. the folders arrived, women in their fifties – Donna (sumo wrestler), Deeanna (arthritic roller derby queen), and Maureen (Bette Davis look-alike). I enjoyed listening to their chatter.

"Said in the paper that Mrs. Doan passed away, ninety-six," Maureen said.

"I liked that corner store," Donna said. "Mrs. Doan was so particular about her hair."

"That wasn't her hair, she wore a wig," Maureen said.

"Noooo!"

"Real hair so thin you could play tic-tac-toe on her scalp."

"I can bear the arthritic hands, the slack breasts, but if I lose my hair that would be unbearable," Deeanna said.

I pulled clean fabric out of a dryer. It smelled like sunshine. When a diplomat or a teacher or a business tycoon goes to bed at night he can never know for sure whether his efforts amount to anything other than self-aggrandizement, but a laundry man knows that the smell of clean fabric does not lie, that through his labors he has taken one small step toward making a sick person a little more comfortable while relieving the burden of the more important medical staff.

The work went on through the day. By 3 P.M., I had reduced Mount Laundry to a hamper mound. By 5 P.M. there would be no dirty laundry remaining in the laundry room. I would leave in triumph, with the equivalent of a victory and a complete game.

My home was Moses, which I parked at a space I rented at the defunct Pinnacle Mountain Ski area a few miles outside of Keene. I was the only tenant. Evenings I drank beer, read books, read outdoor magazines such as *Fur, Fish and Game*, mused over campfires. Weekends I fished, and took walks in the woods. I stayed away from women and baseball; I lived a spare and frugal life; I saved my money.

I called myself a Catholic, I called myself a believer, but I didn't like going to church. The sermons were long and dreary, the rites repetitive and boring, especially now that the mass was in English. Words that sounded magical in Latin seemed mundane in my own language. *Hey, Tsee-guh, your language is not English, it's Canadian French, and don't you forget it*, Memere said. I felt unworthy to take communion. Usually I caught the quicky eight o'clock mass at St. Bernard's, but sometimes I went to ten o'clock high mass to see my parents or perhaps so they could see me. Either way, I felt like a hypocrite when I went to mass. I refrained from questioning my weak faith, because I knew if I started to think about it my religion would seem more like a human fabrication than the word of God.

And so my life went for more than a year. I wasn't happy exactly, but I was no longer haunted by guilt and regret. I was settling down in a mechanical kind of way as I continued my retreat from my old life of ambition and yearning. I could not bear to read about baseball in the papers, nor listen to the Red Sox games on the radio. I grew lonely. I thought about getting a dog, but who would keep the dog from being lonely when I was at work? Eventually, the drudgery of my labors in the hospital laundry wore me down. One day I finished up at 4 P.M. The folders had gone home. I was alone; I had nothing to do for an hour but think about the weight of time on my hands, the ugliness of my surroundings, the knowledge that tomorrow would be the same as today. I found myself wracked with involuntary sobs. I had to make a change. I started reading the want ads in the *Keene Sentinel*. How a town keeps its identity without a local newspaper – I don't know.

Blue, Orange, Green, Brown, Slate

With the help of a recommendation by Keene City Councilor Cormac MacDonald, I landed a job with the New England Telephone and Telegraph Company, as a COEI man, Central Office Equipment Installer. It was inside work; it was not unpleasant, dangerous, nor unhealthy; the pay was decent and benefits were provided; the company was stable; with the help of a union you couldn't get fired without just cause. My father's eyes grew moist when he learned of my good fortune.

"Mother Bell will take good care of you," he said in a reverent tone. "This is a job for life. Make the most of it." He was more proud of me than if I'd pitched in the World Series.

I worked all over northern New England on crews that converted telephone offices to dial systems. I had an expense account that was sufficient to rent a room and eat out at a restaurant every night, as long as it wasn't too fancy. I only used my salary to maintain my truck and to buy clothes and beer, so I was able to save money. I was privileged to see towns in the unique way of one who is neither a tourist nor a businessman, but a worker. For a young French-Canadian American man with no college education it was a dream job.

We would come into a town, like, say, Belfast, Maine, or Nashua, New Hampshire, and we would knock holes in the concrete floors with hammer and star drill, then pound in lead-alloy inserts to bond with the concrete, which held bolts, which in turn held steel bays from Western Electric, Inc., about three feet wide and eight feet tall and that contained rows of relays, panels, and other telephone switching equipment. Our job was to put the "number, please" operators out of business. Not exactly progress, now that I think about it decades later. You could depend on the local operator to provide local information or even a kind word. Try to get that information today from your telephone operator.

On top of the bays we built metal alleyways to hold cables. When all the metal was up, the place looked like an outsized Erector Set. Running cable was the most unpleasant part of an installation. We rookies would be stationed on the metal alleys on top of the bays, our heads only a few feet from the ceiling, and we would drag the cables from bay to bay, hundreds of cables, which ranged from one-half to one-and-a-half inches in thickness, consisting of scores of wires of various colors coiled up and wrapped with gray plastic. The wires were color-coded and very beautiful.

Picture gray cables tied down the side of a bay with a waxy string that we called twelve-cord. On the front of the bay would be rows of relays screwed onto panels. On the rear of the bay were the connection points. At each row, a particular cable would be stripped of its gray sheathing, its colorful wires exposed. The bunched wires gradually thinned out as individual wires were selected to connect to points on the backs of the relays with wiring guns or soldering irons. The wires were kept in place with twelve-cord. It could take weeks to wire and test a bay, which had thousands of connection points.

I present this long explanation because it leads up to something I want to say about a very important person in my life during this period. His name was Harold Archer, and to my way of thinking, he was one of America's unsung heroes.

Harold was only about ten or so years older than I, but in terms of maturity he was an ancient sage, a little guy, with a handsome but not particularly expressive face, dark hair, light brown eyes, clear fair skin. In some ways he reminded me of Alcide – quiet, reserved, dignified in his own way, but inarticulate, or maybe just reluctant to reveal himself with words. Harold always managed simultaneously to appear both serene and alert. He almost never went to the bar after work. Casual conversation did not interest him. His idea of fun was to eat a sandwich in the motel room and talk to his wife on the phone.

I can sum him up with two words: attitude and skill. Harold loved his work. You could read the excitement on his face as he pored over wiring diagrams for a bay he was about to start. He often worked through breaks and into the lunch hour. Harold worked very fast, but also with great precision. He was known for the elegant sweeps of wires he shaped with twelve-cord, the ties exact and equidistant from one another. He devised new ways to tie the wires so that they would look beautiful, and his connections were exquisite. When Harold finished a bay, all the guys would gather around and admire it.

The wires were color-coded and when I voice them today they sound like a poem to me, and I see the colors in my mind, forming a work of art.

Blue orange green brown slate
Blue-white blue-orange blue-green blue-brown blue-slate
Orange-white orange-green orange-brown orange-slate
Green-white green-brown green-slate
Brown-white brown-slate
Slate-white

Harold Archer made me understand in a deeper way the lesson my father had taught me about what it means to take pride in one's work. It ennobles the self, it builds the world.

Mortal Sins

First Mortal Sin
July 1965

Father Gonzaga's ecumenical mission didn't last long. Very suddenly he turned his attention to the protest movement. He grew a beard, wore rosary beads around his neck. People started calling him the hippie priest.

Every Saturday night Father Gonzaga led a march around Central Square to protest the Vietnam War. I did not join in. I told Father Gonzaga that I couldn't participate as long as my best friend, Sergeant Elphege Beaupre, was fighting for our armed forces, but that was only part of the reason. I didn't know what to believe about the war. It didn't seem possible to me that my country could embroil itself in an unjust war, and yet the news – the news gave me pause. I wasn't neutral. I was just confused, unable to make sense of it all. Just as my faith in God and my Catholic religion was weak, so was my faith in my government.

I told myself to forget my priest, forget my God, just live my life as an individual, but the pressures were too great. I felt the need to confess my sins. Again I went late at night. I was surprised to see a neon sign over the back door of the Eagle flashing on and off in psychedelic lettering: CHRIST'S RAPTURE HEAD SHOP – PIPES POSTERS PEACE.

I went inside and started up the dimly lit staircase. At the top, I saw that the chapel had been converted into a head shop.

Through the windows I saw colored lights shining on posters, candles, hippie beads, and strange doodads whose use obviously had something to do with mind-altering drugs but whose specificity I could not fathom.

I walked down the hall. I didn't have to knock on the door of Room 314. Father Gonzaga opened the door. I caught a smell, but it was not incense. The smell brought me back to the late falls of my childhood when people burned leaves in their backyards.

"Have a seat, Jack."

I sat down. On the table was a pipe. I understood now that what I smelled *was* burning leaves.

"You smoke marijuana?" I said.

"Acapulco Gold, very high quality. I'll expect you to try some. It will open your mind."

"My priest a damn hippie!" The sound of my voice, strident and ugly, startled me, but not Father Gonzaga.

"Well, yes, I am a hippie priest – I am *the* hippie priest. I've located my mission in the en oh double-U." Father Gonzaga spoke in a low voice, full of passion, but amused, too. "There are so many issues today – civil rights, the war, the ecology, mind-expanding drugs, police brutality, the God Is Dead movement – and it's the hippies who are out in front of all of them. Where have you been?"

"What happened to the ecumenical mission?"

"It's been absorbed by the Age of Aquarius. You've come for confession."

"Yes." I bowed my head.

"I want to hear you in the confessional, but before we start I want you to smoke some of my Acapulco Gold."

Father Gonzaga rose from his chair and returned with his stole around his shoulders. He sat, lit the pipe, inhaled, and handed me the pipe.

"No, please," I said.

"What are you afraid of?"

"I'm afraid it will change me." I could not voice my real fear, because it was so strange and terrifying, which was that change would take me further away from Alouette in a future lifetime.

Father Gonzaga laughed. "Musing over change is ideation, not prophesy."

It took a few more minutes of persuasion before I agreed to use the marijuana pipe, and it took even longer for me to inhale the smoke. I choked and gagged, and my eyes burned. Soon everything changed. I began to hear the ancient beams of the building groaning, like a sound from my childhood, of Memere's deep breathing during her afternoon nap. I heard the snows of old Acadia falling outside, like millions of tiny wind chimes in a faint breeze. The reflections off Father Gonzaga's glasses grew huge enough to walk into. Distant fires from past tragedies flashed over the hills.

"It's like a 3-D movie," I said.

"Okay, I think you're ready," Father Gonzaga said. "Most people usually don't respond quite so dramatically the first time. You're a natural." The words sounded to me as if they were shouted into a culvert.

Father Gonzaga took a long pull on the pipe, then handed it to me. I drew the smoke into my lungs and put the pipe back on the table. My remorse and the drug had combined to make the world strange and alluring but also frightening. One slip and I would fall into a vortex of color and never come out.

"Father, why don't the French-Canadian Americans and Irish get along?"

"Part of it was competition for jobs in the mills, but mainly it was a problem in the Church," Father Gonzaga said. "The Irish immigrants spoke English. The French-Canadians tied their identity to the French language. They wanted French-speaking churches and French-speaking parochial schools. The Irish wanted to Americanize the Catholic schools. It all led to bad feelings. Jack, what do you think your first mortal sin was?" Father Gonzaga asked me.

"I don't know – masturbation? Maybe my affair with Olympia Troy?"

"No, those sins of the flesh are essentially venial in nature. A mortal sin throws the World of the Self and Loved Ones out of orbit. Think back. You won't have to think too hard. Old sins come from the depths frequently to torment the sinner. Examine your conscience for the specters that rise up to haunt you."

I could see my memere with her rosary beads praying in French, a look of incredible sadness on her face after I'd betrayed her.

"Okay, I know now," I said. "I committed my first mortal sin when I was five years old."

"A splendid splinter of truth. Tell it to me in detail, please." Father Gonzaga was breathing hard.

"In those days we only spoke French in our house, because Memere didn't speak any English and because French was my parents' preferred language. 'I can say more, because I can feel more in French than in English,' my mother would say. My memere pampered me because I was the oldest and the only boy. In fact she believed I was the reincarnation of the son she'd lost. It was a joyous household. Everything changed when my father came back from the service and I went to kindergarten. I could barely speak English, and I talked with an accent. In school I discovered that the French language and French-Canadian people were scorned. I had no courage, Father. I told my parents that I would never speak that awful French language again. My parents held a council and decided to speak only English in the home. My kid sisters never did learn French, and the joy that I had felt in the family never quite returned. My memere became morose. What I did to the family, that was my first mortal sin."

"You are correct. It's not only what you did to your family, it's what you did to yourself. You speak no French today?"

"Only in my dreams. I took it in high school, but I couldn't relearn it," I said.

"Jack, you killed that language inside of yourself and entombed it in your psyche. That self-destructive act to bury your heritage was not only your first mortal sin, it was your first self-imposed penance. You will grieve the loss of the French language until the day of your death and perhaps beyond into the next life and into succeeding lives."

"You believe in reincarnation? That's not Catholic."

"*Catholic* means 'to encompass,' 'to embrace all' – universal. I believe in all the gods and in all the faiths. I forgive thee in the name of the Father, the Son, and the Holy Ghost."

As he spoke, I made the sign of the cross.

"I'm not sure that your telephone company job is sufficiently menial," Father Gonzaga said.

"Should I go back to working in the hospital laundry?"

Father Gonzaga shook his head. "I'll leave the decision up to your judgment. Look for a sign."

From then on, I had it in the back of my mind to look for a sign. With the help of Father Gonzaga, I found some purpose in my existence. He reinforced my determination to devote my life to menial labor.

Another Mortal Sin?

Master Sergeant Elphege Beaupre came back to Keene on leave for the holidays with Katie and their two children, Nate, three, and Amy, two. They were staying a couple weeks at the MacDonald camp on Granite Lake instead of at the new MacDonald house in West Keene, a scheme cooked up by the women to keep Beaupre and Coach from ripping out each other's throats. Coach still hadn't forgiven Beaupre for "stealing my daughter" and Beaupre had called his father-in-law a bullshit artist to his face.

A couple days after Christmas, Katie telephoned me at the telephone office in Claremont, New Hampshire.

"Hey, Katie, how did you track me down?"

"You're not that hard to find. I called your mother."

"You sound a little strained," I said. "Is something wrong?"

"Yes. Can you come over New Year's Eve and stay for supper?" she said. "Beaupre needs you."

"What's the matter with him?" I asked.

"He can't relax. Please, come – please," she said.

Whatever you can say about Coach MacDonald, he was a doting grandfather. Katie had dropped off the kids at the MacDonald house in Keene while she visited her girlfriends from high school days, so when I arrived at the camp only Beaupre was there. I had a vague idea of us ringing in the new and ringing out the old.

I was shocked by the sight of my old friend. I'd always been the lean tall guy and he was the short muscle man with pudgy cheeks and belly, but I had filled out and these days, my weight nudged up around the 200-pound mark, while Beaupre had lost all of his baby fat. His face now was as sculpted as the Indian on an old nickel, his stomach flat, and, just as Coach MacDonald had predicted, thick piston legs, which seemed to want to burst through the trousers at the thigh.

We didn't bother with awkward pleasantries, but just started talking as if no time had gone by since we'd seen each other. Beaupre put his coat on and we both knew without discussion that we would go out onto the ice.

At the hemlock tree beside the camp, we glanced at the thermometer, nine degrees. Beaupre hugged the tree and pretended to hump it.

The ice on the lake was new, but plenty thick enough to accept the weight of a man. In the shallows you could see the bottom magnified, strange and inviting through the lens of the ice. In deep water, the lake appeared black under the clear ice. No bob houses had yet been set up; there was no snow cover, the sky was overcast, and the air very cold with just enough wind to sting. The forlorn mood, like a sad song, suited me.

"Somewhere out there, my memere cracked her head open on the ice," I said.

"Not a bad way to go for an old lady," Beaupre said.

"I watched it happened. She didn't fall, Beaupre. She stiffened and let herself drop, and maybe I helped her along with a push."

"You tell the same stories over and over again. Jack, you were just a fucking kid."

"That's how I remember it," I said.

We walked in silence the rest of the way to Mystery Island and the big maple tree, His Lordship, where we had axed the branch to make Beaupre's bat when we were wiseass fourteen-year-olds. Nature had done a good, if not complete, job of healing the woods where we had cut the trees to make our ladder to reach into the branches of the maple.

"This fucking tree is not as big as I remembered, but it's big enough," Beaupre said.

"I like the bark, gnarly and tortured," I said.

We stood looking up at the tree as if we expected it to speak to us. Then Beaupre surprised me by rolling a marijuana cigarette and lighting it.

"You toke up?" he asked.

I smiled.

"You and me, we're always on the same fucking wavelength," Beaupre said. He rolled another one and handed it to me.

We sat silently for a few minutes until the experience of the marijuana took hold. We talked about the war protestors.

"I have moments when I imagine myself up on the belfry of the First Congo with a sniper rifle just picking off fucking protesters," Beaupre said.

"You think the war is justified?" I said.

Beaupre had a way of speaking in outrage in a calm voice that made his words all the more edgy and threatening.

"The war is shit," he said, "the peace movement is shit, the country is shit, and the other ones are worse, and seriously, if it wasn't for Katie and the kids I'd kill them all, the long, the short, and the tall, and who gives a flaming fuck their philosophical persuasion, they're human beings, aren't they, the fucking scourge of the planet. I'd kill them all and I'd kill myself because I believe in a just, verdant, and peaceful world. I tell you we will never get the verdance and the fucking peace, there's no fucking justice to be had, there never was. Yeah, if it wasn't for Katie and the kids I'd be a fucking war hero, the most fearless motherfucker this side of Audie Murphy, but, Jack, because of Katie and the kids – " And he repeated himself, "Because of Katie and the kids, because of Katie and the kids, I'm scared, I'm fucking terrified. Jack, I'm being sent to Vietnam hell and I'm coming back in a flag-draped coffin."

"You can't know that."

"Don't fucking question me. I know, I fucking know. I might be MIA, I might get blown up or shot up or get jungle fever or accidentally napalmed by a fucking B-52, or some skinny Viet Cong is going to sneak up behind me and slit my fucking throat, or my chute won't open, or more likely I'll step on a mine in a rice field. I don't know how it's going to happen, but I'm not coming back to my beautiful wife and my beautiful kids." He paused, pleased with himself, staring at his reefer. "Cripes, this is good stuff – I'm flying. I wish I could be around in ten years when they fucking legalize it and purify the high, and everybody can get stoned, and my kids will learn in school how to get stoned from the Sisters of Fucking Mercy at St. Joe's."

Beaupre sucked the smoke into his lungs.

"I can't calm my nerves, Jack. It's not me I'm thinking about, it's Katie left with the kids and no man around, or worse getting laid by some suit and tie, and I'm totally forgotten by my kids. I don't know how to say it."

Suddenly, I understood what Beaupre was trying to tell me.

"Listen, Beaupre, when you get yourself killed, I'll marry Katie and take care of your children. I'll never let them forget you, either. You'll always be God the Father, and I'll be Joseph, and I'll treat them both like Jesus Christ."

"You'll do that for me?"

"No, I'll do it because Katie is a great piece of ass," I said.

We both laughed the way we used to laugh when we were kids. It was a private joke laugh that unnerved our friends, because nobody could tell when we were serious and when we were kidding. But we knew; we knew each other the way only best friends can.

On the way back the sky cleared and the wind picked up and we could see ice boats in the distance. They came toward us at fantastic speed, the runners making a loud clacking sound as they whacked against the ice. I'd met these guys before. They were from all over the Northeast. They had a network. At any one time in the winter there would be ice somewhere in the North Country, from Montana to Maine, for their boats. Today it happened to be Granite Lake; next weekend they'd be off somewhere else, all through the winter. It was the way of America during these times of freezes and thaws: Everyone traveling here and there to get high from one method or another – drugs, booze, money, thrills, sex, power, religion, speed, and, of course, war. I was thinking of Chalky, my on-the-road cousin, wondering where his travels had taken him, whether he had found peace without Spud Polix.

By the time we returned to the camp, Coach and Mrs. Mac-Donald had left after dropping off Katie and the kids. I was introduced to Nate and Amy as Uncle Jack. I played with them on the floor in front of the fireplace while Katie and Beaupre hung out in the kitchen preparing the meal and talking, talking, talking.

For supper we had spaghetti and meatballs washed down with cheap Chianti wine. Afterward, while Katie was putting the kids to bed, reading them stories, Beaupre and I yakked some more.

"Katie and I want to thank you, Jack. She'll marry you when I die, okay?"

"Good," I said.

Katie returned. She looked very Irish, like Ann-Margret with freckles.

"Thanks, Jack, thanks so much. Now Beaupre can relax," Katie said, looking me in the eye.

"You know, I haven't felt like this, just free and optimistic, since Amy was born," Beaupre said. "Wait a minute, I'll be right back." He went into the bedroom.

"You sure about this, Katie?" I said.

"Jack, I can love you because I know how much you love Beaupre," Katie said.

"I told him and I'll tell you, if it comes to that, I'll see that the kids will always be his kids. Even in death he'll be their father."

Beaupre returned with his baseball bat. It was scuffed and dented and darkened by time and sunlight, but there were no cracks in the wood. He handed me the bat.

"It's the only thing out of my childhood that means anything to me," Beaupre said. "I want you to hold onto it, and when it happens to me, give it to my kids when they're of age and tell them everything you know about me that Katie doesn't, all the stupid baseball stuff. The home runs I hit with that bat off Whitey Ford in Fenway Park."

"Hell, I will, I'll tell them I struck out Ted Williams on three pitches."

Beaupre and I both laughed. Katie didn't see the humor. How could she?

"Tell them any fucking thing to make them cherish my fucking memory," Beaupre said. "Tell Amy I always respected her mother, and that I was in love with her from the moment I saw her picture on the fridge in this camp back when I was fourteen years old. Tell Nate never back down, never instigate. Listen to me now, Jack, I have to know that you and Katie . . . you understand me?"

"You and me, we understand each – we always did," I said and turned to Katie.

"Beaupre and me, we discussed it," Katie said.

"So you don't mind?"

"Of course I mind, but . . ." She let the words hang there.

"She's doing it for me, not for you. Good night. I'm going to turn in."

He faked a yawn and went into the bedroom. He didn't sleep, though. I know because I could smell reefer.

Katie and I lay on a blanket in front of the fire.

"What I always found interesting about you, Jack," Katie said, "is that you always seemed to be whistling a secret tune."

"Some women look so much better after having children, fuller, more assured and proud of their fertility," I said. "It makes a man want to please them. That's you, Katie."

After that we fucked like mad bunnies. I told her I loved her and she told me she loved me. It was a crazy, holy kind of matrimony, and we both hoped and prayed that we would never have to repeat this act again, because it would occur only with the death of Elphege Beaupre.

Two days later, the Beaupres cleared out. I put Beaupre's bat in my Moses pickup truck, behind the seat for safekeeping.

Beaupre's premonition turned out to be half right. He did step on a mine, but he didn't die. His legs had to be amputated above both knees, which got him out of the Army on disability. I called him and Katie at their trailer outside of Fort Bliss, Texas, where Beaupre's mother had moved in with her latest husband, but Beaupre wouldn't talk to me. Katie told me he was having a hard time adjusting. "He won't come back to Keene until he can walk again," she said, "because he doesn't want people to see him as a cripple. The trouble is, he isn't going to walk again. He's in a wheelchair for life."

"Katie, you sound like you're coping," I said.

"With two kids and one on the way, somebody in this family has to hold together." She paused. "Or at least fake it." After that she couldn't seem to formulate words.

I lay on my camper bed thinking about Katie, what we'd done. I'm ashamed to say that I was excited all over again. Who had committed the mortal sin? Beaupre for persuading his wife to make love to his best friend for his own mad reasons? Katie for committing adultery? The U.S. government for going to war in a foreign land? Me? *Yes, it was you,* Memere said, *but not then – now, for thinking about it with so much enjoyment.*

Beautiful Women

A Sign

One of my favorite telephone towns was White River Junction, Vermont. It was only an hour's drive from Keene, so I could visit my parents or Coach MacDonald on weekends – if I felt like it, which I usually didn't. As Coach constantly reminded me, I owed him for the job I held and all the intangibles that a mentor provides. WRJ might have appeared to be a tired railroad town built on a bluff above the confluences of the White River and the Connecticut River, but to me it was an energy center. The Indians met here for councils. The railroad lines converged here, and so did the phone lines (it was a toll telephone switching center for the region). The future interstate highways 89 and 91 would cross here.

The downtown was out of an old black and white movie. The main feature in the town was the Coolidge Hotel, which overlooked the railroad station across the tracks. The hotel block included a few small shops, a Woolworth's, a bank, a post office, the 100th Monkey Bookstore – one of the best used bookstores in America – and Fancy Felix, a costume-maker's shop operated by one of the great women of Vermont, but hers is another story for another book. Across the street was the WRJ Diner, a barbershop, and a bar.

I stayed at the Coolidge. The rooms hadn't seen a coat of paint or a change in wallpaper in many a year. Huge murals of local scenes by the artist Peter Gish gave the hotel an intimate yet classy appearance, despite its rundown condition. The wood floors were worn from the steps of thousands of guests. The dining room was huge, but only a quarter full on a good night. The separate bar was handy. I could get drunk and not have to worry about driving or even having to go outside. Did I mention that living on the road had made a habitual drinker out of me?

I was making good money working for New England Tel and Tel, and I liked living on the road on a modest expense account, but something in me was restless. I told myself I should start a family. In the French-Canadian American household men were supposed to emulate St. Joseph, Jesus's stepdad. Of course, poor Joe never got near Mary, since from all reports she remained a virgin. You wonder about a culture that chooses an emasculated saint to represent its manhood. I didn't have a steady girlfriend. I couldn't bear to look at, let alone go out with, girls who reminded me of Alouette. It was as if I was betraying her all over again. In the affairs I had, the women were always older, whorish, and bad-tempered. I tried to figure out who I was, what I was, but just when I thought I'd learned something about myself the knowledge would be revealed as irrelevant. The quest for self-knowledge is like trying to catch your shadow.

I usually ate supper and went out drinking with the telephone guys, guys like Famous Papadopolis who would bet on anything. Once in a while I liked to eat alone. So it was in May 1966, a couple weeks after my twenty-fifth birthday, I dined alone at the Coolidge. I picked a table where I could spy on the other diners. Some people ate in spurts and then they rested; others nibbled. Some bent their necks to put their faces closer to the plate. Some constantly wiped their kissers with napkins. Some sat up straight like Mommy taught them. Some made piggy noises.

This particular night, the Coolidge was busy, the clientele apparently coming from Dartmouth College up the road, only a few miles from WRJ, though it might as well have been on the other side of the planet. Few residents of WRJ went to the college town, and few from the college town found their way to WRJ.

A really classy couple came in. The man was about fifty-five, with a full head of perfect dark, graying hair, the woman about forty. Some men, especially members of wedding parties, appear out of place in formal clothes, but this guy looked like he had been born and raised in a tuxedo. Walked with a dignified waddle, a man part penguin and part Cary Grant. The woman wore an evening gown that showed enough cleavage to conceal a leprechaun. To titillate myself I imagined she was Elizabeth Taylor, and for all I know maybe she was. She sure looked like Elizabeth Taylor, when the actress was at her peak.

I never noticed the man eating, because I was fascinated by Elizabeth Taylor. She ordered a huge sirloin steak, which she cut into He-Man-bite-sized chunks. She stabbed a chunk with her fork, stuck it in her mouth, followed up by mashed potatoes and peas. Then she put another piece of steak in her mouth, more mashed potatoes, more peas. This process went on until her cheeks bulged like those of a chipmunk let loose in a peanut factory. I watched her slowly masticate, jaws moving, body perfectly still, eyes in a trance. Elizabeth Taylor must have been remembering some other lifetime when she was a snake digesting a mammal swallowed whole.

On impulse I decided to follow the couple outside to see what kind of car they drove. By the time I'd paid my bill and reached the street, however, they had disappeared. Sometimes I think maybe they were never there, that I made up these creatures as exemplars of the kind of people who ruled the world and who I could never get to know in a real way and who never could get to know me in a real way.

It was quite dark. Across the street I could see the WRJ Diner, the scene under the streetlight framed in my vision like an Edward Hopper painting, or maybe, as I recall it now, a Dennis Hopper painting. The old scar on the sole of my foot began to throb.

"Fuck," I said to nobody. "Fuck."

And then I saw her. Elizabeth Taylor. *No, Jack,* Memere said. As the woman stepped out of the diner and into the light I recognized Olympia Troy.

About the same time she spotted me. I walked toward her. "Long time no see," she said.

"My priest told me to look for a sign – I think you're it."

"Well, then, let's go."

I followed her Subaru in Moses for about ten miles, until she pulled down a long driveway built over a swamp. On a slightly elevated spot was a trailer. Olympia got out of the car and waited for me.

I slammed the door to my rig and looked around.

"Nice place," I said, my eyes scanning the swamp.

As if reading my mind, Olympia said, "My golden meadow, and don't you forget it."

"I thought you were with Pete Dubie," I said.

"We had a parting of the ways."

"Where's he living?"

"I don't know and I don't knows that I give a damn."

Olympia's place was off a dirt road in Perkinsville, Vermont, roughly halfway between WRJ and Keene. No neighbors in sight. I stayed that night with Olympia. I hadn't realized how much I needed the love of a woman. We produced fireworks when we were together. I wasn't lonely anymore. Soon I moved in with her for keeps.

Beyond the swamp – excuse me, the golden meadow – the land steepened and was heavily forested. One particular tree stuck out in my mind, a huge white pine that had no definable trunk but seemed to be a collection of trees that had fused into one. For reasons I could not then discern, it frightened and excited me. Sometimes when I was with Olympia I could arouse myself sexually by thinking about cutting down the tree.

Every once in a while Olympia would disappear for a night or two. She never denied she cheated on me. She'd say, "You knew what I was when you moved in with me." The humiliation added to my belief that I had to live a life of sacrifice and penance. One afternoon we had a picnic under the the big pine. Afterward, I felt more passionate toward Olympia than I ever had and we made love on the blanket with the aroma of pine needles as our aphrodisiac.

"I don't like it that we're just living together. It doesn't seem right to me," I said.

"Are you proposing marriage?"

"I suppose I am."

Olympia burst into laughter. "Jack, I'm fourteen years older than you are."

"I could never be with someone my own age or younger," I said. She waited for me to give her a reason, but I didn't say anything.

"Marry for love, they say, marry for money, marry for nookie, but I say if you want to be happy marry for laughs," Olympia said. "Red Skelton or Sid Caesar are what I've been looking for in a man all my life, but at my age, Jack Landry, you will have to do."

"Will you cheat on me?"

"Ask me no questions and I will tell you no lies."

Out of the blue, a thought came to me: "Olympia, what is Frank Sinatra's theme song for zookeepers?"

"I don't know, and why should I or anybody else care?"

I sang: "Egrets, I've had a few, but too few to mention."

"Jack, are you going weird on me?"

"Takes one to know one," I said.

"You don't love me, Jack, not really anyway, so I don't know why you want to marry me."

"I love you as well as I can. One thing I like about you, Olympia, is I can always tell you what I feel. I can't do that with my parents or Coach MacDonald or any of the girls I've been out with. I guess because you speak your own mind I can speak my own. You're an honest woman, Olympia."

"Honest enough to know when I'm lying."

"I got my own secrets; we deserve each other," I said, but I wasn't looking at her; I was looking at the wolf pine. I could see a burl about thirty feet up, like an eye staring down at me, mocking me.

We decided to elope. Our reasons went unsaid. I realize now that I was secretly ashamed of Olympia, and that shame was part of my punishment for my sins. Olympia had her own reasons for marrying me on the sly, though the story behind those reasons would not come out until decades later.

By now the war in Vietnam had ended, the world had changed, and therefore Father Gonzaga had changed. Though his mission retained ownership of the Eagle Hotel and he kept his room overlooking Main Street, he shut down the head shop and disbanded his gang of protestors. His mission bought pieces of puckah brush and transformed it into a commune that he called Ecology Farm, which was where he married Olympia and me.

The place didn't have a regular toilet, nor an old-fashioned privy. You did your business at the neck of a huge tank called a clivus multrum. The idea was to recycle human waste into mulch for crops. Father Gonzaga and his followers from the mission built houses out of fieldstone and cement. They didn't eat meat, just vegetables, which they grew in gardens all around the place. Working in the fields hardened Father Gonzaga's few muscles, though his face remained gaunt. Olympia kidded that he'd lost all his weight on a "macro acrobatic diet."

I wanted to calm myself down before the ceremony by toking up, but Father Gonzaga forbade it.

"You brought weed into my life," I said.

"The era of mind-expansion through hallucinogens is over, Jack," Father Gonzaga said. "Come, now I will teach you to meditate. You too, Olympia."

"I'm game for any new trick," Olympia said.

We didn't learn to meditate that first time. It took a while, but we practiced and I did it over the years, sort of, but Olympia thought it was a big joke; she thought Father Gonzaga was a big joke.

"I assume you wish to waive the banns of marriage," Father Gonzaga said.

"Why not?" Olympia said. I nodded. I was imagining myself joking with Alouette: Wave the bands of marriage. I pictured bald men playing trombones and sweet-smelling ladies fiddling on cellos and a choir singing "Here comes the bride."

Coureur du Bois

Good Years

It was the 1970s. There were gasoline and fuel oil shortages. People lost faith in the oil markets, and in northern New England, where as far as the eye could see were trees, the populace turned to wood heat. I quit my job as a COEI man. With the money I'd saved working for Mother Bell, I bought a couple of chain saws and a truck big enough to hold a cord of wood. I wanted to buy a skidder, but the price was out of my range and I refused to go into debt. I settled for a secondhand tractor to drag the logs.

I was better suited as a woodcutter than I was as a telephone man. I called myself a *coureur du bois*, which in Memere's crazy French patois meant "man crazy for the woods."

Olympia kept her waitressing job at the WRJ Diner. When Olympia acquired her lot from her gentleman friend, Pierre Dubois, A.K.A. Pete Dubie, she fell in love with the "golden meadow." She never paid attention to the hillside she owned. It had been logged over some years earlier, so the timber had little value and the land was unappealing to the eye. By the time I came into the picture, the trees had grown back, not saw-log size, but perfect for firewood and just for admiring. In places, the old-time loggers had left trees with defects, so there were a fair number of big trees, but all of them were marred, from maples whose cores had rotted out to the single grand wolf pine that I liked to think had consciousness and memory.

The property had everything I wanted. On a narrow back road

near a fishing pond. Small trout stream running through it. No neighbors in sight. Northern exposure so the snow stayed longer. Moss and lichen on boulders that grew like maps of the secret Soul of Creation.

The hillside forest was very dense, second or third or fourth growth, who knows: white pine, hemlock, red spruce, balsam fir, red maple, sugar maple, moose wood, white birch, gray birch, yellow birch, black birch, ash, and beech. In the spring, the ground was a mat of dead leaves through which poked trillium, star flowers, lady slippers, columbines, and a few rare orchids of the north; in the summer, an Eden of ferns (meditating on a fern is a nice way to pass an hour or so); in the fall, sweeps of fresh leaves of varying hues of red and yellow and orange from the hardwoods; in the winter, snow. Snow may hide the earth, but it reveals the wanderings of rabbits, ferrets, foxes, birds, deer, bears, bobcats, voles, and most exciting of all, shadows.

Most of the hills in this area were very rocky, but the highest point on our land was free from any rocks at all. The soil was sandy from a glacial moraine now covered with young white pine trees and a few birches. Here also reigned the old wolf pine with its multiple stems and trunk that the loggers had overlooked in the last couple centuries. You could see why. Ten feet above the eye burl were huge branches, arching helter-skelter. Loggers call such trees "wolf pines" and "widow makers" because the twisted wood is low quality and because when you cut them you never know which way they will fall.

On summer nights, I built campfires, and Olympia and I smoked pot and watched the flames the way another family might watch TV. If it rained, we listened to it patter on the aluminum roof of the trailer, a symphony that soothed me, as best as I could be soothed. In winter we watched snow through the windows. You can learn a great deal about patience and the mind of God by watching weather. In some future time, dear God, bring me back as a tree where I can stay in one spot and contemplate your creation. I had a home that fit my sensibilities at last. Working in the woods made me realize that Memere had been right about me. I was one who belonged in the forest; I was a *coureur du bois*.

It took us five years, but Olympia and I built our modest dream house on the high ground, a three-room cabin of rough-cut pine boards and recycled doors and windows, no cellar. We used the trailer as a shed to hold tools and store the junk a householder collects over the years. Among the stuff in the shed-trailer was Beaupre's bat, stored for safekeeping.

I cut wood through winter cold, wind, snow, slush, and some days of sunshine that made me optimistic and thankful to God for the blessings. I worked in the muddy spring: run-off from snow-melt filling the woods with music; swarms of black flies that made me bleed and got into my eyes, mouth, and up my nose. I worked in the summer heat and humidity when mosquitoes tormented me; poison ivy made me itch so bad that I ran naked into the swamp and rolled in the mud. "Look at you, Jack," Olympia said, laughing at me. "You're fucking the mud." I worked in the fall through driving rain and leaf colors that brought me to my knees in gratitude.

Hard as working in the woods was, it was better than the laundry room at the hospital, better than the telephone offices. The woods made me feel alive and magnificent. And the beauty . . . the beauty could lift my spirits through any discomfort. I wanted so much to pass on my love of the forest to a child of my own, but Olympia didn't want children. "I wouldn't be a good mother – I'm too old and too selfish," she said, "and anyway, there's enough people in the world."

My business was not lucrative, but it was steady. I had more orders for cord wood than I could handle. I started my new trade by clearing my and Olympia's cabin site. Then I did selective cutting on our woodlands. I left the trees that might become good saw logs in ten to fifty years, and I cut the rest for firewood. I made deliveries in my truck. By the time that work was complete, I'd developed the necessary skills with chain saw and tractor that I could call myself a professional cutter of firewood. On the social ladder I was a step down from the loggers, who dealt in quality logs for the sawmill. Placing myself on the lower rung was another part of my penance, my humility journey.

I made it a point to introduce myself to consulting foresters, who would contract with land owners for timber. Loggers would cut the trees and pull out the valuable saw logs on their expensive skidders. I would cut up the rest of the trees into sixteen-inch lengths for firewood. I was a scavenger of the forest products industry.

Building sites were another source of firewood. People were moving out of the cities and putting houses down in the woods. Companies were clearing huge sections for shopping centers, housing developments, and industrial parks. The loggers and I would clear-cut these areas, and then the heavy-equipment guys would come along to scoop out the trunks and rearrange the landscape.

In the eighteenth and nineteenth centuries the mountains from Georgia to Maine had been denuded to grow crops and grass for sheep and cattle, but in the twentieth century the New England farms had been abandoned and the forests had come back, leaving the land in a natural state of mixed hardwoods and conifers. In other places around the planet, the forests were slashed and burned for agriculture, industry, and housing. In my part of the world, the trees were growing back faster than we could cut them down.

It was an optimistic time for Olympia and me. I was at my peak physically, even if my hairline was running scared from my brow. Though I had put on weight, most of it was muscle from eight to ten hours a day of working in the woods. I made decent money, which allowed Olympia to reduce her hours at the diner and devote more time to gardening and cultivating a sunny disposition.

One piece of news that cheered me was a report in the *Keene Sentinel*. Elphege Beaupre had won a wheelchair marathon race in Colorado. The picture in the paper showed him with huge, muscular arms embracing Katie, a woman who grew more beautiful with the years. It was a great picture, and it made my day.

I remained in a buoyant mood when I visited Father Gonzaga at Ecology Farm one winter afternoon to ask him to hear my confession, though I had some reservations. I was afraid he'd say something to depress me, but I went anyway. Keeping in touch with my weak faith was more important than maintaining a peaceful, easy feeling.

Father Gonzaga's acolytes of back-to-the-landers and lost youths had cleared out after the harvest, and he was alone in the Ecology Farm stone house. He was wearing a long brown robe, like a monk, sandals over L.L. Bean wool socks. He had grown a curly beard that was turning gray. He'd lost most of his hair, but what he had was long, in a ponytail tied with a leather thong. His face was gaunt as ever. Working in the fields had given his lean body some definition. Except for his glasses and the inquisitive eyes behind them, he didn't look anything like the fat union organizer priest I'd met back in the finishing room of Narrow Textiles, nor the conformist priest, nor the hippie priest I'd known at the Eagle Hotel. Even his accent was different. He talked in a Bob Dylan Midwestern twang.

I knelt on the oak kneeler he brought with him wherever he went. Father Gonzaga sat in a rocking chair beside the fire in the stone fireplace. I started by confessing that old sin against Alouette Williams and our baby, and as always, voicing the words brought back the old pain and the old regrets. It was a sin that God and the Church might forgive me for, but for which I could never forgive myself.

I confessed my rages when Olympia came home late and I knew she'd stepped out on me. I was afraid that I would hit her. Father Gonzaga made me understand that I was not really jealous, that I knew Olympia was faithful to me in spirit, if not in flesh.

"I guess I knew what she was when I married her," I said.

"Jack, what she was and what she remains is *why* you married her. She is part of your pattern of mortification of the flesh."

"Is that what it is? Is beating myself up part of my penance?"

"You've converted a sin of pride into a neurosis, *garçon*," Father Gonzaga said. I was thunderstruck. He was right.

Father Gonzaga showed me that my anger and despair were not centered on Olympia's behavior but on my ancient fear of humiliation, the brand of my heritage from French Canada.

"You don't really care about what she does," he said. "What you care about is what other men think of you, Jack the cuckold who married the town pump. Let the humiliation go, let your pride ride off into the sunset, and your rage cannot be far behind."

"What about you, Father? Who do you confess to?"

My question jolted Father Gonzaga, one of the few times I'd seen him anything other than in complete command. His answer left me somewhat uncomfortable.

"When I was in Rome I confessed to the Holy Father, and we met for coffee afterward. I advised him to visit our small community of homesteaders here at Ecology Farm."

I knew he was lying, and the knowledge provoked in me a smart-alecky response. "He better not come in winter, because if he kisses the ground he'll be here until mud season," I said. It was the kind of humor that Beaupre would have appreciated, but Father Gonzaga didn't get it or pretended not to.

I told Father Gonzaga that Memere haunted me less frequently these days and that I thought less and less about Alouette. My mind was preoccupied with my work. Inspired by Harold Archer to make a good thing, I had labored to be an artful woodcutter.

Suddenly, Father Gonzaga reached out and said, "Let me touch your hands."

Still on my knees on the kneeler, I held out my hands. He ran his fingers over the thick calluses, his face contorted with emotion. I'd seen the same expression on Olympia's face when I slapped her behind during our lovemaking. "Nothing better than the rough hands of a working man," she'd say. Father Gonzaga traced the creases in my palm. Then he released my hand and looked at his own.

"Is it a *W* for work or an *M* for Mother Mary?" I asked.

"Where does this question come from?"

"From Memere. She showed me." I cupped my hand. "See, in the shape of the creases?"

"Yes, an *M*."

"That's debatable," I said. "Memere told me that when I thought about doing bad I should look at my hand and the *M* would remind me of Mother Mary, and I would not sin, but if I'm pitching a baseball I turn the hand as I cock it behind my ear. From that perspective it's a *W*, which to me stands for Work, capital W."

"I would say that you have transubstantiated the symbol of our heavenly mother for your own uses."

"Is that a blessing or a curse?"

"In truth I cannot say." Father Gonzaga stood, raised his eyes to heaven, and made the sign of the cross.

After he forgave me my sins, Father Gonzaga and I sat by the fire and sipped homemade brandy and Benedictine from ingredients grown on the farm. I felt mellow and, following my confession, purged. I told Father Gonzaga that despite a few complaints I was darn near content with my world, my wife, and myself. Father Gonzaga surprised me by sharing in my optimism.

"I'm beside myself with hope for the future of America and mankind," he said. "Do you know about the Great Awakening?"

I shook my head.

"It was an experimentalist phenomenon in which people everywhere sensed the presence of the Holy Spirit, but since the word was spread by Protestant ministers you didn't hear about it from the Sisters of Mercy in parochial school. I am here to tell you that we are on the verge of a new Great Awakening, when all Christianity will join under our Holy Father in Rome to drive out the atheistic philosophies and convert the Jews and the Hindus and the Muslims, all the religions – even the Pagan New Agers – until we experience a world in Christ. All signs point to a new day.

"The Vietnam War is finally over. Congress has established the EPA to protect the earth from harm and OSHA to protect workers. Black people are getting the civil rights denied them for centuries. With these successes to point to, I predict the Democrats will be in charge of Congress and the White House until the end of the twentieth century and into the twenty-first. Capitalism and communism will fade away, and a gentler, kinder economic *-ism* will be forged out of the hippie counterculture and ecology movement to lead the country and, yea, the world, into a quiet revolution where all men and women will be equal and prosperous and in touch with the good news from Mother Earth and her husband, God the Father. With the help of scientists and the Holy Ghost, the infernal combustion engine will disappear, replaced by tele-transportation devices powered by the sun. Have you been watching *Star Trek*? By the year 2000 our very thoughts will link up into one giant machination of Universal Love. Humanity is evolving toward God, Jack. Witness the words of my Jesuit brother, Pierre Teilhard de Chardin. The day of the Experimentalist is at hand. Let us pray in thankfulness."

And we did.

The Flood

Incident in Taxi Office
Fall 1980

It was a normal rainy fall day. Not a cold rain, but a warm rain, remnants of a hurricane that wandered north from the Caribbean. It was certainly not a day to work in the woods, so I decided to run some errands in Keene in the morning and stack wood in the afternoon for some of my customers that already had deliveries.

I had a long phone conversation with my sister Denise in Portland, Maine, now a certified special education teacher with a master's degree. We talked over old times, which put me in a nostalgic mood.

When I arrived in Keene in my most recent Moses, a cord wood truck, I headed for the dilapidated house where Beaupre had lived as a boy, with his neglectful mother and her strings of no-good lovers and husbands. That crummy house was long gone, and his mom had passed away. In its place was a city park with grass and benches and trails through the meadow where the brook meandered. The park was closed, the stream swollen by the recent rains so that the trails were flooded. A thin fog snaked over dead weeds, dreary and brown at this time of year. I could hear a dog barking. I got out of the truck and walked over to a metal plaque on a rock about four feet high.

I read the words: SITE OF THE FIRST GRIST MILL IN KEENE, 1740. BEAVER BROOK STATE PARK, ENACTED 1978, KEENE

CITY COUNCIL, MAYOR CORMAC MACDONALD. I got back in
my truck and drove the short distance to the Hephaestus Dynamite
building. It had not exactly been renovated, but it had been patched
up, a new roof laid, broken windows repaired. A new gate had been
installed, and the brush in the parking lot had been cleared. New
sliding overhead doors had been built, and over them was a sign:
WINTERS AUTO AND MOTORCYCLE REPAIR, BILLY WIN-
TERS, PROPRIETOR. Beside the garage was Liberty Taxi. I remembered reading in the paper that Coach MacDonald, now Mayor
MacDonald (elected after he had switched from the Democratic to
the Republican party), had leased the building and moved his taxi
business from the downtown.

I hadn't seen Coach MacDonald to say anything more than a
hello in years. I'd failed to help Coach get elected to mayor his first
time around, and after that he had no further use for me. When I left
Keene and married Olympia Troy my status around town didn't
exactly enhance Coach MacDonald's position in the community.
I was relieved to be outside his orbit. However, the sight of the
Hephaestus building put me in a nostalgic mood, and I wanted
very much to see Mayor MacDonald. He had long ago given up
coaching Post 7 American Legion baseball, but in my mind he'd
always be Coach with a capital C.

Mayor MacDonald was at the dispatcher's desk talking on the
phone when I entered. The taxi office consisted of a big cluttered
room with no windows, cement floors, and grimy concrete block
walls. Furnishings included a metal dispatcher's desk and a couple
of couches that looked like they had been rescued from the dump.
Beside the desk was a curtain behind which was a toilet. The office
smelled of stale cigarette butts, doughnuts, burgers, French fries,
sweat, auto fumes, piss, jock itch powder, and sneaker sweat. The
place was in contrast to the MacDonald house in West Keene,
which was clean and modernistic, the vision of Mrs. MacDonald.

On the couches sat four drivers. I recognized Wes Leb, still
wearing fifties-style biker garb after all these years; two other drivers were vaguely familiar faces around town; the fourth driver was

a young kid, who I guessed was a part-timer, a student at Keene State College probably. I nodded to the drivers, and they nodded back. They knew who I was.

The smell; a mess of ancient magazines, newspapers, and Bettie Page pinup calendars from years gone by; and Coach MacDonald's collection of sporting gear – autographed footballs and baseballs, gloves, hockey sticks, goalie masks, et cetera – gave the taxi office a homey feel. The photos caught my eye. There was my team, with Beaupre in the front because he was short, me standing behind him, skinny Chalky and skinnier Spud standing side by side. But the picture that really grabbed me was framed-in by a glass case, a sixteen-by-twenty blow-up of two photographs pasted side by side on posterboard. One was an autographed picture of Ted Williams, swinging a bat; the other a picture of me in my American Legion uniform in throwing position from the mound. The caption at the bottom spanned both photographs. "Jack Landry, 18-year-old phenom right-hand bonus baby from Keene, strikes out Ted Williams on three pitches, 1960, the year Ted retired after hitting a home run in his last at bat." Another item in the case was the news clipping of the interview with Coach MacDonald.

I stared at the montage, which celebrated the pinnacle of my baseball career. Part of me actually believed that I had struck out Ted Williams. If it was in the paper, it must have happened.

"You're with the immortals now, Jack," Mayor MacDonald said, as he hung up the phone, rose from his desk, came over and slapped me on the rear. He shook my hand, squeezed my right biceps, and said, "If I had an arm like that, I'd be a bully."

We talked old times for a while in loud voices for the benefit of our audience, the drivers. My former coach told me the story of how he'd leased the building for ninety-nine years from the Hephaestus family.

"I did a little fix-up, and found myself a good tenant in Billy Winters. He services all my taxis, quite handy for both of us," Coach said.

"Did you find any interesting stuff when you moved into the

building?" I asked. "There used to be rumors of leftover explosives."

"Funny you should ask. Get a load of this." He pulled open a drawer in the dispatcher's desk. Amidst the clutter was a faded red cylinder about ten inches long, fuse at the end.

"Wow!" I exclaimed. "An old-fashioned dynamite stick, just like in the movies."

He put the stick back in the drawer. "I keep it as a good luck piece, and a reminder."

"Of what?"

"Oh, I don't know. It's just a reminder, that's all."

The displeasure in his voice at my question made me wince. Though I was pushing forty, I still wanted to please this man.

I asked about Beaupre and Katie. They were living in Oklahoma outside of Fort Sill. The mayor hadn't exactly forgiven Beaupre, but he had come to understand that Katie was not about to dump her husband even if he was in a wheelchair, so the two men were on speaking terms, if just barely.

"They're doing okay," Mayor MacDonald said. "Katie's the office manager of a sporting goods store, and Beaupre works, would you believe, as a bouncer in a strip club. He tools around in a wheelchair and carries a cattle prod. Anybody gives him a hard time, *zappo*, they get a charge. He's got character, that boy." Coach lowered his voice and whispered so only I could hear. "If you had had his character, you could have made it to Fenway Park, Jack." He raised his voice again. "Mrs. MacDonald and I go down every winter and spend a month to see the grandkids. They're getting big, teenagers, how time flies. That youngest one, well you wouldn't believe." He laughed, the way a person laughs when they know something you don't, and gave me a searching look that unaccountably sent a tremor through me, then he said more to himself than to me, "Let it ride."

"What?"

"Never mind." Coach changed expressions, bland with his politician's smile. "Jack, you still working in the woods?" He turned to look at my picture on the wall.

"That I am, Coach," I said. It seemed to me that his Irish brogue had become more pronounced, but my thoughts about Coach were fleeting. I was thinking about Beaupre's bat, how it had come to symbolize the bond between me and Beaupre and Katie. I decided that it was time for me to return the bat and resume our friendship. Olympia and I would take a vacation by driving to the Southwest to visit Beaupre and Katie.

"I don't coach any more. Call me Mister Mayor. Everybody else does."

"Okay, Mister Mayor."

"I worry about you, Jack. A tree could fall on you, chain saw accident, branch kickback, you could get hurt just like you did when you came down with the sore arm that prevented you from making the big leagues." He spoke up to make certain that the drivers could hear clearly.

I looked at Coach, he averted his eyes, I looked at the drivers. They seemed to want some confirmation from me. No doubt they knew that Mister Mayor was full of beans. I couldn't bring myself to call Mister Mayor a liar in front of his employees. I just shook my head and glanced at my wrist, as if I were wearing a watch, and fibbed, "I have to go."

The phone rang. Mister Mayor jogged to his desk and picked up the receiver. "Liberty Taxi," he said with a good-bye wave to me, but no meeting of the eyes.

I ran errands in Keene, lunched at Lindy's Diner on an Eastern Western, and spent the afternoon stacking wood. Old people or just lazy people with money were happy to pay extra to have good-looking wood piles. I loved touching wood, smelling it, especially the minty aroma of black birch, and it was very rewarding making neat rows in various patterns to enhance the landscaping of a property. Once I finished I would always take a moment to make a mental picture of the house and the wood pile I'd created, and later, lying in bed before going to sleep, I would run a little slide show in my mind of my wood stacks. They were about as close as I was going to come to the art of Harold Archer's bays.

By mid-afternoon, it started to rain again, and suddenly it was pouring. I was soon soaked to the skin. It may have been a warm rain and the temperature outside balmy for the season, but even so, I was chilled. I headed home and turned the heater on. Once I warmed up, I found myself in that easy state of grace between awake and asleep, and I almost dozed off at the wheel when I reached our golden meadow/swamp, except it was neither a meadow nor a swamp. It was now a lake. As I figured out later, the brook washed down sticks and leaves that piled up and created a dam to hold back the water.

My first thought was that Olympia was stranded in our house, which was on high ground but on the other side of the flooding.

I looked out into the new lake. The shed-trailer was just barely visible. It took me another minute before an image popped into my mind: Beaupre's bat.

I stripped to my underwear and went into the water. It was a lot colder than I wanted it to be. It was still raining hard and getting dark, so it was difficult to see. I wished I could swim a fast crawl, but I didn't know how to breathe properly with my face in the water, so I side-stroked, looking up frequently to keep a bead on the shed-trailer. I heard a roar – it was distant thunder – but for a second I thought it was Mister Mayor's Chris-Craft come to run me down.

When I reached the shed-trailer, only the roof was visible. I treaded water, looking around for what seemed like minutes but was probably only thirty seconds or so. I dove down again. The water was murky, and I couldn't see anything distinctly, but one thing was for sure. The trailer had flooded entirely. I was starting to get very cold. *Another rash act, won't you ever learn*, Memere said. I swam for shore. I didn't realize until I was on land how bad off I was. I was shivering uncontrollably.

I made it to the house. Nobody home. I stripped off my clothes, jumped into bed, and pulled all the covers over me. It took an hour before I could warm up. I heated a bowl of Campbell's chicken soup with rice and poured myself a double shot of Four Roses. I called Olympia at the diner and told her the story. After I'd dressed and eaten, I was overcome with weariness. I lay down on the couch and fell asleep. Next thing I knew, I was dreaming about Katie MacDonald Beaupre. When I woke it was morning, and she was standing over me, but it wasn't Katie, it was Olympia.

"Look," she said, pointing to the picture window that over-looked the swamp.

Sometime in the night, the dam burst and the water drained out. The lake was no more. The shed-trailer still rested on its concrete block foundation, but with the water line above the windows. Later, I went through the trailer; the bat was gone. My best friend had given me that bat for safekeeping. I'd lost it. He had been a soldier who fought for our country. I'd let him down. I'd let down America. I was ashamed at the idea of seeing my best friend and his beautiful family, so I changed my mind and refrained from connecting with them.

The Wolf Pine

A year went by. One bright fall day I showed up at Father Gonzaga's farm for confession. I wanted to talk to him about Beaupre's bat. The flood and my sense of loss and guilt soured me on life and wore on my marriage. I needed Father Gonzaga's counsel. I wanted to ask him, What is a sin anyway? Good intentions or self-delusion, or a combination of both, often can cause more harm than a premeditated act of malice. How many sins do we fail to confess simply because we do not know that they are sins? How does heaven judge the sinner who does not know he is sinning?

The apple trees were heavy with unpicked fruit. Weeds had taken over the gardens and now lay flat and thick after a frost. The windows in the Ecology Farm stone house were boarded up, the front door padlocked. NO TRESPASSING signs were tacked to trees. A cold snake of dread slithered through my spinal column.

I contacted one of Father Gonzaga's followers, and she told me that he had gathered his flock after Sunday mass a month ago and shocked them all by saying good-bye, that he was going on retreat. He didn't say where or what his purpose was, only that the world was changing yet again, and he had to climb the mountain where God would send the Experimentalist on yet another mission.

Through November and December I flipped-flopped from euphoria, as if Father Gonzaga's absence had freed me from the entanglements of God's politics, to despair, as if Father Gonzaga's absence had freed me from the entanglements of God's politics. I didn't want to talk to Olympia, I didn't want to sleep with her. I was sick of her – she was getting old, and I was getting stupid.

It all came to a head on a Friday night in January 1982. Olympia should have been home from the diner by 11 P.M. It was almost dawn before I saw the headlights of her Subaru turn off the main road, onto the long drive through the swamp and up our driveway. A few snowflakes had started to fall. I went onto the porch in the death-chill air. Olympia was so drunk that she left the car door open and walked zig-zaggy as an ant up the path to our home.

"Where the hell have you been?" I shouted.

"Go fuck yourself," Olympia said.

The hand on my pitching arm seemed to rise by itself to my ear and doubled into a fist.

Don't hit her, never hit a woman, never hit anyone, Memere said. *Open your hand and look at the 'M' and think of Mother Mary.*

Teach her a lesson, my cock said.

Olympia pointed to my upraised arm and said, "Well, are you going to swing that thing or what?"

I punched air through the screen door, missing her on purpose, but coming close in an attempt to scare her.

"Good one," Olympia said, and zigged past me into the house. Her calm further infuriated me.

I followed her to the bathroom. She zagged in, hoisted her dress, and sat on the potty.

"Where are your underwear?" I asked.

"I don't have no idea," she said. "Hey, how about some privacy?"
I turned my head away while she peed.

When she finished, I followed her to the bedroom. She plopped
down on the bed.

"Well?" I shouted. "Well?"

"Well, what?" She lay on her belly, face half-buried in the pillow.

"I'm going to cut down that wolf pine," I screamed, as if for
help.

"Good idea," Olympia said.

I waited for a minute, trying to think of mean things to say. By
then Olympia's breath was rough with sleep. She'd made a complete fool of me, or I'd made a complete fool of myself.

I see that old self in wood-cutting gear – chain saw, yellow hard
hat, gas in red can, chain oil, gloves, belt ax, and twenty-one-inch
bow saw tied to a backpack containing a water bottle.

My first act was to check the temperature gauge that I'd hung
on a hemlock outside in the shade, inspired, of course, by Coach
MacDonald's outside thermometer at Granite Lake. It was five
below zero. Sky gray, just starting to snow lightly. The forecast was
calling for an inch or two. It never snowed big when it was this
cold. I was always amazed by how varied snowflakes can be. That
morning they were like tiny lightning bugs flying every which way
in a fickle wind that could not seem to make up its mind which way
to blow.

A thaw a week before had flattened the snow on the ground,
and walking was easy on the hard crust. Young pines stood at attention like old soldiers on the reviewing stand as their retirement
parade passed them by. When I arrived at the wolf pine, I sensed a
presence and stopped in my tracks. I had the crazy idea that Mister Mayor's Chris-Craft had evolved into a land creature that was
now in my woods, hiding behind the trees, ready to jump me. I
whipped my head around. Nothing there. The mocking eye of the
wolf pine stared me down. Of course, the Chris-Craft was not up
the tree either. I was, so to speak, the one up the tree.

The snow was fine and swirly like musical notes searching for a scale in a modernistic opera. The top of the wolf pine vanished into a whiteout. For all I knew the tree might reach to the stars. When I cut it down, it would fall across the world, leaving a great gash. I heard the caw of a crow in the tree, and I listened for an answer from one of its compatriots, but none came. Not a good omen.

I had never cut down a tree this large and unwieldy before. Who could say which way it would fall?

I walked around the wolf pine to determine where to make the hinge cut. I determined that despite its many branches, which seemed to grow on their own and without the direction of any central planner, the tree as a whole was perfectly balanced. That's the way it is with most trees. They might appear to be weighted to one side or another, but look closely and you'll see that the tree's heavier branches will be opposite the lean of the trunk to balance the tree. The wind at ground level was not a factor, but no doubt it was blowing harder higher up, though its direction changed by the second. My experience was that trees want to fall downhill, and that was where I would design the cut. However, the incline here was not great, so my confidence was limited.

The hinge cut was no problem. One thing about white pine is that it cuts easily compared to most of the hardwoods I sawed for firewood. The problem was going to be the felling cut on the opposite side of the tree. My chain saw bar was not long enough to cut through half the tree.

I made a series of cuts. When I least expected it, the tree sat down on the saw bar. I was thinking that I was going to have to return to my shed to fetch my backup chain saw, when the wolf pine shuddered for a moment, a good sign that it was ready to go. Sometimes a tree falls with no warning or splits and springs out at an odd angle. That's when a woodcutter in the wrong place can be crushed. I jogged back a dozen steps.

The crow flew out of the tree, uttering complaints. Odd to see a lone crow. A slab of crusted old snow the size of a man shook loose from high up and crashed at my feet. It might have brained me if it had fallen on my head, hard hat or no. The eye of the tree winked. A deep creaking sound issued from inside the trunk. Memere spoke to me now, but in her French gibberish. I hollered in my mind: *Speak English so I can understand you. Speak! Speak!*

The tree was trying to fall not down slope, but up slope where I stood. I dodged to one side. The tree's eye seemed to seek me out, but gravity was too much for the tree, and it started to go at a forty-five degree angle from my position. The whoosh of the falling tree whipped my face. After the crash, the earth shook beneath my feet and a cloud of snow rose up, so that for a moment I was in a cold fog.

When finally the snow had settled and I could see, I started to shake but not with trepidation. I was giddy with relief and triumph. My chain saw had freed itself without harm. I grabbed it, climbed on the stump, and admired my work. The fallen wolf pine had smashed through a mess of smaller pine trees and a couple of white birches. One of the birches splintered down its trunk. What was left stuck up twenty feet high, like an upraised sword, which brought back a memory of a high school play where my sister Gemma was Lady Macbeth and my cousin Chalky had been Macbeth. I heard his voice with its deep upcountry accent: "Is this a daggah I see befowah me?"

Chain saw in hand, I leaped from the stump to the largest of the multitrunks. I made the jump all right, but I almost slipped off when I landed. I righted myself and walked down the trunk until I came to a snare of branches, some birch mixed in with the pine. I lowered the sound mufflers of my hard hat, pumped the choke of the chain saw three times, flipped the slide from off to on, and pulled the starter cord. The machine roared to life and I made the first cut. I had done this work a zillion times, if never with a tree this big. I was thinking that I would find a partner, sell the tractor, buy a new truck and maybe a secondhand log skidder, and start cutting saw logs, when I was suddenly airborne.

In the following seconds, time slowed. I watched my chain saw slowly migrate outward from my hands. The crow was back in my vision, perched on top of the flagpole at MacDonald's camp on

Granite Lake, its wings expanding hugely as it prepared for flight. The snowflakes gathered in pentatonic scale and began a score for an off-Broadway play memorializing the working man. I thought: *So this is what the Church means by eternity.* When you die your soul leaves the body and time. The soul observes the material world as an exquisite slow-motion movie that flashes back and forth in time. I wished Father Gonzaga was here so I could bring up this matter for him to comment on.

It was pain that brought me back to present-time. The chain saw had shut off and was lying at my feet on the snow-crusted ground. My right leg below the knee was extended at an angle that would have shamed a contortionist. Apparently the saw cut I'd made had released a branch bent by the fall of the tree and it had whipped my knee and broken my leg. I blacked out for a minute or two. When I came to, I was cold and hurting more than I can describe in words. I reached behind to my pack and pulled out the Mother Marys, poured a handful in my hand, and sucked on them until they gave me some strength. I crawled, pulling with my hands, pushing off with my good foot.

Olympia's Triumph

Change of Scenery

Olympia saved me. The sound of the chain saw woke her and when it went silent and I did not return for a long while, she knew something was wrong.

A month later there was a thaw not only in the weather but in us. We were making love again, and it was better than ever. One Sunday afternoon I stood outside leaning on my crutch, looking at the carcass of the trailer in the golden meadow still covered with melting snow. Olympia joined me out there, handing me a cup of coffee just the way I liked it, one cream with a dollop of maple syrup.

"You think Beaupre's bat will ever make like a rutabaga and turn up?" I said, not really addressing Olympia, but that fifteen-year-old girl in my past whose love I could never forget.

"Every once in a while, Jack, you come out with the strangest shit," Olympia said.

"I'm sorry, I don't mean to go weird on you," I said.

"Actually, weird is the part of you I like second best," she said, paused, and looked me in the eye. "Do we get a divorce?" Her voice was even and without hysteria, though I thought I detected a hint of sadness.

"Do we still love each other?" I said.

"Jack, I never loved nobody, and you never loved me," she said. She wasn't looking for pity. Just telling the truth, as she perceived it.

"I loved you as best I could," I said.

"Me, too. I didn't cheat to hurt you, Jack. I was just following my urges. I don't know no other way. I'm too old for you. You can do better with some young stuff. I wouldn't hold it against you if you moved on."

"You took care of me when I was laid up – you pulled me out of those woods."

"Yeah, and I had a hangover, too."

I laughed out loud at that and we both knew we'd stay together. I knew what I had to do. I pointed with my crutch, and said "If I can't work in the woods, I don't want to be in the woods."

Everything came together after that. We sold the property for a good chunk of change to some people from down country. A tricky legal deal because Pete Dubie technically was half-owner, but Olympia's lawyer friend in Keene (one of her many former boyfriends) brought us through the legal maze, and with our savings and the profits from the sale of property we bought the WRJ Diner. My only regret was the new owners of our swamp/golden meadow tore down our cabin and built a new old colonial house.

After we signed the papers, Olympia said, "This is my chance to prove that I can run a business. That I can be somebody. That my star will shine. Bless your heart, Jack, for riding piggyback on my dream."

"How about doggy-style?"

"That's okay, too," Olympia said, and we laughed.

"However you want to put it, I'm behind you all the way," I said.

"All the way is the only way I have ever known," Olympia said.

The WRJ Diner was authentic, which meant it had been built by the Worcester Diner Car company back in the 1920s, with an assigned number.

From the outside, the diner looked like a train car with windows you might peek out of. It was silver colored with red trim and sat right off the Main Street sidewalk, within spitting distance of public parking and the Coolidge Hotel. Never mind that foot traffic in downtown White River Junction was light on the best of days.

WRJ's anchor store was a Woolworth's obviously on its last

legs. Most people in the area shopped across the river in Westboro at the Kmart.

Once when Olympia and I made one of our occasional visits to Coach MacDonald's camp on Granite Lake, Mister Mayor, as he liked to be called, advised us to invest our money in Kmart because, "and remember where you heard it, Kmart will rule the world."

We did not invest in Kmart. Neither Olympia nor I had any grounding in the stock market. We put our money in the bank and collected the meager interest on a savings account. We were descended from factory workers, and we didn't understand nor trust the world of investment. Once I began to read, I realized that Father Gonzaga had been right: the main -*isms* of my time – capitalism, communism, socialism, even Catholicism – were not only flawed but also only accidentally useful to honest people. You had to be some kind of crook or insider to profit from an -*ism*.

If you walked into our diner, you would smell fryer food and stale cigarette smoke and something else that made it unique, a faint aroma of the White and Connecticut rivers that probably rose up from our dank cellar.

You would see a tile floor of little black and white squares and silver counter stools with red swivel seats. Behind the counter would be food warmers, coffeepots, a short-order cooking grill, and shiny steel pots to hold oil for French fries and genuine Northern Southern fried chicken.

On the walls you would see old black and white photographs of WRJ when it was a hopping railroad town.

You would see a sign that said COFFEE NEVER MORE THAN 30 MINUTES OLD. True. Another sign had our motto on it. NO REASON TO CONTINUE THE FRAY IF THERE IS WORK TO BE DONE.

You would see a sign that said CATS AND DOGS ALLOWED. NO HORSES. NO COWS. NO RACCOONS. NO SNAKES, SKUNKS OK ON LEASH.

You would see booths made of oak darkened and enriched by time.

Attached to the diner was a crude two-story wood-frame addition that included storage and our upstairs apartment, which was cramped but handy.

Olympia threw herself into the work of making what had been a good diner into a great one. It was odd, but Olympia and I were more relaxed with each other as business partners than we had been back at the meadow as a kinky couple, not that we stopped our kinky coupling.

The work for me wasn't as strenuous as woodcutting, which was a good thing for a man with a wrecked knee. I'd come to that age where I'd gained quite a lot of weight and lost quite a lot of hair.

Directly behind the diner ran railroad tracks, and only a few hundred yards away was the railroad station. Trains came in daily from Montreal going south and from New York City going north. You'd think people who live in big cities, where there's everything you need, would stay put, but they don't: They wander. I've never understood the lure of travel. There's enough variety in day to day living to keep up anybody's interest if they pay attention. Most people go to the party of life and circulate. I stayed in one spot and let the party circulate around me.

Neighbors on our connected strips of buildings included Famous Smoke and Sundries, Shorty's Barber Shop, the Touche Adult Book Store, and Close Encounters, which was a drinking club that catered to people searching for one-night stands. "Are you tempted?" I asked Olympia.

"At my age, the boys don't exactly throw flower petals at your feet," she said.

After Olympia pulled me out of the woods with a broken leg and we decided to stay together and not argue and I was touching her again, Olympia didn't cheat on me anymore. At any rate, I didn't see any evidence of same.

Olympia did all the brain work in the business. Kept track of the accounts with the help of an Atari ST computer, which she called

Sir Lancelot. She dealt with vendors and rode herd on our wait-resses, dishwashers, and cooks and made decisions for big-ticket items, such as a paint job to freshen the look of the restaurant and the new sign.

OLYMPIA'S DINER.

When the sign went up, the look on her face made me almost love her.

I shopped for food from Olympia's daily list. I filled in as a short-order cook or dishwasher when necessary. I bounced out the late-night drunks who shot off their mouths or bothered a waitress. I mopped the floors and fixed this and that. I waited on tables if a waitress didn't show.

Unfortunately, White River Junction continued to decline and business faltered, so in 1987 I had to take a second job to supple-ment our income. I worked 4 to 6 A.M., seven days a week, as cus-todian of the Library Restaurant in the university town up the road.

One day a man came into the diner with a strange request.

"How do you do," he said politely. "My name is Ralph Goings. I'm an artist and I want to paint that ketchup bottle and those salt and pepper shakers." He pointed to one of our booths.

"Be my guest," Olympia said. Years later I saw a painting of our diner by Mr. Goings on the Internet. It was very accurate; it brought a tear to my eye.

The fun part about running a diner is that it's like a baseball game: You never know what's going to happen next.

One hot July night, I was filling in as a cook when a scraggly-looking guy came in. From his unwashed appearance and dunga-rees stiff with grime, I knew right away where he'd come from. A handful of homeless men lived under tarps in the woods between the river and the town. Something about the face of the man under the graying full beard looked familiar. I came out from behind the counter.

"Chalky – Chalky?" I said.

It was my cousin Chalky all right. He was drunk. He had come into the diner to beg for food. I gave him a plate of eggs and ham.

"You think I'm going to act grateful, well fuck you," he said, and walked out.

Chalky was the most embittered human being I've ever met, but I found something admirable about his pessimism. Maybe it was that he didn't try to be liked.

One late morning he was eating a free breakfast at the diner, and I joined him at his table with a cup of coffee. I tried to act cheerful, but he saw right through me.

"The world's a shit sandwich, and every day you take a bite, so stop smiling," he said.

"That's not very original," I said.

"The original part is I mean it."

"Why don't you just get it over with and kill yourself?"

"I stay alive to spite you and to spite God." And he laughed, but he wasn't laughing on the inside.

"Didn't you get a high from your travels?" I asked.

"I been to every state and I hated 'em all."

"Well, at least you don't play favorites." I got up and went to work. I couldn't stand being in his presence.

Chalky remained a denizen of the woods down by the river. I wanted to talk to him about the old days, baseball and hot fudge sundaes at the Ice Creamery, but he laughed at me. The only time he showed any softness was when he talked about how pretty and private it was below Wilder Dam, a couple miles up the road on the New Hampshire side. Occasionally, he'd work in our kitchen as a dishwasher to get money to buy beer. Olympia had a theory about Chalky. She said it wasn't unresolved grief and guilt over his complicity in the death of Spud Polix that crippled Chalky's growth as a human being, it was his failure to accept his sexuality.

"For you, everything is about sex," I said to Olympia.

"Well, yeah, of course. Is there something else I've missed?"

Library Restaurant Custodian

Higher Education
September 1991

I don't quite know how to gauge the diner years, especially in comparison to the *coureur du bois* years. I had loved my job as a wood-cutter when I was at my physical peak. I had built up not only my body but my mind. I had discovered me. I never would have made the big leagues, because I didn't really want that kind of life, on the road with strangers in strange places, playing a kid's game, and for what? For amusement, for distraction, so people wouldn't face up? What I had liked about pitching from my boyhood on had been the practice, the work, owning a feeling of excelling honestly earned. Victory, glory, even money diminished the art of pitching as I had defined it.

Harold Archer had showed me that true success was in the creation of a thing, the passion you put into your labor in that thing. I had found my contribution as a woodcutter. Dealing in firewood had brought me a decent living, warmed my house, exposed me to the beauty of the forest, and allowed me some pride because I always did my best.

Petty jealousy had led me into the woods to cut down the wolf pine, which I believe was a manifestation of God, and God had punished me by ruining my knee and my career as a woodcutter.

He could have killed me, but He didn't. He wanted me alive and of some use to Him. But what use? I didn't know until Olympia confessed a deep yearning to start her own business. I understood then that God wanted me to put aside my desires and please my life mate. The ensuing years were not my best, but they were not bad either; they were as good as I deserved.

After my injury (the result of yet another rash act), my body suddenly was less reliable. I stood at the beginning of decline. I kept very busy with my two jobs, but I didn't exercise the way I used to when I was a young stud cutting wood. Result? Another thirty pounds. My frame carried it well enough, but there was no denying that I was overweight. I agonized less over my weight than I did over the loss of my hair. I used to have good hair, thick and wavy like Alcide's. He recommended Glover's Sarcoptic Mange medicine. I shampooed with the stinky stuff, but it did no good. I tried for a while to maneuver what hair I had to cover as much of my scalp as possible, but I wasn't fooling anyone. By 1991, I quit trying and just kept my hair buzz cut short.

During this period, my parents retired and lived modestly on Social Security and savings in their house in Keene. I'm ashamed to say I rarely visited them. They didn't approve of Olympia, and she wasn't about to go out of her way to appear to be anything other than my mother's worst fear, a loose woman with pagan ideals. I'd lost touch with my sister Gemma, who had a family out West. We exchanged Christmas cards and brief notes, and that was all. Occasionally, I drove to Portland, Maine, to visit with Denise and her partner, a divorced mother of two.

After Mister Mayor left politics he and Mrs. MacDonald retired to Florida. The MacDonald daughters kept the camp on Granite Lake as a meeting place for the now quite large clan.

I was surprised to learn that Beaupre broke his promise never to return to Keene until he could walk again. Beaupre and Katie took over Liberty Taxi when Coach retired. I couldn't bring myself to visit them, because I'd lost the bat Beaupre had given me for safekeeping. But they didn't contact me either. I thought at the time it had something to do with my marriage to Olympia. I should have guessed what the real problem was, but it would be years before I learned the truth.

I continued to read and take notes with pleasure, if not with speed. I had decided on a daring new plan. In the same way that I had taught myself to pitch a baseball, through devotion, persistence, and hard work, I embarked on a plan to educate myself to a higher plane. My job as custodian of the Library Restaurant gave me an idea of how to go about the task.

The restaurant was designed to look like an old-fashioned library from the late 1800s, with dining tables resembling library reading tables and old books lining dark shelves built into the walls. The books in the restaurant were real books; I knew because I had dusted their backs, though out of a strange reluctance I hadn't touched the pages. I could tell by their worn and faded covers that the books had already been handled and no doubt read, so I would not be the first. In my fantasy, I would remove a book from the Library Restaurant, like you'd take a book out from a real library, and I would leave a note for the owners, the Knight brothers, "Have borrowed book, will bring it back when finished," and I would sign it Joseph Jacques St. Vincent de Paul Landry, Night Custodian, Library Restaurant. I would read the entire library of the Library Restaurant. I hatched a vague plan to get myself into the *Guinness Book of Records*: the man who read every book in the Library Restaurant. I set a deadline for what I hoped would be the beginning of my higher education, the day after Labor Day of 1991, the year I turned fifty and the year that Olympia bought her first new car, a Buick LeSabre.

I didn't need an alarm clock to get me out of bed at 3:30 A.M. The train woke me. Not the sound per se, but the vibration. It shook the building, shriveled my morning hard-on, and stirred my brain cells to leave me with half an idea that it was Doomsday.

Olympia lay beside me. I loved the delicate way she snored, the sound like a kid's electric train. The real train rarely woke her, not because she was a particularly heavy sleeper but because she was so exhausted when she hit the rack at 11 P.M. after twelve or fourteen hours of labor in her diner. She claimed she loved every minute of it. I believed her.

My knee was a little stiff, as it always was when I woke, but I wouldn't have any problems doing my work at the Library Restaurant. To be on the safe side, I took a couple aspirin.

Before I left, I did some dishes that had piled up in the sink. For a second, the dreariness of our apartment weighed me down. The plywood floors were covered with linoleum, a design of swirls that were supposed to be modernistic but that looked to me like scattered puke. In the linoleum's defense, I'll say that it hid dirt. The wallpaper was not only yellowed, it was cracked from train-rumble shakin' and bakin' the plastered lath.

I hopped into my Ford Escort – Little Moses – and headed for work. The university town was only five miles from White River Junction, but during the day the sidewalks could be crowded with strangers and Main Street clogged with traffic. Finding a parking place could be a hellish experience, but not when I arrived for work at 4 A.M. The town was deserted, restaurants and stores shut down. I imagined myself in that old movie *On the Beach*, the last man alive – with Ava Gardner, of course. I enjoyed the feeling. I used my key to let myself in, which said a lot about the trust the Library Restaurant owners, twin brothers from Long Island, Eddie and Donnie Knight, had in me.

The waitpeople had put the chairs on the tables, and I had a routine down to mop the floors, so it only took me an hour to do the dining room. I was almost done with the tavern section and was cleaning the toilets when a man surprised me by walking into the men's room.

He wore a black suit with a black shirt and a white Roman collar; he was clean-shaven but on his head was a Reagan-red hairpiece that you'd see on the head of a United States senator. If it had not been for the thick glasses, I would not have recognized him.

"Father Gonzaga?" I said, as he walked to a urinal and unzipped.

"Every time I pass a bathroom, I have to do it," he said, staring straight ahead at the wall with a blank face. "Goes to show how so many of our actions are involuntary."

"How did you get in?" I said, mop in my hand, like a staff.

"I have a key," Father Gonzaga said after a pause, turning, zipping up. "Let's have a drink."

Mop on my shoulder, I followed Father Gonzaga to the tavern section. He went behind the bar and reached for a bottle of tequila.

"Father, you'll get me in trouble."

"It's all right, Jack. The Knight boys are among my parishioners. In fact, I have a financial interest in this little restaurant. I'll explain everything to them." He pointed to a bar stool. "Now sit. I'll make you the specialty drink of the house. I'm dying to hear your confession and to tell you about my latest mission."

We sipped Long Island iced teas in tall glasses while Father Gonzaga heard my confession. I spilled out my grief and remorse for the old and terrible sin of my youth against Alouette and our child.

"How about some new stuff?" Father Gonzaga said, great impatience in his voice.

I told him how my jealousy had led me to cut down the wolf pine. I told him about the secret resentment of these last years in my role as Olympia's gofer at her diner. I talked about the return of my cousin Chalky.

"You never liked Chalky – why do you put up with him?" Father Gonzaga asked.

"He's family."

"No, there's more to it than that. Examine your conscience."

"When he works for us washing dishes, he does a lousy job and it infuriates Olympia. I get a secret satisfaction from her frustration."

"Good, very good," Father Gonzaga said, and he gave me absolution.

Afterward, we drank and talked at the bar.

"The return of Chalky does not bode well," Father Gonzaga said, a grave look on his face.

"What do you mean?"

"I can't give you the details, Jack. Sometimes I get these pre-monitions from my guardian angel, but he never fills in with the nitty-gritty. I can't plumb the depths because there are no depths. We live in a postmodern world of surfaces, repetitions, decon-structions, and the inglorious spectacle of irony."

"How come you left Ecology Farm, Father, and the counter-culture lifestyle? I feel, well . . . I don't know how to say it."

"You feel betrayed." Father Gonzaga said. "Believe me, it wasn't easy for me to make the transition, but I had to go where Jesus and our Polish Pope were leading me. I used to think that the future of the world was among laborers, and that was why I was a union activ-ist. For a brief time I tried to be a conformist priest, a time much like the one we live in today. Then I discovered mind-altering drugs and the wonders of the hippie generation. That evolved into the ecology movement and the counterculture's attempt to reform American values to be tied more to earth than to commerce, but the Age of Aquarius was spent rather quickly, and Father Ecology found himself marooned. Now, I believe I have discovered where one must look to save souls."

He had me on the edge of my bar stool, and he knew it. I waited. He went silent. Finally, I said, "Well?"

Father Gonzaga laughed. "Hell is other people, is it not? Jack, our world is now in the hands of yuppies. I shaved my beard, cut my ponytail, bought this toupee, ingratiated myself to the boss clergy until I was back in the good graces of the Church. I incurred debts when the head shop went bust. I was forced to sell the Eagle Hotel, except Room 314, which I've leased as a refuge. I sold Ecol-ogy Farm. I returned to my former hobby of photography with my trusty Leica, trying once again to capture those decisive moments in the lives of the children of rich Catholics. I've been rewarded with good tips in the stock market. I am now a wealthy man again. I've put every penny into dot-coms and I expect to rebound big time, if you will excuse the current vernacular. With the profits I will accrue, I will build stadia-churches all over the world and spread the word of God. My congregation here at Dartmouth loves my sermons, which I've altered by combining the styles of Protestant ministers and late-night self-help TV pitchmen. Eleazar Wheelock would be delighted."

"You've been here all along, and I'm only five miles away, and I didn't know it – I'm astounded," I said.

"Ah, the gap, the gap, between here and there, it's the one problem we cannot find a solution to," Father Gonzaga said.

As he always had, Father Gonzaga turned my world upside down – the gap. Suddenly, I was thinking of Alouette Williams, how we hoped our love would bridge the gap between her kind and my kind, how we'd failed. The gap had morphed into The Gap, a department store. I had only one recourse left, to educate myself. I told Father Gonzaga about my goal to read all the books in the Library Restaurant.

"It's an amusing thought, but . . ." Father Gonzaga shook his head. He seemed about to say something, then stopped, apparently having changed his mind. "I have to go now. You're on your own, Jack," he said, and he left quite abruptly, and the only sound was the background whisper of the Universe from the remnants of the Big Bang, as manifested by all those words in the books stacked on the shelves of the Library Restaurant.

It was now almost 6 A.M. I was tired; my knee had swelled up again and it hurt. I stared at a bookshelf, but I could not bring myself to approach it.

I saw myself reflected back from a mirror behind the bar. In shadow was a figure in a red-and-black checkered shirt.

The colors of old Acadia, Memere said.

I peered into the mirror for a better look. Nothing there. My mind playing tricks. Had Father Gonzaga actually visited me, or had I just imagined him? The sight of the two empty glasses reassured me that I had not been talking to myself. Or maybe I had. Maybe I had been talking and drinking for two. I shook away the disturbing thoughts and put myself back on track. It was time to return to my original task: to begin my higher education.

I walked over to a bookshelf. For a moment I froze. I told myself that I must conquer my fears. I grabbed a book and jerked it out of the shelf. I gasped. The mutilated book that rested in my hand mocked my aspirations. The book, all the books in the Library Restaurant, had been cut in half vertically to fit the shallow shelves. They were just for show, their content eviscerated to create more room. It wasn't just me that suffered from partial literacy, it was the world.

Now I knew that I had good reason to be afraid. I went all weak and dropped to the floor in a sitting position, the mop falling in my lap. I held the wet mop head as one might hold the head of a distraught friend that one is attempting to comfort.

A Cousin's Revenge

The Fire
August 1992

As usual, Chalky was late for a dishwashing shift that I had talked Olympia into allowing, and as usual, I filled in for him, except this time he was an hour late instead of only half an hour. In her normal life (is there really such a thing?), Olympia was droll and casual; in her love life, creative and passionate; but in her business life, she was, how can I put this delicately? Okay, she was a tyrant, who could reduce a waitress to tears or wobble the legs of a cook with withering sarcasm. She even turned on me once in a while. The worst thing you could do with Olympia was to take her on and argue back. She only grew more abusive and wild-eyed. Her saving grace was that she never held a grudge, and when she calmed down she always made right what she'd wronged. Anyone who worked for Olympia learned to take her criticism with a sense of humor in the knowledge that she'd be back in half an hour with a "Geez, I'm sorry, I don't know what got into me." We all knew how much this diner meant to her. Olympia never took offense to insults to her person; she took offense to insults to her business.

At the moment Chalky walked into the diner, I happened to be running an errand next door at Famous Smoke and Sundries, operated by my former telephone company workmate, Famous Papadopolis. He'd retired and had bought this small store. Famous hardly cared about the goods he sold and the meager profits he earned from them. His true business was to take and place bets.

First thing that caught my eye as I walked in were the tabloids, *The Inquirer* and *Midnight*. Headline: 80-Year-Old Octogenarian/ Likes Young Poontang.

"Hey, Famous," I said.

Famous was on the phone. He gave me a bare nod and pointed to the cash drawer.

I went behind the counter, grabbed two packs of Mother Marys, a carton of Old Gold cigarettes, a *Midnight* and a *Twin State Times*, published out of Westboro, New Hampshire. I rang up the sale on the register – loved that sound since the days of Mrs. Doan's store – put the bills in, and removed my change. Famous gave me a wave of the hand, and I left the shop.

When I walked into the diner, I could hear Olympia sounding off, which wasn't unusual. The recipient of her tirade was Chalky. He towered over her, while she shouted insults up at him. In an odd way, the image threw me back in time. Where Chalky stood was I as a boy, where Olympia stood was my mother chewing me out.

"You ungrateful bum," Olympia said.

Chalky gave Olympia a murderous look. I thought for sure he was going to strike her, but when he saw me he turned his back on her and stormed out.

Olympia and I then had one of our infrequent fights. I tried to defend Chalky, but it was no use. In the end I had to relent. My cousin would no longer be welcome in our diner.

After that, everything seemed to return to normal for the rest of the day and into the early evening. My knee felt better and I sacked out at 10 P.M. to get some sleep before my shift at the Library Restaurant. Around midnight, I was dreaming of the poison ivy along the banking of the railroad tracks. In my dream it was peak foliage and the poison ivy was very beautiful, scarlet and russet, and I was making love to a homeless woman in the poison ivy. I woke to Olympia's voice, her hands on my shoulders shaking me.

"Jack, grab your pants, we gotta get out of here," Olympia said.

I quickly dressed and ran out into the street. The fire had started in the basement of the Touche Adult Bookstore at the end of the block. I could see smoke illuminated by a small burst of flame from a window. A crowd had gathered. The fire trucks were just arriving.

"They'll contain it," I said.

"Wanna bet?" Famous said, still in his pajamas.

A minute later the flames licked into a storage room where paint and turpentine were stored. There was a *whump* sound and vibrations under my feet that felt like Granite Lake in the winter making ice. Soon the adult bookstore was gone, Encounters nightclub was gone. Shorty, the barber of Shorty's Barbershop, made whistling noises as his barber pole burst into flames. I put my arm around Olympia's shoulders as our diner and apartment evaporated before our eyes. For a while it was as if I were tripping on some powerful marijuana. I was seeing the Acadian hell fires of my childhood. They hadn't been so vivid since the fires I saw through the windshield when Alouette and I played our own version of chicken.

By 3:30 A.M., the block had been reduced to black jagged beams and a collapsed roof.

Olympia and I walked across the street to the Coolidge and registered. Took the weekly rate. Our room had a pull-chain toilet, a hot plate, a mini fridge, and an old-fashioned four-poster bed above which was a faded movie poster of *Way Down East* with Lillian Gish. Olympia called our insurance agent. We had some fire insurance. Enough to rebuild? Maybe, maybe not. After my shift at the Library Restaurant, I returned to our room in the Coolidge and tried to get some shut-eye.

We slept fitfully until 11 A.M., when I drove to the Dunkin' Donuts shop across the river in Westboro. I returned with our breakfast, which we ate sitting up in the double bed watching TV. In a way, it was kind of a treat. We'd worked so hard over the years that we rarely indulged ourselves in luxuries such as breakfast in bed and television shows, certainly not daytime TV, *America's Most Wanted*. Then the local news came on. There were pictures of the fire, and then the fire chief said the cause of the fire was under investigation.

Something dawned on Olympia, and she turned to me and spoke in an accusatory tone. "It was Chalky. Your screwy cousin burned down my diner."

I was thinking the same thing, but I said, "We don't know that."

"I'm going to call the cops," she said.

"Look, let me talk to him. I'll find out – okay?"

"You're going to warn him."

I didn't say anything.

"Blood is thicker than water," Olympia said.

"Give me an hour," I said.

"I'll think about it."

I left Olympia in our room and walked across the street and the tracks to the railroad station. It occurred to me that I had never created a mental picture of our diner from this vantage point, and I never would because now it was gone forever. Police had cordoned off the area. It was a warm summer day, but I could still smell the fire, sour and acrid.

I walked past the Victorian railroad station, through the rail yard, and onto a spur that left the main tracks and knifed through some dense woods for maybe a couple hundred yards before it crossed the river on a bridge in poor repair into Westboro, New Hampshire.

In the brush just off the path some guys had set up a little village of poles and tarps that my father would have called a Hooverville. There I learned that Chalky was last seen crossing the bridge on foot into New Hampshire. I had a good idea where he was going, the secret place where he liked to drink alone.

I got into my Moses, crossed the Connecticut River into New Hampshire, and drove a mile north to the small parking lot across the road from Wilder Dam, which held back ten or fifteen miles of water and generated electricity. Canoeists were halted at the dam and had to portage over a path that led to steep stone stairs. As I descended the steps, my knee began to throb. Afraid my leg would kick out from under me, I grabbed bushes to slow my momentum.

I made it to the river level and was greeted by an awesome sight, acres of driftwood from the size of toothpicks to entire trees, the bark stripped off by water and ice, a driftwood paradise. My first thought was to drop everything and set up housekeeping among these incredibly beautiful objects.

Chalky sat alone on a log in front of a fire pit, just a few strings of smoke rising from it. He stared into the tiny fire. Beside him was a quart bottle of beer. His long beard and long hair looked like the tangles of sticks in a beaver dam. His blue jeans were no longer blue, but dirty brown and shiny from where he wiped his filthy hands. I could smell fire on him. He'd seen me coming, and when I arrived, he spoke calmly.

"You won't need a dishwasher anymore, now will you?"

"You know for a brain-fried drug addict, you're quite shrewd," I said.

"I'm not a drug addict, I'm an alcoholic."

"Sorry, Chalky."

I reached down and snatched his beer from him.

Chalky glared up at me, deciding whether to take me on or not.

"Lemme have a last drink, will ya?" he said, his voice full of need now.

I returned the beer to Chalky's hand. He pulled his dead eyes away from me, looked into the dead fire, and took a long swig.

"No love life, no family, no work ethic, living on booze, Slim Jims, and dumpster scraps: That's you, Chalky," I said.

"Admit it, you envy me."

It was a simple declaration, and the kernel of truth in it caught in my throat. I did envy Chalky and his pals under the tarps. I saw nobility in their simple, easy-on-the-ecology lifestyle; I saw resistance to the powers of conformity.

"I won't envy you when you're in jail," I said.

"Even when we were kids, I hated you, Jack. Jack Landry, the big fucking hero. You didn't make it to the bigs, did you now? You didn't have it in here." He tapped his chest where his heart should be.

"I struck out Ted Williams," I said.

"So fucking what?"

In his dissipated state even a fat man like me could out-quick Chalky. I put a hand on his shoulder, then I hit him as hard as I could in the middle of the face with my right fist. He tumbled backwards, fell, writhed, went still.

I pulled him to a sitting position. He brought his hands to his face to protect himself. I was going to hit him again, but it was clear that that action was not necessary. Chalky had problems breathing; he was huffing and snorting, blowing blood and snot onto his hands. He stared in fascination at his blood.

I thought of just the right thing to say, to hurt him worse than a punch. "What, me worry?" I said.

Chalky started to cry. "I'm sorry I set the fire. I'm sorry. I'm sorry for everything."

I helped him to his feet and we started walking toward the portage trail up the stone steps.

"You know, once when I got really into it, you know, when you drink so much you can make yourself sober, I saw him," Chalky said. "He was in heaven, Jack. 'Spud,' I said, 'you made it.' 'It's nice up here,' he said. Do you have to be good to go to heaven, Jack?"

I didn't have an answer, but I remembered something that Father Gonzaga had said during one of our confessions. "Nobody's good all the time, Chalky, so either heaven is empty or God forgives us our sins, if we can forgive those who sin against us. That's key. Maybe if you repent, you can make it."

"I don't think so, Jack. See, I can't forgive, I can't forgive Olympia for ragging on me, I can't forgive Coach for being a lying sack of shit, I can't forgive my mother for her sickening sweetness, I can't forgive my father for boozing every night and slapping us around, I can't forgive myself. I'm not going to make it to heaven. I'm never going to see Spud. And you know what, I don't care. I don't care if I ever see heaven. I want to go to hell because it'll feel more like home." He rolled his tongue inside his mouth, spat some blood out. He appeared pleased with himself.

"You ruined my perfect game, and you did it on purpose. Go ahead, admit it," I said.

"Okay, I admit it. It was my first big thrill in life. I'm not sorry. You helped make me the man I am." He startled me by breaking into a smile, the "What, me worry?" smile that is the soul of American triumph and tragedy. "Jack, before you turn me in, let me have one more high."

"One more high? What do you mean?"

"You know. Let's tie one on. I always wanted to go drinking with you, but you wouldn't have anything to do with me."

I bought a case of beer and we drank it in the car parked in the viewing area above Wilder Dam on the New Hampshire side. Chalky and I both knew the woods behind was a meeting place for gay men, but the subject never came up. Chalky drank two beers for my one. Finally, when he was good and drunk, he said, "I gotta take a leak."

"Go ahead, I won't look."

I watched him walk into the woods and disappear. I was giving him an opportunity to get away. He was gone ten or fifteen minutes. I was about ready to drive off, relieved that I wasn't going to have to turn him in, wondering what I was going to say to Olympia. Something else, too, that I'm ashamed to admit: A feeling of immense satisfaction flowed through me. It was as if it had almost been worth it to lose the diner just so I had an excuse to punch somebody out. It wasn't Chalky I hit. It was . . . who? I didn't know. *Your problem is you don't know the identity of your nemesis,* Memere said. I was pondering this matter when Chalky came out of the woods, hopped in, and said, "Let's go." I drove him right to the police station, where he confessed to setting the fire that burned us out.

For a week or so, I was a hero in the twin states; I was even on Channel 31 TV. It came out that the fire in our block was not the first that Chalky had set. I got a call of congratulations from Coach MacDonald in Florida, along with an "Isn't it too bad about

Chalky?" and "What do you expect, given the people he came from?" It was one of those (many) moments when Coach had complete control over me, so that I was incapable of speaking my mind. I just agreed with everything he said, even though I knew that afterward I would feel dirty all over. I remained quite full of myself until I heard the news on the radio, a week after I had knocked Chalky on his ass and brought him in. Charles "Chalky" Landry had hanged himself in his cell.

I was so messed up in the head that I didn't have the courage to attend his funeral and face my aunt and Uncle Three Fingers. Meanwhile, my marriage to Olympia began to crumble. She wouldn't let me touch her. Then, out of the blue, we were contacted by an attorney who represented the estate of Pierre Dubois, who had recently passed away from natural causes. It seemed that Olympia had never really held a title to the golden meadow property. The court proceedings dragged on for six months. All of our insurance and savings went to pay for a settlement to the Dubois estate and attorney fees. We were broke and too full of anger to comfort each other. One day I returned to the hotel to find a note that Olympia had written on a brown paper bag from the liquor store where we bought our booze in Westboro. She had big bold handwriting that reminded me of the days when she was young and had the body of a voluptuous movie star:

"Jack, did I ever tell you that I fucked the overseer? Well, I did. He gave me the clap, but I got over it thanks to penisillin. And I fucked Hiram Williams – he gave me money! And I fucked Mister Mayor when he was a young buck! He liked the French thing. I fucked them all, Jack, but if it'll make you feel better I never fucked Alcide. He wouldn't have me. You're the best man I ever knew, Jack. Coarse that ain't saying much since I never knew too many good men. I loved you, Jack. Too bad you couldn't love me for real. You tried – I'll give you that much. I'm leaving the divorce papers. Sign 'em, honey, and you'll be free. I got the LeSabre and the money, what there is of it. You got your freedom. It's what guys all say they want. You're welcome to it. I'll take the car and the doe." She meant "dough," but I read the word the way she'd written it, a beautiful female deer.

Surprise Visitor

By the River
Summer 1993

I didn't sign the divorce papers. I knew that Olympia was griev-
ing the loss of her diner in the only way she knew, and that she had
a right to be angry with me. In six months, a year, maybe two, she
might come back, and we could get on with our lives. I had no
job, no money, no wife, no home, no Father Gonzaga to confess
to, no one, really, who needed me, and for the first time in my fifty-
two years, no curiosity about the future. Somehow I had managed
to screw over the two women in my life, and I was an accessory
in the death of my cousin. The next big thing had come along like
an eighteen-wheeler and run me over. I was flattened, a two-
dimensional man.

I put most of my stuff in a self-storage unit, and when spring
arrived I moved out of the Coolidge into a tent with just the bare
necessities below Wilder Dam. The driftwood made spectacular
designs, God's way of showing us a glimpse into His mind and
heart. Here I would build a new self, one that did not need love.

To earn a few dollars, I hauled some of the prettier pieces of wood
to my Ford Escort, Moses, and sold them to artisans and wood
sculptors who lived in and around the college town. It wasn't much
money, but my expenses were low and I made enough to feed
myself, smoke weed, and keep my car running. My clients lived off
university jobs, spousal money, or trust funds, but their true voca-

tion was art. They were self-absorbed, but also sympathetic to other people and the human condition. They were friendly and polite, but had no real interest in me, any more than I had any real interest in them or their quirky art objects. That's the way it goes with a working man. He's never really part of inner circles.

At night I made campfires and got high, staring at the flames the way another man might stare at his TV. All the sound and fury of human existence was in my fire. When I felt a need for human contact, especially the love of a woman, I'd strip naked and jump in the river.

As the months went by, I began to change physically. I grew a beard and long hair, becoming a bald gray-haired man with a ponytail, very much like the ponytail Father Gonzaga sported back in the 1970s. I was getting plenty of exercise hauling wood, and my hands thickened with calluses. Without diner food always available, I ate less and lost weight. I'm not going to say I was skinny, but I no longer resembled the fat man who mopped the floors of the Library Restaurant. Without all that weight to carry, my knee responded by calming down. My right hand where I punched Chalky healed, though arthritis parked in the knuckles. Late at night I would be awakened by a tingle under the scar where I'd stepped on a twenty-penny nail oh so long ago.

One morning in the middle of September a light frost coated the driftwood. The sight was very beautiful, but it also reminded me that I couldn't live out here through the winter. I considered moving south for the cold months, but I felt duty bound to stay in the White River Junction area in case Olympia returned. Did I really want to see her? She had left me, why not just sign the divorce papers? I wasn't sure of the ethical course of action, so I waited for a sign.

So it was that on a cool September night I sat by my fire meditating the way Father Gonzaga had taught me, praying to St. Anthony. Of course, I had a little help from my only friend, marijuana. I told myself I had achieved my purpose in coming here: I had cut myself off from intimacy with other people. I was an island, happy to be without hope, desire, and fraternity. For music, I listened to the birds, the occasional wail of a coyote, the fall of water over the dam. The river, quiet at this time of low water, carried other sounds at ground level, and the night magnified them, so I was well aware that someone was approaching me before I saw the glow of the flashlight. The intruder could see me by firelight. I thought it might be one of Chalky's pals from the Hooverville, coming back to avenge his death, but I was willing to bet Famous that it was Father Gonzaga. I stayed put, seated on my log stripped of bark and smooth to the touch, my motto bringing me strength: Never back down, never instigate. I watched my fire and waited.

The flashlight beam scanned the ground littered with driftwood as someone slowly came toward me. Finally, the flashlight clicked off.

"Jack, is that you?" It was a woman's voice.

"Olympia?" I called, though I knew it wasn't her.

She stepped into the light, a woman in her fifties, a little overweight but very pretty, carrying a manila envelope in her right hand.

"Katie?" I said. "Katie MacDonald?"

"Katie Beaupre."

I stood and we embraced for a moment, the manila envelope between us. Katie didn't feel right in my arms, her body stiff with nervousness, as if she'd touched me with great reluctance.

"Have a seat," I said, pointing to the log.

She sat down. "I like the fire, it's soothing," she said.

I sat down on the log beside her. "How did you find me?" I looked at her pained face in the fire glow, skin prematurely wrinkled, a woman who had spent too much time in the Western sun when she was younger.

"You're not that hard to track," she said. "Everybody in Keene knows about Chalky, that your wife left you, and – " She suddenly caught herself.

"And?" I coaxed her.

"That you're a homeless man."

I was angry now. "Hey, I'm here of my own free will."

"I can smell the wacky-tobbacky," she said.

"Did you come down to preach to me?"

"No, that would not be appropriate," she said. I heard something in her voice, then, a tenderness, a frailty. Whatever it was, it made me realize I was overreacting.

"I'm sorry I was rude, Katie. I don't talk to many people these days. Where's Beaupre?"

"He's in the car." She pointed to the bluff, in the general direction of the Wilder Dam parking lot. "He has a special rig to allow him to drive with his hands. He can do just about anything a normal man can do, though coming down here on this treacherous ground in the middle of the night is not one of them."

"Yet, you did it, and in the dark . . . to see me?"

"It was a snap judgment we made tonight. We didn't wait, because we thought we might change our minds. We want you to come back with us, Jack."

"You don't have to feel sorry for me."

"There's more to it than pity. Beaupre and I, we did you a disservice over a period of years. We feel we must make amends."

She sounded so sincere, so – how can I put it? – so deep, as one speaking from a well of anguish. Those old feelings for her nudged me.

"Go ahead, I'll listen," I said.

"Four years ago, we – " she stopped, to catch her breath " – our youngest, we named him after my dad."

"Cormac – you named a child Cormac MacDonald?" I couldn't help but chuckle.

"Yes, Cormac MacDonald Beaupre. He was tall and handsome with jet black hair, and he played baseball. He was a center-fielder."

She opened the manila envelope. "Father Gonzaga took this picture. Take a look," she said.

Inside the envelope was an eight-by-ten black-and-white glossy.

Katie shined the flashlight beam at a photo of a soldier in uniform. I was startled by the familiar face.

"Could be me when I was young, except he's better looking," I said.

"The picture was taken shortly after his twenty-second birthday, and only a month before he was killed in a stupid Army training accident. Do the math, Jack."

I didn't have to do the math. I knew how to count the months.

"I'm sorry, Katie, I'm so sorry." We hugged, and she began to hiccup with emotion, but stopped abruptly.

"I promised myself I wouldn't cry," she said.

"Did you tell him, did he ever know?"

"We didn't know ourselves until he hit his teens and it became obvious from his looks. My parents, they knew – they didn't say anything. I told them what happened between you and me and Beaupre that night. I don't think they understood. I don't understand myself, but, Jack, despite the pain, I don't regret what we did, and neither does Beaupre. 'Let it ride,' my father said. So, we did. And suddenly Cormac was dead. If we had done the right thing and told him who his real father was, maybe he never would have joined the service, because he did it to be like his dad, like Beaupre. For these last years, we've been suffocating in our sorrows and guilt. We didn't have room for anything or anyone else. Now we've realized life has to go on. Can you forgive us, Jack?"

I could not grieve for a son I never knew, but I could feel for these good people. They had more than my forgiveness, they had my love.

"You know why I never visited? Because I lost Beaupre's bat in a flood," I said.

We both laughed at the absurdity. "The things that keep us apart . . ." Katie said.

I led her through the driftwood, up the river bluff, to the parking lot and the car where my best friend waited.

Liberty Taxi

A Hug a Day

I returned to Keene in the fall of 1993 and I went to work for Liberty Taxi as a driver.

Beaupre and Katie didn't own the Hephaestus Dynamite building, but they acted as if they did; they had fifty years to go on a lease that Mister Mayor had negotiated. The owners, heirs of the Hephaestus family (A.K.A. "the ugly ducklings of the Fortune 500"), lived out of the country and showed no interest in the building as long as the rent was paid.

The Beaupres expanded the operation to include Liberty Transportation, a franchise bus station for the Twin State Transit Authority. Much of the old factory was gutted, and a ticket counter, waiting room, and snack bar were installed. Katie managed the bus station and Beaupre the taxi stand. The bus station was modern and clean, because Katie was a neat freak. By contrast, the taxi stand retained the atmosphere of a pool hall, because Beaupre had promised Mister Mayor he wouldn't make any big changes as long as the old baseball man was still alive. Only a wheelchair ramp had been added. The Bettie Page pinup calendars were still on the wall, and former Coach MacDonald's collection of sporting memorabilia, including the montage of yours truly and Ted Williams, remained in place.

Beside the taxi office was Winters Auto and Motorcycle Repair, owned and operated by Billy Winters (a pacifist during the Vietnam War) and his son, Earl. Billy and Earl maintained our fleet of Ford Tauruses, all of which had many miles on them. At any one time, one of the vehicles was likely to be in for maintenance or repairs.

I often went next door to the bus station for a bite to eat, and my right instep always tingled, because the snack bar was in the same area where Beaupre and I had had our adventure decades ago.

Liberty Taxi was open from 6 A.M. to midnight Monday through Thursday, from 6 A.M. to 2 A.M. on Fridays and Saturdays, and from 8 A.M. to 9 P.M. on Sundays and holidays. Our goal was to keep a half dozen cars in service at any one time. I drove sixty hours, sometimes more, a week. Beaupre, the main dispatcher, employed four full-time drivers and varying numbers of part-timers. The full-time drivers included myself, Wes Leb, Jules Bonneau, and Buck Reynolds.

Wes was the aging biker cat, who these days dyed his thinning hair jet black and greased it down into long sideburns. He wore black engineer boots and a motorcycle jacket. He put all his spare cash and time into his Harley-Davidson hog, riding it year-round through downpours, blizzards, ice storms, hail, and volcanic eruptions. He never instigated, but he never backed down, either. Many years ago, Wes couldn't decide whether to be Elvis or Marlon Brando in *The Wild One*, so he tried to be both. Actually, Wes was not wild at all. He mumbled like Marlon Brando because he was painfully shy, and though he had a baritone voice like Elvis, he could not sing. He never married, but he did pay child support to two different women, which left him impoverished. He lived in a run-down mobile home in one of the poorer towns of the Monadnock Region.

Beaupre and Katie were proud to have Jules Bonneau, a graduate student at Keene State College, among their drivers. He was a local celebrity because one year he had finished in the top twenty in the Boston Marathon, which was where he met Beaupre (who was doing the marathon in his wheelchair). When Jules wasn't driving, he could be seen jogging all over the city. He annoyed me by running in the street and not on the sidewalk. I called him on it one day, and he said he stayed off the sidewalks because he would become so wrapped up in his thoughts that he feared he would run into a pedestrian.

Jules lived with his girlfriend, an anti-nuclear power activist and organic farmer. Jules could be argumentative. He had no patience with anyone who disagreed with him. He liked to lecture on the corruption of elected officials, the remoteness and coldness of corporations, and the dangers of nuclear power. I didn't necessarily disagree with Jules, and I was happy to have him on our driving crew, but he got on my nerves, because he was such a know-it-all.

Buck Reynolds was Beatrice Reynolds, but everybody called her Buck. She was in her twenties, short but powerfully built. I'd seen pictures of her as a teenager, and she was drop-dead cute with blond hair, a pixie face, and a nicely turned ass, the body of a cheerleader. Somewhere along the line she decided she didn't want to be cute. She stopped wearing makeup. She pumped iron and went on a high-protein, high-fat diet to gain weight. By the time she was twenty-five, she had succeeded in altering her looks until she resembled a fair-haired Yogi Berra.

Buck lived with a girl named Lyla and Lyla's mother and grandmother, both named Lyla, and half a dozen Siamese cats, also named Lyla. The women were working to pay for, as Buck put it, a "secret enterprise." Buck was ambitious, but what she was ambitious for I did not know. Beaupre, who never quite got over the paranoia he picked up during the war, worried that Buck and the Lylas were scheming to start a competing taxi company.

Beaupre, who now sported a Fu Manchu mustache streaked with gray, and I worked out four times a week at the YMCA, so I was in good shape. Beaupre had built a powerful upper body, which allowed him to lift himself from his fold-up wheelchair to his jerry-rigged Dodge Ram pickup truck so he could drive it. Beaupre was sometimes tactless on the phone, and he had a foul mouth, but he was good-natured around the office.

I usually drove Car Four. Driving taxi in a small community was not like driving taxi in a big city, where the customers were visitors or people of means. Our customers could not afford cars or were denied access to cars: welfare mothers, retarded people, crazy people, the elderly, the blind, the crippled, drunks, people busted for DUI, people who had had their licenses revoked, sick people, and once in while people with hang-ups about driving. Occasionally, you would take fares from transplanted Manhattanites who had never bothered to learn to drive. They tipped 15 percent, unlike the locals, who didn't tip at all, because they were low on dough.

People who possessed something they valued – money or power – or who had loved ones who depended upon them or who were super selfish developed powerful defenses to prevent the real world from divining who they really were inside. If they did reveal themselves, it would certainly not be to the taxi driver. It was as if you were invisible to them. You picked up those types of customers from the airport. You always opened the rear door for them, because the back seat was where they wanted to sit. The only time they related to you in any personal way was when they worried you were going to screw them out of a few dollars by driving the long route, which I never did, though I was tempted, not for the money, but on general principles.

By contrast, most of my local customers sat in the front seat, and they liked to converse, mainly about their problems – the bills they owed, the medical problems they endured, their disabilities, their drug addictions or the drug addictions of their loved ones, their sick mothers, their crippled children, the no-good rotten spouses who had walked out on them, the drunk husbands who knocked them around, the fathers who had abandoned them.

I'd found a job that fitted me in this epoch of my life. Merely by listening, I was doing my customers some good beyond transporting them from Place A to Place B. I loved driving taxi.

Olympia returned in 1998 – what was left of her. She'd had a breakdown from booze and smoking that brought on a stroke resulting in brain damage. I don't know how she found me in the condition she was in, but somehow she showed up one day at the taxi office, thin, demented, wasted. "Jack," she said, "Jack." She wasn't looking at me; she was looking at the picture of me and Ted

Williams. She was only seventy-one, but she had the body carriage and demeanor of a ninety-year-old. She couldn't take care of herself, and I couldn't take care of her and still make a living. I had to put her in a nursing home. Thank you, Medicare and Medicaid, thank you.

Over the next few months, I discovered that what Olympia required from me was simple, a hug a day. No matter how busy I was, I made it a point to go to the nursing home on Court Street. I'd usually find her in a rocking chair in the parlor, staring at fish in a small aquarium. She'd rise and hold out her arms. "I need it, I need it," she'd say. I'd embrace her, and she would put her arms around me. We would lock for a full minute, until I felt her body relax, and then I would slowly release her. At first, I gave her a hug a day out of my duty as a husband, but as the weeks, then months, passed, I realized that I needed those hugs as much as she did.

Part Three
Fate

Footprints in deep snow lead to and from the grave
of TRUTH, where someone has left flowers.
– Memere

A Virtual Cartier-Bresson

Defining Message
March 1999

The day was messy, a sloppy snow falling, the forecast for a swift turn to bitter cold in the night. The roads were a little slippery, but there was no reason to put chains on the cabs. Keene did a good job of keeping the roads plowed, sanded, and salted, thanks to such men as George Glines, John Ranagan, and Earl Wilber. It was 2 P.M.; not much taxi business at this hour on a day like this.

We had a routine for communicating over the two-way radio to avoid confusion, since all the drivers could hear one another and the dispatcher. The driver began his conversation with the word "check," followed by his car number, and the dispatcher addressed the driver by his or her car number. One of the rules was never to swear over the two-way radio, because the customers in all the cabs could hear you, a rule that Beaupre constantly broke.

I had just dropped off one of my favorite customers at her apartment on Central Square. I didn't know her name, but I remembered her pinched face. She'd worked in the office of Narrow Textiles, Inc., and had given me papers to fill out my first day on the job when I was sixteen years old. To me she was the Doll (Dignified Old Lady). She referred to me as "young man," though I was pushing sixty.

Beaupre's voice crackled over the two-way radio, "Four, where are you now?"

I picked up the mike and talked into it. "Check Four. Central Square, just finishing with my fare."

"Four, buy a bottle of Raynal brandy, and bring it to the Eagle, Room 314."

"Check Four. That's Father Gonzaga's old room."

"Four, the name he gave me was Cartier-Bresson, and he sounded like a Frenchman, and I don't mean Quebec, I mean Old France. Does that ring a bell?"

"Check Four. Yeah, Cartier-Bresson is a famous French photographer. His thing is the decisive moment."

"Four, fuck that. Make sure you get your money before you give Mister Bresson his booze."

"Check Four."

"Four, one more thing."

"Check Four."

"Four, he asked for you by name."

"Check Four." I put the mike back in the cradle. What did one of the great photographers of the century want with a lowly working man?

I drove to the new state liquor store, where I was a familiar face. The clerks who didn't know I was a taxi driver must have thought I was quite the drinker. Actually, since I'd quit smoking marijuana I'd become a three-beers-after-work man, and hard liquor didn't appeal to me except on special occasions.

The cocktail lounge in the Eagle Hotel had long ago closed; there was talk of demolition. On the walls of the staircase were the outlines of paintings that had been removed. No evidence remained of Christ's Rapture Head Shop. The smell was musty. The new landlord (a bank, I believe) had put weak bulbs in the light sockets, so the place was gloomy year-round.

I'd had deliveries to the Eagle Hotel before, but never on the third floor, which I thought had been closed by the city for safety reasons. It certainly appeared uninhabited. The only light came in from a single window at the end of the hallway, the outlines of those discarded paintings in the dim light like commentaries on the inevitable failure of corporeal matter.

At 314, I paused at the door for a long moment, intimidated. Father Gonzaga had introduced me to the work of Cartier-Bresson. Had the good priest sublet his room to the French photographer?

Finally, I knocked. Long quiet interlude. I was about to knock again when the door opened. For a moment I was blinded by the light, because my eyes had grown used to the relative dark. The room faced the street, where two tall and wide windows let in the cool but strong light.

The old man was plump in an angelic kind of way, wearing black pants and a white shirt, pink slippers that matched his complexion. His thin gray hair, what there was of it, was slicked back. No toupee. Because of the glare of the light off the glasses, or maybe because the face had fallen with age, whatever the reason, I didn't recognize it. What I recognized was the voice, speaking now in a Parisian accent: "Bonjour, Jack, put the bag on the table by the window, *s'il vous plaît.*"

"Father Gonzaga?" I said.

He laughed, a witness-to-a-century laugh. "Father Gonzaga is no more. He lost his mission and his fortune when the dot-coms went bust, an awful fit, it was. Thank God and human ingenuity for the clothespin clamped on the tongue, or I might not be talking to you right now. With the money went the influence of Father Sebastian Gonzaga. Jack, I've been excommunicated from the Catholic Church."

"I'm sorry. What happened?"

"I was canon fodder for the philosophical wars of the church hierarchy."

"But the name?"

"Sebastian Gonzaga was a focal point for identification, not an identity per se. I go by Cartier-Bresson now, a comfort for a virtual man. Sit down, have a brandy with a refugee from reality." He reached for the Raynal.

236 · *Never Back Down*

"Let me use your phone," I said. I dialed the taxi stand and asked Beaupre to get along without Car Four for a while.

Virtual Cartier-Bresson poured the brandy into snifter glasses. We sat by the window. Between us on a table was the booze, a pack of Gauloises cigarettes, a propane lighter, a tablet of seizure medication, the clothespin, a pair of binoculars, and a tripod holding a Leica camera aimed through the window.

Virtual Cartier-Bresson lit a cigarette, turned his gaze away from me to the window, and said, "It's a great view of Main Street, is it not? Take a look."

He pointed to eight-by-ten black-and-white glossies held by thumbtacks on the wall: a young couple walking, the boy's bare hand over the girl's mittened hand; an old woman, who I recognized as the Doll; a couple of boys wearing Keene High School jackets. None of these pictures particularly arrested my attention as part of some important or unique action. The photographer had missed the decisive moment. Where were the great photographs by the great photographer?

"So you sit here all day smoking and drinking and snapping pictures of the street?" I said.

"Yes, for the last two months I've been making a record for a book I'm putting together. It's a visual world, *bonhomme*. I came back to this town because of this room – the views of Main Street."

I'd already finished the brandy and glowed inside from its marvelous effect. Virtual Cartier-Bresson poured me a refill. I was thinking: special occasion. Virtual Cartier-Bresson had not touched his glass. It was another moment before I realized it was my turn to speak.

I quickly brought him up to date, telling him about the son who had died in a training accident in the military and how I could not grieve for him because we had never met, that all I felt was an emptiness.

"Yes, I remember photographing him. Those who cannot grieve carry the burden from lifetime to lifetime," Virtual Cartier-Bresson said.

Those words propelled me into memories of the childhood dreams of fires in old Acadia, of the girl I'd loved and lost over multiple lifetimes.

I mentioned the spooky corridor of the hotel with outlines of the paintings. "It made me sad," I said. "I miss the real paintings."

"I do not," Virtual Cartier-Bresson said. "The outlines are the greater art."

"What do you mean?"

"Those empty spaces framed by grime tell a truer story than the decorative pictures that inhabited the spaces. We live in an age where only virtual reality can get us through the day."

"I guess that makes a kind of twisted sense," I said.

Virtual Cartier-Bresson sipped the brandy, then looked over at me the way you would look at a cat that had used your couch as a scratching post. "Jack, you have not made peace with the Church."

"I have trouble with the bottom lines: Jesus as the son of God, rising from the dead, salvation, heaven, hell, purgatory, limbo, the Trinity. You, you believe, and look what they did to you."

"Of course I believe. It was my belief that set the stage for my excommunication by the enemies of Jesus Christ. Jack, when was the last time you went to confession? Don't answer, the look on your face tells me everything."

"I have to go back to work." I stood. I didn't want to confess to a madman.

"All right. You will confess when you are ready."

After that reunion I saw Virtual Cartier-Bresson irregularly. He sometimes called the taxi office for liquor, and he always asked for me. I'd see him on the street wearing a long black overcoat, earmuffs under a backward Red Sox cap, chin tucked into his chest as he bucked a wind, sometimes when there was no wind. In a sense he was always with me, because I knew that most of the time he'd be at his window with his camera on the tripod and he would recognize my taxi. I hoped he was taking pictures. I wanted to see my cab in some future book. At night, I'd drive by and his light would always be on. When I asked him why he didn't shut off his light or pull the shades, he said, "The philosopher's great fear is the dark. Alas, it's also his living."

When I visited Cartier-Bresson I'd always stay until the bullshit was too thick for me to take, and then I would be disgusted and I would get out of there. I knew the symptoms. I'd worked in Seton Unit at DePaul Hospital.

One afternoon, in the summer of 1999, I had gone to the nursing home to give Olympia her daily hug, and she had not recognized me.

That night I drove down Main Street. As usual, Virtual Cartier-Bresson's light was on. I could see him in the window. I parked, got out of the car, and waved. I wondered if he was taking my picture. Minutes later, I was at the door of 314.

"You're upset, I can tell," he said, as I entered.

"I've carried divorce papers for years," I said. "Olympia signed them, and I am tempted to sign them now – I don't know what to do."

Cartier-Bresson poured two brandies and lit a Gauloise for himself. We sat by the window. "Do you want to confess?" he said, and I heard that strange desire in his voice.

"It just dawned on me why you became a priest, so you could hear confessions," I said, remembering that Olympia believed that Father Gonzaga lived with a secret perversion.

"Sins are the most interesting things about people. God, the true God, not the fake God we make up to assuage our fears and satisfy our desires, created man so that He, God, could know sin – in an intellectual way, of course. We are his research subjects into that topic. Do you want to confess?" He was starting to breathe hard.

"I just want to talk."

"Conversation is akin to confession. I'll take what I can get. Talk."

"All these years, Memere has been with me. What is she? Is she a demon?"

"I don't have answers for such questions, nor even better questions," Virtual Cartier-Bresson added, with a twist of sarcasm. "Let's attack this problem of conscience in a different way. I know your claim to fame in Keene. Do you? Do you know what they say about you?"

"I do, yeah."

"You struck out Willie Mays."

"No, no," I said, insulted, "it was Ted Williams. Willie was the greatest all-around player of my era, but Ted was a better hitter. Probably the best of all time."

"And you struck him out."

I gave him a noncommittal shrug.

Virtual Cartier-Bresson laughed and laughed. I must have had a hurt look on my face, because Cartier-Bresson reached over and gently took my arm.

"Jack, I'm not laughing at you, I'm laughing at the predicaments brought on by human absurdity."

"I've been thinking," I said, though I hadn't been thinking. I didn't even know what I was going to say, only that certain ideas had been brooding inside me, and now they were ready to come out.

"My whole life so far has been guided for better and for worse by the penance you gave me so long ago."

"The penance you gave yourself. I was merely the accrediting agent."

"I don't know exactly how, but it's come between my wife and me, and between me and the world."

"What do you want from this ancient defrocked priest, Jack? You want me to take it back? You want me to be the Jesuit priest, Sebastian Gonzaga, all over again?"

"I guess, yes. That's exactly what I want. Just tell me I'm free to live my life in another way than through menial labor."

"You don't believe in God, but you believe in me, a broken-down, excommunicated, alcoholic, schizophrenic, epileptic, aged priest living in virtual reality?"

"Not in you. I believe in that moment that changed me, that

gave me some meaning. I believe that a word from you can help me find . . ." I struggled for a word, but it did not come. I looked at him, pleading with my eyes.

"You want me to release you from the penance, so you can start anew."

"Yes, that's it, release. I want release so I can start anew."

"No."

"No?"

"That's correct. My answer is no. Without your penance you would be doomed to eternal damnation." He stood and turned his back on me. I could see his glasses flashing in the reflection in the window. I hesitated, waiting for him to say something or make a gesture in my direction, but he continued staring out the window, and I continued staring at his reflection, the glasses that threw off light preventing me from seeing the eyes. Finally, I left without a word.

The next night I was driving down Main Street in Car Four, imagining that Virtual Cartier-Bresson was photographing my taxi. Without thinking about it, I glanced up at Room 314 to look for that reassuring light. The room was dark. Dread rolled over me. I drove around back of the Eagle, parked, took the flashlight out of the glove compartment, and went inside.

For the first two floors I didn't need the flashlight, but the staircase to the third floor was dim and by the time I reached the top it was dark. I switched on the flashlight and jogged, huffing and puffing, down the hallway to Room 314. I knocked. No answer. I knocked again. Waited. I shouted, "Cartier-Bresson, let me in. Father Gonzaga! Gonzaga! Sebastian Gonzaga!" The sound of my voice deafened me, as if I were hollering into my own ears. I waited. Waited some more. Finally, I calmed down a little bit, and I tried the door. It opened. I switched on the light.

Virtual Cartier-Bresson's things were gone, including the photographs on the wall. All that remained were the smells of booze, cigarettes, and body odor and one object, the purple stole, which lay on the windowsill. I picked it up and carried it out with me.

In the hallway I was relatively calm, able to think straight. I shined the flashlight on the walls. Cartier-Bresson had been right about spaces holding a more defining message than the paintings, and he was right not to remit my penance. The only meaning I was going to find in my life was as a common laborer.

Millennium Blast

On the Ice Again

Cormac "Skitzy" MacDonald – Mister Mayor, as he preferred to be known – passed away peacefully in his sleep on Christmas Eve of 1999 at his home in Delray Beach, Florida. His body was shipped to Keene for the funeral in St. Bernard's Church, which was filled to overflowing. Before the interment, Katie showed Beaupre and me the will. Coach had left Beaupre the ancient thermometer on the hemlock tree outside the Granite Lake camp. I was stunned to discover that I, too, was named in the will. Coach had left me the Chris-Craft, which needed repairs and had not been in the water for many years.

"I get a thermometer that won't reach 98.6 even if I stick it up my ass and you get Coach's primo possession, you bastard – I'm hurt," Beaupre said, and only I knew the depth of his sarcasm.

After the funeral, the long line of cars, lights on, went in procession to St. Joseph's Cemetery. Coach's plot was beside his Scottish father, his French-Canadian mother, and the priest-uncle he was named after. Though he spoke with an Irish brogue all his life, Cormac MacDonald had never been to Ireland and had no Irish ancestry. The ground was covered with a thin crust of snow.

While the MacDonald family wept over the loss of their patriarch, Beaupre and I lurked in the background.

I bent down and whispered in his ear, "Hey, Beaupre, Coach told me you worked as a bouncer in a strip club and that you carried a cattle prod as an enforcer, is that true?"

"Yeah, right, and you struck out Ted Williams. Do you think Coach was crazy, cagey, or an ignoramus?"

"Just a dreamer – maybe," I said. "Too bad he had to hurt so many people."

"His kids loved him, Katie loved him. He never lied to them or fucked them up. Every time I told her how full of shit he was, she went ballistic, so I stopped bad-mouthing him. I wonder if he stopped bad-mouthing me."

"He's dead, Beaupre. He can't fuck you up anymore."

"Oh, yeah, then why did he will me the fucking thermometer and you that fucking tub?" Beaupre said, outraged, then suddenly his face softened. "Skitzy was as close to a father as I ever had. In a weird kind of way, I loved the man, which I think is the only reason that Katie could love me."

"I loved him, too, but I wish I hadn't. Love's like belief in God; it doesn't make any sense, but sometimes you can't help it."

"Keep God out of this," Beaupre said, moving back into outrage mode. "Religion is all lies; as for love, who the flaming fuck knows, you just piss in the wind and call it Mariah."

"I don't know what that means, Beaupre, but you're right."

"No, I'm not right, but I'm never wrong either. Jack, I don't understand why you fuck around with religion. I know you don't believe it."

I was angry now. "There are times when I have to pray, okay? You understand?"

"No."

"Remember when Katie came down to the driftwood city and told me about your son, my son, our son? That stayed with me. My only flesh and blood and I never knew him, I never fucking knew him. I've had a lot of bad things happen in my life, and I don't know if that was the worst, but it lingers. I know it lingers with you, too. I get through it by getting down on my knees until they hurt, and praying. So, yeah, I find it impossible to believe what I'm supposed to believe, but I believe in prayer and I believe in penance. It's the closest I'll ever come to faith, glory, and the man upstairs."

Beaupre looked up at me from his wheelchair, and he cracked a smile. "You and me, we fought the same battles, but with different tactics, and we both lost, but we never ran."

"Never back down . . ." I said.

"Never instigate. Geez, I haven't had a Camel in twenty-five years, but I wish I had one now."

We watched the mourners for a minute, then Beaupre said, "Listen, Katie and the family are going to be in Florida with Grandma MacDonald for New Year's Eve, and I'm baching it. What do you fucking say you and me go out to the lake and get smashed? You know that stick of dynamite from the old Hephaestus shop that Coach left in the drawer? Let's blow it the fuck up for Coach Mac-Donald and the bullshit millennium."

I didn't have do anything but grin; we both knew it was a go.

Beaupre gave himself and me the night off for New Year's Eve and assigned Jules Bonneau duty behind the dispatcher's desk. Months earlier Jules had been dumped by his girlfriend and he had taken up with Amy Beaupre. She'd been a low self-esteem fat girl, with a bad divorce behind her, but Jules had gotten her to start running and these days she was slimmed down and full of confidence and beauty.

Beaupre and I drove out to Granite Lake in his Dodge Ram. I wore Alcide's watchman's hat. The accelerator and brakes were on the steering wheel. Quite a rig. Beaupre wheeled himself to the cab, opened the door, reached for the grab bar, hauled himself behind the wheel, picked up the wheelchair, folded it, and put it in the slot in the back of the seat. He did all this work in one fluid motion. He made it look easy, but it took strength and agility.

We brought eggs, sausage, fake New York bagels, steaks, potato chips, a case of Bud, a bottle of Four Roses, and one Camel cigarette. Beaupre threw away the rest of the pack. He made noises about getting stoned, but the fact was that these days we were both so far out of the drug scene that we didn't know where to buy the stuff anymore. We were going to ring in the new and ring out the old in the time-honored fashion, with booze and our unique fireworks display.

We drank beers on the way to the camp, arriving around 6 P.M. We stopped at the hemlock tree. It said twenty below zero on Beaupre's outdoor thermometer. Estimated actual temperature forty-five degrees above, unusually warm for a New Year's Eve in the North Country.

"Why do you think Coach left you that stupid mercury?" I asked.

"Who the fuck knows, who the fuck cares?"

"I think Coach had a sense of humor," I said.

"More likely he had old-timers' disease." Beaupre tapped his temple with his index finger.

We went into the camp. It was colder inside than outside. The water had been shut off, the place closed for the season. I built a fire. It took a couple hours to warm up the living room. Meanwhile, we drank steadily. When a good bed of coals collected in the fireplace, I pulled the top off the gas grill, outside on the porch, and propped it up over the fireplace coals on some bricks. Beaupre got down off his wheelchair onto the floor, moving around on his knuckles like an ape.

"How do you want your steak, motherfucker?" he asked me.

"Medium-rare."

He cooked those steaks to perfection on our makeshift grill. We ate the steaks with potato chips and washed down the meal with beer while we sat on the floor and conversed. It was probably the third-best feed I've had in my life. By then it was 10 P.M.

"Where do you propose we set the dynamite stick?" I asked.

"On the lake someplace, maybe out to the island," he said.

I was wondering whether Beaupre could wheel his chair on water-slicked ice for half a mile, but I knew better than to raise that subject. Instead, I said, "You think the ice is safe?"

"No."

"You just want to do it anyway."

"That's right. I've been living a cautious fucking life so long I've forgotten what it feels like to believe you're going to die in about three minutes. I want that feeling back."

"Are we going to pop that stick at midnight?"

"I don't give a fuck when we do it. I just want to go to war again and see if I'm still scared. Did I ever tell you I was scared? Well, I wasn't."

"You're a liar and a drunk, Beaupre," I said.

"Fuck you. Millennium, what a crock. Let's go outside, climb trees, and go swimming under the ice. Where's the dynamite stick, where's the fucking dynamite?"

"If it was up your ass you'd know," I said.

"If it was up my ass I'd have a right to know."

It was great to be drunk and with Beaupre, like we were kids again, just raising hell and having fun.

Though I'd been in the artillery in the Army, I had no idea how to arm a dynamite stick, but Beaupre had learned quite a lot in his training with the airborne. He hooked up the dynamite into a package that looked like something the UPS man would bring, except for the wires sticking out. I removed the battery from the Dodge Ram. Beaupre's plan was to place the package on the ice, run the wires to a safe location, and detonate it with the help of the truck battery.

"Did you ever think about blowing things up for profit, like a bank safe, for example?" I asked.

"Of course, but I'd start with the churches."

"That's not for profit, that's for spite."

"No, it's for profit. The fucking churches have more money than Carter's got little liver pills."

"You ever take a liver pill?"

"You have to if you're pissing in the wind."

I laughed, Beaupre laughed, and God laughed loudest of all at these ridiculous, aging men.

We left our bomb in the camp, put on our winter coats, and went outside to reconnoiter the situation. Some snow had fallen a week ago, but it had flattened during the warm spell. The ground was crunchy here and slushy there. Shallow puddles on the lake ice glowed under a half moon and starlight.

Beaupre's wheelchair slipped and slid, but he controlled it with skill. "Watch this," he said.

Beaupre let the brakes go on his wheelchair and it sped down the hill. He spilled at the bottom, rolled around on the wet snow, and came to rest at the base of the flagpole. The tattered Old Glory had long ago been taken down and never replaced. Beaupre lay in a clump at the base of the flagpole. I took my time walking to him. "You look like a monkey fucking a football," I said.

"No, I am the football, and the monkey is fucking me. Give me a fucking hand."

I clapped my hands as if applauding.

"If I had a gun, I'd kill you," Beaupre said.

"How would you get back in that wheelchair if I was dead?"

"No problem, you want to see?"

"No." I held out my hands.

He grabbed them and used them for levers to lift himself into the wheelchair.

He wheeled and I walked to the dock. The Chris-Craft – my Chris-Craft, I reminded myself – rested inside a cradle that hung from stanchions on the dock. There was a winch that would lower the boat onto the water or, in this case, onto the ice. The boat showed signs of serious rot on its wooden hull, and the finish was faded.

"How's the engine?" I said.

"Probably gummed up. It hasn't run in five fucking years. Jack, it'll cost you a small fortune to float that sucker."

"I guess nobody in the family had any interest in it after Mister Mayor retired."

"It wasn't running when he left, and my sister-in-law has got a ski boat, and the young people are kind of embarrassed by it. They call it an old man's stink pot."

"It's mine now." I pictured myself wearing a captain's cap, tooling around the lake in the Chris-Craft, drink in hand, cigar in mouth; I tried to put Alouette Williams in the picture, but she wouldn't resolve. Instead, Hiram Williams took her place. I shook the image out of my mind.

The lake ice was new, and it appeared iffy to walk on. If I hadn't been drunk, I wouldn't have trusted it. In the mood I was in, I didn't care if I fell through or not. Some of the ice rippled between puddles, but in other places it was as smooth as if a Zamboni had run across it. Beaupre did wheelies on his wheelchair.

"You remember Chalky and Spud?" I said.

"Those crazy bastards made you and me seem sane."

"If they'd had seat belts, padded dashboards, and safety steering columns like they have today, Spud wouldn't have died, and Chalky might have had a chance for a decent life," I said.

"You're wrong, they were going to die fucked up one way or another."

"You're a mean motherfucker, Beaupre."

"It gets me by, it gets me by."

We avoided eye contact. We both knew how to hurt each other's feelings. Cruelty was part of our love for each other.

I stood on the ice and looked at the Chris-Craft on its cradle.

"Coach left me the boat to get back at me for joyriding it to impress Alouette Williams," I said.

"Coach was like that. He held a grudge for years, especially if you were French. He didn't trust anybody with a French name, even though he was half French himself. Boy was he fucking pee-ohed when Katie ran off with me, but something happened to him in old age. He wanted somebody to run his business, and he picked us. I know what you're fucking thinking. You're thinking it was pity or patriotism that moved him because I was blown up in the war, but it was something else. I wish to fuck I knew."

"You were a hell of a catcher, Beaupre. He trusted your pitch calls." I took a pull of Four Roses.

"I wasn't that good, and he wasn't grateful. You going to fix the boat? You can keep it here as long you want. I don't think anybody in the family will object."

I asked myself if I really wanted the boat. For a moment, my mind was a blank, and then I knew – I knew! "I want to blow it up with the dynamite," I said, "and I do care about the time – midnight at the millennium. I want to start the next thousand years of my life without the curse of Evil."

"That's the booze talking." He looked into my eyes. "That's not the booze talking. You really mean it."

"You're fucking-A I really mean it."

We both cackled, our laughter coming back in echo as hyenas mocking the moon.

Beaupre cranked the winch while I guided the boat down onto the ice. It rested there, huge and ungainly and hapless. We went back to the camp for the bomb, the coil of wire, and the battery. Upon our return to the lake, we held a conference on the ice beside the boat.

"Rip out as many floatation batts as you can. Put the charge in the bow," Beaupre said. "If it blows too far aft, the engine will drop straight down through the hull and the fucking boat won't sink because of the fucking flotation."

"Yeah, and what about the ice? Maybe it won't break open to sink the boat." I jumped up, and when I landed a crack rippled through the ice.

"Do it again," Beaupre said.

"I don't think so. I wonder if that dynamite stick still has some energy in it."

"Jack, it doesn't fucking matter if the ice doesn't break, and it doesn't fucking matter if the dynamite doesn't go off. I'm committed, you're committed. We're going send Mister Chris-Craft on a sightseeing tour of the bottom of Granite Lake one way or another."

"Have you been drinking?"

"No, have you?" Beaupre looked at me with a straight face.

"No, of course not. I deplore the stuff."

"He deplores the stuff. Let's get to fucking work."

The hardest part of this job was pushing the damn boat on the ice fifty yards, to where it would be over deep water. Beaupre at turns cheered me on, mocked me, gave me deliberately false advice, and tried to push. I huffed and I puffed and I pushed the boat. I never would have been able to move it if the ice hadn't been so wet and slippery. Finally, I stopped when I could see Shinbone Shack, the former Williams mansion. It had been bought up by a Pentecostal church, which used it as a conference center and summer retreat. At the moment it was dark and uninhabited.

Meanwhile, a few other camps on the lake started shooting off fireworks, just an occasional colorful incendiary. No doubt they were saving their best stuff for midnight.

We returned to the camp, stoked the fire, warmed up, and continued to drink. Beaupre talked about young Cormac, and I talked about Chalky, and we toasted Coach, and we wondered who would be next among our loved ones to pass on. Older you get, the more people you know who share your memories die. If you live long enough, you'll find you are alone and maybe even the memories are gone. In the end, forgetfulness is the only blessing remaining.

At quarter of twelve, we went down to the lake again, and I planted the bomb in the bow of the boat. The wires ran a hundred or so feet away on the ice, to where Beaupre sat in his wheelchair, the battery in his lap. Beaupre spliced the wires together, ripping plastic covers off the copper with the edges of a vise grip. He joined the wires and twisted them clockwise.

"Pretty sloppy wiring, Beaupre; didn't the Big Red One teach you better?" I said.

"Fat leg, ugly leg, dirty leg," Beaupre said, mouthing an old insult that paratroopers reserved for soldiers who didn't jump. "It'll do the fucking job, okay?"

I was thinking of that unsung hero Harold Archer and his beautiful wiring jobs on those old Number Five Crossbar bays. I was thinking of myself struggling to achieve the norm of a thousand connections a day, reaching the goal, and the pride I felt in my workmanship, though I knew I would never be as good as Harold Archer. I was thinking of the artful woodpiles I made for my customers back in my heyday. They were pretty and true – were they art?

"You know something, Beaupre? The real reason I quit baseball was because I knew I would never be as good as Smoky Joe Wood so they would never name a street after me."

"Yeah, and I was no Roy Campanella. You ready to blow this thing?"

I looked at my watch. "Two minutes to twelve."

"Okay. See this wire? And this wire? Just put them together." He made an X with the wires, but without touching. "And we'll see what happens."

At midnight, three or four amateur fireworks displays filled the sky with colors and popping sounds. Beaupre lit his Camel and took a deep drag. I put the wires together. There was a bright flash and a split second later a loud *whump*, almost like the sound the wolf pine made when it hit the ground.

What followed was very satisfying. The ice rippled under our feet, or I should say, under my feet. Following the explosion were grunts and groans from the boat, like a woman makes when she pushes out a baby. The bow nosed into the crater made by the explosion. The stern rose up, and then the hull slid bow first into the deep and disappeared.

Before going to bed that night I took Nate Beaupre's hangover prevention remedy – two aspirins, a multivitamin, and a tall glass of water. I slept well that night on the couch in the camp, rising once to pee and to throw some wood on the fire, and woke in the morning without a headache. After a breakfast of sausage, eggs, and bagel, Beaupre and I went down to the lake. I picked up all the boat debris that the explosion had scattered on the ice and put it in the back of Beaupre's truck. Eventually, it would find its way to the landfill.

All that winter I returned at odd times to check out the grave of my nemesis. After a few snowstorms, meltings, and freeze-ups the ice there didn't look any different from the rest of the lake, and I began to lose interest in my triumph over evil.

Lost and Found Keys

Bonsoir, Tsee-Guh, Bonsoir
February 1, 2003

I was on the late shift for Liberty Taxi the day the Columbia shuttle went down. Not one of my customers mentioned the news. They all had problems of their own to deal with. By now each driver had a cell phone, and regular customers could call their favorite cabbie direct. Around 9 P.M., my phone vibrated in my pocket. It was the hospital.

"Liberty Taxi, Car Four," I said.

"Joseph?" The sound of my real first name sent a chill through me.

"Mummuh?"

"Yes, this is your mother."

"Are you feeling all right?"

"I am fine, because they have given me morphine. Joseph, I am going to die tonight. I want you to come. Call Al. Call your sisters. Tell them to come." She hung up. Seconds later I telephoned her room. A nurse answered.

"This is Jack Landry, Jeanne Landry's son. May I speak to my mother?" I said.

"She's sleeping."

"Sleeping? She was just talking to me."

"She's been medicated."

"She told me she was going to die tonight."

"She may be right. She's very spiritual, your mother, and very much in touch with herself."

"Call a priest," I said in the same commanding tone I used to employ when I bullied my cousin Chalky.

"He's already heard her confession. He just left."

An hour later, my father and I gathered at the new Cheshire Hospital for the death watch. I'd telephoned my sister Gemma, in Washington state, and my sister Denise, in Portland, Maine. They would be arriving when they could. My mother lay on her back, eyes closed, head on a pillow, spine so crippled by osteoporosis and arthritis that she could not sit up, let alone stand or walk. Both my parents suffered from osteoporosis, probably from lousy diets growing up poor, but Alcide was spared the arthritis that wracked my mother's body. Each joint of my mother's thin fingers was swollen. A plastic oxygen tube ran from her nostrils to a machine that made an indecorous gagging sound.

I pulled up a chair beside the bed. My father remained in a chair against the wall, his hands on his knees.

Around 1 A.M., breathless, Denise walked into the room. She was still beautiful after all these years, though I thought her hair was cut too short. Gemma would not arrive until later in the day.

We took turns brushing my mother's blue lips with a sponge on a stick dipped in water. She drifted in and out of consciousness. She seemed aware of our presence, but did not respond to our questions.

My father didn't look all that well himself. He had a bad cold and his voice was weak. Another hour went by before my mother suddenly opened her eyes.

"Al, are you here?"

I got up and my father took my place in the chair beside the bed. My mother wrapped her hands around his left hand and whispered something to him. He started to cry.

"No, no, Alcide," she said, "not in front of the children."

My father stopped crying.

"Denise," my mother called.

Denise took my father's place in the chair. My mother whispered to her. Denise bent and kissed her. It must have been a heck of a soothing kiss, because my mother was instantly asleep, and she appeared very serene.

"What did she say?" I asked Denise.

"She said I've been a good daughter irregardless and to bring Daddy home. I think she's right. Jack, he's exhausted."

"Okay," I said, though I was uneasy at the prospect of being alone with my mother, especially if she died with only me in the room. I was not worthy of that privilege. My sister and my father left. Time went by. I remained in the chair beside the bed sponging her lips.

Though I wasn't sure if she could hear me, I talked to my mother, just rambling on out of nervousness. "I remember the doughnuts you made, so much better than what you can get at Dunkin' Donuts, and the dogs came for miles for a handout. Today they won't let a dog roam free. I used to love watching dogs on their business, unless I was on my Schwinn and their business was chasing me."

My mind went blank, and for a couple minutes I couldn't think of anything to say, until a few words came to mind. "I remember how calm you were when I came in crying with a nail hole through my foot. I've always been prone to rash behavior."

Another blank space in my thinking . . .

"I remember picking flowers for you, that wonderful feeling of a boy's love for his mother," I said.

My mother opened her eyes. She'd been listening all along.

"It was frustrating," she said.

I was startled and pulled away.

"Don't be afraid, Tsee-Guh." She tore the oxygen tubes out of her nose.

"I'm not afraid," I said, but it was a lie. I was afraid, but of what I did not know.

"What did you mean 'it was frustrating'?" I asked.

My mother smiled. "You always picked the flowers with the

stems too short to put in a vase, but that is all right. I loved you all the more. Are they gone?"

It took a sec before I realized she was not talking about the flowers.

"Yes, Denise is taking Dad home. She'll be back."

"I sent them away because I have something very important to tell you about the family," she said, her words fading to a whisper. I tried to put the oxygen back into her nose, but she turned her head away.

"Shut the machine off – I want it to be quiet," she said.

I shut off the oxygen, and it was quiet. It was as if I had stepped into the deep woods after a snow. I realized later that actually it was not quiet. The noises of the hospital were constant.

"You, you were the only one who wanted to know about Pepere," my mother said.

"Yes, the St. Vincent de Paul side of the family. Memere never said anything about Pepere."

"She was ashamed."

"I surmised that, but why? Tell me about your family."

My mother said something, but the words were no more than breaths articulated with the tongue.

"I can't hear you, Mummuh. Listen, I've already figured out that the family shame has something to do with where Pepere came from. I look at your dark skin and my dark skin, and I wonder maybe if Pepere was not Italian or French but Indian or even maybe part black."

"It is worse than that," she said in a whisper. "He was . . . oh, it pains me to say it. He was" – and she started to break down, but pulled herself together – "he was Irish."

"Irish?"

"Not just Irish, Protestant Irish. Memere met him in Halifax. He was just off the boat from Belfast. She made him change his name and convert."

"What was the name?"

"I do not know."

"Was it MacDonald?"

"I do not know. Memere was the hero of our family. She brought us to the States – "

I interrupted, "Us, who do you mean by us?"

"Riding the train from Trois-Rivieres to Suncook, New Hampshire. Your Pepere, my father . . ."

"Yes, tell me."

"He was Irish. Oh, the shame. The shame."

"That's it, that's all – he was Irish?"

"That is it."

Disappointed, but hardly shaken by the news that I was part Irish, I pressed on. "There's another secret, Mummuh, what you were doing from age eighteen until you married Dad five years later. You never talked about those years."

"Oh, that, yes. I suppose it's time you knew. I will tell you the secret." My mother smiled. "Your sisters have lives of their own; you, you do not. The secret will do you some good. It will make you think, it will make you feel and examine your beliefs." Her voice grew in strength, but her eyes rolled back into her head, and her entire body trembled. She reached out, and I took her ice-cold hand in both of mine.

"Speak," I said. "Speak."

And speak she did, in a calm and clear voice. It was the voice I remembered as a child in that language I abandoned so long ago.

"Mummuh, I don't know what you're saying. Please talk English."

My mother went on for almost half an hour, but her speech was in French. I kept interrupting her, begging her to talk English, but she was deaf to me. She went on until her voice began to fade. It was only her last words that I grasped: "Bonsoir, Tsee-Guh, bonsoir." She shut her eyes and suddenly her body was still. She was gone. My grief was sudden and overwhelming. I'd lost more than a mother. I'd lost a key to my very being.

An Old Sailor's Story

It was December 2004, and I was alone in my taxi, driving down Main Street the week before Christmas, light snow falling, only 5 P.M., but already night. Out of habit I looked up at the third-floor windows at the Eagle, hoping I'd see the light on in Father Gonzaga's room, but of course it was dark. I was now living at the Eagle myself. During the taxi years, I was quite the skinflint, saving my money for retirement. I enjoyed my spare existence, no TV, no computer, nothing but a radio, a few books (I had discovered Eric Hoffer), and my journal to chronicle the events you are reading now.

"Four, where are you now?" It was Beaupre on the dispatcher's desk.

"Check Four. On Main Street. Just past the Eagle."

"Four, I called your father to see how he was getting along. He didn't answer his telephone."

"Check Four. He's probably turned his hearing aid off. I'll have a look anyway."

"Check Four."

The lights were off in my father's house on 19 Oak Street. I didn't have to search for a key. My parents never locked the door. The house keys had been mislaid decades ago, and no one bothered to replace them. I walked in, snapped on the kitchen light. I smelled the wonderful heat from the radiators. I remembered sitting in a chair beside a radiator reading my favorite magazine, *Fur, Fish, and Game*.

"Pop? Pop? Hey, Al, crank up that hearing aid!" I called out. No answer.

I looked in the bathroom right off the kitchen. There was no shower, just a sink, a tub, and a toilet. In front of the tub was a scale.

It was as if I was a kid again, and I stepped on it – two-twelve. I kept in reasonable shape at the gym with Beaupre, but I wasn't exactly svelte.

I heard my footsteps on the linoleum floor of the kitchen as I left the bathroom. Everything in the parlor and dining room (it was the playroom when we kids were growing up) appeared normal. I glanced up at the shrine of St. Anthony, patron saint of the lost things. "So, where is he?" I asked. The saint did not answer.

Off the playroom was my bedroom, which had been turned into my mother's room when she could no longer navigate the stairs, and which was now my father's room.

It was neat and bare as a monk's cell. My dad always liked things Navy – "squared away" – bed made with perfect hospital corners, slippers lined up under it. On the dresser were framed snapshots of myself and Olympia when we were in our prime, Denise with her partner and their daughter from her partner's marriage, and Gemma with her husband and kids. The top drawer of the dresser was slightly open because the wood was warped and it did not fully close. I opened the drawer. Inside were all of Dad's black socks, folded and lined up. What Dad liked about the Navy was its insistence on cleanliness and order; essentials only. I took after him in that way.

After my mother's funeral, my sisters had cleaned out her things. They fought over her clothes, sewing, and personal effects. All I ended up with was her rosary beads. I opened the closet door, and was accosted by the old-man stink of my father's clothes. His 1940s wide ties hung on the back of the door. I remembered how when he came back from the war he used to dress in a suit and tie and sit in a chair all day long.

I went up the stairs, which opened directly into what used to be "the girls' room," where my sisters slept. They envied me, because I had my own room. It was because I was a boy, they whined. Boys get all the goodies. And so forth. It was now a storage room, full of the junk my father acquired from the Publishers Clearing House Sweepstakes. I remembered the day I'd found a Playboy tape lying on the kitchen table. I asked Dad if he had run it. He answered, "Not yet, I'm working my way up to it."

Beside the girls' room had been my parents' bedroom.

"Pop?" I said, hesitantly, to the closed door. No answer. I took a deep breath. For a moment, I could not enter. A part of me expected to find my parents young again, thrashing around on the bed.

"Oh, cripes!" I said aloud, and barged in.

As a boy I thought of my parents' bed as huge, edifying or terrifying, one or the other or both; a swamp of love, you could get mired in there. Now the bed seemed ordinary and small as double beds went, with a modest maple headboard from the Furniture Factory.

Some doofus like me or my father or Three-Fingered Willie logged the maple tree, hauled the logs to the saw mill, operated the band saw that milled the logs, trucked the boards to the furniture factory, made the boards on a table saw, ran two-by-twos through a lathe to make the slats, drilled holes, routed grooves, mortised the side boards, joined them with glue, sanded and shellacked, inspected the work, and on down the line to packers and forklift operators and truck drivers and accountants who fudged the paperwork and the salespeople and those mysterious powers behind the scenes who made the decisions and took home most of the profits and the government whose minimum wage and other laws protected the working people, sort of. No OSHA, though – too bad, Uncle Three Fingers, too bad. The trail of the product ended with my parents, who held their own jobs to earn money to pay all those who made a bed, so they could lie in it. That headboard comprised the only understanding I had of our economic system.

I found my father in the cellar. He was half-reclining, half-sitting on the concrete stairs, eyes closed, either dead or asleep.

"Pop, are you alive?" I asked.

No response. I touched his skinny arm and shook him gently. I almost expected his bones to rattle.

His blue, blue eyes opened. He gave me a whimsical smile that said, *it's about time*. Suddenly, I was contemplating my father's strategy for survival in this cruel world. He knew from the start that as an honest man with little formal education and only an ordinary body and mind he was overmatched. He would provide provide provide, never never never complain, and cede the executive duties to loved ones with more calculating minds. The strategy had been a success. My mother and to some degree my sisters and I had taken care of him.

"That's a relief – you're alive," I said.

"I can't hear you. I got the gizmo turned off." He reached for his hearing aid, moaned, and passed out.

My father had broken his hip. While he was in the hospital and then the convalescent home recovering, he signed over durable powers of attorney to me. He also signed papers notifying his care-givers that should he grow ill and unable to answer for himself, he wanted to receive palliative care only. I sold the family house. It languished on the market for six months while I kept lowering the price. When we finally had an offer, Connie Joyce, our real estate agent, told me, "Jack, this is the cheapest house in Keene. Nobody wants to live in this neighborhood, especially women."

When he was back on his feet, I moved my father into a room on the bottom floor of the Eagle Hotel rooming house, so I could keep an eye on him.

Liberty Taxi and Liberty Transportation continued to expand. Nate Beaupre joined our force, managing a car rental unit. The old fleet of Ford Tauruses was traded in for new Toyotas. Beaupre was going to junk Car Four, but I claimed it for my personal vehicle when my most recent Moses finally succumbed to rust. Car Four needed a ring job, burning a quart of oil to a tank of gas, and its exhaust pipe polluted the air with black smoke, but I loved Car Four as much as I had loved my cord wood truck, my camper-pickup, and my Ford Escort. I loved all my Moseses.

The old penance hung over my head. It was my link to the possibility of a God, the He or She or It that oversees our actions and judges us accordingly, and if there was no such being it was my cry in the wilderness. Without my penance, I had no voice, no substance, no mission, no reason to grind on with the ages.

Alcide Landry tooled around the hallways of the Eagle pushing an aluminum walker. He treated women with a courtly manner that charmed them. He made his own breakfast, toast and coffee. At noon the Meals on Wheels driver brought him a huge plate. He ate half for lunch, half for dinner at 5:30. By 6:30 he was in bed. God love the Meals on Wheels driver, God love all the Meals on Wheels employees. Once a week the visiting nurse gave him a bath, cut his toenails, flirted with him. God love her, God love all the visiting nurses. And while you're at it, God, give out an extra dollop of love for those nursing home people, most of whom are underpaid women. They are among the unsung heroes.

Since Dad never complained, I constantly had to quiz him to determine his needs. I asked him what he missed the most about the bygone days.

"A woman's comfort," he said, and then he added, "I've been thinking. I'd like to get a girlfriend, maybe advertise in the paper."

"That's not how you get a girl," I said.

He looked at me for an answer, I in my position as his power of attorney, as future executor of his will, as administrator to his life, as his only son, a man of the world, at least compared to him.

I shrugged. I had no answers. All I had were questions. I wanted to ask what happened to him in the war to break him down, to leave me as a small boy confused, disconsolate. I started to formulate my question, but held back. In the end, all I could say was, "Pop, what are you looking for in a woman?"

"One with a car," he said.

The best thing I did for my dad was take him to a motorcycle dealership that featured a facsimile of the Indian motorcycle that he used to ride as a young man. He stared at it for the longest time. When the saleswoman came over, he turned his attention to her. When he discovered she had a French name, he talked to her in French, and she answered. They talked and laughed. I wanted desperately to join in on the conversation, but of course I could not. Eventually, he got around to showing her how to count to ten in Lithuanian.

Middle of July 2005, weather hotter than usual, Alcide caught a cold. A few days later, he was too weak to get out of bed. I called 911 and he was taken by ambulance to the hospital. Diagnosis: bacterial pneumonia. He refused treatment.

"Pneumonia is the old man's friend," he said from his bed in the hospital.

"You don't want to come back to the Eagle?"

"There's a lot of good-looking nurses around here." His voice was a register above a whisper, and I had to bend to hear him. It was as physically close as we'd ever been.

"Pop, before you ride off into the sunset, I have a question."

"Fire away."

I could tell by his blue, blue eyes that he knew what I was going to ask him, but was he ready to speak the truth?

"You were drafted to the Navy late in the war and you never saw any action, but when you came home, you didn't go to work for six months. You dressed up every morning in a suit and tie and sat in a chair by the window."

"That's right. I did that. I had to think it through."

"Think what through? What happened to you in the war?"

My father talked to me then as never before. He was a sailor on a small transport ship that moved men from one island to another in the Philippines. He worked in the engine room at the bottom of the ship. Somewhere in the Pacific the ship hit a rock and hung up. They were there five days, until another ship arrived to pull them off. My father was the only seaman stationed in the engine room when the ship began to lurch back and forth. He was thrown from one bulkhead to another. He tried to go topside, but he couldn't open the hatch.

He realized then that they had locked him in. If the engine room flooded, he would drown. What screwed up his head was not the panic he felt, which was brief and passing; not the fear of death; it was not even that he'd been locked in – he understood that the ship and its crew were more important than one man in the engine room. What troubled him was that they had not informed him. He would have volunteered, he said. They had robbed him of the opportunity to distinguish himself. For the rest of his hitch, he remained alienated from his fellow sailors but especially from the officers.

"Last question, Pop."

"Yeah, I've been waiting for it."

"Where was Mom during those missing years?"

"I'm not sure exactly."

"What are you sure of?"

Alcide's face broke into a big smile. There was warmth that spread through his entire face that I had never seen before. It was as if I were seeing into him for the first time, and then he shocked me. He said, "I'm sure that I love you all." It was the first time that I'd ever heard him use the word "love." It took me a moment to recover my breath.

"What else?" I whispered.

But there was nothing else. He had fallen asleep. I waited for him to wake, but he never did. Alcide Landry passed on two nights later. Beaupre, in his cruel but truthful way, said, "He died the way he lived – clueless."

I learned a lot as a witness to my epoch, but not enough. For every new insight an old one was lost or forgotten. I just didn't have room in my head to hold all the necessary information for health, happiness, and what have you.

I put in more hours behind the wheel of my cab and awaited the next big event.

The Lake Turns Over

Return of the Specter

In the fall of 2004, Buck Reynolds had left Liberty Taxi and moved with the Lylas to San Francisco. They returned to Keene a year later and Buck went back to work as a cabbie, now a he after a sex-change operation.

Meanwhile, Katie retired and Nate, who had a degree in accounting, took over Liberty Transportation. He tried to get Beaupre to clean up the taxi office, but Beaupre wouldn't do it. The taxi office remained a memorial to Coach Cormac "Skitzy" MacDonald, Mister Mayor, as he wanted to be remembered.

In the fall of 2005, the big hurricanes smacked the Gulf Coast. All the old memories of my betrayal of Alouette Williams stormed back. The thought of her made me want to help the dispossessed. But how? I had no special skills. I was sixty-four years old, no longer young and full of energy. I yearned to do something, but I'd probably serve no useful purpose. All I had going for me was a working man's grit.

I remained in a state of torpor when November arrived with news that Jules Bonneau and Amy Beaupre planned to "Signify Our Vows." Those were the words on the wedding invitations.

After the ceremony at the First Congregational Church in Keene, the wedding party drove to Granite Lake for the reception. Afterward, Beaupre suggested we "roll down to the water and smell the Four Roses."

It was that time of year when the lake turned over. The water, usually clear, was murky. I didn't want to go near dirty water – something about it frightened me – but I went down to the dock anyway; I wasn't about to back down.

Beaupre had removed not only the thermometer from the hemlock tree, but the tree itself. Even the stump was gone, ground up by one of those marvelous machines they used in woods work these days.

The wind was blowing in, raw and nasty from the northwest. Several people I didn't know, young handsome men and pretty women in their thirties and forties, runners all, and friends of Jules and Amy, stood on the end of the dock.

Beaupre introduced me.

"Are you *the* Jack Landry, the guy who struck out Ted Williams?" asked one of the younger guys, his voice excited, probably more because of the effects of drink than meeting me.

"That's my claim to fame," I said.

"How did you do it?" the guy asked. The young people looked at me as if I were a celebrity.

"Oh, I don't know – I forget after all these years," I said, keeping my voice even. I was thinking that false modesty is a subtle craft. You want to under-do, but you don't want to overdo the under-doing either.

"Jack was the best arm to come out of these parts since Smoky Joe Wood," Beaupre said in a bit of a put-on Irish brogue that reminded me of Coach MacDonald. "I personally saw Jack strike out Williams. It was a spring training intrasquad game. This was before Jack hurt his arm. He burned Williams with two fastballs on the outside corner, then jammed him with a fastball, high inside, just barely in the strike zone."

"It was a change-up," I tried to interrupt, but Beaupre talked right over me.

"Tall guy like Williams, crowds the plate, can't handle that pitch," Beaupre said. "It's dangerous to throw. A couple inches off and it's a gopher ball. What I remember most about that day was how cool, calm, and collected Jack was."

One of the women turned to me. "Must have broken your heart when you hurt your arm?"

"It wasn't baseball that broke my heart," I said, and decided I better change the subject. "Did Beaupre tell you about his job as a bouncer in a strip club?"

"No kidding," said one of the men, turning to Beaupre.

"I needed to make a living for my family after getting blown up," Beaupre said. "I had an advantage as a guy in a wheelchair. I could sweet-talk a drunk. If they gave me a hard time, I zapped them with a cattle prod."

Everybody laughed.

"You guys were really something in your day," said one of the women. I heard the condescension in her voice.

"Yeah, in our day," Beaupre said.

I looked at Beaupre and he looked at me, and we were laughing at this young crowd, how gullible they were, and no doubt they were laughing at us. It didn't matter. We were going to go our way, and they were going to go theirs.

"Hey, get a load of that," said one of the men, pointing at the lake.

I looked out at the water. In the chop was a huge menacing shape, almost entirely submerged.

"What is it?" said a woman.

"Looks like the wreckage of a boat," said a man.

"Hey, Jack, guess what?" Beaupre said.

It was my Chris-Craft. I tried to think of a reason why it would surface. "I bet the wood rotted, and without the engine's weight, the flotation allowed the hull to rise up when the lake turned over," I said.

"I fucking doubt it," Beaupre said.

"What is that thing?" asked one of the young men.

Beaupre motioned to me with his hand. I bent to the wheelchair, and he whispered in my ear. "Should we tell them?"

"No. Please," I said.

Beaupre glared up at the young man and said, "None of your fucking beeswax."

All my shame and weakness was in that wreck. I made plans to haul it into shore, burn it, and scatter the ashes all over Cheshire County. I hopped into Car Four and drove to town to buy a winch. By the time I returned to the lake, the reception was over, everyone was gone, the wind had shifted, and the Chris-Craft was nowhere in sight.

Later that night, I woke in my bed in the Eagle with the realization that I had been so wrought up that I had not visited the nursing home to give Olympia her daily hug. I was still awake an hour later when I had a call on my cell phone from the hospital. Olympia had had a stroke. By the time I arrived at the emergency room, she was gone.

After the funeral, I drove out to the MacDonald place, launched the MacDonalds' ancient Old Town canoe, and paddled around the lake looking for the wreckage of the Chris-Craft. I went every day until the lake froze over. The boat was out there somewhere, its sole purpose to haunt me. It occurred to me that while the existence of a rational and merciful God might be in doubt, evidence for the existence of Satan was overwhelming.

HandsOn

One Who Showed the Way

In early March 2006, I had a talk with Beaupre. We met at an eatery in the Colony Mill Marketplace in Keene, the brainchild of Emile Legere, the French-Canadian American man who saved Keene.

"So, Jack, what's the crisis?" Beaupre asked, as he sipped his hot chocolate, right pinky extended.

"What makes you think there's a crisis?" I said. I didn't care what his answer was, because I knew what I was going to say. I just wanted to study him as he spoke.

"When the biggest cheapskate in the Monadnock Region offers to buy me lunch, I figure I'm being set up," Beaupre said.

I laughed. "Beaupre, I'm giving you my two weeks notice."

"You want to fucking retire?"

"No, I could never retire. I'm going to work until I drop. I want to go down to the Gulf Coast and volunteer my services."

"Bullshit, you're looking for that girl."

"A day hasn't gone by when Alouette wasn't on my mind."

"Jack, she'd be sixty fucking years old. Even if she's alive, she's not the same person you fell for and you aren't the same person she fell for."

"You're wrong. We're both Old Souls, but I'm not going down there looking for Alouette Williams. I just want to do my part for those people who got walloped by the hurricanes. Beaupre, my wife is gone, my parents are gone, Chalky is gone, Uncle Three Fingers is gone, my sisters have their worlds far away from Keene. All I got in this town is you and Katie and a reputation as an old jock based on a lie."

Beaupre laughed. "People are so fucking stupid. They want the lies. They don't care about the truth because truth is too boring. Just accept that and they won't hurt you so much."

I didn't say anything, but my face must have conveyed my state of mind, because Beaupre grew serious.

"Listen, Jack, you have friends in this town, the welfare mothers, the retards, the old folks, the sick, the lame, the fucking halt. What the hell that does that mean, the halt? The nutcases, the drunks, and just Joe and Jill Schmoe who need somebody who won't interrupt to tell their troubles to. You've been there for all of them. You're a caring kind of cab driver and they know it, and they appreciate it, and they don't give a flying fuck whether you struck out Ted Williams or not. They are your fucking people. But go, if you have to, go to the Gulf, you have my fucking blessing."

"Okay, Beaupre, thanks a lot," I said. "Every man needs a good woman and a best friend."

"Fuck you," Beaupre said.

Me and Car Four, my stinking, polluting Ford Taurus, said farewell to Keene and I set out with a suitcase, a sleeping bag, and two cases of motor oil. On impulse I brought Father Gonzaga's stole with me. I half expected he would reappear in my life, and I would return it to him. Maybe the Church would reinstate him, and I would find the faith again.

In Memphis I picked up a frantic mom and dad and their two daughters who mistook my rig for a local taxi. I started the meter and drove them to Graceland. Were they surprised when I told them no charge.

"I'm a tourist like you," I said.

Graceland was not a real mansion, just a good-sized house, gaudy at first glance but plain Jane at the core, kind of homey and dull in its own Elvis way.

I slept the night in a Motel 6 on the road – "We'll leave the light

on for ya," says Tom Bodett – then headed for New Orleans: French
Quarter with ga-ga tourists drinking "hurricane" cocktails; St.
Charles Avenue with its streetcars and fine homes; Tulane University; DePaul Hospital (now part of the Tulane Medical Center); the
levee where small boys flew kites above the masts of mighty ships
sliding silently around a corner of the Mrs. Ippy; and Monkey Hill,
primates copulating and complaining about their plight as captive
entertainers.

I turned down South Carrolton and soon everything changed.
Many houses, no one living in them. No pedestrians on the cracked
sidewalks. Few cars on the cracked roads. You'd come to a major
intersection and instead of a traffic light there would be a makeshift
stop sign stuck in a bucket of sand. Mile after mile of abandoned,
gutted homes. Shopping centers and apartment houses with shat-
tered windows. Part of me wanted to stay here, the ruination
reminding me of the driftwood graveyard where I'd camped as a
homeless man, live out my days in my broken-down taxi, limit my
contact with other human beings, build campfires at night and try
to find God in the glow.

I spent a couple days looking for the black people I'd worked
with so many years ago – Glenda Bethanny, Charlet Gibson,
Alphonse Pierre – I found no trace.

Next day I drove out of the city and headed east on Route 90,
the road that ran along the seventy-something miles of the Mississippi coast. Route 90 was as close to the ocean as any road in the
USA, though it was not an exciting coastline. No rocks to frame
crashing waves. No surf, which was blocked by the barrier islands.
I pulled over in Long Beach, walked across the grimy sands to the
shore. The water, still roiled from Katrina seven months earlier, was
dirty, cool, and scummy to the touch, reminding me of Granite
Lake turning over. I almost expected that damn Chris-Craft to
materialize out of the greasy depths.

I drove the entire length of Route 90 in Mississippi. In my
memory I saw motels, restaurants, shops, houses – including many
mansions. Now, for more than seventy miles, there was only one

building remaining standing, a mini-skyscraper casino in Biloxi that was closed for renovations. The bay bridges at each end of Route 90 had been destroyed.

In Biloxi, I cruised some of the flooded neighborhoods, marveling at houses with blue plastic tarps for roofs, strips of refuse waving in the breeze, high up in trees where the storm surge had left them. I came across a crew of fix-up volunteers wearing blue T-shirts that said "HandsOn. Be the Change. Volunteer. Gulf Coast." I liked the "hands" and "on" united into one word.

Headquarters for HandsOn was a Methodist Church on a busy, commercial road. I liked Biloxi, the home of Keesler Air Force Base. It was a working man's town. I offered my services and the services of my taxi to HandsOn, a ragtag army of volunteers, most of them college-age. Some tutored in elementary schools, a few walked traumatized dogs from the Humane Society, which was loaded with refugee mutts and felines, but most filled crews that gutted flooded houses and scrubbed out mold spores to prepare the frames for builders. We ate cafeteria-style in the church hall, the food and water donated by businesses. I wanted to give the corporations a pat on the back for pitching in, but they ruined it all by advertising their largess. The cooks were airmen from the Air Force base, volunteers like everyone else. We bedded down in sleeping bags in the hall; we waited in line for the toilets and showers. Because I had a car, I sometimes ran errands in my taxi. During off hours, I borrowed various laptops and cruised the Internet in search of you know who. I hadn't lied to Beaupre about my motives for coming down here. I had lied to myself. Now I was following my truth.

Nobody called me Jack. They called me Pops, Pops Landry. The name had a ring to it. I liked it. There was a spirit of joie de vivre among the crews. The young people sometimes burst into song. They joked. They sang camp songs around a campfire at night. They critiqued American culture. They told sad stories of crushed love lives. They desperately wanted . . . something. They were waiting for the big event to set them on a life course. They were young, I was old, but I was waiting too. My moment came three weeks into my service with HandsOn, in the evening, when the leaders were plotting the next day's schedule. One wrote on the black-board, "Bay St. Louis."

I didn't wait to be assigned to a crew. I pointed to the map and announced my desires. "This one, this house right here on Esta-brook. I want to work on that house." I hesitated. "It's personal." The response was a gratifying subdued *uh-huh* from the group. Nobody questioned me. They understood. They too had their own secret reasons for volunteering for a no-pay job.

Our crew consisted of half a dozen young people, plus myself. Our leader was a college dropout named Darrell. He'd been here since the hurricane hit. He was wiry, nervous, sardonic, a smoker, and he was the one who nicknamed me Pops. Like the other vol-unteers, he was a little bit crazy. Older I got, the more I admired crazy. Darrell was the me I would have been had I gone to college.

The house was only a short walk from the St. Rose de Lima Ele-mentary School, where our crew stayed the night. The entire neigh-borhood had been flooded. Half the houses were abandoned, with windows and doorways boarded up or window casings just empty holes, yards overgrown with weeds and grass two feet tall. Other houses had been rebuilt from the inside out, lawns mowed, gar-dens tended, cars parked in the driveways, FEMA trailers scattered here and there. The most distinguishing feature of the neighbor-hood was huge piles of debris from gutted buildings stacked on the street sides. Our crew would add to that debris. Periodically, trucks came by to haul off the rubble, but they couldn't keep up with the trade.

Eight feet up, along the white clapboards of the shotgun-style house, was a line of grime left by God to signify the high-water mark of the flood. Almost obscuring the house, very close to the street, were tall healthy azalea bushes in full bloom. The azaleas and other spring flowers were in their glory. Best display in years, the local folks told me. A strong hurricane season, disastrous for human beings, was a godsend for the flowers.

Which brought me to the subject of just what God sends and

why. From what I could see, God did not particularly favor one species over another. He'd arranged the universe like a Rube Goldberg machine to run at random by itself so that He was constantly surprised and entertained. The material world was God's matinee movie.

We on the wrecking crew wore gloves, hard hats, plastic goggles, and dust masks. We carried crowbars, pinch bars, claw hammers, nail pullers, wrenches, screwdrivers, pliers, wire-cutters, stepladders, and so forth. The front door had already been removed, along with the furniture and appliances. The place smelled musty. The flood had washed out any color or personality from the house.

Darrell was not a drill-sergeant type of leader. He advised, and he taught when necessary, but mainly he let the group find its own orientation. We just picked a spot and went to work, and in that fashion everything got done. Two girls in the crew took the bathroom, a girl and two guys took the kitchen and dining room. I and a college boy from Dartmouth who hailed from Hong Kong took the living room. We'd do the bedrooms last.

I asked the kid from Hong Kong why he chose to spend his spring break helping Americans. He said he wanted to see the U.S. Southland. We started with the ceiling, pulling down plaster and lath with our crowbars. Slabs fell on the floor and raised dust. (There's good reason to wear the masks.) When the plaster was so deep on the floor that it was a nuisance, we hauled it outside. I ignored the complaints of my back, my neck, my trick knee, and the arthritic middle knuckle on my right hand. The Hong Kong kid, half my size, worked steadily, seemingly without effort, and his output was greater than mine, although I was huffing and puffing and he was not.

After the ceiling was down and carted away, we started in on the walls, a more "fun" job because it didn't raise so much dust. The walls were wood. I didn't know Southern trees, but I'm guessing the paneling was some kind of hard pine. It reminded me a little of the fir cabinets in my parents' house on 19 Oak Street in Keene. I used a pinch bar to pry boards off two-by-four studs.

I hated to see this wood go to a landfill, but that was how the world worked. Everything had to be new, nothing was reused. A good example of waste was the management of drinking water. Instead of carrying water canteens, we went through plastic water bottle after plastic water bottle, which of course had to be disposed of.

The main feature of the living room was a stone fireplace with a mantle over it. The Hong Kong kid and I discussed whether to rip out the mantle or leave it. His accent, half-Chinese, half-England English, made me believe he was very smart. We decided the mantle should remain. However, in tearing up the board walls we accidentally pulled down half the mantle, so it ended up outside, with the rest of the innards of the house, for burial at the landfill.

Around 11 A.M. I took a break, went outside for some air. In the shade of a live oak tree lay an old dog. Beside him was a pan of water and a bowl of food, untouched except by flies. From the look on the old dog's gray face, I'd say he was anxious and perplexed by the activities around him. I went over to him, got down on one knee, and spoke softly. "Old dog, I know how you feel. Great powers beyond your understanding have cut your balls off. I am sorry for that and other indignities." I could see that he would tolerate being patted, but he'd rather be left alone, so I backed off.

By the end of the day, our crew had gutted the ceilings and walls. Tomorrow we would return to coat all the inside wood surfaces with a chemical to kill mold spores.

We spent the night in St. Rose de Lima Elementary School with other HandsOn volunteers. Like every building in this neighborhood, the school had been damaged during the hurricane. It had yet to reopen. I laid out my sleeping bag in a classroom, under a hole in the roof. I didn't care if it rained. I wanted to fall asleep staring up at the sky. I drifted off thinking of my boyhood years reading *Fur, Fish, and Game*, daydreaming of living in the wilderness like a voyageur of old.

Next day I was on a mold spore crew, same house, same leader, different volunteers, except for me. Darrell instructed us. We donned white, throwaway jumpsuits, goggles, and respirators that covered our mouths and noses. We looked for mold spore invasion on the wood, splotches of white or black or yellow or blue that resembled modern art.

You scraped the infected area with wire brushes. That failing, you used a power sander. Then you put on surgical plastic gloves and wiped down every square inch of wood with a rag dipped in a chemical. By late afternoon, our work was done. Carpenters would rebuild around the shell we had prepared.

We gathered in front of the house by the now ten-foot-high pile of debris. Along the way, the azalea bushes had been sacrificed. I was the last one out. Darrell lit an American Spirit. I was about to remove my respirator when the old dog limped toward us. Behind him was a slightly plump woman with tanned skin, about sixty, wearing a flowered dress. She wore her long white hair in braids; her quizzical mouth was in a half smile, and her almond eyes seemed to be searching for adventure. I recognized her right away.

She shook hands with each member of the crew, said a thank-you and a few kind words. "I'm Alouette Belliveau, and this is my house. I don't know how to thank you." It was the same voice I heard decades ago, except that her Southern accent had deepened. *You are not worthy of her, you never were*, Memere said. I was trying to figure out a way to slink off when she approached me with her hand extended. I took it. Her handshake was firm, mine slack, because I was afraid of accidentally hurting her.

Darrell yelled, "Hey, Pops, show her your kisser. It's not that bad." Everyone laughed.

"Yes, please do," Alouette said.

I pulled down the respirator, reached through the slit in my jumpsuit, removed a handkerchief, and wiped the sweat off my brow and bald head.

She read my craggy face, with its gray, two day stubble. "I guess you're not a college student."

"I guess not," I said, trying to sound not like me.

"That's Pops Landry," said Darrell. "He came all the way down here from the North."

276 · *Never Back Down*

"I know who he is," she said, and turned to me. "I've known since you arrived two days ago. Jacques, Jacques, I've waited for you all these years."

"Alouette, you and my memere were the only ones who called me by that name."

"Jacques – Jacques, I love the name, I can taste it."

I was over my nervousness. I was – how can I put this? – I was grateful to God for this moment, and I did not want to screw it up.

I reached through the slit in the white jumpsuit into the right front pocket of my shirt, produced a pack of M&M's, and held them out to her.

Alouette took one, popped it into her mouth, and crunched it.

"Thank you, Mother Mary," she said. "What do you call a girl who drives a fancy car?"

"A Lexus," I said. "Sing the dirge that Frank Sinatra sings on behalf of zookeepers."

"You got me on that one," she said.

I sang, "Egrets, I've had a few, but too few to mention."

Alouette laughed, and I thought her laugh must be what heaven was like.

"I've been waiting forty years to spring that one," I said.

The HandsOn crew backed away in respect, but they were still listening.

"What do you get when you cross a North France provincial post office with a major American author?" Alouette said.

"I give up."

"Norman Mailer."

"I thought he was the copy king," I said.

"That would be Gnomon Mailer."

I handed my respirator to Darrell, removed my jumpsuit and threw it on the refuse pile.

Alouette led me through the backyard, into the St. Rose de Lima cemetery for a short ways, to another lot. Under a live oak tree was a FEMA trailer on concrete blocks. Surrounding it were weeds, tall grass, and flowers, then the cemetery.

"Where the trailer is now used to be my greenhouse and retail outlet for herbs and flowers," Alouette said. "The storm surge destroyed everything. Even so, look. Some of the plants are back without me even trying."

Following us was the old dog, his tail wagging, or anyway trying to wag.

Entering the FEMA trailer was like walking on a boat. The structure was not anchored to a foundation, so the floor trembled slightly with each of our footfalls. Everything in miniature you'd expect in an American home could be found here – electric stove, fridge, microwave, propane heater, shower, flush toilet, and air conditioner. The trailer was cramped, however. Two people could not pass one another in the passageway between stove and booth-style dining table without rubbing tummies. There was no place to store stuff. Cardboard boxes were stacked here and there and everywhere. "Excuse the mess," Alouette said.

On the wall was an Old World drawing of a young woman and man at a well. "Hey," I said, pointing, "that print used to be in the Eagle Hotel."

"I know, I bought it on eBay from Father Gonzaga," said Alouette.

"Do you know where he is?" I asked.

"He's in China, a missionary for a church he founded."

"I guess China is where it's at today for an Experimentalist philosopher."

Alouette gestured for me to sit down at the booth-style dining table, a tight squeeze for a man my size. The old dog went into the bedroom.

"Nice pooch," I said. "He looks a little zombified."

"He's a stray I took in. Who knows who his people are and what happened to them. I'm a bit of a Chablisaholic these days. May I offer you a glass?"

"I'm a bit of a beeraholic, but the wine will do just fine," I said.

She served the Chablis in elegant glasses. We sat at the table. The walls were bare except for a photograph of the Williamses when they were a young family. In the picture, Alouette was perhaps six or seven, a beautiful girl with alert eyes and a mischievous smile. I couldn't help myself and I touched the picture.

"Is your mom still alive?" I asked.

"No, she died several years ago in Utah."

In the next two hours, Alouette and I went through that bottle of wine and ate the best shrimp salad I ever had in my whole life. I told her about Olympia, Chalky, Father Gonzaga, Beaupre, Katie, and Cormac, the son I never saw; I told her about Memere. I told her about my various occupations. I told her about my penance, how it shaped my life as a working man.

"You ever feel tricked?" Alouette asked.

The question made me stop and think, but in the end I knew the answer. "I may have been tricked, but it doesn't matter. I did what I had to do to feel right about myself."

After that, Alouette told her story. She recovered from her nervous breakdown after her miscarriage by reading *The Story of a Soul* by St. Therese until she'd memorized most of the book. She joined an order of nuns in South Louisiana. Alouette – Sister Therese – was a nun for twelve years. During that time she prayed, did penance, including mortification of the flesh, and became an expert in horticulture. Slowly, she recovered her senses and memory and began to understand her own heart. She never wavered in her Catholic faith, but she questioned whether God wanted her to remain a cloistered sister.

She discovered the women's liberation movement, and within a year she'd left the convent and become a businesswoman, operating a plant nursery specializing in herbs. She took her mother's Cajun name, Belliveau. Her love life was at turns ecstatic and despairing until she met an older widowed man with four children to raise. They married and had a "pretty good" life. He died of a heart attack while watching TV. Alouette was proud to say that she had a dozen grandchildren, though none were hers by blood.

When the hurricane came she took it as a sign.

"A sign of what?" I asked.

"That you would find me, Jacques; Evangeline knew right here" – she put her hand over my heart. "All I had to do was send you my thoughts and wait. I loved you for hundreds of years, Jacques Landry. You and I were fated."

"Maybe it's better not to know your heritage, so you can start anew," I said. "That's what my parents used to say."

"For many people, that's probably true, but some of us carry the trauma of past generations in our DNA. I am one of those carriers of trauma, and you are another. Jacques: You and me, we remember things we are not supposed to know. I am Evangeline and you are Gabriel. We were lovers separated by Le Grand Derangement. Now we've found each other again."

"It could still be our imagination."

"That was what the psychiatrists told me. That I was crazy. They were right. They're so much smarter than we are. I know that even the Cajuns make fun of the Evangeline myth. I know she's not real. But it doesn't matter. I didn't start to get well until I decided to follow my heart, and in my heart I am Evangeline."

"All right. You follow your heart, and I will follow you." The moment I spoke the words I knew they were my destiny, and that my penance finally was complete. I was free, I was forgiven. I would follow this woman and she would lead me to my new mission in life.

It was sunset when we went outside, walked across the weeds, through what used to be a gate, into the cemetery. The old dog, head bowed, followed us. We walked among the gravestones.

"Can you forgive my dad for firing your dad?" Alouette said, as we strolled.

"Sure, he was only doing his job – what else can a person do?" I said.

"I want to pray," Alouette said. She took my hand and we knelt in the moist grass.

"I have my mother's rosary." I pulled the rosary beads from my pocket and passed them to her.

Alouette raised her eyes to heaven, and prayed aloud, "Hail

Mary, full of grace, the Lord is with thee. Blessed art thou among women, and blessed is the fruit of thy womb, Jesus."

"Holy Mary, Mother of God, pray for us sinners now and at the hour of our death. Amen," I answered, completing the prayer. We said all five decades of the rosary.

The drone of our prayers ferried me away. I was thinking about the live oak trees that surrounded us. They stood up to the hurricane and survived the flood. It was a comfort to know they would be around long after our own epoch had run its course.

We returned to the FEMA trailer and went into the cramped bedroom. We didn't have to talk about making love, it just happened as naturally as morning glory petals open with the sun.

I worked another two weeks for HandsOn, and then Alouette and I were married. I'd hoped that Father Gonzaga would pull another of his miracles and show up to perform the ceremony, but it wasn't to be. We were married by the pastor in the St. Rose de Lima church. We lived in the FEMA trailer until the house was ready for occupation. Meanwhile, we worked together to rebuild the greenhouse and plant the herbs. We worked all through the summer to establish the business. In September, after Labor Day, we took a vacation and visited Keene and the Beaupres and then went on to Nova Scotia.

Halfway to the Canadian border Car Four quit – blown engine. We junked it and bought a "preowned" Honda Civic in Bangor, Maine, that the salesman insisted had been owned by the Etienne Roi family. We were back on the road – me, Alouette, and the old dog – when I realized I'd left Father Gonzaga's stole in Car Four. I wondered if it went to the metal crusher with the car or was saved by a curious workman. It didn't matter. My dependence on my confessor had faded away.

In New Brunswick, I bought a book of photographs by Henri Cartier-Bresson, decisive moments not of Keene, New Hampshire, but of Paris, France. I liked to think that Father Gonzaga was on the verge of finding the -ism to save humankind.

I baptize thee in the name of the Father, the Son, and the Holy Ghost,
Memere said.

"What?" said Alouette.

"I guess I was talking to myself again," I said.

"Yes, I like that," she said, and we drove on.

My genealogy, done by my sister Gemma, showed that the first
Landry had arrived in Acadia in 1640 and settled in the town that
would be known as Grand-Pre. In 1755 our ancestor was not deported like so many Acadians. He got away, remained in the woods
with a few others to fight the English for a couple years. In the end,
the rebels were overwhelmed by a greater force, and he found his
way to Quebec in time to find a wife and carry on his clan.

We reached our destination, the Grand-Pre National Historic
Site in Nova Scotia on the shores of the Minas Basin of the Bay of
Fundy. There was a small stone chapel with a steeply pitched roof,
but the main feature of the site that caught our attention was a
statue of a farm girl, the Evangeline of the poem.

"Looks just like the you I fell in love with at Granite Lake,"
I said.

"I know," Alouette said.

Grand-Pre was still farm country after all these centuries, with
fields, crop lands, and orchards. I thought it was about the prettiest place I'd ever been, but it scared me a little, too, because it was
so familiar.

"I've been here before," I said.

"I know," Alouette said.

"When I close my eyes, I don't see the fires anymore. They've
burned out with my childhood."

Alouette nodded. "I feel at peace, too. I used to imagine myself
back in time here with my lover, but I don't care about that anymore.
Home is Bay St. Louis, my yard, my herbs, my business now you."

"Yes, and our dog."

Our vacation was over, and it was time to go home to Bay St.
Louis. After a lobster meal, we returned to our guesthouse, where

we dozed in rocking chairs on the porch that overlooked Minas Bay, the old dog between us on the floor.

Alouette and I popped awake at the same time.

"Something's on your mind – I can tell," Alouette said.

"I can't get those Harold Archer bays out of my head," I said. "They were as well-made and beautiful to look at as any piece of sculpture. They're gone now, melted down no doubt, or rusting and abused in some salvage yard."

"They're not gone, Jacques. They exist in our minds. We lost our baby; that's our tragedy, but it's not our end. We have so much to do. The only mistake you made, Jack, was demeaning yourself. There's no such thing as menial labor. All labor is noble if it serves other people."

I looked at my hands, and I saw the nimble hands of the web boy laboring over his web horse. I saw my ruined baseball career. I saw the hand of the artilleryman pulling the lanyard on the eight-inch howitzer. I saw the thick, rough hands of the woodsman. I saw the raw hands of the laundry man, the dishwasher, and the custodian. I saw the skilled hands of the telephone man making a connection for long lines. I saw the right-hand punch I threw at Chalky for truth, justice, and the American way. I saw the careful hands of a careful cab driver. My salvation was not in my confession and my penance; it was in my hands.

Look at your palm, the 'M' for Mother Mary, Memere said.

"Memere, to me it still looks like a *W* for Work," I said aloud.

"Jacques, Jacques," Alouette said and took my hands into her own and kissed them.

ACKNOWLEDGMENTS

What bothers me about writing acknowledgments is all the people
I will leave out because I get preoccupied and selfish when I'm writing and forget those who've helped me. To those of you whom I've
overlooked, please accept my apology.

Below is a list of people who have my gratitude during the years
this book was put together. In no particular order, they are: Connie Hébert Hamel; Warren Johnston; Lael Ryan; Nicole Hebert;
Dayton Duncan; Terry Pindell; David R. Godine; Susan Barba;
Sally Brady; my colleagues and students at Dartmouth College; the
spirited *pistoleros* of the Writers' Table in Hanover, New Hampshire,
with a special nod to Linda Kennedy, who started it all by persuading me to join a Dartmouth College fix-up crew that worked
with HandsOn Gulf Coast in the Katrina cleanup; and Robert Per-
reault, who prodded me into thinking about my Franco-American
heritage. I have a lot in common with my protagonist in *Never Back
Down*, Jack Landry (in fact Landry is a name that appears in my Acadian ancestry). I lived half of Jack's adventures. *Never Back Down*
dances back and forth between memoir and pure fiction. I've been
a lot luckier in love than Jack was though, thanks to my partner,
best friend, and wife of more than four decades – thank you,
Medora, for everything.

A NOTE ON THE TYPE

NEVER BACK DOWN *has been set in Galliard, a lovely and lively Renaissance face deisgned by Matthew Carter after the sixteenth-century models of Robert Granjon. Originally introduced by the Mergenthaler Linotype Company in 1978, it was the first type of its kind made exclusively for phototypesetting. The italic is especially felicitous – and just a little quirky – harking back to chancery scripts. Both the roman and the italic have a notable heft on the page, a distinct advantage over other types (Garamond among them) with Renaissance roots.*

DESIGN & COMPOSITION BY CARL W. SCARBROUGH